book one in The Grand Valley Series

"A sexy, smart romp that will appeal to both romance and sports fans."

—*RT Book Reviews,* 4 stars

"*First Step Forward* by Liora Blake is an entertaining read, filled with charming characters and plenty of humorous moments."

—*Harlequin Junkie*

"I loved this story! It's a football romance with actual football! But it's more than that. It's an epic opposites attract love story that had me laughing out loud the entire time. From Cooper's filthy mouth to Whitney's granola view of life. I loved every second!"

—*Two Book Pushers*

"This book is funny, sweet, smart, and sexy. Being inside the heads of these two characters as they navigate the challenges in their own lives while moving toward each other is pure joy."

—*Literary Gossip*

"I love books that when I finish reading them leave a smile on my face or a sigh escapes me. This is exactly what happened with this novel."

—*Mrs. Leif's Two Fangs About It*

"*First Step Forward* is a funny, witty, sexy, sweet, and just a bit quirky contemporary romance. It will make you smile, it will make you ache, and it will make you swoon."

—*Literati Literature Lovers*

"The author set up a fantastic series with this first book. The only problem . . . it's going to be hard for her to go up from here. This was pretty much contemporary romance perfection in my opinion."

—*Smitten with Reading*

"I loved this seriously sweet, romantic, sometimes silly, sometimes hot read!"

—*Cocktails and Books*

"Deeply affecting and absolutely outstanding."

—*Always Reviewing*

"Contemporary romance at its very best, heartfelt and light, something you start and cannot put down!"

—*Ramblings From A Chaotic Mind*

Praise for Liora Blake's True Series

True North
True Devotion
True Divide

Available from Pocket Star!

"Blake's debut is a heated, sexy romp that will entice readers to want more."

—*Library Journal*, starred review

"Highly recommend . . . adult romance full of love and forgiveness."

—*Harlequin Junkie*

ALSO BY LIORA BLAKE

The Grand Valley Series
First Step Forward

The True Series
True North
True Devotion
True Divide

LIORA BLAKE

Second Chance Season

POCKET BOOKS

New York   London   Toronto   Sydney   New Delhi

Pocket Books
An Imprint of Simon & Schuster, Inc.
1230 Avenue of the Americas
New York, NY 10020

First Pocket Books paperback edition June 2017

POCKET and colophon are registered trademarks of Simon & Schuster, Inc.

For information about special discounts for bulk purchases, please contact Simon & Schuster Special Sales at 1-866-506-1949 or business@simonandschuster.com.

The Simon & Schuster Speakers Bureau can bring authors to your live event. For more information or to book an event, contact the Simon & Schuster Speakers Bureau at 1-866-248-3049 or visit our website at www.simonspeakers.com.

Interior design by Bryden Spevak

Manufactured in the United States of America

10 9 8 7 6 5 4 3 2 1

ISBN 978-1-5011-7535-0
ISBN 978-1-5011-5515-4 (ebook)

Second Chance Season

1

(Garrett Strickland)

If you want to get to know someone, there are a hundred different ways. Drinking games and personality tests, or the long haul of good old-fashioned *time*. But where I'm from, there is one thing that's more efficient, less complicated—and never lies.

Your truck.

From the make and model, to the number of dings and dents, these things say a lot about who you're dealing with. Take the guy who's cruising around in a brand-new rig, bright like it just rolled off the assembly line, with wheels so clean it seems they haven't seen a dirt road and likely never will. My bet would be on its owner being just as slick and polished. The sort of guy who likes his beer *crafted* and his beard *coifed*.

But a beat-to-hell one-ton with a permanent layer of dust on the dashboard, a flatbed loaded with bales of hay, and a border collie riding shotgun? I probably know that guy. He might be someone I grew up with or someone my dad grew up with. Here in Hotchkiss, odds are that if your truck only sees water when it rains and sounds like it needs a new muffler in the worst way possible, then I've probably known you my whole life.

As for me, I drive a 1996 Ford F350. Crew cab, diesel, and enough sheet metal damage to make it clear this is no show truck. Lifted to serve purposes when I'm out in a field, but not so much that it looks like I'm compensating for what's behind my fly or between my ears. The odometer has long cleared two hundred thousand, but despite all those miles, I'd bet on it being more reliable than any throwaway import on the road these days. It can tow like an ox, too. No hesitation, no delay, nothing but power when you need it.

But, no, my truck does not have a name. Only complete tools do that sort of shit.

Most important, I own it. Free and clear, pry the title from my cold dead hands, it's a piece of shit, but it's mine. And nothing beats the peace of mind that brings. Because losing the shit that matters to you . . . it sucks.

So what does my truck say about me?

Today, it says one thing: that I'm smarter than Braden.

Because if I were Braden, right now I'd be stuck, watching the tires on my Dodge spin deep ruts into the mud in the field we hunted geese over this morning. I'd be pissed off and muttering "*fuck*" on repeat. Just like my best buddy is currently doing.

Thankfully, I do not drive a Dodge. I drive a *real* truck.

Casting another glance in my rearview mirror, I enjoy the sight of Braden's scowling face reflected in his side mirror for a few more seconds before hooking reverse. Steering with one hand, I come to a stop next to him so that our windows are side by side. I shove my truck into park, but keep the motor running, because we both know how this is going to go down. He'll tell me to fuck off, try to power himself out again, then give up and beg me to tow his ass out of here.

Perhaps "beg" is overstating it. More like grunt and cuss like a pissed-off moose surrendering to the inevitable.

I roll down my window but say nothing, simply drop my forearm to rest on the trim panel and tap my fingers casually. Braden eases off the gas and the roar of his overtaxed motor descends into a low whine, which makes it easy to hear his oh-so-cheery acknowledgment of my arrival.

"Fuck off, Strickland."

I force myself to hold back a chuckle. And so it begins.

He's in an exceptionally pissy mood already, but that makes giving him shit even more fun. First, he overslept, which Braden *never* does. We started our morning later than planned because of it and found ourselves setting up at sunrise—about an hour later than we should have. Success in goose hunting means you're in the field well before first light, so that when you set out your decoys it's still dark. Anything later means the real birds can see what you're up to, and once they do, you've effectively ruined your chances for a decent hunt.

Second, his bird dog—a gorgeous toffee-colored Chessie girl named Charley—listened . . . well, not at all. She was wiggly and wild, all over the place, and did a bang-up impression of a deaf dog by ignoring every command Braden issued. I spent most of the morning sneaking her pieces of venison jerky as reward for her bad behavior.

To top it all off, Braden missed just about everything he shot at. I'm mean, he missed *everything*. As in, the broad side of a barn would have been safe. Something I was happy to point out each and every time he skunked it.

Yup, good times. Good, *good* times. For me, anyway.

I grab the Hostess Fruit Pie—apple flavor, natch—that's sitting on my dashboard and tear the wrapper open.

"Now, now. No reason for that kind of language. I'm just checking on you. Looks like you're having a bit of bad luck out here. I *care*, Braden, that's all."

Braden hits the gas again and the truck's tires give everything they can, launching dirt so violently that my windshield quickly looks like a freak mud storm just rolled through this field. I take a large bite of the apple pie goodness and wipe a few flecks of sugary glaze off my chin using my coat sleeve. Charley scents my snack from the passenger seat and proceeds to crawl over Braden, standing on his lap so she can stick her head out the window, craned forward to see if she can figure out a way to lick my face from this distance. Braden immediately lets off the gas and flops backward into his seat, his head tipped skyward.

I take another bite and wait it out. After a few more grumbled cuss words, Braden gently but pointedly shoves Charley back into the passenger seat and starts to roll up his window.

"Hook it," he growls.

Ah, there's the grouchy, defeated moose I knew would show up eventually. His window is halfway up when I tilt my head toward him, cupping my ear. "What's that? Say again?"

He stops the window and shoots a hard look in my direction.

"I picked a weird spot to park. That's all. Just fucking hook it, Garrett. I've got to get to work."

"See"—I raise an index finger, pointing it his way—"*that's* where you fucked up. Should've brought your work truck in the first place."

Braden is a game warden for the state of Colorado, and his work truck is a Ford, thus a smart use of my state tax dollars. Why he spent good money on a Dodge for his personal use, I'll never understand. We're friends because we both like to hunt, I'm good for his surly disposition, and I appreciate the way he tells it like it is. Plus, he owns a trailer full of quality goose decoys.

I take the last bite of my pie and toss the empty wrapper back on the dash, then make a show of straightening my coat and ball cap before putting the truck in reverse again. And, while I won't admit it out loud, someday when I'm the one who's stuck, I know exactly who I'll call. Braden will show up without question—no matter the time or place—with his Cummins motor and a few insults at the ready.

I feather the gas pedal of my truck, revving the motor for no reason other than to prove a point.

"Two words, Braden." He flops his head forward and visibly grips the steering wheel tighter. I grin. "Power Stroke."

⁓

Twenty minutes later, we're both on our way. Braden heads east on Highway 92 toward the Parks & Wildlife offices, and I head west to my place to grab a quick shower and a change of clothes. Braden's job means he can show up at work decked out in camo from head to toe if he wants, but I work at the Hotchkiss Co-op, where jeans and a duck jacket are a better choice.

Cranking up the radio a touch louder so I can hear it better, I waggle my pinkie finger a few times in my ear, hoping that might fix what's left of the dull buzz in my head. Braden's payback for my lording my Power Stroke motor over him was to blast his horn right when I hunched down to hook a tow rope to his front bumper. Fucking juvenile—but exactly what I would've done in his place.

I give the heater dial another nudge higher and aim the vents toward my still-thawing-out fingertips. Late-January mornings are always cold, but a cloudless sky like today's means the air turned crystalline and frigid at sunrise. But despite the weather and the fact goose season is coming to a close, I love this time of year. When I was a kid, hunting was all about bag limits and the excitement of a good shot. Now I couldn't care less if we come home empty-handed or not. It's the entire experience that gets me out of bed at four a.m. to set decoys in the dark and tuck myself into a layout blind in the middle of a freezing-ass-cold cornfield. Because the silence of first light is deafening in a way only waterfowl hunters can understand. Just like the stillness that comes with the ritual of waiting for something to happen. Even if it never does.

I slow the truck at the county road that leads to my place, then hang a right onto a long dirt driveway. The place I rent is nothing special, just an old modular set on a raggedy patch of dirt. But it's quiet, clean, and set back from the road enough to feel secluded even though I'm only a five-minute drive from the heart of Hotchkiss. I've got plenty of room to shoot my bow outside and wrench on my truck, but no yard to mow in the summer or sidewalk to shovel clear in the winter. Basically a dream come true for a twenty-five-year-old redneck bachelor.

Inside, I strip off my gear and duck into the shower for a quick rinse, craning under the shower head that's set too low and was clearly not installed with my six-foot-four height in mind. I'm out and dried off in record time, tugging on a pair of battered jeans and grabbing a shirt from the towering stacks that line the shelf of my tiny closet. After grabbing a refill from the coffeepot in the kitchen, I'm back in the truck, barreling down the driveway because I've realized how close I'm cutting it this morning.

I hit the gas and my beast starts to rumble. Just ahead I spot a car pulled onto the side of the road, the four-ways on, blinking bright amber against the burgundy metallic paint color. I slow my truck and ease toward the center line because while it's technically on the shoulder, the car isn't over quite enough to be safe. Which doesn't surprise me once I'm closer, because I see it's a Lexus. One of those crossover SUVs that are often owned by very rich—potentially unpleasant—old ladies. I crane my head as I pass by, spotting only dark-tinted windows and out-of-state plates.

Tourists, I'd guess. Lost and confused vacationers whose original destination may have been the ever-ritzy ski town of Aspen. And if I'm right, they're about a hundred miles off course and in the wrong fucking county.

Or maybe they overshot the town of Paonia or Palisade, where the wineries, orchards, and a bunch of crafty artisan businesses are the big draw in this once quiet part of southwestern Colorado. While the Grand Valley used to be nothing more than an afterthought in the state, now—thanks to whoever dreamed up the concept of agritourism—it's a *destination*.

Regardless of why they're here, the driver of that Lexus has their four-ways on, which means something could be wrong. And if it were my grandma or my mom out there, lost and confused while trying to find that quaint vineyard with the simply *fabulous* red wine she's heard so much about, I'd want a guy like me to stop.

Fuck it. I'm going to be late opening the co-op anyway, so I hit the brakes and flip a U-turn. Once I'm close enough, I ease off the road and pull to a stop in front of the car.

Illinois plates. The top of a woman's downcast head is visible through the windshield, but she doesn't even lift her head, despite the way my truck announces itself a good mile before you can actually see it.

I put a little extra force behind my truck door when I shut it, thinking that might draw her attention. No luck. Dirt kicks across the tops of my boots when I deliberately drag my feet on my approach to her driver-side door, because if she's ancient enough that too much of a surprise might cause a heart attack, I sure as hell don't want that on my shoulders.

Once I'm next to her door, the thump of music blaring inside explains why she can't hear me. And whatever it is that's on blast in there sounds eerily similar to the goose-calling DVDs I bought to improve my honking skills in the blind—not exactly what I'd expect to hear coming from a ride like this.

I give a quick rap to the door glass. A sharp squeal and her head whips up. Through the dark-tinted glass I see the shadow of her pressing one hand to her chest before moving to turn down the radio. The window hums to life and descends.

Well, shit.

Definitely not an old lady. Nope. Not even close.

Instead, this Lexus Lady is a woman my age, maybe a few years older. And—*welcome to Hotchkiss, why don't you stay awhile*—she's beautiful.

Shiny and soft-looking chestnut-colored hair comes to just above her shoulders, mostly straight but with a few wavy pieces that frame the fair skin of her face. She's wearing a pair of eyeglasses, black frames that are shaped like Wayfarers and give off a Clark Kent vibe. Specs I might declare utterly geeky if it weren't for the gorgeous big brown eyes behind them. A half-eaten Twizzler hangs out of her mouth. Those brown eyes lock on mine and she reaches up to yank the Twizzler from her lips.

"Jeez. You scared me."

Her left leg is bent, with her bare foot perched up on the seat, positioned in the lazy way that girls with an automatic sometimes drive. She's wearing a pair of light-colored jeans, in a dusty sort of pink color, and a heap of plat maps are sprawled across her lap, some half-folded and the rest askew. All of them unexpected, since plat maps show farming section lines, landowner names, and acres owned—but they don't make the best road maps for someone from out of state.

But even with the maps in the way, it's still easy to deduce how she's built. It's a safe bet that if this girl unfolded herself from that seat and stepped outside the car, she'd be damn near my height—and nearly all legs. Picturing that turns my brain mushy for a second because you can keep all those curves and handfuls that some guys can't get enough of—for me, long, lean legs are like kryptonite.

Christ. This scenario is not what I was expecting. But my inner Boy Scout led the way, and now I'm goddam glad of it. Because one thing about living in the small town you grew up in is that meeting new women is nearly an impossibility. And one who's beautiful, your age, and sitting on the side of the road just down from your house? *That* never happens. Which means it's time to see if I can earn my merit badge in community relations.

I set one hand to the roof of her car and drop my chin to focus on her.

"Didn't mean to scare you. Your four-ways were on; just wanted to make sure you aren't stuck or something. I passed you once, then turned around and drove back here. My truck is usually loud enough to wake the dead. Most days it sounds a lot like an industrial wood chipper."

She cuts her gaze to the windshield and takes note of my truck sitting there covered in mud and dwarfing her little SUV. Her eyes widen in a way that looks like she's half horrified and half fascinated. I lean forward a bit, lifting one side of my mouth up into a lazy grin.

"Your music was blasting. Either that or you have a huge bag of pissed-off farm cats in here, engaged in some sort of feral cat choir practice. Not sure which."

She lifts one brow wryly, then leans back in her seat, removes the Clark Kent glasses, and tosses them on the passenger seat.

And that's not particularly a good thing, because now her entire gorgeous face is on display, along with her expression turning intent. Her eyes travel down my chest, landing at my waist and staying put for longer than I would have expected. Not that I particularly mind if her gaze is glued to the space inches from my dick, but it's worth wondering what she finds so fascinating. I might be country, but I'm no cowboy, so I'm not sporting some trash-can-lid belt buckle. It's just a regular belt, the same one I've had for years. I hook one thumb into the waist of my jeans and her eyes shoot back up.

"It's from *Lakmé*," she says, as if that one obviously foreign word will clear up everything.

I nod slowly. "Sure. Lakmé. So, the cats are here on a passport?"

Reaching toward the radio console, she turns the volume back up. A woman's voice belts out a long high note just as she does.

On second thought, that noise is less like cats or geese and more like an elk bugling. Loudly. And in the rut.

"No cats, no passports." She fiddles with radio again and the wailing fades into the background. "Opera. It helps me concentrate."

I give up a chuckle. "Good to know someone finds that racket soothing." Another lift of her one eyebrow, annoyed this time. Not the best reaction if I want to earn that merit badge. "So do you need some help? Directions or something? Paonia is a ways back. If you're looking for Palisade, you need to keep driving."

Quickly, that annoyed eyebrow of hers sinks. Her head drops to the seat back with a defeated thump and she directs her gaze out the windshield for a beat, then cuts her eyes my way, along with another pass of her eyes skirting toward my belt.

She needs to stop doing that. If she doesn't, I'm bound to give in and start indulging in a fantasy where the gorgeous girl in the very expensive SUV finds me and certain areas of my body all too interesting.

"Are you from here? Hotchkiss?"

She dips a hand into the open bag of Twizzlers sitting in the center console and slips one between her lips, eventually taking a small bite. Short of the biting part, my dick likes the scene a little too much, so I remove my hand from the roof and straighten myself up.

"Born and raised." I outstretch a hand. "I'm Garrett. Garrett Strickland."

When her hand meets mine, it's all I can do to let go within a reasonable amount of time. Her fingers are long, nails manicured and done up with those white tips. The sort of nails I love—and combined with the softness of her hands, a few very non-PG thoughts cross my mind before I can stop them.

"Cara Cavanaugh." She pulls her hand back and looks up. "And I do need some help."

Great. My favorite kind of nails, legs for miles, and now she's all doe-eyed and looking up through her lashes at me to tell me she needs help. I'm hoping and praying that her next words will somehow follow the shitty script of some low-budget skin flick. Nearly any story line will work. Randy college girl gone wild. Stranded motorist gone desperate for a redneck in a beater Ford truck.

But I keep my voice steady, just to be sure I don't do or say anything that might signal exactly how many months it's been since I was this close to an age- or situation-appropriate woman—let alone how long it's been since I got laid.

"I'm a helpful guy. Consider me at your service."

Intrigue flashes in her eyes, disappearing just as quickly. Cara leans over to rustle around in a bag on the passenger floorboard. This means that half of her ass comes into view, along with a few inches of very soft-looking skin on her lower back when her T-shirt rides up. I nearly let out a whimper when she rights herself into the seat and hands a scrap of paper my way.

"I'm having trouble finding this address. I managed the drive all the way from Chicago without getting lost once, but the minute I passed through Paonia, my GPS wanted me to turn around. The system must not have the right data for this area. Do you know where this place is?"

I glance at the paper.

Then again, just to be sure I'm not imagining things. Nope. Fuck.

Do I know where this place is? Yes. I know exactly where it is. I could probably walk there in the middle of the night, drunk off my ass, under a moonless sky. Muscle memory and autopilot have already been known to take me there on occasion, pulling into the driveway as if it's still the place I belong, even when years have passed and I've worked damn hard to bury the ache that comes with understanding how much was lost.

My hand crumples the paper slightly. I cast my eyes back to her.

"No one lives there anymore. You sure this is the right place?"

She snags another Twizzler and points it my way in offering. I shake my head.

"I know it's empty," she mumbles, answering around a mouthful of licorice. "A family friend owns it, and he said I could stay there for a few weeks to work on a project."

So much for my lucky day, because this is bound to get a little awkward. A beautiful girl and her equally beautiful legs arrive in town and I decide to Boy Scout my way into her orbit, only to find out she's about to crash in the house I grew up in. The family farm I had to sell, even when I would rather have done anything but that. The land my dad busted his ass on to make it through one year after the next, but in the end was too debt-ridden for me to keep afloat after he died. The life I rarely let myself remember—if only because my dad never believed in looking back and he raised me to do the same.

So I ignore the sting of emptiness that's centered itself in my rib cage as I hand the paper back to Cara. Her fingers graze mine again, making it easier to focus on what lies ahead: a beautiful girl in from out of town, who—you never know—might be up for some fun while she's here.

"Well, City, I think this is fate. I happen to know everything about this place."

Her eyes light up. "You do? Oh, this is perfect." An exhale visibly releases from her chest. "How do you know about this place?"

Leaning forward, I latch both hands to the roof of her car and let my entire body drift closer. Those damn eyes of hers seem to eat up the advance of my body, drawing another long exhale out of her, but shakier this time. She wets her lips.

"It used to be *my* house."

2

(Cara Cavanaugh)

Maybe this was a mistake.

And not just the decision that brought me to this tiny town in Colorado, but *everything*—all the choices I've made over the past few months that led to this moment.

Like six months ago, when I broke up with my foregone-conclusion-but-not-quite-yet fiancé, the same man I'd been with for years. Or the one where I walked away from what I always thought would be my dream job at a major newspaper, then accepted a freelance writing gig that was based three states away from my home in Chicago.

That one was a doozy.

Not that I quit my corporate journalism job impulsively. Not at all. I did what I always do. I sat down and brought up the handy pros-and-cons worksheet I have saved on my desktop—with its perfectly sized columns and rows strategically designed to put my world in order by way of Microsoft Excel. I hashed it out until I was sure that while I hated my job, I still wanted to write as much as I always did. I just didn't want to file one hundred stories a month, most of which were nothing more than words churned out of a journalistic meat grinder and cited Facebook as a source more often that I care to admit. I also didn't want to read the daily reports from management that detailed my online stories' Google Analytics. Because writers often survive on the very idea that someone, somewhere, is reading their words and feeling *something*—and when know-it-all Google informs you that your audience spends an average of ninety-three seconds "reading" your articles, the delusional ruse of affecting a reader becomes a little hard to keep up.

What I *did* want to do was write comprehensive pieces on people and places and things that mattered, the sort of stories that were worth more than ninety-three seconds of someone's time.

Enter the slightly self-righteous, impossibly niche, and wonderfully in-depth world of a quarterly journal called *Purpose & Provisions* based out of Asheville, North Carolina. I'd been stalking the job listings on a freelancers' site for months already, hoping to find a post that might justify leaving corporate news for something I could sink my heart into.

And one day, there it was:

WRITER NEEDED. CAPOTES, NOT COURICS, PLEASE.
MUST BE WILLING TO RELOCATE.

Looking for a spirited and heartfelt writer to report on the changing face of agriculture in the Grand Valley area of southwestern Colorado. This diverse region is home to both traditional ranching families, organic and conventional farmers, plus a host of fruit orchards and vineyards. Yet the graying of the American ag producer is as much a threat to land use here as it is in the cornfields of Iowa or the wheat fields of Kansas. The right candidate for this assignment will immerse themselves in the Grand Valley community for up to eight weeks, provide weekly updates to our editor, and return with a long-form piece worthy of our publication's discerning readership.

Purpose & Provisions is dedicated to a sincere appreciation of all things crafted and created—and the narratives we owe those artisans. We aren't beholden by word counts and believe white space always trumps advertising space.

Forward a cover letter with writing samples to submissions@purposeandprovisions.com.

A little research and I found that while they might take themselves just a little *too* seriously, *Purpose & Provisions* was also exactly what I had been looking for. The articles were evocative and interesting, the design was modern but warm, and once I had my hands on a print copy, I sort of wanted to sleep with it under my pillow and wait for the writing fairy to work her magic.

I sent off my cover letter and two spec pieces I'd written on northern Illinois food producers. The editor replied hours later, we Skyped the next morning, and he offered me the assignment one day after that. I gave my notice at the paper, trudged through my two weeks, and started making a plan for my temporary relocation to Colorado.

Fast-forward one month and here I am. Trying on a new life so different from the one I mapped out for myself since I was twelve that it's no wonder I'm having trouble with the most basic tasks.

Like opening a stupid padlock.

My dad insisted on having my stuff shipped out here from Chicago in one of those transportable storage pods, which arrived in Hotchkiss yesterday. I wanted to rent one of those cute

U-Haul tow-behind trailers—an idea my mother claimed would make me look like a vagabond, and vetoed before I could argue my point any further. I have the only key for the lock I affixed to the metal box after loading it full with a microwave, boxes of clothes and shoes, and assorted kitchen goods, plus my Pilates reformer unit. But somewhere between Illinois and here, the lock seems to have amassed enough dirt to make it now impossible to open.

Although perhaps some of the problem is all the inconvenient hormones zinging through my body. Any strength I might derive from proper blood flow has reoriented itself toward the more erogenous areas of my body—brought on by a roadside encounter with a guy I suspect possessed a set of abdominal muscles you could easily round out a zydeco band with.

Wash. Board.

There was a moment when I considered reaching out and lifting Garrett's shirt to see if I was right. Even without my laptop and worksheet handy, I was still able to pro-and-con the scenario in my head.

PRO: Technically, it would be research. A way to get to know the locals . . . to *immerse* myself in the community.

CON: It's also a way to firmly establish myself as crazy on my first day in town. Or get arrested.

PRO: I've never actually seen *abs* before. As in, multiple muscles that are defined from one another and exist without flexing or filtering. Not in *real* life.

CON: I wouldn't know what to do with the reality of a six-pack, anyway. Pet it with the flat of my hand? Poke it with my index finger to assess its durability? Take a picture?

Abs aside, Garrett seemed like a guy who could, with one night, permanently obliterate all memory of the tepid sex I've experienced to date. Because his truck was both jacked up and broken down, his body appeared as if it had been corn-fed and well worked, and his hazel eyes were puppy-dog soft and bedroom trouble. All of this meant I spent most of our roadside conversation letting my eyes drift where my mind wandered, even after he claimed the "Flower Duet" from *Lakmé* sounded like feral cats going at it or something.

Cats.

And I *still* couldn't stop thinking about what he looked like underneath that battered T-shirt he was wearing. He, on the other hand, seemed to know I was lost, overwhelmed, and attracted to him—and he was enjoying every minute of it, right up to the moment when he climbed back in his truck, gave a slow grin and casual wave my way, then drove off—leaving me with only the directions he'd provided and a slightly confusing case of lust-itis.

I give the padlock another good yank, hoping a little exertion might cure my lust-itis affliction, while bracing my entire body against the pod to see if that provides the leverage I need. Nothing. I shake it back and forth. Whack it against the metal a few times. Still nothing.

Just before I land a frustrated kick against the box and inevitably break a toe, my phone rings. I drop my head to the cool metal and tug my cell out from the center pocket on my pullover and put it to my ear.

"Hello?"

"Cara Jane! Can you hear me all the way out West there? Are you safe?"

My sister. I'm convinced she possesses a finely tuned meltdown radar, because no matter where I am or what I'm fretting over, she will call or show up exactly when I need her to. She insists it's not radar, rather the result of simply being my baby sister. She spent so many years watching me and itemizing my every personality quirk that she's like one of those dogs that can sniff out their owner's seizures before they happen. Either that or she's clairvoyant. A Narciso Rodriguez–clad, Fendi bag–carrying clairvoyant.

"Amie Jane, I think you're a witch." I say, "Like Fairuza Balk in *The Craft*, but prettier and not bonkers. But just as unnerving. How do you always know when I need you?"

My sister and I share the same middle name, which we enjoy making use of whenever possible. *Jane*, for our great-grandmother on our father's side. He'd insisted, likely prompted by the fact she'd established sizable trust funds for both Amie and me before we were even born. Regardless, our mother hates it. She's convinced people will think it means she was either too lazy or too dim to come up with different middle names—or worse, that she was attempting to be ironic, and my mother simply does not *do* irony.

Amie laughs in her utterly feminine way, light but full-bodied, somehow sweet while never sounding silly. "I've explained this to you before, my Cara Jane. My earlobes itch when you're in trouble."

"Oh, yes. The earlobe thing. Nothing at all witchy or weird about that."

"I prefer to think of myself as more of a fairy godmother. Cinderella style."

"Well, if you could bibbidi-bobbidi-boo this padlock off my storage pod, I would appreciate it. I'm about ten seconds away from driving back into town and buying a lock cutter. But my first trip through town was eventful enough."

She snorts into the phone. Just like her laugh, even her snort is cute. Yet another disparity between us, as my laugh and snort are, let's say, *heartier*.

As sisters go, I'm sure our DNA matches up, but at first glance anyone with eyeballs can see we're cut from two very different patterns. Amie's follows my mother's: golden, sun-kissed complexion and honey-blonde hair, button nose and green eyes, with petite measurements that fulfill all the ideals of traditional femininity. I—in keeping with my father's side of the family—trump all their lovely porcelain doll traits with dark eyes and even darker hair, and an Olive Oyl–esque frame that made junior high *boatloads* of fun.

" 'Eventful'? Were there cows blocking the road or something equally rural? A tractor dawdling along the shoulder with a hot cowboy operating it?"

"No tractors, no cows."

"What about the hot cowboy?"

Garrett and his abs launch themselves to the forefront of my mind again. No Stetson, no shiny belt buckle, and I couldn't quite picture him on a horse. The jeans were cut the way you might expect, but the boots were lace-up work boots. So "cowboy" isn't the word I'd use to describe him.

"He wasn't a cowboy. More . . . redneck?"

Amie lets out a dejected groan. "Ugh. Like *Duck Dynasty*?"

"No?"

There's a pause on the line before Amie lets out a tinkling laugh.

"Oh, wow. My earlobes are itching again. Must be the way you said 'no' but phrased it as a question. Sounds like you found yourself some *trouble* already, Cara Jane."

Her tone is teasing, but it sends a rush of heat to my cheeks.

The reason why is simple: My ex-boyfriend, Will Cahill, has a twin brother named Tayer. And Tayer is engaged to Amie—so any talk of Garrett's trouble-like qualities feels like some sort of betrayal to the Cahill boys. *Our* Cahill boys.

From country day schools to cotillions, our family histories were so intertwined it was as if there were no other choice *but* for us to pair off. First, it was Amie and Tayer, followed by Will and me, a year later. I was nearly finished with my undergrad in journalism at Northwestern while Will was basking in his acceptance to Yale Law, and under the haze of too much celebratory prosecco, we looked at each other and things felt . . . inevitable.

And for five years, not much changed.

Except for one thing: I finally realized how much I didn't want to become my mother. Unfortunately, that's exactly the sort of woman Will would eventually need in his life. When he inevitably left the law for politics—as his father, grandfather, and great-grandfather had done—he would need a flawless society wife, a woman with poise and grace to spare.

And unlike my mother and my baby sister, poise and grace do not come naturally to me. I have to focus my attention on every detail of how I walk and talk and *breathe*, when life calls on me to be the Cara Cavanaugh my family expects. Because we come from the sort of money that has so many strings attached it's like being ensnared in a spiderweb of expectation. Those trusts Granny Jane set up for Amie and me? All part of what started out six generations ago as a steel baron's money, earned with hard work, ambition, and resourcefulness—the same traits expected of us as inheritors now.

But while our family holds to an industrious code of conduct, in the Cahill clan, women simply don't have careers. They might dabble for a few years after college, but that's about it. And whether Will would admit it or not, he doesn't stray far from the Cahill norm on that topic.

So I broke up with Will because, in the same way I knew I hated my job but still loved to write, I knew I would hate the woman I'd become if I tried to be who Will needed to love. And just like everything else that happened during the time we were together, Will and I parted ways dispassionately—no hard feelings, no awkwardness between our families, so much that it's been easy for us to fall back into friendship.

Amie finally tires of how I've gone quiet, breaking into my lost thoughts with a laugh.

"Silence, huh? This guy must be some seriously excellent trouble."

I force my own laugh, hoping it sounds effortless and unaffected, then slip down and flop cross-legged onto the dirt driveway in front of the farmhouse.

"I have no idea if he's trouble or not. We had a five-minute conversation. He insulted *Lakmé* and gave me directions. But in a plot twist only to be found in small towns, it turns out this farm used to be his. He's about our age, so I'm guessing he grew up here or something."

"No. Way." Amie hums in thought. "Tayer said that his uncle Davis bought it from an estate; the family couldn't afford to keep it. Davis snapped it up without even seeing it because it's apparently a good area for their supposed elk hunting trips. But I think all they're really *hunting* for are more excuses to plow through their precious bottles of Pappy Van Winkle without any nagging women around."

Because the history between the Cahill and Cavanaugh families mimics that of a backwoods holler in Kentucky, the man who owns the farmhouse I'm staying in—Garrett's former home— happens to be Tayer and Will's uncle.

Davis Cahill has more money than he quite knows what to do with, and even after Will and I parted ways, Davis insisted that I was as much family as always. When word made its way to his ears about my freelance assignment, he offered this place as a base. At the time, the fact that he owned a house in the area seemed like divine intervention confirming I was on the right track.

As Amie continues to extol the many reasons she believes the Cahills like bourbon whiskey more than big game, my eyes land on the farmhouse.

Faded white paint covers everything but the wide front porch, which is flanked by dark stacked-fieldstone pillars. The same stones form the foundation and patches of decades-old limescale speak to how many years have gone by since this house was built. A window shutter on the second floor appears to be hanging by a solitary nail set in one corner, the rest of the wood rattling loosely against the siding. Beyond the house, I spot the edge of what I think is a long-neglected hayfield, a few Canada Thistle peeking tall above the stalks of overgrown yellowing grasses. The entire property shows its age, neglected in a way that looks lonely and forsaken.

Amie finally ends her rant. "Anyhoo, I expect a full report if the hot redneck causes you any trouble worth discussing, OK?"

I give up one of my hearty snorts. "Doubtful. But I'll be sure to keep you updated."

"I've got to go, Tayer's home. There's an arts league benefit tonight and we're going to be late as it is, which won't look good seeing as I'm on the board."

In the background, there is the faint clink of ice hitting a glass. I can picture Tayer in the kitchen of their condo, pouring himself a drink before settling into his spot on the couch, happy to know Amie is his and contented enough to wait it out, no matter how late she makes them.

"And, Cara?"

Homesickness settles deep in my belly. "Yeah?"

"Try the lock again. I've sent some good juju your way."

When we hang up, I stare down the lock and take a deep breath.

Bibbidi-bobbidi-boo. The lock slides open, so effortlessly only a fairy godmother could be to blame.

3

(Cara)

Less than an hour later, I've unloaded nearly everything from the storage pod and familiarized myself with the layout of the house, plus decided which of the three upstairs bedrooms I'll sleep in. The inside of the house is as sparsely furnished as Davis warned me it would be, as this place is still awaiting his wife's scrutiny and the lavish renovation that will inevitably follow.

Through the front door is a living room with a faded brick fireplace, containing one couch and a coffee table. A large flat-screen television is the only thing hanging on the walls. A wireless modem, a satellite receiver box, and a rat's nest of power cords have been shoved into one corner of the room, all covered in a layer of dust.

Beyond the living room is a dining room void of any table or chairs, followed by a tiny kitchen where I've set about unloading a cooler I had stowed in the back of my car, crammed full of cold goods I picked up at the Whole Foods in Basalt on my way here—leaving out the makings for a late-afternoon protein shake. While it might be easier to dig into the remaining stash of road trip food I have in the car, I've consumed far too many Twizzlers, Sour

Patch Kids, and Cheez-Its in the last three days, and if there's one thing my mother's always reminding me of, it's that crap about a minute on the lips and a lifetime on the hips. Even if I would gladly take a little *anything* on my hips to give my reed-like frame some curves, I've spent twenty-seven years being brainwashed by sample-size expectations.

I drag my trusty Vitamix blender out from a cardboard box and glance around the kitchen. Electrical outlets are at a premium, and the one along the main countertop already has the microwave and my electric moka pot plugged into it. I won't need the moka pot until it's time for my morning coffee, so I unplug it and slide it over to make way for the blender. In the pitcher, I toss in a scoop of vanilla shake powder, an equal amount of almond butter, then some soy milk and a banana. I turn the dial to high, but the familiar hum lasts only a few seconds.

Suddenly, there's a loud pop, the sole light fixture in the center of the ceiling snaps off, the microwave's digital display goes dark, and my blender whirs to a stop.

"Shit." I freeze in place, all except my eyes, which skirt the room rapidly as I try to figure out what just happened.

Given I'm not schooled in the way of electrical mishaps, I come up with pretty much nothing. Although in the part of my brain where random information is stored, I think this may be a situation where a breaker box is important. Unfortunately, I don't know what a breaker box looks like. I don't know where one would *find* a breaker box. And I definitely don't know what to do with said breaker box once I find it.

While I grew up in an old house, it wasn't this kind of old house. Our house was a six-bedroom, nine-bathroom, two-acre English-style manor in the Chicago suburb of Kenilworth. There was a foyer and a fountain, a sculpture garden and a wine cellar—

and probably more than one breaker box. I'm sure Mac, the man who handled all things maintenance in our house, would know exactly how to fix this.

What I wouldn't give for a Mac right now.

In the spirit of resourcefulness, I decide to take a look around for anything that might scream *breaker box*, but after ten minutes of searching—including time in the cobweb-ridden basement—I find nothing.

My last resort is to call for reinforcements. Davis provided the contact info for a local real estate agent who has been acting as a de facto property manager and said I should call her if anything came up with the house. And, no matter how modest a house I'm happy to stay in, Amish I am not.

I, and my Vitamix, need power.

~⌒~

Janet the Realtor is both sweet and kind, but a font of electrical information she is not. She and I quickly realize that our two heads will not be enough to tackle this problem. She offers to call a local guy who has handled odd jobs at the house over the years to see if he can help, but warns that since he has a regular job in town, it might be a bit before he stops by.

A few hours later, a loud rumble sounds outside, followed by gravel crunching on the driveway.

Thank God. The electrical cavalry has arrived.

I peek down at my outfit and consider my mother's horrified expression if she could see me now. She raised us to only answer the door when absolutely necessary—read: the housekeeper had the day off—and then, only when dressed appropriately. My current outfit would not qualify. Because I'm about to answer the door in bare feet, wearing a pair of very *short* yoga shorts and a very loose

V-neck tee that drips low enough to hint at the butter-yellow lace of the bralette I have on underneath. Definitely wouldn't pass inspection in my childhood home.

I tug up on the neckline of my tee and remind myself I haven't lived at home since I was eighteen and today—sloppy or not—my mother can't see me.

Padding over to the door takes me past a large picture window in the living room that faces the driveway, where the source of that loud rumbling is parked, looking a little menacing, a lot big, and entirely too familiar.

No.

No, no, no.

Who'da thunk it? I *should* have listened to my mother. Because unless there happens to be another truck exactly like Garrett's in town, then he's the local sent over to save the day. And I'm dressed for anything but another round of Garrett and his abs. I wasn't clad in evening wear when we met earlier, but I also wasn't wearing what suddenly feels a little too show-and-tell for the audience. Give me a hard-of-hearing, half-blind geriatric electrician in some grease-stained coveralls and I'd probably feel fine in this. But Garrett? Not a good idea.

A knock sounds at the door, and out of some impossibly irrational reaction, I end up scurrying forward until I'm tucked under the back side of the staircase in the foyer, leading to the second floor. Maybe there's a way I can bolt up the stairs for a costume change without being seen. If I duck low and belly crawl across the floor, then drag myself up each riser like a zombie, then . . . Oh my God, this is insane.

Grow up, Cara. Think of the moka pot. Think of tomorrow morning. Think of being without your coffee. All you have to do is open the damn door, let him fix the power, then send him on his way.

I roll my shoulders back resignedly, then wiggle my arms about before stepping out from behind the staircase and make my way toward the front door. When I look up, Garrett's face is staring back at me through the traditional farmhouse door, thanks to the large glass insert across the upper half. I'm sure the fact I emerged from behind the stairs did not escape his attention, and it's also possible he saw me skulking my way over there in the first place. Damn glass and its inherently revealing properties.

His gaze stays fixed on my approach until I swing the door open.

Garrett gives a half grin and lets his eyes pass over the length of me, slowly enough that a prickle of awareness flares on my skin. I take a measured breath and mentally cloak myself in a nun's habit, a potato sack, *and* a large black trash bag.

"Heard you're having some electrical trouble," he drawls.

He's dressed exactly as he was this morning, and with the exception of a light layer of dirt that's spread across the chest of his T-shirt, he looks as distracting as he did a few hours ago. The canvas work coat he's wearing hangs open, one side of his shirt is half tucked into the waist of his jeans, and the spot where the two meet his belt draws my attention again. The space that looks flat and taut and like a whole handful of trouble.

Amie's freaking earlobes must be on fire right now.

Garrett clears his throat. My eyes shoot up. A lift of one eyebrow, combined with the way his mouth has curled into a sly tilt, makes it clear that while he doesn't mind the way I'm staring, he wants to be sure I'm aware I've been caught. *Nun's habit, potato sack, trash bag.* Despite the mental cloaking, one of my nervous habits kicks into high gear, the one where I tuck my hair behind my ears and usually end up talking more than I should.

"I was trying to make a protein shake but didn't get very far. I've existed on junk food for three days and needed to eat something that didn't include an expiration date into the next century, you know? But the blender was on for about ten seconds before there was this loud pop and then nothing. Now nothing works in the kitchen."

He stares at me for a beat, bemused but fascinated, like I'm a creature he can't quite identify.

"Sounds familiar." Garrett gestures toward the interior of the house. "Can I come in?"

I can't imagine how strange this situation must be for Garrett, even if he doesn't look the least bit weirded out. Here he is, asking *me* for permission to come in when this was once his home and I've been here for a grand total of three hours. I take a quick step back from the doorway and wave him in.

"Of course. God, yes, sorry. Come in."

He steps across the threshold and points toward the kitchen. "Did you check the breaker already?"

I shrug, waving my hands about aimlessly because I'm not sure how to explain that I might have graduated with honors from every school I've attended, but I can't find my way out of a proverbial paper bag when it comes to a breaker box.

"No. I couldn't find it. I looked, but nothing jumped out at me. I'm not sure what it looks like or where—"

Garrett chuckles and holds up his hands, palms out. "Relax, City. No offense, but I'm not shocked to find out you aren't the kind of girl who knows a lot about home maintenance shit." He starts toward the kitchen. "Follow me. I'll give you the lowdown on the quirks of this place."

In the kitchen, he comes to a stop in the center of the room, turns in a circle to survey everything crammed atop the limited counter space. He points to my Vitamix.

"Is that what you had running when the power went out?"

I nod. "Blender."

He lifts it up and cranes his head to inspect the underside of the base. "OK, this is a big part of the problem. It's probably drawing a shit ton of power when it's running. So you can't have this and anything else plugged in at the same time. Especially the microwave." Garrett sets it down again and points to my moka pot. "Or whatever that is."

"It's a moka pot."

Garrett gives up a snort. "A what?"

"For making espresso."

He gives me a blank look, and then lets his mouth curve as he answers by way of a slow nod.

My mind reels through a few potential follow-ups to his condescending little smirk, but all of them seem to highlight the obvious. That even if I'm not a Paris Hilton–type socialite who doesn't know what Wal-Mart is, it wouldn't take much to figure out what kind of life I come from. My car, my inability to find a breaker box, and now my preferred method for brewing my morning coffee—all of it sends a message. And if Garrett sees it, then so will everyone else, which means it's going to be hard to get the farmers and ranchers I came here to interview to talk to me about anything more significant than the weather.

Before I'm able to source the right retort, Garrett swipes one hand under the collar of his jacket then slips it off entirely, tossing it on a lone spot of empty counter space.

"Fucking hot in here. Did you turn up the thermostat?" I nod. "It's not very accurate. Just take whatever you think you want to set it at and subtract ten degrees; that usually works. Unless your goal is to get everyone who steps foot in here to start shedding their clothes."

He cuts a look in my direction, and my expression must reveal my first thought: that if Garrett started shedding his clothes, I wouldn't mind a bit. Because when our eyes meet, he winks.

Immediately, I want to advise him that the smirk was bad enough, but winking? There shall be no winking. It's cliché and lame and borderline smarmy. Who does that? This isn't a cartoon, which is the format I associate with winking. Like Tweety Bird. Or Pepe Le Pew, right before he sloppy smooches his way all over the wriggling lady cat's furry body.

Garrett's only reprieve is that my insides are doing weird things at the moment.

Fluttery, bubbly, perky things.

Also, he's just pulled the microwave out from where it was pushed up against the tile backsplash of the counter, and every muscle along his arms—the entire length from his wrists to his collarbones—leaps to work when he does. His biceps are especially problematic, as they are evidently under the misguided notion that the microwave is a lot heavier than it actually is, because they seem to flex in size twice over.

He cranes forward and inspects the outlet, then returns the microwave to its original position.

"Outlet looks good. Let's go have a look at the breaker."

Garrett grabs his coat off the counter and strides off down a short hallway toward a door at the back of the house. I follow, dazed but able to keep from bonking into the wall or stumbling over my feet. He sets one hip up against the door to brace his weight, grabs the handle and lifts upward, then uses his other hand to twist the dead bolt open. All the while, his biceps continue to overcompensate.

"This sticks a little. Gotta make sure you're pushing in and lifting up at the same time to work the dead bolt. If that drives you crazy, you're safe to leave it unlocked. Our crime rate is pretty much nonexistent."

A set of concrete steps leads out to the backyard, and Garrett clears them with a practiced half step, half jump. "The breaker box is out here. Come on over and I'll show you how to—"

Garrett stops short when he notes that I'm still standing on the top step, slack-jawed, looking out at the landscape ahead, my eyes doing their best to soak up the last moments of russet-orange sunset light behind the mesas in the distance. The neglected hay field encompasses what would normally be a backyard, stretching deep toward a bank of cottonwood trees. At the center, there's a break in the trees, and with the sunset glow alighting that clearing, I swear I wouldn't be a bit surprised if a yellow brick road suddenly materialized in front of me.

"Not exactly what you're used to seeing back home, I'm guessing?"

I allow a slow shake of my head. "Not even close."

Garrett stays silent, simply relaxes his posture and shoves his hands into the pockets of his coat, apparently content to let me stand here until I've taken my fill. After a few moments, I allow myself to exhale fully.

"Question," Garrett says. "I know you said you're here to work on a project, but I can't even guess what would bring a woman like you out here from Chicago. What is it you do?"

"I'm a freelance writer. Contracted with a quarterly journal— *magazine*," I clarify, a passive-aggressive retort for his smirk at my moka pot, "to write a piece on the ag industry down here."

A flicker of admiration lights in Garrett's eyes and I suddenly want to tell him more, prove how I might be an outsider, but I've also done some research and I want to get it right when I tell Grand Valley's story.

"This is a unique place. The microclimate means there's a banana belt where you wouldn't expect one, luring in all these new arrivals who've relocated to grow fruit and make wine because of it."

Garrett grins and gestures toward the far edge of the hay field, to an opening between the trees. I spot the hazy evidence of wintering trees planted in rank and file rows not more than a quarter mile away.

"You'll have plenty of options when it comes to interviews. You can't throw a stone around here without hitting someone who's making their living off the ag business. The newbies are interesting, yeah, but don't forget the old-timers. Some families have been here for a century, and they have plenty of stories." He gives a good-natured eye roll. "Just don't let them bust into a case of Natural Ice while you're there. They'll drink you under the table and it'll be midnight before you can get out of there. Trust me."

I give up a laugh. "Too much Natural Ice can mean trouble—I'll try to remember that. But I definitely want to talk to some of the old-timers. That's part of our focus, too—the changing face of this business, the way we're losing more and more farmland every day. Farmers passing on, families who can't or don't want to keep the land, how deeply that digs at . . ."

My words trail off when Garrett's expression shutters, his face going blank except for the faint twitch of his jawbones flexing. Crap. Talk about killing the vibe we were building by shining a spotlight on what Garrett knows all too much about. Silence falls between us.

Garrett blinks once. "Sounds interesting."

His flat delivery indicates he does not find what I just said *interesting* at all. He may find it insensitive, judgmental, or exploitative, but he sure as hell does not find it interesting.

I look away, letting my eyes track back to the tree rows,

knowing that if I tried to explain myself better, all I'd likely do is make things worse. The early evening light seems to dim in a rush, driving goose bumps across my skin. The fact that I'm out here in an outfit that both my mother and the winter temps apparently don't approve of snaps my attention into focus. I cross my arms over my chest, then run my hands up and down to stifle the chill. I allow a quick glance in Garrett's direction and find him tracking the motion of my hands, the shuttered mask he was wearing now replaced by a little wrinkle in his brow line.

"Are you cold?" He moves as if he's about to shrug a shoulder out of his jacket.

I wave him off before starting down the concrete steps. "I'm fine. Show me this breaker box thingy."

He rights his coat, lets his expression turn easy again, and walks toward the corner of the house where a metal box is affixed to the siding. Garrett points toward the box and threads his index finger through a metal loop to yank open the panel cover.

"This is the breaker box *thingy*, as you call it. Come on over."

A flick of his wrist to encourage me forward until I'm close enough for him to put one hand on my waist, gently urging me in front of him so I'm face-to-face with the box.

And despite what just happened, my words and his reaction, with the full span of Garrett only a half step away, it's impossible to ignore how well matched our bodies are. My height doesn't threaten to crest his, not even a bit. The breadth of him, the way he's broad without bulk, means I'm standing next to a man who can make me feel both on par and still feminine.

Garrett starts pointing at different parts of the box. "Each of these little levers controls a certain part of the electrical in the house. See this one? The one that's facing the opposite way from all the others?"

I spy the one he's talking about and give a nod. He flips the paddle so it's lined up with the others.

"When there's too much of a load, it shuts itself off. You just have to flip it back the other direction to reset it."

My forehead furrows up because with all those levers and bits, I expected something far more complex than this. Cautions about arcs and watts, or repair guidelines that required brain-numbing mathematical conversions—volts to amps to quadrangles to . . . something. But I feel like a regular journeyman electrician all of a sudden. At this rate, I'll be a Jill of all trades before I know it. Rewiring the house in my spare time, changing my own oil when needed, and building a dresser to store my clothes in.

"That's it?"

Garrett shuts the front cover. "That's it."

He doesn't move right away, and neither do I. The awareness of our bodies, his seemingly closer than it was before, quickly tramples over my newfound electrical prowess and the missteps I made earlier. When I hear Garrett's breath catch, mine does the same. I tuck my hair behind my ears in my typically nervous way, but keep from babbling by forcing my body to turn and face his.

Garrett *is* closer than before. Close enough that a Catholic school dance chaperone would remind us to leave room for Jesus. My gaze settles on his mouth, the part of him that's in my direct line of sight.

And, God, it's a *good* mouth. His bottom lip is fuller than the top, but not in a feminine way—just a teasing, feel free to nip or tug or play here, way. Soft but firm-looking, a combination that makes no sense in theory, but does when it's right in front of you. Because I'd guess Garrett's very good mouth is capable of doing and saying some very bad things on occasion.

The good mouth moves. "Any questions?"

Very. Bad. Things.

I manage a shake of my head, observe the slow bob of his throat over a labored swallow before cautiously peering up at him. His voice turns rough.

"Let's go check our work, then. Make sure you have power."

Another hitch of someone's breath. His or mine, who knows.

Garrett follows the dirt path back to the set of concrete steps into the house. I follow, issuing silent instructions along the way.

One foot in front of the other, Cara. Do not swoon, stumble over your feet, and somehow end up on your knees at his. He's a guy. A guy who winks and doesn't appreciate *Lakmé*. This is just some inconvenient glitch in your hormones.

Garrett waits as I mount the steps, then props the door open. His tongue ticks across the seam of his very good-bad mouth as I step past him, and the move reads like reason battling with temptation.

One foot in front of the other.

Do. Not. Swoon.

4

(Cara)

Inside the house we find the kitchen light fixture ablaze again. Garrett gives a chin nudge toward my blender.

"Remember, one thing at a time in the outlet. Same thing upstairs. You can't plug in a hair dryer and a curling iron or whatever beauty torture device is in these days—not at the same time."

I let out a snort at his utterly male assessment of female hair-styling. "I don't use a curling iron."

Garrett's gaze flits over my hair, inspiring the need to tuck it behind my ears again. He raises his arm up and makes a vague circling motion with his hand. "So it just does that?"

"What?" I will not tuck back my hair again, no matter how strong the pull is to do so. I cross my arms over my chest instead, digging the tips of my nails into the flesh on my arms to keep them there.

Another swirly move with his fingers. "The little curly pieces around your face. You just wake up that way?"

"Pretty much."

His arm drops heavily and a muttered curse leaves his mouth. Garrett looks past me, toward the front of the house.

"I should go. You need help with anything else?"

Yes. I need help with your shirt. It's been in my way since I met you.

Crap. No. Do not say that.

Before anything inappropriate comes out, I remember that I do have a task Garrett might be able to assist with. One that does not involve his clothes coming off.

"Actually, I do need something else." Garrett's gaze turns strangely unfocused for a moment. "I have one last thing in my storage pod outside that's too heavy to get in here by myself. Could I get you to help me before you take off?"

He looks amused and then shrugs. "At your service, City. Let's go grab it."

We head for the door and Garrett holds it open, clicking the front porch light on when we step outside. It's dusk now, making it even colder out. Garrett stops at the edge of the front porch.

"You want to grab a coat? It's pretty cold now."

I shake my head and make my way toward the pod. "My jacket is still in a box somewhere. I'm fine; this won't take long."

Fumbling with the lock, I twist it to insert the key and it frees up on the first try. Slipping the padlock off, I reach down to the handle, but before I latch on, Garrett grumbles and steps closer.

"Here. I can't watch you shiver again." His coat lands over my shoulders. Then he nudges his body ahead of mine, wordlessly shooing me out of the way.

Whether the coat thing is some lame attempt at orchestrated chivalry, I don't know, but when I slip my arms through to pull on Garrett's coat, I nearly groan. The inside is lined in a quilted flannel that is so broken in it's almost silklike, and I have stop from wiggle-burrowing into the fabric further. And it smells like a mix of something spiced, something soapy, and something dirty. Actual dirt, dirty. Mud, maybe? Sweat and silt? Grit and dust? Whatever the blend, from the smell to the heat, it's patently male and entirely new to my olfactory senses. I'm more used to how a designer *thinks* a man should smell—the sorts of cologne that always smell a little like someone dropped a bottle of pine-scented household cleaner into a barrel of Scottish single malt.

"Is it for sex?"

My head jerks up. "What?"

Garrett chin-nudges in the direction of my reformer. "That thing looks like it's designed with either torture or sex in mind." He looks over his shoulder. "Which is it?"

"It's a reformer."

"That doesn't clear anything up. 'Reformer' could apply to either. Torture or sex."

"It's for Pilates." I huff. "The only form of exercise I can stand."

He steps in sideways and works his body behind the machine, then gives one corner of the unit a test lift.

"You sure about this? This thing's heavy. I could bring my buddy Braden over tomorrow."

Rational reasoning hits hard at the mention of Garrett returning. No way. If we start making a routine of this, I'll find myself calculating ways to steal his coat or some other article of clothing, all of which are best left on his body.

I yank up the coat sleeves and move into place on the opposite side of the machine. "I'm stronger than I look."

"I don't doubt that, City." He takes hold of his end. "On three?"

I mimic his posture and deadpan my response. "Go team."

~⁓~

The lack of furniture in the house means we easily make our way inside, setting the reformer down in the middle of the empty dining room. Once it's in place, Garrett grips his hand around the foot bar, attempts to shake it, and then steps off to one side.

"How does it work?"

I get a little thrill at his question. "The carriage travels when you lie or stand on it. There are a bunch of different things you can do, different poses and moves, but it's your own resistance doing the work, so your muscles end up long and lean. Like a dancer's workout. I guess that's the best way to explain it."

"Can't picture it." He crosses his arms over his chest, eyes running over the length of the machine.

I slip off his coat and hand it his way, then kick off my shoes and step onto the machine. Placing the arch of one foot to the foot bar, I stretch my other leg out to set my heel against one of the shoulder rests. Slowly, I lean forward to grasp the foot bar with both hands, find my balance, and press the carriage out behind me until I'm fully extended. Essentially, I'm doing the splits—and after being cooped up in a car for so many hours, the release is a relief. I tamp down a loud groan that wants to escape into something quieter. Unfortunately, what ends up coming out sounds a little more *satisfied* than I planned on.

"So it's stretching," Garrett offers.

I move into another position, both feet on the carriage shoulder rests, my hands still fastened to the foot bar. "It's harder than you'd think."

Letting one foot rise off the shoulder rest, I point my toe and drive my leg up toward the ceiling, then slowly pull it in toward my chest, before repeating the sequence. The moves are yoga-like, akin to warrior three and royal dancer—and the combination of balance, movement, and tension means the whole sequence is far from easy.

On my fifth pass-through, just as my body starts to ache in a way I like, Garrett grunts, a low, rough sound that's indecent enough to draw my focus in his direction.

His rapt attention is fixed to my legs, eyes taking in every move I make. Normally, this would be a moment when the instinct to make myself smaller would take over. Too many years of my mother reminding me—usually when I am trying to enjoy my favorite banana frozen custard from Scooter's—that tall and skinny is one thing, but tall and *not* skinny was another, so I should probably put the spoon down. Or her insisting I always sit down in family photos, hoping that might make it so my height wouldn't *overwhelm* the picture. In her eyes, I'm like a towering sequoia, and all she wanted was a dainty magnolia.

But Garrett's gaze is appreciation mixed with interest, and shying away from it is the last thing I want to do, so I take a few more passes before sitting down cross-legged on the carriage.

"Do you do mat work, too?"

"Sure, sometimes. I like this better because . . . " I pause and narrow my eyes. "Wait. How do you know about mat work?"

Garrett laughs, his voice giving way to the lighter sound, then his mouth curves up guiltily.

"I was fucking with you; I knew what this thing was when I saw it. I went to school up in Fort Collins, had a part-time job at this sporting-goods store and there was a Pilates studio next door, with these huge plateglass windows along the front. It's impossible to be a straight guy and not look inside when you walk by. Plus, we sold a cheap-ass version of these things at the store I worked at." I let out a little huff and he widens his grin. "Figured I could play the country bumpkin for your benefit. And mine."

He stretches one arm out, palm open so I can take his hand. I work to keep a glare on my face, but when his fingertips strum across the inside of my wrist and my entire body heats, I realize it's a futile endeavor.

"You're *impossible*."

Garrett tips his head. "Come on, don't be mad, City. I'm sorry."

But his tone says he's not sorry, he enjoyed every second of what just happened. I sigh and slip my feet back into my shoes.

"Thank you for your help. Fixing the power, moving the reformer. I appreciate it."

"Not a problem. Happy to help." He shoves one hand into his back pocket and extracts his phone. "In fact, give me your phone and we'll swap numbers. That way you can text me if you need something."

I look down at his phone and hesitate. Garrett finally shakes the phone about, a prompt I take even when I know I shouldn't. A direct line to Garrett? Garrett with a direct line to me? This is trouble. Double trouble. Or worse. Fivefold trouble.

After I dig my phone out from the depths of still-unorganized things strewn across the coffee table in the living room, I meet Garrett near the front door, where I think it's best we remain. Adjacent to an opening where I can boot his charming, troublesome self outside as quickly as possible. I hand him my phone and set about entering my info in his.

Garrett hits the contact button on my phone.

"Cara, you only have five contacts in here." He reads them out loud. "Amie, Dad, whoever ICE is, Will, and some spa with a weird name I can't pronounce."

I peer at the screen and shrug, knowing it's considered peculiar to have so few people in my phone. When I was at the newspaper I had a cell they provided, which was littered with hundreds of contacts, and it was just another thing I was happy to be rid of when I quit. Now I can keep who matters on speed dial and relegate the rest to voicemail or, even better, email. I decide not to overthink the implications of Garrett's info being included in my inner circle.

"I believe in small circles. The spa is for getting my eyebrows threaded and my nails done. Important girl beauty *torture* things."

"I'm sure," he chuckles as he starts to key in his information. "Who's ICE?"

"My mother."

A snort from him. "Should I ask?"

"Technically, it stands for 'in case of emergency.' They say you should do that so if you get in a bad car accident or something, the hospital can look at your phone for an emergency contact. But it *is* my mother, so whatever double meaning you think applies, does."

I resist surreptitiously scrolling through his contacts. It's probably littered with entries that lack proper names, only vague descriptions. *Hot girl from bar. Blonde/Short Dress. Long Hair—Likes Coors.* After typing in my info, proper name and all, I lock the face and we exchange devices.

"All right, now you can hit me up when you need me. How long are you here for, anyway?"

"Eight weeks or so. I'll head home at the beginning of April."

Garrett shoves his hands into the pockets of his coat and opens his stance, stepping his feet wider. "That's a long time to be away from home. Expecting any visitors while you're here?"

"Visitors?"

"Yeah, *visitors*. Bound to be people who hate not being able to see you for two months. Maybe whoever this *Amie* is?" He waggles his eyebrows—which is nearly as bad as the winking—and his voice husks over a notch. "Or maybe *Will* wants to visit."

Ah, there we have it. Circuitous line of rambling for him to get to the point, which my sex radar indicates is about determining if I'm single. I open the front door and hold it ajar with my foot.

"Amie is my sister, and she's busy planning a wedding. As for my parents, Dad's a Boeing executive and Mom's a very dedicated executive wife. Aspen is about as far into Colorado as they'll venture."

Garrett lets my answer hang for a beat, ignoring my polite cue with the still-opened door. The tip of his tongue peeks out, grazes the center of his upper lip.

"What about Will? If he's the polo shirt–wearing investment banker back home that's missing you, I'd prefer to know that straight out of the gate. That way I don't misinterpret any late-night texts you send my way."

I lock my eyes on his, a steady gaze to match the one he's giving me. "I'm good with words. If I send you a text, it won't be open to interpretation."

He lowers his voice. "Don't play like that. You're good with words? So use them. Tell me what's what here."

Maybe it's the nearness of that very good-bad mouth, the scent of his stupid coat, or the tease of his tone, I don't know, but an answer tumbles out before I can stop it.

"Will is . . . family. I'm single. *That's* what's what. No boy-friend. No husband."

One side of his mouth curves up, gratified by this tiny coup over my best efforts to send him off shortchanged. "Thank you."

And with that, Garrett saunters through the open front door—just when I decide I might not want him to.

5

(Cara)

Day one.

My first day on assignment, doing the work I came here to do. I've channeled all the great storytellers I can think of—Joan Didion, Tom Wolfe, Gay Talese—to remind me why I made this leap, out of traditional journalism to what they called New Journalism, the place where a literary writing style and reporting can exist together, where the writer's experience can be as much a part of the story as her subjects.

I spent yesterday deciphering plat maps and then driving around to make sense of what the maps showed. After three hours, I was only slightly better oriented. But I did find a coffee shop in Paonia, one worth the lost time that led me there. Beans roasted on-site, Chemex-brewed coffee that bloomed while the café owner shared more than I ever wanted to know about the summer he spent as a Rainbow Family member. Despite that, I'm going back—the coffee is that good.

This morning, though, I brew my own. *After* making some oatmeal in the microwave. *After* making a protein shake. All while holding my breath to stave off any electrical dramas. Then I spread out a plat map and settle on where to go first.

I decide that my first stop will be south of town, where a quarter section of ground is owned by someone named Earl Kidd. By cross-referencing a topo map of the same area, I can see that his land sits below a small mesa, ripe with ridges and ravines throughout. While it doesn't seem suited to farming, he may have some cattle on it. My main hope is that this isn't a *gentleman's* ranch belonging to some Silicon Valley exec, retired at thirty-two, with enough money and time on his hands to become a well-meaning nuisance to the locals, full of ideas and initiatives to help the community—all of which will likely destroy a way of life that predates any of the apps he's developed by hundreds of years.

After a twenty-minute drive, I slow the car as I spot a lone mailbox along the road, its address numbers stenciled on in white spray paint on the side. Just beyond the mailbox is a large piece of plywood nailed to a makeshift sign post. Large block letters declare the terms of Earl Kidd's property.

PRIVATE PROPERTY
POSTED—NO HUNTING
NO TRESPASSING

I stop my car next to the sign and think over my choices. I even consider calling Will, posing the question to him about whether driving up there and knocking on Earl Kidd's door is considered trespassing or not. But Will would probably tell me two things:

a) He's a securities litigation attorney, a field where the SEC meets the law. He reads a lot of thick documents full of little type in order to figure out how the Bernie Madoffs of the world operate. Trespassing isn't exactly in his wheelhouse.

And b) that the big-ass sign erected here is my answer. Will's logical, law-loving brain would tell me this isn't worth it.

But my nosy, journalistic brain disagrees. I love other people's stories, always have—whether real or imagined, logical or not. And given that my master's degree is in comparative social sciences, I also want to know *why* Earl Kidd feels the need to post such a dramatic sign. He's an outlier, it seems, since no one else seems compelled to put up signs like this one, at least not that I've come across in my drive around the outskirts of town.

Time to go find out why. And keep on asking, until I discover the real reason.

Slowly, I let off the brake pedal, looking out of both windows cautiously as I cross a cattle guard and head up the dirt road. The road eventually curves up an incline at the base of the mesa, then narrows its way up several switchbacks, where the dirt turns craggy and jarring. I hit a particularly deep divot and wince when a loud thud sounds from underneath my car. I glance in the rearview mirror to see if something important-looking from the undercarriage of my car now lies in the roadway. Nothing but ruts and gravel, thankfully.

An open livestock gate comes into view, along with evidence that I've arrived at someone's domicile. A large travel trailer sits inside the gate, a heavily faded tan color with blue stripes running down the center of each side. Affixed to the rear of the trailer are two flags. One is a Gadsden flag, the signature bright yellow background and the image of a coiled rattlesnake in black, along with the tagline "DON'T TREAD ON ME" at the bottom. The other flag is navy blue with a colonial-era soldier surrounded by a ring of stars printed in white.

Suddenly, my time spent covering a few very rowdy Tea Party protests for the paper is proving pretty useful. Because to some those images are just a return to a bygone era of hearty American patriotism . . . but to others they're freak flags for politics that are a hell of a lot more volatile. So those two flags being flown together, atop a travel trailer parked in the middle of nowhere, could spell trouble for me. I'm potentially about two minutes away from finding myself besieged by a guy in fatigues who was *not joking* with his signage down by the road. And he's not likely to be a very understanding fellow.

On cue, the sound of a roaring motor and gravel spitting into the air causes me to whip my head toward the rear window of my car. Through the haze of dust billowing there, I spot a red four-wheeler barreling my way, looking as if the driver plans to plow straight into the back of my car. Just in time, he hooks a hard turn to the right, speeds down the side, and veers left so he can come to a stop directly in front of me.

The driver is standing on the footwells, dressed in fatigues as I expected. A black helmet covers his head, with the word "KIDD" stenciled in red letters across the top. Attached to the front of the four-wheeler is a metal caddy of sorts, designed to hold smaller-sized cargo. Just right for the short-barrel shotgun this guy's currently toting around.

The four-wheeler's motor putters to a stop, but the driver doesn't step off of it. He simply stands motionless, defiant and terrifying.

Pleasure to meet you, Earl Kidd. You are everything I thought you would be.

Slowly, he removes the helmet, revealing a full head of white hair underneath, cut short into a military style. His head is shaped liked a concrete block. Piercing eyes fix on mine—in all the wrong ways.

I lift my hands from their death grip on the steering wheel and hold them up in front of me, palms out. He squints to take in the gesture but doesn't lean in or relax his stance. I point toward my driver door with one hand, and then move to slowly open the door, stepping out on legs that feel a little fawn-like at the moment.

Decision time. Do I keep the opened door in front of me as a shield? Or step around it to show I'm not hiding anything? Not sure if this guy would actually think a girl in a Lexus hybrid would come up here packing anything other than a snack-sized baggie of raw almonds, but I can't be sure. Probably for the best to keep everything out in the open here. Very deliberately, I shut the door behind me.

"Can't you read?"

"Yes. I'm sorry—"

"If you can read, then is English not your first language? Are you some pale-skinned half-breed? All *gracias* and *de nada*?" Earl crosses his arms over his chest. When he does, the gun holstered to his belt comes into full view.

Screw all the other great storytellers I channeled this morning, I need Hunter S. Thompson for this one. His gonzo journalism style suits this situation perfectly—along with his knowledge of firearms and ties to the Hells Angels. Also, my heart rate could do with one of those barbiturates he was so fond of.

Absent of all that, the only thing I can do is lie. Attempt to fib my way out of here with all my limbs still intact.

"No. I'm a freelance writer. I thought this was the address for a cattle rancher I'm supposed to interview, but I must have written it down wrong. I'm very sorry to have disturbed your privacy; I'll just get in my car and go." I take two steps backward, reach behind me, and blindly swat about with one hand until I'm able to grasp the car door handle. "Again, I'm so sorry."

"You do that. Get in your rice can." Earl reaches forward to extract the shotgun from the metal caddy, gives it a practiced flip in his hands so that the barrel is facing away from me.

This seems like a good thing, right up until he rams the stock into one of my car's headlights. The shattering sounds like every bad action movie I've ever watched.

". . . And get out of here. If you trespass on my property again, I won't give you a second chance."

My shaking hands yank the car door open, fumble across the console for the keyless start button and press down. I jamb the car into reverse, keeping my speed reasonable as I back up, then once I'm headed straight I all but floor it. The undercarriage bounces against the dirt more than once, but if any parts are scattered on the road, I wouldn't know it. Looking back is the last thing I want to do.

Day one. A hell of a start.

6

(Garrett)

The Saturday shift at the co-op during the first weeks of calving season can be a killer. No matter how much ranchers prepare in advance for this busy time of year, their best laid plans sometimes don't work out—guys might find they need to change a mineral supplement to deal with illness and nutritional changes, or replace calving equipment that ends up damaged or disappears unexpectedly. Everyone is short on patience and time, so things can get hairy quickly—especially when I'm working solo and my last nourishment was almost nine hours ago, in the form of a shitty frozen breakfast burrito that wasn't even heated all the way through. Add in the fact I haven't slept well for the last few nights and at this point my body insists there are only a couple of options: fuel up via sugar rush, or crash. Hard.

Normally, I wouldn't be on my own, but my boss, Bart, is stuck on the other side of the Divide, waiting for Cottonwood Pass to reopen. He took his saint of a wife on an anniversary trip to the hot springs in Nathrop, and the night before they were supposed to come home a winter storm blew through and shut down the pass. The high school kids who might normally be able to jump in and help out are all working at their own family ranches. So flooding my body with caffeine, sugar, and calories appears to be the only choice to make it through the next few hours. And the gas station across the street has all three. I just have to finish up with Kenny Euland, then I can beeline my way over there for a hot dog and a vat-sized vessel of Mountain Dew. Perhaps a Snickers bar—or three.

"Worst calving season of my life. Can't get a damn thing to go my way," Kenny grumbles.

He slips a twenty from his wallet and hands it my way, adding in a few muttered curse words from under the brim of his straw cattleman's hat.

Kenny's a third-generation rancher with a large parcel of land west of town, not far from my friends Whitney and Cooper's organic orchard. With plenty of seasons under his belt, any claim that this is the worst one yet isn't a good thing. Kenny might be barrel-chested and burly, and prone to griping more than chatting, but he's not a drama queen. If he's complaining, there's truth in it somewhere. And even though my dad was a farmer, not a rancher, I've spent enough time around cattle guys to know that when things go to shit, it's all at once and in some exceptionally fucked-up way.

I hand back his change and slide the bottle of calf claimer powder he came in for across the counter. "I'll come over on Monday and give you a hand. Can't do anything tomorrow because I've got to head up to Grand Junction for my mom's birthday, but Monday I'm off and around all day."

Kenny wraps one hand around the back of his neck, kneads the thick roll of skin at the base of his skull, and sighs.

"Come on, kid, you have better shit to do on your days off. I appreciate the offer, but you don't need to do that. Stay the night in Junction, find yourself one of those Mesa girls to keep you company." He lands a good-natured shoulder punch for emphasis.

I shake him off. We've played this game more than once. He claims that I don't need to help, and I tell him to pipe down. If I weren't about to face-plant into the countertop from hunger, I'd go through our usual charade.

Truth is, I want to help far more than Kenny needs me to. The co-op is just a job—a good one, but it's nothing more. Out there, no matter who the land belongs to, the work is honest in a way no *job* can be. Dirt is a righteous equalizer; you can't fake your efforts or fib your way through what it takes to make a living that way, and that—the harsh and authentic reality there—is what I miss the most about working the land.

I slam the cash register drawer shut, then cross my arms over my chest.

"Geese are out of season, so I can't go hunting until turkeys open in March. And listening to some college girl run her trap about Snapchat all night isn't worth any company she might offer. So as I see it, I'm pretty sure I *don't* have anything better to do. I'll see you on Monday around six. Tell Barb if she happens to make some of that monkey bread she's known for, I'll be more than happy to eat it."

Kenny shakes his head, pushes out a long exhale from one side of his mouth, then turns to head for the door.

"Don't get into cattle, kid," he throws out over his shoulder. "When you get some of your own dirt, stay away from the damn cattle. Your dad had it right. Wheat. Corn. Sugar beets. Screw these damn cows; they make a man miserable."

When the front door shuts behind him, I grab my coat and pat my back pocket to be sure my wallet's there. I clear my way around the counter and out the front door, hanging the "Will Return" sign on the front door after setting the little fake clock hands to fifteen minutes from now.

The sun is high in the sky, casting bright across everything below. I tilt the bill of my ball cap down to cut the glare and give Kenny a parting wave as he pulls out from the co-op parking lot.

Whether what Kenny said about my dad getting it right was true or not, I'll never know. But with how things ended up after he died, I'm not sure I can say he had it all figured out. No disrespect to my old man, but whether it was shit luck or bad timing, either way things didn't go the way they should have.

Three years ago, I was a few semesters away from finishing my ag sciences degree and had an internship lined up at a major seed company where I was supposed to spend the summer working on drought resistance seed science, learning about solutions I could eventually bring home to the farmland I grew up on. Instead, my dad collapsed in the middle of July, in a field full of knee-high corn rows, dead at fifty-one from a massive heart attack.

I came home to a farm leveraged so deep there wasn't a way out. Not for a kid my age, at least, no matter how many people knew I was able and willing. Try getting any bank—even the one your dad carted you into atop his shoulders every Saturday to make the weekly deposit—to carry a loan for a twenty-two-year-old guy without a degree or a savings account. Looking back, the fact that I had no idea where the farm stood financially was proof enough I wasn't ready. I was more than just a bad risk. I was a joke.

The estate attorney, also known as my dad's best drinking buddy, gave it to me straight. No sugarcoating it, nothing but the three fingers of Crown Royal he poured me to take the edge off.

"You have to sell. That's your only option here, son. There isn't any cash to pay off these debts, and no matter how great of a kid you are, the bank isn't willing to let you take over the loan. So you sell, bank whatever might be left after all the loans are paid off, and

go back to Fort Collins. Finish your degree and go get a good job. Walk away knowing you did what you had to do. We both know what your old man always used to say: there ain't nothing behind you worth worrying about. He'd expect you to move on from this, no regrets."

I followed *most* of his instructions.

Sell? Done. I sold our farm to a guy I'd never met, who had enough money to buy it sight unseen, and until Cara arrived a few days ago, the house had been empty since the day I moved out, turning shabbier by the day.

Bank the cash that was left over? Done. I have a savings account now—one I haven't touched since the day I opened it and deposited that check. I've yet to need something enough to touch it. All the things I might want, a new truck or a new shotgun, aren't worth what that money stands for.

But I never went back up to Fort Collins to finish my degree; instead I stayed put and went to work at the co-op. Probably couldn't explain why, even now. Maybe because coming home was always part of the plan anyway. I always figured that, after a stint at a big ag company and a few years getting to know the right girl, she and I would find our way here. A girl who understood this life, loved it, and didn't want much more than to wake up next to a guy who did, too.

As for moving on? That was easy. Even when things were hard, when I missed my dad and wondered what I'd done wrong in life for shit to turn out this way, I sucked it up. Because anything less would have disappointed the one man I never wanted to let down. Even now, when I get to thinking about what might have been, I remind myself that what I have is good enough.

Most days, it is.

After waiting for a grain truck to rumble past, I dart across Main Street to make for the gas station on the corner, where all my poor food choices await. I stride past the three pumps and scan the lot absently, but pause when my eyes snag on the back end of a burgundy SUV.

An expensive-looking burgundy SUV.

With Illinois plates.

The SUV that—unless fate, or this grave bout of starvation are messing with me—belongs to a certain woman with big brown eyes, a sharp mind, and the longest, prettiest legs I've ever had the pleasure of seeing up close.

Immediately, my dick starts to wage war with my stomach. Certain less-rational parts of me are pointing due north, intent on creeping around that gas pump to see where Cara is. My stomach, though, doesn't give two fucks about a woman, any woman, right now.

Stomach wants a hot dog. Dick wants to be the hot dog to Cara's . . . bun . . . or something.

Christ. I have to eat. Now. Before I end up letting my dick lead the way and then allow my mouth to say any of this crap out loud. I strike a bargain with my junk. We'll go inside, procure food, and if she's still out here when I'm less likely to make an ass out of myself, we'll consider it fate.

All parties involved—brain, stomach, dick—agree to this compromise, although some less agreeably than others. I yank the store door open and almost stumble into a pack of college-age girls blocking the doorway, who then seem to decide that giggling and gawking about in my way is cute. Normally, I might play along, but not today. I need to save my flirt for the woman who's outside. I make my way over to the hot dog roller, where one sad but edible hot dog remains. Bun, hot dog, mustard, a spoonful of pickled peppers. One huge bite and my eyes roll back in my head a little. When my eyes return to center, I spy my next course in this gas station buffet.

On a display positioned right where the sunlight streams in from the storefront's large plateglass windows, a tall rack is stacked full of single-serve packs of Honey Buns. My second favorite snack cake after the ever-tasty Hostess Fruit Pie. Even better, these are *sun-warmed* Honey Buns. Definitely need one of those. Snickers bar be damned.

Yanking one off the display, I sneak a peek out the window on my way to the cash register.

Excellent. Overpriced SUV hasn't moved.

After pocketing my change, I swipe a coat sleeve over my mouth and slip out the front door to weave my way around the gas pumps. And there's Cara. Looking even better than before.

Shit. I think I wanted her to seem, I don't know, less appealing than she did a few days ago. Less beautiful, less polished . . . fuck, maybe if she were just *shorter*, that would help.

But nope, not even a little bit. She's dressed in a pair of loose cargo-style pants with a drawstring waist, the bottoms tucked into a pair of lace-up boots that don't appear built for roughing out hard terrain or slogging through mud. A tight long-sleeve top with a deep neckline shows off her tiny waist and the slant of her delicate collarbones. Her hair is pulled back, leaving the long slopes of her neck exposed.

So, basically, she looks awesome. Fucking gorgeous. Like some sort of super-misty slow song should be playing in the background as she pumps gas into her seventy-thousand-dollar ride.

"Hey there, City."

Cara flinches, then grips the handle on the gas nozzle like it's her only anchor from toppling forward. Her already-fair skin looks more pale than it should, and when she locks her eyes on mine, my entire body reacts to the wariness there, heart thumping into my gut, hands tightening into crab claws—including the one still grasping what's left of my half-eaten hot dog.

Cara presses her free hand to her forehead, using the heel of her palm.

"Hi," she offers, then struggles to paste on an entirely fake smile.

I narrow my eyes, leaning in a touch closer. "You look a little dazed. Did you zap yourself trying to flip a breaker or something?"

She doesn't laugh, just closes her eyes and works to regulate her breathing, and now she's starting to freak me out a little bit. All of a sudden I'm not hungry anymore, so I toss the half-eaten hot dog in the trash can and tuck the package of Honey Buns into the inside coat pocket of my jacket.

"No. No electric mishaps. More of an interpersonal mishap."

I have no idea what that means, but before I can ask, the gas pump trips to a stop and Cara pulls out the nozzle to set it back on the pump. "Do you know Earl Kidd?"

Immediately, my eyebrows raise up high enough to nearly meet my hairline. "The crazy survivalist prepper dude? Drives an old Suburban that's spray-painted camo, with a bunch of minute-man propaganda plastered all over it?"

Cara nods. "I didn't see the Suburban . . . but yeah."

My brows descend, wrinkling tight lines across my forehead.

"I don't *know* him, not well, at least. He's been into the co-op a few times. But I've heard enough to know what he's about. Why?"

She sets her gas cap in place and gives it a twist, then slams the fuel door shut—way harder than necessary.

"I went up to his place today."

The fuck? Why she would do that, I don't know. But it does explain the Casper-like shade of her skin, given she probably just met her first sociopath. If Earl Kidd isn't writing ten-page editorial letters to the local newspaper, then he's wallpapering parked cars with his latest manifesto on liberal agendas and conspiracy theories. When he isn't busy with all that, he's poaching big game on the national forest land adjacent to his property. Boldly, too. Because he claims that the entire premise of federally owned land is a sham to begin with, the result of a government gone wrong. He's *batshit*.

"Christ," I mutter, taking a step closer to her. "Hold on."

Gently, I place one hand on her shoulder. When she tenses, I drop my hand and step back. After taking inventory of her from head to toe, I crane my head a bit so I can make a show of inspecting her back. She eyes me over one shoulder with a narrowed gaze.

"What are you doing?"

"Looking for holes. Stray shot where one doesn't belong. Like on your ass." She laughs, and while it's a little shaky-sounding, it's also evidence of her relaxing. "Are you OK? Did he do anything?"

One of her arms gestures toward the front of her car, where the right headlight is smashed in.

"Other than that, he mostly yelled at me. Told me to get in my rice can and not to come back." Her eyes rise up to meet mine. "What's a *rice can*, anyway?"

"He's commenting on your car. Asian manufacturer." She purses her lips and gives up a frustrated sigh. "Don't let it get to you. He's nuts."

"I know. It's just . . ." Cara's voice trails off.

I cross my arms over my chest, wait for her to finish without me having to push and drag it out of her, even when a hundred different parts of me want to dig in and do exactly that. Cara yanks her printed receipt off the gas pump and stuffs it in her back pocket with a sharp jab of her fingers.

"This was day one. Day one and it's a fucking mess. I managed to find the loosest cannon in the county, get my headlight smashed in by a sawed-off shotgun, and have my life threatened. On day *one*. I'm not exactly off to a good start here."

Her expression turns frustrated, then becomes almost blank as her gaze settles in the distance, like she's not sure whether she wants to holler or bawl. Then she slumps to rest her back on the car, eyes dropping to fix on the asphalt below our feet.

And I have no idea what to do. I want to do something, but who knows what a woman like Cara needs right now? Does she need someone to tell her not to worry about it, that it's all going to be fine? Does she need me tell her to forget that shit and get on with plan B? Does she need a hug?

Fuck it. I'll just throw it all out there and see what sticks.

"He's crazy, Cara. Don't worry about it," I tell her. She nods at the ground, obviously unconvinced, so I try another approach. "Screw Earl Kidd; he's a one-off. You just need to move on. Go knock on some more doors."

Her shoulders rise and tense, but she still doesn't raise her head. I'm down to my last option. I tip my head, hoping to see her expression better, then grin a little—that way my voice is sure to sound easy and relaxed.

"You know what might help? My friend Whitney swears by hugs as a legit treatment for anything. Now, bear in mind, she's a tree hugger with a nose ring, not a medical professional. But I'd be willing for us to test out her methods right now, if you want."

Cara sputters and laughs, her downcast head and shoulders bobbing a little when she does. The laugh tapers and she brings her head up. "I'm good. Thank you, though."

My dick and I are disappointed at being denied even some tame body-to-body contact with Cara—can't lie about that. But I won't ask again. After the day she's had, the last thing she needs is me pushing my way into her space.

She heaves herself up from resting against the car, and when it becomes obvious our conversation is about to be over, my mind starts to work overtime and words tumble out before I can think through what I'm offering—or why.

"On Monday I'm planning to go help out a cattle rancher for the day, Kenny Euland. You should come along. This is calving season, so you can see how it all works, ask Kenny some questions." I shove my hands in my pockets awkwardly, watching as Cara scans my face, looking for evidence of I'm not sure what. Next thing I know, I'm talking again.

"And my friend Whitney? The hug-ologist? She and her boyfriend, Cooper, own Delaney Creek Orchards. Whitney's a hippie who up and decided to buy an orchard on a whim, and Cooper's a former Texas cattle ranch kid. Both of them are good people who I'm sure wouldn't mind giving you some time. I could set something up, take you out to see them."

More of Cara studying my face like either it's interesting or I have mustard somewhere it doesn't belong. Christ, hopefully she jumps in here soon—otherwise I'll end up inviting her to my mom's birthday dinner or some shit. Finally, one side of her mouth curves up into a near smirk.

"Aren't you helpful," she deadpans. "Will you write the story for me, too? I know you have a job in town somewhere, but I don't know what it is. Are you also the plucky and charming local newspaper reporter?"

I drop one hand to the roof of her car, lean lazily, and tip my chin down to match her smirk with my own.

"Nope. I work at the co-op. I'm just the guy who knows everybody and wouldn't mind getting you up in my truck for a few hours, while I make some introductions. After that, you're on your own to write the story."

Her head cants as she considers my offer. *Say yes, City.* We could have a hell of a good time together. Stop thinking and say yes.

After a few moments, Cara rights her posture so her back is ramrod straight.

"OK," she says, confidently but also cautiously. I keep the high five I want to throw her way to myself, giving her a satisfied grin instead.

"*But*," she continues, eyeing me skeptically, "the getting-me-up-in-your-truck part isn't necessary. I'll drive. You're helping me; it's the least I can do."

I glance at her car and note the little blue *H* on the nameplate, working out the best way to say what I need to.

"I should drive."

"Why?" Her eyes narrow. "Because it's a rice can?"

"I won't say that. But yeah. And it's a *hybrid*."

"God, you have to be kidding me," she sputters. "I'd like to know what is so wrong with a hybrid. I mean, I know it's a Lexus, I know it has out-of-state plates and I'm from the city, but how in the hell is the fact I'm conserving fuel that can now be used in tractors and combines somehow a *bad thing*?"

Defense sparks in her eyes, and I realize how much I like that fire, the way it lights and colors everything about her. I *really* like it. Probably a lot more than I should.

"Nobody thinks it's a bad thing. It's just . . . I don't know, not our way. Let's take the path of least resistance this time, OK?"

Cara's shoulders relax, but I can tell there's a complex transaction taking place in her mind. All of what happens inside this woman's head is probably way over mine, and pretty fucking impressive to boot. A little nod tells me she's on board with my plan.

"So I told Kenny I'd be there early. Does five thirty work for you?"

"Yes. And thank you, Garrett. I appreciate your help." She

pauses. "I'd throw out the offer of my own thank-you hug, but I'm not sure if it's a good idea."

I respond by angling my eyes skyward then opening my arms wordlessly and flicking my wrists to encourage her. Cara chuckles and steps forward, wrapping her arms around my waist, and I know I have to keep myself from tugging her closer, so I set my arms around her shoulders loosely. Cara does the opposite, dropping her grip lower and tighter on my waist. I tip my head to hers, lowering my voice.

"Careful, City. You're about to smush my Honey Buns."

Cara goes stiff. Quickly raises her arms up to ensure they're clear of my ass, and then starts to wrangle away. Her cheeks are a touch pink when she mumbles an apology and steps clear. I tuck one hand to the inside of my coat, pluck out the plastic wrapper of sugary goodness, and jangle it about in front of her.

"No one enjoys having their Honey Buns manhandled." Cara flops her hands over her face with a groan. I start across the parking lot backward, tearing open the wrapper as I walk.

"Dress warm and wear boots. And whatever else you won't mind getting covered in blood, cow shit, and mud."

7

(Garrett)

My mom lives in an apartment. An *apartment*.

Or, as I prefer to call it, a jail cell. I'd live almost anywhere else before I moved my crap into an apartment. A hut. A lean-to. A tent. Shit, give me a tarp, a couple of trees, and a handful of stakes to work with, and I'd be good—at least that way you have plenty of blue sky around you, not just the hint of it through a few cereal box–sized windows. Here, it's just hundreds of human beings piled together like rats in a science lab.

What hurts is that this isn't even one of the *nicer* apartment complexes in Grand Junction. Although it is better than the place she rented after she and my dad split up almost ten years ago. I was fifteen when they divorced, and shared custody meant I spent more weekend nights than I ever wanted to in that first near-ghetto dump, which probably has a lot to do with why I hate apartments.

Now that I'm a bill-paying adult, I get why she couldn't afford much more. Any alimony from my dad had to be a joke given the state of the farm, and there weren't any full-time jobs to speak of in a small town like Hotchkiss, so she took the only decent gig she could get, cashiering at a big-box hardware store in neighboring—and significantly bigger—Grand Junction. Since then she's found a better job with the city and moved here, to the Grand Glen Lodge, where shabby siding is covered in flaking paint and the landscaping consists of ugly bushes seriously in need of a good whacking with some hedge clippers. Technically, it was moving up, but without fail, every time I pull into the parking lot all I can think about is how it isn't *grand*, or part of a *glen*, and doesn't look at all like a *lodge*.

But I love my mom. She's the only parent I have left, and even if she lives in what I think is the equivalent of a hamster cage, as long as she does, I'll keep making the hour-long drive from Hotchkiss to see her.

One lonely parking space is available in the guest lot, small enough that I may have to roll down my window, crawl out the opening, drag myself onto the truck's roof, then leap into the truck bed and over the tailgate—all to avoid dinging the Mazda or the Honda boxed in on either side of me.

Fucking hamsters.

I avoid all that shit by creaking the door open slowly and side-stepping my way out between the cars, holding my mom's birthday present up above my head. A short walk and up three sets of stairs, I round the corner and head down an open-air walkway to my mom's door, where a decorative sign hangs: "Holy Spirit, You Are Welcome Here" penned in fancy cursive writing, surrounded by colorful painted flowers. After the divorce, my mom found religion. Although she claims she just found it *again*, back to the faith she grew up with, instead of the one my dad believed in. Weather was Dad's church and the only thing he would pray to—but he was devout, no question.

I give three knocks on the door and almost immediately, it swings open.

"Garrett! Good to see you, son!"

Randy, my mom's boyfriend of three years, opens his arms and grins. He's wearing a chef's hat, white and billowy, atop his balding and perpetually sunburnt head. I stick one hand out for a perfectly acceptable handshake, hoping this might be the time we leave it at that.

But Randy does his usual: latches on to my hand and yanks me forward into a bear hug, complete with a hearty, hammering back slap that always knocks my breath away. My theory is he's trying to prove something when he does it: that behind the goofy chef's hat and the bald spot, he's a guy's guy. Which is pointless because Randy sells life insurance for a living. He sports chinos with polo shirts and boat shoes, and a pinkie ring on his right hand. He drives a used red BMW convertible . . . that he calls *Scarlett*.

And you just can't back-slap your way away from all that.

Also, he doesn't need to try so hard, because I already think he's a decent guy. Short of the times I catch him leering at my mom in a way I'd rather not see, he treats her right and loves her. He's also been trying to convince her to move into his place with him, which I think is a good idea because I'd much rather see her shacked up with Randy than here. So whether I would or would *not* want to go fishing with him, doesn't matter.

I catch my breath and lean back. "Hey, Randy. Good to see you, too."

My mom pops her head out from around the wall to the kitchen, where something smells damn good. "Peanut, get in here. I want my birthday hug, but my hands are covered in cracker dust."

It's her birthday, but Mom loves to cook, so she'd take slaving away in the kitchen any day over any trip out to a restaurant. Do

I have a list of top-pick dishes I'm hoping make an appearance at the table today? Selfish or not, I do. Her Delmonico potatoes are one, as is a certain broccoli-cheese casserole that's topped with a butter-soaked crumb topping made out of Ritz crackers, evidence of which I can see all over her fingers at the moment. I'm an only child, so there's always a strong chance my mom will indulge my favorites, even if it's not *my* birthday.

I slide past Randy and make my way into the kitchen, slinging one arm over my mom's shoulder and tucking her into my side for a hug, the top of her blonde head reaching only to the middle of my chest. Balancing her birthday gift in the palm of my free hand, I present it to her with as much flourish as a boring gift set of bath products can justify. Thank God for Bath & Body Works, especially the one located three miles away from her apartment complex.

"Happy birthday, Mom. Ta-da, bubble bath and shit."

"Don't curse, Peanut." She leans in to peer at the bottles, her dangly turquoise earrings tinkling quietly when she does. "Ooh, gardenia. Thank you, sweetie."

Randy strides through the kitchen and flips the latch to the slider door that leads out onto the so-called balcony. I'm not sure what the exact definition of "balcony" is, but somehow I think that a six-by-four-foot space that overlooks a dingy parking lot doesn't qualify. Randy grabs a bright red apron off the back of a chair by the kitchen table and slips it over his head, slightly deflating his chef's hat. Today's polo shirt is yellow, so adding in the red of that apron means he's one seriously colorful being right now.

He thumbs toward his chest, where the words "KING OF THE GRILL" are printed on the apron.

"This guy's going to fire up the grill." Randy realigns his chef's hat and pats the sides to pouf it up properly. "We picked up some rib eyes at the store. Sound good, Garrett? We went with choice. Nothing but the best for my Paula."

He throws a pleased grin my way, followed by a wink for my mom.

Note to self: Stop winking at girls. It's lame.

But Mom laughs, throaty from the Camels she smokes but swears she's someday going to give up. Then she smiles big for Randy, with a tilt of her head that confirms she truly does feel like he's giving her the best.

Moments like these make it hard to ignore how much has changed in those years since my parents divorced. It's more than the apartment—it's everything.

When Mom left, I couldn't understand a thing about what she was doing. I knew my dad was a stoic guy, but even if he didn't say much, when he did I listened—he taught me every farming, hunting, and life-living lesson I've ever needed, and as a kid I believed the sun rose and set on his watch. Which is why no one questioned whether I was going to stay with Dad in Hotchkiss or move with my mom.

And after I watched him go from stoic to silent in the six months after the split, during one of those shared-custody weekends at my mom's first apartment, she and I argued over something stupid and I snapped. The next thing I knew, I was telling her exactly what I thought about what *she'd* done. That she was heartless and hateful, that I hated coming to her shitty apartment, and she didn't deserve my dad anyway.

She cried. Big, fat, silent tears. And for the first time since the split, I could see how she was hurting as much as my dad was.

The second those tears started, I wanted to take back every word. Then she tried to explain how a girl from town could fall for a kid from the farm and want desperately to love the life he did, but after twenty years of trying, had to accept that she hated being a farmer's wife and for all the years she'd thought it would grow on her, it didn't. It wouldn't. She said Dad knew it, too. And his way of dealing with it was to *not* deal with it. He shut her out until they had grown too far apart to find their way back.

I understood better then, because love might grow your heart, but it doesn't rewire who you are, and even the fifteen-year-old me could see how expecting another human being to be happy where they don't belong was too much to ask.

And my mom belongs here. With Randy, who makes her happy, and working a nine-to-five job doing payroll for the city.

Now, this doesn't mean I can overlook *everything* about her life these days. When Randy squeaks open the slider door to light— translation, plug in—their grill, I have to stop from rolling my eyes. Their grill is electric. Not charcoal, or a pellet grill, not even propane. It's electric, endorsed by the illustrious George Foreman, and putting three steaks on there will be a tight fit, although given the size of that balcony, anything bigger would be a joke anyways. The fact that the steaks came nestled in Styrofoam and wrapped in plastic is even harder to bear.

Growing up, my dad did his best work on a Traeger, and more often than not, what landed on there were elk steaks and antelope burgers. When beef did make an appearance, it was from Euland's or the Mahon's ranch, not the Kroger grocery down the street.

Still, I try to play along when my mom opens the refrigerator door to extract the large plate of steaks.

"Those steaks look good, Randy. I should get over here more often," I manage, watching as Mom shakes on a healthy dose of Lawry's Seasoned Salt, then hands the plate off to Randy when he steps back inside.

Mom slips the broccoli casserole into the oven and gently smacks my arm with an oven mitt. "You should. I miss seeing my boy."

Randy chimes in with an agreement from outside, where the saddest-sounding sizzle rises in the background as he puts the steaks on. "Tell me what's going on with you these days, Peanut."

I snag a handful of shredded cheese out of the zipper bag on the counter before she puts it away, then slip off my coat and hang it on the back of the chair.

"Not much. Work is same, same. Nothing to hunt until turkeys at the end of March. But I need to spend some serious time shooting my bow before then. I'm trying out a new release, so I want to make sure I'm ready when the season opens. Need to change the oil in my truck and swap out the plugs, shit like that."

"Are you helping Kenny Euland out? I'm on Facebook with Barb, and things don't sound good. If things keeping going this way, they might end up losing eight percent this season."

That helps explain Kenny looking like shit and sounding like gloom and doom. Losing eight percent of his calves would be a huge blow to his year, even in an operation his size, not to mention the mental kick in the gut that comes with watching that many little ones die. Commodity or not, even the toughest of ranchers can't watch that without feeling it.

"I saw him yesterday and he didn't look good, but I figured it was just the usual. I'm planning to head over early tomorrow, see if I can get Kenny the hell out of there for a while. Do what I can to help."

"I'm sure he'll appreciate it. I still remember how those guys need all the hands they can get this time of year."

I make to steal a Hawaiian roll out of the basket she's about to put on the table, but she dodges the move and I come up empty-handed. A stack of place mats, napkins, and silverware are in the middle of the table, so I start to set them out. Mom's *all hands* talk reminds me of the extra set of hands I'm taking along for the ride tomorrow, and even though I might regret bringing it up, the idiot inside me wants to mention Cara. Why? I have no fucking idea.

"Well, I happen to be bringing another pair of hands with me. Not sure if Cara's going to be any help, but—"

"Cara? Who's Cara?"

Yep. Regretting it already. I can practically hear the whip of Mom's head in my direction, along with the pitter-patter of her grandmotherly instincts firing to life. Given that the last girl to meet my mom was my high school girlfriend, I should have known better than to think she might play it cool when I drop a woman's name in conversation. Not that I've been considering the priesthood or anything over the last few years, I just haven't dated anyone seriously enough for it to matter.

But now, two syllables (*Ca-ra*) and Mom's possibly already trying to determine if we should plan a fall or summer wedding. Which isn't even a question, because when I do find the right girl, there is no way I'm getting married in the fall—that's prime big-game hunting time, after all. Any woman I marry will have to accept hunting widow status from Labor Day to Christmas. As for the specific woman in question, Cara is about as unlikely a candidate for a hunting widow as exists.

I sigh. "Simmer down. Cara is a reporter out here from Chicago, and she's writing a story on the ag industry. I'm helping her out with a few introductions so she can interview people, that's all. So you can stop knitting those baby hats or socks, or whatever, in your head."

She cocks a hip and sets one hand there, looks at me squarely. "Is she cute?"

I groan. *"Mom."*

"Is 'cute' not the right word? Pretty? Hot? Maybe smokin' hot?"

Idiot mouth of mine and those two innocent syllables. I can't even explain how much I want this conversation to be over.

"Jesus Christ. Stop. There's no way I'm going to have a conversation with you where I tell you that I think she's hot."

"You just did. And don't say JC's name unless you're praying."

"I am praying. Praying you'll stop asking me these questions." I cock my head in the direction of the balcony. "Wait, did you hear that? I think Randy needs my help. Maybe the George Foreman singed his apron. I should go check."

She cuts me off at the pass when I head for the slider door, narrows her eyes as I try to avoid her unflinching mom stare. Another tilt of her head. Then a raise of her brows, and I crack.

"Fine. Yes, she's hot. Gorgeous. Beautiful. *Tall*," I answer, giving in because there's no other way out of this conversation.

And it's like I can suddenly hear those baby-bootie-knitting needles clacking away in my mom's head. Outside, Randy is whistling the theme song from *Bonanza*. Fucking apropos, really, given the way my pint-sized emotional-gunslinger mom is grinning at me.

8

(Cara)

By the time Monday morning rolls around, I'm feeling appropriately optimistic. I've put the Earl Kidd debacle behind me, my travel mug contains moka pot–brewed espresso topped off with boiling water to create the best Americano there is, and I have my new Sorel boots on—and, more important than good coffee and dry boots, I have a source. An "in" with the locals, a guy who, as he put it, is *the guy who knows everyone*. If he isn't full of shit, then getting in good with Garrett is bound to pay dividends. I just haven't figured out if those dividends could, or should, include the kind where we're naked together.

I spot the headlights on Garrett's truck from where I sit on the front steps, under the glow of a bright halogen porch lamp, plumes of exhaust visible against first light dawning in the east. When he pulls to a stop, I catch his grin through the windowpane of the truck just before he jumps out, leaving the motor running to chug away in the quiet morning air.

"Morning, City."

Oy. Garrett's morning voice. Gruff and rough, a touch hoarse, and addling to my sanity. Maybe I need to find another tour guide. One with a dad bod and an unkempt beard, old enough to be my grandfather, and who calls me "darlin'." Because if Garrett being my "in" involves too many early call times like this, I won't be held responsible for my actions. He's merely standing there holding the edge of the open truck door and leaning forward casually, yet after one gas station hug session with him, I'd swear I can envision every muscle in his lean body flexing underneath his clothes. One hug was all it took. I memorized the ridges my hands traced, then filled in the blanks on the rest with my imagination. My *vivid* imagination.

Sigh. I'm simply far too undercaffeinated to make good decisions at this ungodly hour.

"You ready?"

I stand up and haul my messenger bag over one shoulder. "I'm ready."

When I step off the porch, Garrett gives in to a slow inspection of my form, and the sleepy pace he employs is even harder to manage than his morning voice. His gaze is a slow trickle, starting with the gray scotch cap on my head, complete with little flaps to keep my ears warm—a cute, themed purchase I made before I came out here, with a morning just like this in mind. Then a pass over my zipped-up shell jacket, past my jeans-clad legs, and ending at my boots. When he's finally done, Garrett steps to the side of the opened door, leaving barely enough room for me to crawl inside without touching, bumping, or jumping him.

Barely.

Garrett drives through town then continues north on Highway 133. The radio hums quietly, tuned to an oldies country station broadcasting what sounds like a never-ending playlist of Dolly Parton and Kenny Rogers.

Just as those two start to croon the doozy that is "Islands in the Stream," Garrett switches on the dome light and the entire cab goes bright. After my eyes adjust to the change, I take in the interior, and for an old truck owned by a young guy, it's not exactly what's expected. Yes, plenty of dust covers the dashboard, and there are clods of dirt on the floor mats, but there aren't empty fast-food wrappers or soda cans littered about. The bench seat's upholstery is worn without being shabby, and in the center, there's a length of duct tape on the seat back where he's repaired it.

"I brought you a pair of work gloves and some hand warmers." Garrett hooks a thumb toward the crew cab's large backseat. "They're behind my seat, on the floor there, if you want to grab them."

With my travel mug in one hand, I scan the cab for a cup holder. Garrett sticks his hand out.

"Cup holder broke off a couple of years ago. Hand it over. Fair warning that I might not give it back. My Mr. Coffee and I had a disagreement this morning, mostly about the fact I forgot to buy more coffee, so I'm running without my usual high-test."

I pass the mug his way. "Go for it."

He takes a sip and groans. "Is this from your fancy pot thing?"

"You mean my *moka* pot? Yes." Shimmying toward the center of the bench seat, I rise up on my knees to reach over the backseat.

"It's damn good. A stupid name, but it definitely does the job right." He takes another drink before moving the mug to his other hand. He manages to steer with only two fingers, still grasping the mug, then uses his free hand to adjust the heater dial. "Makes sense why you would drag it across a couple of states with you."

A set of work gloves and some Day-Glo orange plastic packets with HotHands printed in large black letters are piled in an open shoe box that's sitting on the floorboard behind Garrett, shoved into the corner there. With my belly resting on the seat back, I work my upper half toward the shoe box, but the big ol' truck's size means I have to stretch out and lean down, and even that doesn't quite get me there. I edge my way closer, near enough that my hip nudges Garrett's shoulder . . . which puts my ass in the same vicinity.

Great. If only my mother could see me now.

I latch on to the box edge and drag it a few inches forward, intent on scooping up the contents as quickly as possible so my butt returns to where it belongs, firmly planted on the upholstery. Just as I do, the truck hits a rumble strip.

The combination of Garrett overcorrecting, the jostling, and my not expecting any of it means I end up swaying off balance, driving my nether regions into direct contact with Garrett's face. I swear I can feel the imprint of his nose on my . . . just all sorts of places I shouldn't. Garrett's right arm shoots out to brace the backs of my thighs, mumbling an apology as he does.

I grab the gloves and return to my side of the seat, my back straight as any etiquette teacher would demand, and set the very undainty work gloves in my lap as daintily as possible. Garrett hands my travel mug back, which adds another element to the things I need to oversee gracefully. Two hands for this one.

Garrett flicks the dome light off and I catch a glimpse of him before the cab goes dark. A quirked grin is fighting with the rest of his sheepish expression, and I almost wish he would spit out the obvious, killing the adolescent awkwardness of what just happened. That I had my ass in the air, he was looking at it—and he nearly wrecked the truck.

~⁓~

Ten minutes later, we arrive at the Eulands' ranch without further incident. I'm sure gluing myself to the opposite side of the bench seat aided to that end.

About halfway down a long driveway, we cross paths with a red Ford truck that's headed out. Garrett slows the truck and rolls down his window.

The young guy driving the red Ford does the same. He's a big kid—that's noticeable even from here, given the way the top of his head nearly rubs the headliner. His dark hair is too long and too floppy, yet his adorable attempt at a beard is unfortunately patchy, in the way guys that age always seem to have their facial hair grown in—like their hormones can't decide from day to day if they're old enough yet. What this kid is apparently old enough for, though, is exhaustion. The dark circles under his eyes belong on someone at least a few decades older.

Garrett gives him a chin nudge in greeting, but the pleasantries end there. "Give it to me straight, Tanner. What am I walking into?"

The kid blows out a weary breath while rubbing his eyes with the heels of his palms.

"Ten came last night, right after the snow started. Lost two before we could get them warmed up, and another two needed the hot box. We've also got one that we'll have to graft up. The other five are good."

Garrett curses under his breath and looks toward the ranch. The kid finally drops his hands from his face, but allows his head to fall heavily to the headrest before dropping it our way. He spots me and a quizzical look settles across his already world-weary expression.

"Shit. Sorry." Garrett leans back in his seat, floats his hand my way. "This is Cara. Cara, meet Tanner. This is his family's place."

I offer a small wave and greeting to match, which Tanner returns before rolling up his window a few inches.

"I gotta get to school. Good luck with my old man. I told him I could handle last night's watch on my own, but he didn't listen. I think he's coming up on twenty hours since he last slept, so he's in rare form."

Then he's off, roaring down the dirt road at a speed I certainly wouldn't encourage my kid to drive at.

"Is that kid in high school?" I ask.

Garrett nods and the implications take a second to sink in. "And he was up all night with the cows? On a school night?"

Garrett rolls his window up the rest of the way.

"Welcome to the life of a country kid."

~⁃~

When we crest a low hill at the end of the driveway, the Euland ranch comes into view. Sunrise is in full swing behind the two large barns set in the distance and the large corrals that span between them. Opposite those is a newer but modest brick ranch house without a front lawn, only a concrete pad poured in front of a two-car garage and a few long-ignored shrubs in whiskey barrel planters near the front door. Garrett pulls to a stop in front of a smaller, vinyl-sided building and shuts off the truck. With the engine off, the sound of cows and all their assorted noises—mooing, snorting, and snuffling—is an impossible-to-ignore soundtrack.

I take a sip of my coffee, then hand it Garrett's way. "This looks like quite an operation. How many head does he have?"

I give myself a silent high five inside because of my rather smooth use of the ranching-type jargon I've studied up on. *Head* instead of *cows*. Like I *know* things.

Garrett drains the rest of the coffee. "OK, lesson number one, City. Never ask a rancher how many cows he has."

"What? Why?"

"It's like asking him how much money he has in his checking account. Same thing around here because cows *are* money. So I've never asked him. My guess would be that he's running close to a thousand these days."

So much for knowing things.

"A thousand sounds like a lot for one guy to manage. So Tanner helps when he doesn't have, you know, *school*—what about Kenny's wife? Does he have employees? Is *that* OK to ask?"

He snorts. "That's fine to ask. But I can tell you he does most of it himself, only uses a part-time guy when he has to."

Garrett steps out of the truck and I follow, coming to a stop when he pauses a few paces away and then bends over at the waist to loosen the laces on his boots. He tucks his jeans into them and retightens the laces.

"His wife, Barb, works in town as a nurse, which is pretty much the norm. There's an old saying about *behind every great farmer or rancher is a wife with a job in town*. Not many folks are big enough or rich enough to have this be their only income."

And my viewpoint of his innocent clothing adjustment while he talks means I can better understand Garrett's earlier steering blunder. I'm having some trouble listening and I'm forced to clamp my mouth shut when a bit of drool becomes almost inevitable.

What's worse is that he isn't even trying—he can't be. He's

dressed as he has been every time I've seen him, in the uniform of choice around here. Nothing but the ever-practical jeans, ball cap, work coat, and T-shirt, although today he's added a hoodie and swapped out his usual coat for a sherpa-lined duck vest, a combination that should, at best, cause a neutral reaction from me. I certainly shouldn't want to stumble into him—or *onto* him.

Garrett stands upright again, tugs down on the bottom edge of his vest and up on the waist of his jeans. And catches me gawking.

Gentleman that he apparently is, there's no winking, no smirking, no asking if I like the view. He just tips his head toward the vinyl-sided building and heads that direction.

Inside, we walk past a row of straw-lined stalls, metal shelves full of supplies, and a small room where a cot is set up with a limp pillow and a wool army blanket in a heap at the foot. Past there is a larger open space with a couple of long work tables and a metal washbasin where a stocky man is hunched over with his back to us, grumbling as he scrubs an enormous set of steel pliers. At the sound of us approaching, he gives up the grumbling and drops the pliers into the washbasin, where they clang noisily.

"You ever wonder what it's like to live in the suburbs? Maybe down in Boca? You know, where someone mows the damn lawn, the one they watered the shit out of without thinking about how stupid it is to waste water that way? Where the worst part of your day is discovering that the newspaper kid didn't hit the porch and now you have to walk your sorry ass all the way to the end of the driveway?"

"Fuck no. Sounds terrible." Garrett chuckles before turning a thumb in my direction. "Cara might be able to enlighten us on the joys of suburbia, though. Hope it's still OK that she came along."

The man cranes a look over his shoulder and I can see Tanner in so much about him. The hair, the eyes, and most of all the exhaustion. He wipes his hands on his heavily stained bib overalls and turns to offer one my way.

"Of course. I'm Kenny, darlin', good to meet you. Just ignore ninety percent of what I say today."

I take his hand. "I can't speak much to the lawn watering, even from my days in the suburbs. And I live in a condo now, so walking down the driveway for the newspaper is foreign, too. But thank you so much for letting me tag along. I appreciate it."

Kenny cracks a tired grin and drops our handshake. Tucking his hands into the front bib on his overalls, he leans back against the washbasin. "Garrett said you might want to ask a few questions. Interview me or something?"

I start to answer, but Garrett inserts himself by simply stepping forward half a step.

"You just said she should ignore ninety percent of what you say, so I don't think today's the best day for an interview. We're here to be useful; we can come back for the chat. Right, City?"

I'd have to be beyond thick to miss the cue. As much as I might be gung-ho to get going on an interview, Garrett wants Kenny to find his way to the nearest bed or recliner.

"Another day, absolutely. I'd just love to see how things work. Help, if I can."

Kenny starts to protest, but Garrett lands a halfhearted punch to his upper shoulder.

"Go on in the house. See if you're still able to identify what your bed looks like. Tanner brought us up to speed on last night, so we'll take a drive and see where we stand this morning, then go from there." He points toward the straw-filled stalls. "All these little ones need bottles?"

"Yeah." Kenny seems to give up the fight with that one word. He points listlessly to the corner of the room where a beat-up folding table sits. "Barb made breakfast burritos before she headed into town for her shift. Coffee and monkey bread, too." He looks my way. "You like monkey bread, Cara?"

On the table is a small, dirty-fingerprinted microwave with a stack of foil-wrapped burrito-shaped items sitting next to it. I have no idea what monkey bread is, but the mound of dough balls sitting on a plastic platter and glistening with caramel sauce seems to be a likely contender. The whole setup isn't exactly sanitary or food-safety-oriented, so I attempt to cast off his offering as politely as possible.

"Oh, I'm not hungry. But thank you so much for offerin—"

Garrett's arm lands over my shoulder, pulling me in with a rough tug that cuts off the rest of my babbling.

"Cara loves monkey bread. I might have to duke it out with her just to get a bite."

Kenny nods and, after a few instructions, shuffles off, his boots sounding heavier with each step. Garrett waits for him to clear the room, keeping his arm over my shoulder, before pulling me close enough to put his lips to the shell of my ear.

"Lesson number two. Someone cooks for you? Offers you something to eat or drink? Short of being deathly allergic, you take it. You don't politely decline or beg off—just say thank you and eat up."

I resist the urge to roll my eyes. And I thought the social mores I grew up with were hard to handle—the litany of *don't do this* and *don't do that* ways of our world that I had a hard time keeping straight as a kid and found maddening to deal with once I was older. But here, no matter how different the rules are, no matter how much I wish I knew them better, it feels different when I botch them up. Less like failure, and more like learning a new language.

I have Garrett, after all.

9

(Cara)

Half a burrito and far too much monkey bread later (delicious, sugary, *meet my new love* monkey bread), we're back in the truck, slowly bumping our way out to a grazing pasture. Garrett is finishing the other half of my burrito and steering with one hand, slowing when we crest a small hill and see a large group of cows just beyond.

He stops the truck and shifts into park, studying the herd silently. And all of a sudden it feels like we're doing something important, I just don't know what the hell it is. For a while I try to figure it out by watching Garrett, attempting to track his sightline to see what he sees, but his gaze doesn't stay put, never remaining in one spot long enough for me to catch up. Also, *cows*. I'm sure they aren't all the same, but their unique qualities are lost on me. It's a sea of brownish blobs out there. Maybe a nonstop voice-over from him is too much to ask, but I'm also not out here for some bucolic getaway.

"OK, come on, Garrett. Give me something here. Tell me what we're doing."

He pops the last bite of the burrito in his mouth and balls up the foil wrapper, dropping it in the map pocket on his trim panel. A half turn of his head in my direction and it's as if my question pulled him out of a pleasant trance.

Good God, he's dreamy. That's the perfect word, too. "Dreamy." Cute, *plus* hot, *plus* focused, *plus* still a little sleepy-eyed. Thus, dreamy. If I were here for a cute little rural retreat, he'd make the best tour guide *ever*.

"Where should I start?"

His question means I'm forced to stop dwelling on his dreaminess. *Back to work, Cara.*

"I don't know, the beginning? As if it weren't completely obvious, I'm a novice here. I have no idea how the milk gets in the carton or the steak gets on my plate. Tell me how Kenny does all of that."

"Well, first off, Kenny doesn't do that. This is a cow-calf operation. Those aren't dairy cows, they're beef cattle, but he doesn't put your steak on the plate. Eventually, yeah, his cows probably end up there, but that's not his game."

I drag my bag off the floorboard and unzip it, pulling out a notebook and a pen. Garrett watches as I flip pages until I come to a clean sheet.

"You look very serious now. Where are your glasses? I think you should put those on."

The little quirk of his brows when he mentions my glasses tells me he's got a thing for them. As in a *take them off while you shake your hair around and unbutton your top* thing.

And for a beat, I consider doing it. Endeavoring on some spectacle where I'm the coy but contrived seductress and he's my rapt audience. What is it about this guy? He's dreamy, yes, but this is too much. I click the end of my pen and make as if I'm all business.

"I only use those when I'm doing a lot of reading. Focus, Garrett."

He gives a little snort and turns back toward the herd.

"A cow-calf operation is pretty much exactly how it sounds. His business is breeding cows, then selling off the stock to other operations. You can think of these guys as the backbone of the beef industry."

I scribble down a few of his words as he continues on.

"Kenny's setup is AI." I give him a look that asks for more. "Artificial insemination. Cows have a nine-month gestation period, and most guys around here run spring calving, so all the AI is timed to accommodate that. February through April is calving season, but just like humans, you don't know exactly when they're coming. It's an all-day-all-night proposition until every calf is on the ground, monitoring for anything that goes wrong. Taking care of sick calves, helping along the cows that are having trouble, plus keeping up with all the usual feeding and watering. Add in a snowstorm like we had last night and that throws a wrench into things."

I think back to last night's heavy, wet snow, apparently quite typical for spring in Colorado, and I feel a little guilty now for enjoying the view outside my bedroom window, all snuggled up under a warm blanket and sipping a hot mug of tea, knowing now that Tanner and Kenny were out here in the middle of it, worrying about whether their calves would make it through the night. This morning, most of what was left behind has turned to water. No snow piles, only puddles of mud.

"Even though it didn't drop below freezing, it was still cold enough that any brand-new babies born last night would have needed warming up. Sounds like Kenny lost a couple last night before they could get to them."

Garrett drops his forearm to the steering wheel and points toward the left side of the herd. "See that gal over there? The one that's off on her own, near the big aspen tree?"

I sit up straighter and try to track his gesture but can't quite see what he's talking about. Garrett pats the space next to him on the bench seat. I shimmy over until I'm near enough to see—and close enough to Garrett that our legs are nearly touching. His eyes drop for a split second, then the spread of his legs widens, his thigh pressing firmly to mine. The heat there is both real and imagined, so I consider all the reasons I should move my leg, but don't.

"Her tail flicking around, the way she wants to be alone—those are good signs that she's getting ready to deliver." One of his fingers swirls in the air, pointing toward the cow's hind end. "See that white thing hanging out?"

I force myself to focus on what he's pointing out, even when my instincts say to look away.

"That's the water bag. Probably see a couple of little hooves next, as long as everything goes well."

Oh Jesus. *Hooves.* I take a deep breath.

"Do we go help her? Are we, like, her midwife?"

Garrett chuckles and pushes up a sleeve on his hoodie, checking his watch.

"Not unless we have to. Best to let her be. We'll check in after a few hours and if she's having trouble, we might have to pull it."

"*Pull* it?"

Garrett gives the steering wheel an amused look I'm guessing is *not* intended for the steering wheel, since it's an inanimate object and I'm the woman who just posed that last question with a mixture of horror and fascination.

"Just like it sounds. Pull the calf out." He starts the truck and begins to back out of the pasture slowly. The cow in question pops her head up and locks her gaze our way, then gets up and moves to another spot farther away.

I send a silent prayer out for mama. And another for me.

Because this city girl isn't ready for all that.

Another pasture, another herd of cows. While it goes without saying that I can't tell the difference, Garrett explains that this group is all first-calf heifers, as in first-time moms. Given that, they're kept separate from the other cows, graze on the best-quality pasture, and get a little extra attention—and a few bonus calories.

Garrett is ambling through the herd, carrying a tub filled with feed pellets. Evidently, these protein-packed bits are the bovine equivalent of a Twinkie to a pothead. Because the moment they figure out what he has, they come running—well, not running, as much as clomping and plodding. But with a slobbering, unwavering gait and a penetrating gleam in their big cow eyes. It's hilarious and terrifying at the same time.

Garrett, however, isn't the least bit scared, and is able to avoid losing a hand or a finger to the more overzealous gals of the group. I can see his mouth moving, but with all the mooing and the fact I've stayed back by the truck while he works, I can't hear what he's saying. Chances are it's the cow translation of flirting. Because Garrett.

At the edge of the herd, he manages to turn my way and lifts the tub high in the air. "Cara! Bring me that other tub of pellets, will you? The girls are hungry."

Oh, time to be helpful. Watch this city girl slay. I push off the dropped tailgate of his truck and haul forward the second pail sitting in the bed, but it's heavier than expected, so I have to brace my hips and use both hands. Once I swing it down, I start Garrett's way while avoiding the largest mud puddles. Garrett meets me halfway and immediately swoops in to take the pail. I turn around to head back to the truck, but I'm in the middle of the herd now, gazing out into a sea of bobbing cow heads. I try to stay cool and collected, even when I now have a close-up view to the size of their mouths and the bottom row of big, flat teeth working away inside those mouths—while knowing the only tool available for swatting or shooing is my scotch cap.

Speaking of swatting, my body goes rigid when I feel a nudge of something against my lower back. I can't quite identify what's at play here, but whatever it is starts to move southward.

Is that . . . ? No. Can't be.

This gentle pressure, now squarely centered on the back pocket of my jeans, cannot be Garrett. He is not copping a feel. Not here, not now. Not absent of *any* attempt at seduction. Like, by way of dinner and a movie, some excuse to end up on the couch together when he drives me home, then using that to lean in for a kiss. Only after that would he go for the ass grab, right? He's a raised-right country guy. Those rural roots alone must trend toward slower courtships.

And slow courtships would not involve descending his touch from my jean pockets to a place lower and more . . . between my legs.

Must. Set. Boundaries.

That's what I need to do. Quickly. I don't care if he does bring about lust-itis symptoms I can't quite keep in check. This is not my speed—the fast-forward, skip-a-few-chapters, here's-the-money-shot speed. I take a deep breath and turn, fully prepared to lock eyes with Garrett and spell out my boundaries. Clearly and firmly.

Except Garrett isn't next to me. I spot him fifteen feet away, carrying on another one-sided conversation with the cows. Most important, his hands are occupied—one gripping the pail handle and the other scooping out pellets.

A snort emerges from behind me, followed by my mind freight-training through the essentials of what's happening right now.

Garrett is way over there.

I'm in the middle of a herd of cows.

And something is touching me in a far-too-familiar way.

All this is followed by a not-so-subtle poke in the ass—by a cow that either really likes me or really doesn't.

Followed by me screaming.

My screaming does two things: elicits a very wet-sounding grunt from my cow paramour and prompts Garrett to whip his head our direction. He freezes, all except for his jaw dropping open.

Another poke in the butt and I'm off, with only one objective in mind: to make it back to the truck so I can barricade myself inside. Whether cows lack opposable thumbs or not and locking the doors might be unnecessary, I don't care.

I barely register the mud bogs in my path because my feet are working at a squirrelly *Flintstones* pace, so what happens next is pretty much inevitable. Because when I plop a foot down in what looks like another shallow puddle, I find it's actually a gully. A swamp-sized bog. A *quagmire* of epic proportions. Large enough to obscure the rock lying in wait to turn my ankle and fling me face-first into a pond of mud.

The fall and the cold and the mud take my breath away. Wet dirt seeps between my splayed fingers, splashes onto my face, and begins to soak the front of my clothes. And it doesn't smell as if it's composed entirely of dirt. Other stuff is mixed up in here. Other, more odorous stuff.

Garrett appears, sweeping to a stop in front of me before crouching down.

Then he poses an obvious question. The inevitable, stupid, rhetorical question nearly anyone would feel compelled to ask in this situation. And he asks it with a look on his face like he's dying to burst out laughing, but knows that wouldn't be wise on his part, which makes the whole thing even worse.

"City. Whoa there. Are you OK?"

Point proven. The obvious answer to this obvious question would be to claim that I'm *fine*.

But I'm not.

My clothes are soaked through with sludge, my already tiny chest feels as if the impact may send me back into a training bra, and my face—where it isn't covered in mud—is hot from humiliation.

I push myself up and onto my knees. After a deep, shuddering breath, I stand up, take two steps to the right, where drier ground lies, then give my form a once-over to assess the situation.

Verdict is in. The situation sucks.

"Cara, answer me. Are you OK?"

I flick my gaze over to him and pin it there, biting my tongue both literally and figuratively, hard enough that tears are welling in my eyes. Garrett's face falls, all traces of his stifled laughter having temporarily dissipated. He puts his hands to my upper arms, grips them gently.

"Fuck. Don't cry, OK? Don't cry, don't cry. Just nod so I know you aren't hurt."

Just *nod*. This fucking guy. Mr. Rational Instructions Guy. Dreamy or not, he's within striking distance, and I'm pissed at *everything*.

I take another deep breath and lay it on him good. "No! Of course I'm not OK! I'm covered in mud and cow shit!" I jab a finger in the air toward him. "And you're trying not to laugh, I know it. Just laugh; you know you want to."

Then I stamp my foot. Because I'm mature like that. More mud sloshes and lands on the backs of my hands.

And that's all it takes. Garrett starts to howl, laughing so hard he doubles over, bracing his hands on his knees—and he doesn't even have the decency to hold back his cackling, just lets it all out for what feels like a good ten minutes. When he's finally able to breathe and stand upright again, his still annoyingly pretty hazel eyes are watering with gleeful tears. He wipes them away with the heel of one hand.

Garrett cups my face with his hands. "You're fucking ador-able."

"You're *not*," I huff.

He tugs his hoodie sleeves down over his hands and starts to wipe the mud off of my face.

"If it makes you feel better, you wouldn't believe how jealous I was of that heifer. That was a bold move she pulled. Knew what she wanted and went for it. Not the girl-on-girl action I usually go for, but still."

He grins, a few residual laughs escaping him, and I groan. Garrett scans the front of my body, then takes my hand, leading us to the truck. After rustling around in the back, he extracts a stack of clothing from under the driver seat. Garrett holds up a pair of jeans, swinging a look between me and the pants. He drapes them over his forearm, tosses a T-shirt and a hooded camo sweatshirt onto the pile, and extends it my way.

"Redneck shenanigans often involve mud. This means always being prepared with a change of clothes. Come on, we'll find a place for you to change."

A storage closet becomes a changing room back in the building where we met Kenny. I strip off my boots, jeans, and coat, kicking them into a pile in the corner. Garrett's jeans are too big, but I make it work by cinching my belt to the last hole, then rolling up the bottom hems to keep them from dragging on the floor. The thermal shirt I had on under my jacket survived unscathed, so I don't need the T-shirt Garrett provided, but I tug the sweatshirt on to make up for my now lack of a coat. And, when I do, the moment is a bit like when he put his jacket over my shoulders the first day we met. Since I'm alone, I give in and do exactly what I want to. I bunch up some of the material right under my nose and breathe in until I've had my fill.

Seriously, someone needs to bottle this.

After tossing my dirty clothes into a plastic bag, I step out of the closet and peek around for Garrett. When I hear his murmuring voice, I follow the sound.

". . . that's it, sweetheart. Such a good girl. Yes, there you go. . . ."

I find him in one of the makeshift stalls, sitting down in a pile of hay, legs outstretched and his back resting against the wall, with a baby calf nestled in his lap, her muzzle upturned to suckle from the bottle he has in one hand. A few more sweet nothings before he looks up and sees me.

"Well, look at you, City." Garrett runs his tongue over his lips while scanning me from head to toe. "Who knew you'd look so good dressed like a country girl?"

It's a good thing I'm not interested in tangling with another cow today. Because while the calf is adorable on her own, when Garrett's eyes meet mine, doing that sleepy-sexy thing so well, I have to tuck my hands into the center pocket on the hoodie, just to keep from walking over there and using them to shoo that calf out of the way—all to make room for me.

⌒～⌒

By the time Garrett drops me off at the farmhouse, the sun is setting behind the mesas in the distance. I'm starving and beat, more than ready for a shower and a hot meal. After my costume change, I stood by while Kenny and Garrett pulled a calf and later worked some voodoo to help an abandoned calf secure a new adoptive mom. Unlike human adoptions, this involved sprinkling some sort of powder on the calf to entice a prospective cow mom.

Which is nothing compared to the alternative, a technique that was described to me as taking the skin of a calf that didn't make it, then draping it over the orphaned calf, effectively duping the cow into taking him on. Even so, they still sometimes have to tether the new adoptive mom cow's leg so she won't kick the calf when it tries to nurse.

And I thought my mom was difficult to please. Turns out she's no competition for nature.

When Garrett follows me up to the front door, he plants one shoulder to the house siding as I unlock the deadbolt. If my brain weren't so fuzzy from fatigue, I might figure out a way to invite him in without it sounding like I'm planning to return his clothes by stripping them off in front of him. Fortunately or not, I'm too tired to try.

Garrett lazily rests his head on the siding. "Did you at least get something worthwhile out of today? Aside from playing in the mud and the randy advances of that heifer?"

The key finally turns in the lock. "I did. I got some good notes and a better understanding of how the family dynamic works for these guys inside of their business. And Kenny said I could buy him breakfast this week, pick his brain some more. Thank you for taking me."

Garrett nods and shoves his hands into his pockets, drops his gaze to his boots.

"I was thinking, there's a young couple that's farming a small section over near Delta—Corey and Brooke Winsor. I know they'll be in the store this week to pick up some seed they ordered, and if you wanted, I could see about setting up a visit to their place next Monday. Might be nice for you to talk to some farmers. Different industry, different challenges. Either that, or we could go see Whitney and Cooper over at the orchard."

He absentmindedly scratches his jaw with two fingers across

a clean-shaven face, and I find myself wondering what he looks like after a few lazy days, whether his scruff grows in quickly or if it takes a bit.

I decide it takes a few days, but when it shows, it probably looks good. And *feels* good. Not too skritchy, but coarse enough to always remind you that he's a guy—a guy's guy who looks good, a little too good, in the low light glowing behind him and is a little too close for my hormones to deal with. He tips up one side of his mouth in an easy smile, no pressure or production about it, just his very good mouth suddenly becoming impossible to ignore.

All the arguments I might make if I were less tired elude me at the moment, hijacked by pure curiosity and trumped by my ongoing fascination with Garrett's very good mouth. So I do the only thing I can think of.

I kiss him.

10

(Cara)

It's official: I've found my place.

My HQ, my base camp, a command center of productivity. As every freelance writer or aspiring creative knows, finding your place is critical. The coffee shop or bar, the café or bookstore that feels so right, it seems even the chairs were ergonomically designed with you in mind, that way you can settle in and do what you do—whatever that is. Even if you're mostly surfing the net and *thinking* about what you're going to do, once you have your place, that's enough.

Revolution Coffee is the same coffeehouse I discovered the day before my Earl Kidd fiasco, although I decided not to let any associations with that situation cloud its potential. Two days ago, I came back with my laptop in tow and drafted two thousand words about my day at the Eulands'. After I was done, I still had the energy to organize the photos I'd taken into folders on my laptop and email my first weekly update to the *Purpose & Provisions* editor. Really, given how long I've been here, what I've accomplished so far is respectable enough: acquainted myself with the general area, survived a run-in with the local crack-pot, spent a day on a ranch, and made sure to properly *thank* my "in" with the locals. While kissing Garrett was not on my Grand Valley to-do list, it was *so* worth going off-task for a moment.

Today, I get to cross off five items on my actual to-do list, including *Interview Kenny Euland*. So, who's the superstar of the day? This gal. Who's having a piece of strudel made with local Grand Valley pears as a reward? This gal.

Over a two-hour breakfast at a local greasy-spoon café, Kenny shared the nuances of his business, both the good and the bad. I also learned that not all ranchers hope their legacy and land will continue on with their kids.

"I'm praying Tanner doesn't come back. My boy has a full ride to study international politics at DU. International politics, can you believe that? He's too smart for this shit. Garrett was the same way, but had some shit luck and now he's stuck. Kid like that shouldn't be working at the damn co-op."

Without prodding much, Kenny went on to give me Garrett's story. The high school wrestling star carrying a 4.0 in high school, who left for college with both scholarships and ambition, only to lose his dad, abandon his future, and give up his farm and childhood home—all within a three-month time span.

For a guy like Garrett, who must have cut his teeth on a bootstrap way of life, it made no sense. Give up on finishing his degree? Sell his family farm to a guy who never made the time to see it? All without looking back or presenting anything but a happy-enough face to the world? Not buying it. I might know the facts now, but I still don't understand the story. And as with all things Garrett, I haven't been able to stop thinking about it.

My phone shimmies about on the tabletop, set to vibrate, and Amie's smiling face appears on the screen.

Even at the risk of being *that* person in the coffeehouse, I answer. The place is empty except for a small table of high school girls who are too focused on their own phones to worry about me talking on mine.

"Hello?"

"Cara Jane. Tell me how you feel about monograms. Always elegant? Or a stodgy reminder of Granny Jane?"

Given the barbed tone and her lack of a playful greeting, I'd guess Amie's dealing with yet another of our mother's—or her soon-to-be mother-in-law's—wedding-related demands. Not a day has gone by in the last few months that my sweet sister hasn't had to manage a never-ending wedding to-do list and mediate a new drama. And contrary to conventional expectations, none of the dramas are because of her; instead, the mothers involved have picked up all the slack in that department. Thank God Amie has a heart of gold, an agreeable nature, and a maid of honor—*me*—who plans to buy her a pony if she makes it to the altar before losing her sweet mind. Or a bottle of Wild Turkey. She's earned it, either way.

"Depends on the application," I offer. "Pillowcases? Stodgy. That goes for all linens in general. But, like, barware? Not too terrible."

"So, flasks for the groomsmen? Yes?"

I take a bite of my pear strudel and consider. Tayer's groomsmen are a pack of Duke boys with all the pompous titles one would expect: Dr., Esq., Cpt., and CEO. Flasks will do just fine.

Because my mother hired Chicago's most sought-after and kick-ass wedding planner, my task list as maid of honor is composed of two things: keep Amie sane and organize the bachelorette party. While the first is an ongoing endeavor, I'm nearly done with the second. Since our twin cousins from New Orleans—the forever bad-decision duo Mindi and Mandi—are the only members of the bridal party who might enjoy a wild weekend of strip clubs in Vegas, I've planned a long weekend in rural Wisconsin, of all places. We'll be glamping it up on three hundred acres of forest land that surround a secluded lake. When I first pitched the idea to Amie, she gave me her frozen-faced *I adore you but this sounds terrible* smile, which thawed when I showed her pictures of the luxury "tents" with en suite bathrooms (complete with soapstone tile, steam showers, and enormous soaker tubs), the moon-and-candlelit dining pavilions, and the camp butlers. And she was all in when I showed her the spa menu and a description of their signature Himalayan salt stone massage.

As with the glamping, Amie eventually breathes a sigh of relief when I assure her the monogrammed flasks are a perfect choice. When I start to press her for more wedding update details, hoping to reassure her as best I can from hundreds of miles away, she casts it off and redirects the conversation.

"Distract me with an update on your adventures. Keep talking until I tell you to stop."

With a laugh, I launch in. I tell her about Earl Kidd, finding my place, and, of course, Garrett.

I decide *not* to mention the part about how I attacked Garrett with my mouth three days ago. How one of his arms was around my waist a split second later, how he lifted my entire body up until my toes were barely grazing the porch, and I was between him and the side of the house, so I couldn't go anywhere. Not that going anywhere was part of my plan. Because Garrett Strickland kisses like a starved man who just stumbled into a Wonka-like wonderland of his favorite things and doesn't want to waste a single morsel—greedy and reverent with every nibble, taste, and lick he takes.

Still, mind-blowing kisses aside, I keep my current story focused on my misadventures with Mr. Kidd.

"I go tearing down this road away from Hotchkiss's own version of Cliven Bundy–meets-the-Unabomber, and pretty much drive highway speed until I'm back in town. I needed to stop for gas, and even though I was still trying to calm down, hoping I didn't throw up or cry, Garrett showed up, offering hugs and—"

"Stop." My mouth clamps shut. A purr of interest curls in Amie's voice. "Who's Garrett? And why is he familiar enough to be offering hugs?"

"I told you about him, remember?"

"What? Wait, is this the redneck? His name is *Garrett*?"

A prickling sensation ripples through my chest. "Yes and yes. Why do you say it like that?"

"Because Garrett is a totally normal name. We know other Garretts. I figured his name would be, I don't know, Cletus. Jethro. Ricky Bobby."

I laugh at the mention of Ricky Bobby, picturing Will Farrell pontificating about his excellence. *"Here's the deal: I'm the best there is. Plain and simple. I wake up in the morning and I piss excellence."* My laugh is loud enough to jerk the high school girls' attention from their smartphones to peer at me quizzically, as if I've just materialized out of thin air.

"Nope. Garrett Strickland."

"Good name." She hums a little. "It sounds sturdy. Does he look sturdy?"

Amie draws out the word with mischief, like she knows the answer before I give it: that Garrett is most definitely sturdy.

I temper my voice, hoping to tame my sister's curiosity before it gets out of hand. "I don't know . . . He's tall, but not big. Not skinny or anything, just strong in a practical way. He can go from helping lug my reformer into the house to holding a calf in his lap while bottle feeding it. Does that help?"

She squeals. Uh-oh. So much for taming her curiosity. I

was going for an objective description, but instead I must have sounded like there was a little bit of drool sneaking out of my mouth. Amie then demands evidence.

"Evidence?"

"Like a picture. I know you took some with that fancy camera Dad bought for you. Send me one."

She's right. I do have pictures. They *may* be stored in a folder called "GARRETT" on my laptop. There *may* be more images in that folder than in the others, titled "LANDSCAPES," "CATTLE," and "HOTCHKISS." There *may* be one in which Garrett and Kenny are leaning against the bed of his truck and chatting, Garrett in profile with a perfect smile on his face. I *may* have saved a copy in which Kenny has been cropped out. Perhaps this photo exists.

Regardless, I try to protest.

Amie goes for my emotional jugular. "Cara Jane, I need this. Did I tell you that Mom and Mother Cahill demanded that I show them the lingerie I bought for the honeymoon? Demanded. Then they vetoed it, telling me red was absolutely not my color and I should go with a demi-cup over a teddy. I mean, if I don't deserve some fun distraction and giggling over a boy with my sister, then who does?"

By the time she utters the word "vetoed," I've hit send on a photo of Garrett and started looking for some sloth gifs to send her later.

"Check your in-box," I mumble.

Another squeal, now combined with a short round of gleeful applause. Then silence. A gasp. Another squeal.

"Holy mother of *Duck Dynasty*. He's adorable. In a hot, sturdy, amazing way. And if you have any pictures of him holding this newborn calf, I might need a minute alone."

A stupid smile takes over my face. Even though he isn't mine, even if there's nothing other than one kiss between us, I love hearing the proof that it isn't the altitude or something, that my weak-willed hormones aren't solely to blame for the way I get around him. Garrett is hot. Objectively, undeniably hot.

"He wouldn't let me take pictures with the calf. He said it would ruin his rep."

"Please tell me there's something going on with you two. Something that illuminates exactly how strong he is in a 'practical way.'"

My meddling conscience rears up and ruins the fun. Wasting a few minutes giggling at a picture of Garrett is one thing, but anything more isn't right. I close the laptop and tap my fork on the empty strudel plate.

"We shouldn't talk about this, Amie. It's weird."

"Why is it weird? We've always talked about these things. About everything."

I sigh. "Sure. In theory. As in, *I'd devour Chris Evans like a gratuitously buttered, warm-from-the-oven pumpkin muffin.* But this is different. I know it doesn't make sense, but it feels I'm stepping out on Will and telling you about it. Too close for comfort."

"Cara, stop," she groans, before taking a deep breath. "You and Will are on good terms. You're staying in Davis's house, for God's sake. If the whole Cahill family weren't OK about this, he wouldn't have extended the offer. So there's no need for you to drag around some stupid guilt complex. Because that could get boring rather quickly. Celibate dramatics and gloom-doom would not be a good look on you."

I sputter a laugh, and a weight previously so heavy in my heart, starts to lift with a few words of permission and encouragement from the girl who's always known what I need.

"So go forth and copulate, please," Amie continues. "Do it for me. Because the dopamine and such will be good for your already fab complexion and you'll look amazing in my wedding pictures."

Amie knows I'll do just about anything for her. And even though I've never been one for sex with people I barely know, or flings with guys in towns where I'm essentially passing through, my typical *no thank you* thoughts on the subject are fuzzy at the moment.

Because Garrett Strickland might just be the best way to ensure I look rosy-cheeked and blissed out in front of the wedding photographer's camera—better than any oxygen facial or La Prairie serum there is. Oh, the sacrifices a maid of honor must make. But for Amie? I think I can find a way to persevere.

11

(Garrett)

Archery hunting isn't an easy proposition. Unlike using a rifle or a muzzle-loader, hunting with a bow requires a closer range, a stealthier approach, and a far better understanding of the animal you're after. Mule deer are especially adaptable and crafty, with a knack for eluding predators that exceeds most other big game. They're smart, use all their senses, and rarely let their guard down—with one notable exception.

A buck in the rut? Brainless.

During the rut—those early fall months when mule bucks are focused exclusively on finding the ladies—these same wily creatures are driven to distraction, and more than one of them has ended up on my dinner table because of it—an outcome that makes sense to me now. Because it's possible I'd follow Cara Cavanaugh's jeans-clad ass straight into the path of a rifle shot or a broadhead without pause or enough good judgment to avoid certain death. I'd bumble my way forward like a moron, with her as my only objective.

Which means I'm a shit conversationalist at the moment. But Corey Winsor hasn't noticed yet, so I must be holding up my end of the conversation well enough to keep from outing myself as a ridiculously rut-minded creature who can't focus on much else other than how Cara's soft, yielding lips felt on mine. Or the press of her thighs when I picked her up against that siding. Or the feel of her fingers grasping the hair at my neckline with a groan. Or the way . . .

Christ. I'm fucking doomed.

The dry, tan-colored wilts of last year's corn surround us, with a light dusting of snow covering the field ground between. A few straggler geese have landed in the distance, picking at whatever leftover grain they can find. Corey plucks at a particularly large cut stalk, then crumples the withered husk in his hand.

". . . These guys have an efficiency bonus of almost a hundred pounds of nitrogen per acre. I'm sold on the idea, except we'll be in for a long-haul investment before we see any benefit. Brooke isn't convinced yet."

Corey and his wife, Brooke, own Sunlight Farms just outside of Delta, where they grow corn and wheat on the modest acreage they purchased five years ago. While Brooke's roots are deep in farming, Corey is an adult-onset farmer, come to it out of his own curiosity after a few years as a mechanical engineer. He met Brooke after going back to school to study soil management and ended up with an internship on her dad's farm in Iowa. After that, cue the cute and wedding bells, because the farmer's daughter fell hard for the half-lumberjack bearded intellectual who likes busting his ass in the dirt.

A fist suddenly lands squarely against my shoulder, not hard enough to hurt, merely enough to get my attention. I turn to meet Corey's amused expression.

"Sorry. I was listening." I scrub a hand down my face. "No-till can be a transition, for sure. But nitrogen isn't getting any cheaper. You let the soil do its thing and as all those microbes build up and reach full efficiency, the MRTN is a no-brainer. Not to mention the soil erosion benefits and water savings. From what I hear and the articles I've read, if you can tough it out, it's worth it."

Corey grins. "If I provide the beer, will you come to dinner next week and lay all that on Brooke? Maybe an objective third-party voice would help win her over."

"Depends on the beer. If you're pouring that shitty, overpriced craft shit, I'm out."

I cut my gaze back over to where Cara is standing. She's apparently decided it's important she get a close-up look at the corn header on the combine that Brooke's showing her. This means she has to bend over at the waist and then wiggle her ass around to shimmy forward without tipping over headfirst into the huge piece of equipment. Her jeans are snug-fitting without looking painted on or uncomfortable, in faded denim I suspect came with a hefty price tag to make it look that way. Up top she's wearing a button-down plaid flannel shirt with a thermal layered underneath and a cute scarf around her neck that somehow shows off her neck while also covering it up. How women manage to make things like scarves tempting and sexy, I will never understand. If I put a scarf on? I look like an idiot. She puts one on? I want to tug her closer with it, then lick and bite the soft skin under there until the goddam sun goes down.

Not that the darkness of sunset would do a thing to keep my head in check, anyway. This morning, in the unlit cab of my truck, she smelled like orange something and I sat there trying not to think about the Creamsicle Popsicles I loved as a kid, even though that was the best comparison I had for the scent surrounding me. If I let that thought take off, Cara suddenly became my very own personal frosty confection. Maybe I'll start calling her Creamsicle, instead of City. Might be fun until she asks me why I'm calling her that. And there is no way to explain that without sounding like an asshole. Inside, I groan. Because I'm screwed. Totally and completely screwed.

Or maybe the groan doesn't stay inside, because Corey laughs. Chortles, more like. He sounds like a tipsy but youthful Santa Claus.

"Blink, Garrett. Otherwise you're going to get a migraine." Another chortle, this time quieter. "Also, staring at her doesn't actually accomplish anything, no matter how hard you do it. Trust me, I wasted months boring a hole through Brooke's clothes before I made a move."

I sigh. "It's fucking pathetic, I know that. If she weren't so . . ." My words trail off and he smirks. "So *what*?"

"I don't know. Smart. Tall. Out of my league."

Also, if she didn't taste so good. Maybe if she wasn't prone to letting out the sweetest little needy sounds when you tease your tongue against hers—that might help. I probably shouldn't have kissed her. Or let her kiss *me*, then kissed her back and shoved her up against the side of the house so roughly I had to be sure my arm was behind her to keep from doing it again. Harder.

But I did, and now I know too much. I know how easy it is for my mouth to find hers. How I barely have to tip my head, proving true every suspicion I've had about how awesome it is to be with a woman whose body is evenly matched with mine. How good her narrow waist and trim hips feel in my hands.

And how my cock naturally settles right where it belongs.

Knowing that means I can imagine how easily we could have gone at it right there, Cara pressed up against the wall of the house, her leg pulled up to set in the crook of my arm and my dick sliding home with one push forward. No bending my knees, no adjustments, no getting her boosted up to take what I want to give her.

Yep. The kissing was a terrible idea.

Not that Cara or I have brought it up either way. Not when she texted me to see if the offer to come out here today was still on the table, or when I left her a return voicemail to say it was, or when she called me back so we could finalize a plan. And even this morning there wasn't a word between us about the fact that the last time I saw her, she was skedaddling into the house with her lips a little swollen and a satisfied smile on her face. Nope. We just sat there in the slightly awkward quiet, passing her travel coffee mug between us while I worked on tamping down images of what I would do with my very own Cara Creamsicle.

Corey crosses his arms over his chest, juts his chin toward Cara. "OK. So if she were stupid and short, and in your supposed 'league,' then you wouldn't find the pockets on her jeans so fascinating?"

"It would help," I mutter, watching as Cara and Brooke step back from the combine, then embrace in a new-acquaintance girl hug, swift and friendly.

Cara turns my way and waves, then points toward my truck with a questioning lift of her brows. When I give her a thumbs-up, she smiles. Right at me. Like we're the only two people around, like it wouldn't matter even if we weren't because no one else matters. I can practically feel the double-lung hit of an arrow as I stand here, stuck and stupid over a woman smiling at me. With a quick wave in Corey's direction, Cara heads toward the truck. Corey returns her wave and gives up an amused huff for my benefit.

"Good luck, kid. I've been married ten years, but I still remember what it was like to get *that* look for the first time."

I force my gaze his way. His is trained on Brooke, where she sits on the porch steps to their house, gathering up their seven-year-old daughter on her lap with a laugh and a hug. Eventually, he drags his eyes away and takes in the confused look on my face. He smirks and crooks one eyebrow.

"The one that means you've got a shot."

Back at the truck, I find Cara sitting on the passenger side with the door open and her legs dangling out, the heels of her boots thumping against the sill plate as she scribbles notes onto a messy-looking legal pad. Of course, instead of skirting around and putting my dumb ass in the driver's seat, my dick draws me in her direction. I stop in front of her and set one hand on the top of the opened truck door, the other to the roof. Cara tosses her notepad atop the dashboard and grins.

"We're best friends."

"You and me?" I ask.

"No." Cara shakes her head, continues to grin. "Brooke and me. Or at least, I *want* to be her best friend. She's the coolest. I learned so much."

Thank fuck. For a second I thought this was the speech where we finally acknowledge the big-ass kissing elephant in the room and she says it was a mistake then declares we should just be friends—not sure I could've handled that.

Cara swings her boot heel forward a few more times before slowing it to tap gently against my leg. I drop my eyes to that spot and watch as her foot curls around my calf.

"Let me buy you dinner, Garrett. As a thank-you for today."

A gentle pull of her foot to my calf follows, like her body is urging forward the answer she wants. Raising my eyes to hers, I keep my face carefully blank as she grabs a fistful of my T-shirt, even when I'm all but one second away from diving on top of her, right here in front of one of Corey's grain bins, where we're hidden enough to go unnoticed. When she gives a playful downward tug on the cotton but doesn't keep going, I shake off the idea of laying her out across the truck seat long enough to reply.

"Hell, City, you don't need to do that. My freezer's full of Hot

Pockets. And I'm sure Hotchkiss's dining options don't offer the cuisine you're used to."

A hint of hurt crosses her eyes, but she blinks and it's gone, replaced by the fire I like seeing in her expression.

"You'd take a Hot Pocket over dinner with me? With that cheese that's never anything in between molten hot or blobby cold? And the creepy meat-*ish* fillings? Really?" A smile starts to crack across my face. "Come on, you name the place."

Her hand is still gripping a fistful of my T-shirt. She presses her hand forward to bump against my chest and keeps it there, my entire body soaking up that touch, no matter how small it is. I scan her face, trying to read exactly what's happening in this moment, then give her a searching look.

"You like barbeque?"

Cara doesn't answer. Her mouth curves up, one side at a time, sly and slow, confirming what Corey just told me wasn't a bunch of bullshit.

That I've got a shot.

12

(Garrett)

She's wearing a dress.

Not a regular dress, either. A *date* dress. Even I can tell the difference.

After leaving Corey's, I dropped Cara off at the house with plans to return in a few hours to pick her up for dinner. And in that time, Cara went from jeans I'd already stumble toward my own death following her around in, to *this*.

A date dress that sort of looks like a button-down shirt, but all flowy and pretty, made out of a silky-looking baby-blue material that my fingers immediately itch to reach out and touch. The dress ends above the knee by a stretch, and around her tiny waist is a thin leather cord belted loosely. Add in a pair of dark brown high-heeled riding boots, and it takes a second for me to process that she's already locked the house door behind her and is headed down the walkway toward the truck, where she's bound to open her own door—in a date dress—if I don't get it together.

Quickly, I set the truck into park and crank up the heater as far as it will go, because it's twenty-two degrees out and Cara's legs are bare from her boots up to her hemline, then bail out of the truck, making it to the passenger door just in time. Cara hoists herself into the seat and the rise of her dress when she does is almost more than I can take. Because the truth is, she's probably too much for a guy like me—in general. At all. In any way.

And until today, knowing that made flirting and messing around with her nothing but a fun way to pass the time. Harmless, because as much as I think that the two of us hooking up while she's here sounds like a damn good time, the odds on that happening were not in my favor. A woman like Cara is too focused for a fling and too smart to pretend otherwise.

But now she's wearing a date dress, her hair looks a little poufier than usual, and she's giving me that no-one-else-for-miles smile again. When I put the truck in gear, I realize how right Corey was and how screwed I really am. I might have a shot here—but the hell if I know what to do with it.

After a short drive into town, we head into True Grit BBQ and find a spot in line to place our order at the counter. Cara idly starts to chew on one of her thumbnails as she peruses the menu, and a glint of something sparkly around her eyes captures my attention. I take a better look, to be sure I'm seeing what I think I am.

That Cara is wearing make-up.

Look, I'm not a Mary Kay rep—but my mom was. I endured one too many weekend afternoons as a kid watching her slap a million things of junk on women's faces at our kitchen table. So I can't ignore how the goldish-bronzy shadow on Cara's eyelids is more than what she wears on a routine day and the way it catches the light in this not-fancy barbeque restaurant where she's about to eat dinner from a Styrofoam container using a plastic fork. I know the effect a curler and a mascara wand have on a set of eyelashes. I also know what lip-glossed lips look like. I'm fucking evolved like that.

We place our order and Cara follows me toward one of the many picnic-style tables inside, then excuses herself to the bathroom. I set our trays down and slide onto one of the benches, trying to keep the panicked loop of *shitshitshitthisisadate* in my head to a minimum. I'm a grown man acting like a kid, all sweaty palms and nerves because some woman put on a dress and some goddam eyeshadow. Christ.

I shrug my coat off, tossing it and my ball cap to the bench space next to me, leaving room for Cara on the other side. I set about acting like a man by taking a long slug off the beer I ordered. Once I've quenched that need, I feel a little better. Enough to start arranging our table properly—because real men set the damn table, just like their moms taught them how to. I flip open the lids on our Styrofoam containers of barbeque, place a set of the paper-napkin-wrapped plasticware by each, and arrange our drinks.

Cara went with the pulled pork and cheesy corn, plus an extra piece of Texas toast—a choice that I both admire and appreciate. Some guys might think the whole bone-sucking-rib-slurping sideshow act is somehow hot, but I'm not one of them. For me it's the usual, a double portion of brisket and a side of slaw. I also don't think a woman should have to sit across from a man who's smacking his greasy mouth across a plate of ribs.

Just as I get everything in order on our tabletop and move to take another draw off my beer, a grumbling voice I know too well interrupts my focus.

"I planned to go home and eat with my friend Jim Beam, but seeing as you're here, I'll unload my shitty day on you."

Another tray flops to the tabletop. A heavy coat lands on the bench. Followed by a set of big hands slamming aside the tray as

Braden crawls over the bench to take a seat across from me. The wood bench creaks under the assault of his six-foot-five frame when he drops heavily on to it. My palms start to sweat again.

Any other day, this would be fine. I'd welcome the company, and we'd give each other some shit, talk about work, and maybe make a plan to shoot our bows somewhere later in the week. After that, we might finish up our food and round the corner to the Elks Lodge for a few more beers.

Tonight? I'd prefer if he would fuck off. And quickly.

"Why aren't you eating?" Braden shoves a heap of brisket into his mouth and then points his fork toward my plate. I start to work out an explanation, one that includes the words "scram, buddy," hoping I can get it all out before Cara returns.

No such luck.

"I have to say, the 'Little Ropers' versus 'Little Barrel Racers' signage on the bathrooms does nothing for someone like me when it comes to determining gender. I had to wait for someone else to go in before I knew which one to use. Apparently, I'm a *little barrel racer*." Cara slides in next to me, lays a paper napkin across her lap, and notices Braden. She gives a little wave. "Hi. I'm Cara."

Braden doesn't respond, just lets his jaw pause midchew, an enormous mouthful of brisket now protruding from one of his cheeks. His gaze starts to volley between Cara and me, moving nothing but his bewildered eyeballs. Slowly, his jaw loosens enough for him to start chewing again. Finally, he wipes his mouth with a napkin, all politeness, none of which is for me.

The paper napkin crumples in one hand as he extends the other toward Cara. "Hi. Braden."

Cara's hand disappears into Braden's enormous man paw and I start to worry about her pretty fingers getting crushed until he finally releases her.

She skirts her gaze over his uniform. "Are you a game warden?"

"Yes." Braden offers, full-stop-style. He gives Cara a once-over and finds nothing that explains who or what she's about, so he squints before moving on. "And you are *a* . . . ?"

She lifts one hand to daintily obscure her mouth as she finishes chewing a bite of Texas toast. Braden cuts a look my way as she does, using the opportunity to remind me of what's at play here, that I haven't even mentioned the name *Cara* to him, yet here she sits next to me in a date dress. In my defense, we're not guys who talk on the phone to each other—surprise, surprise—and I haven't seen him in person for a couple of weeks. What was I going to do? Send him a text?

Need to talk. You bring the wine, I've got the bonbons. #IMetAGirl

That's happening, um, *never*.

"I'm a freelance writer," Cara answers. "Out here on assignment to put together a piece about the Grand Valley ag industry. Garrett's become my local source of sorts, and I'm buying him dinner as a thank-you for introducing me to so many people. I'd be weeks behind without all his help. Not to mention I'd be in the dark. Literally."

Cara nudges her elbow to my upper arm, calling out the inside joke with that little gesture. Braden's eyebrows work upward damn near into his hairline, and his face contorts into an irritating look of horror, confusion, and dumbfounded repulsion. He looks like a seasick cartoon character, the kind who can't quite figure out what's going on, but he knows it's bad news.

I haven't taken a single bite of my food yet, something I realize when Cara reaches for the array of sauces in the center of the table. Her hand lands on my bicep when she figures out it's too far away, giving it a squeeze as she uses her free hand to waggle her fingers toward the bottles. Braden catches on before I do and moves the spinning bottle holder her way. He sets his napkin on the table, then tips the lid closed on his takeout container.

"I'm going to head out." Braden grabs his coat and starts to put it on. "Stick to my original plan, the one where I tell my troubles to Jim."

The grouchiness in his voice is harsh, even for Braden. Add in the way he keeps mentioning Jim Beam and I realize I'm not the only one who can't find right-side-up tonight.

"Dude, you don't have to leave." I grab the edge of his tray when he goes to pick it up. "Stick around, eat with us."

He flicks one of his hands toward the space between Cara and me. "*That* is happening."

Cara follows the gesture and her forehead furrows up. "*What* is happening?"

"The same-side-sitting thing. If I stay, I'll have a front-row seat to what I think is about to become a Strickland seduction scene, and that's something I've never wanted to see. I suspect it's like watching him call in a hen turkey, which is embarrassing for everyone present."

A little snorting giggle from Cara, and I can't decide which one of them I'm more annoyed with at the moment. Braden continues on. "And my problems will still be around tomorrow. Next month. Next *season*."

My brows furrow up at his cryptic mutterings. "Well, shit, now you have to talk. At least give us the short version. We want to know, don't we, Cara?"

"I'm all intrigue and anticipation over here," she deadpans, following with a forkful of cheesy corn and the droll lift of one brow.

She starts to chew, then gives her plate a pointed and pleased look. "Oh my *God*. This corn is everything I've ever wanted from a side dish. It's like a bowl of *cacio e pepe* had a love child with *cotija*-covered Mexican corn. And *Velveeta*."

Cara shovels in another bite and groans. Braden and I send blank stares her way, but I have to bite back a laugh. I don't know what the hell *cacio e pepe* or *cotija* is, but she's so captivated by her now third mouthful it's kind of adorable. Eyes closed as she swallows, she finally opens them and sees us both staring at her.

"Sorry," she offers, then flicks her empty fork our direction. "Braden has problems. Edge of seat, bated breath, and such. Carry on."

Braden's shoulders slump as if someone's set a sandbag there and he looks my way. "You know who Amber Regan is? From the Afield Channel?"

My eyes go wide. Do I know who Amber Regan is? Is he screwing with me? Does a bear shit in the woods? Yes.

Amber Regan is the blonde bombshell with her own hunting show on a premier cable channel dedicated to all things outdoors. We're talking a Texas beauty queen with big blue eyes, covered in camo and taking down everything from caribou in Quebec to ibex in Kyrgyzstan. The specifics of how she's built would be skeezy and sexist to talk about, but let's just say that a less tactful asshole could spend days on the big-rack jokes.

Braden quickly figures out from my expression that Amber Regan requires no introduction and carries on with his story.

"Apparently, they want to spotlight Colorado on one of her episodes for next season. She and her *team* are coming out to scout locations. I drew the short straw to *liaise* with them for our units."

Braden uses air quotes and draws out what he clearly finds to be the worst of the words he just uttered.

"There were actual straws involved. Boss man cut up a handful of plastic coffee stirrers and made us all choose one. I won. Or lost, if you have any fucking sense in your head."

"Who's Amber Regan?"

A shit-eating look crosses Braden's face at Cara's interjection. *Go ahead, tell your girl here who Amber is.* Choose your words carefully. I curl my lip on the side of my mouth that Braden can see.

"She has a hunting show on cable. Spends most of her time in front of the camera, talks a lot while she does it. Braden is not only averse to hunting shows, he's prickly about humanity in general. This is like his worst nightmare."

Braden slaps a hand to the tabletop and nearly everything atop it rattles under the impact. "Because those shows are a goddam disservice to hunting. They make us look like assholes and idiots. You. Me. All of us. And all that fucking *whispering.*"

He drops his voice into a stage whisper and adds a thick Southern accent. *"Hey, Bobby-Joe-Billy-Bob! Looky! A whitetail. Think we should bait it with a salt lick and an open bag of corn? Roll down the window on the truck!"* Braden's voice returns to its usual growl. "Here's an idea: You're in the woods. It's quiet. Now shut the fuck up."

I let out a snort. "Maybe it won't be as bad as you think."

"Impossible. These people think hunting's something that always ends in a trophy. They hunt for points and mounts, nothing else. I'll be lucky to keep my job with what's bound to come out of my mouth."

"Calm down, George Clooney. You need to be ready for your close-up, and all that scowling is going to wreck your skin with wrinkles. Remember, HD is unforgiving."

Braden tosses a scowl my way before turning to focus on Cara. "Pleasure meeting you, Cara." He stands and starts to gather up his things. "Strickland, you are an asshole as always, but I will see you on Sunday, when I plan to kick your ass shooting some foam . . . and I don't look like George Clooney. At all."

I ignore the comment about his threatened ass-kicking when

we shoot our bows at his place this weekend, because I'll outscore him like I always do. Instead, I offer a thoughtful, mocking nod of my head.

"True. You're less pleasant and professional than Clooney. Less classy. You're more like . . ." Nothing comes to mind, even as I take inventory of Braden's hulking stature and glowering scowl.

"Joe Manganiello," Cara pronounces.

We both cut our eyes toward her. She shrugs. "*True Blood*? *Magic Mike*?" Neither of us responds. She sighs. "He married Sofia Vergara?"

No clue who Joe is, but as with Amber Regan, I do know who Sofia Vergara is. Braden simply blinks, because he doesn't have cable television and relies on an antenna to pick up the one local channel he sometimes watches, so the Sofia reference doesn't help him. I'm sure the only reason he has any idea who Amber Regan is is that she's also always splashed across advertisements in hunting magazines, and Braden does read—a lot, in fact. Everything from hunting magazines to wildlife biology research journals to big, fat hardcover books about natural history.

Braden directs another goodbye to Cara, another insult to me, and stomps out.

Cara slowly finishes chewing a bite of pulled pork. "He's rather intense, isn't he? This Amber girl is in for quite a ride. How long have you guys been friends? Has he always been like this?"

I watch Braden hulk his way through the restaurant, then hold the door open for a group of middle-aged women who all give him a second look and smile, which he doesn't return. And I'm comfortable enough with where my dick finds true north to acknowledge that Braden's a good-looking dude. If he weren't so dead set on living the life of a curmudgeon, he'd have no trouble finding someone to crawl under his rock with him.

"Braden's a solid guy, you just have to look past half of what he says. I met him a few years back, right after he took over as the game warden around here. He tried to ticket me for something that was bullshit and I told him so—been friends since then. 'Intense' is a good word for him, though. But you can count on him. Always."

Cara allows a smile to crawl across her face. "I just met your bestie, didn't I?"

"Men do not have besties. We have drinking pals and hunting buddies. Braden is both. And good people, no question."

Another smile, paired with Cara lowering her voice to a near whisper and leaning in so close, I almost forget we're in the middle of a restaurant.

"He's your *bestie*. Be careful, Garrett. We keep going this way and by the end of the night, I'm going to know *everything* about you."

13

(Garrett)

The town of Hotchkiss doesn't offer much in the way of entertainment. No movie theater, no entertainment center, not even a bar that isn't the Elks Lodge. This lack of anything to do is how we end up leaving True Grit and driving straight back to the farm.

That and the fact I've decided to make the most of whatever this is with Cara and her date dress, which means an empty house suits me fine.

After pulling into the driveway, I edge to a stop by the front door and put the truck in park, the engine at an idle to keep the heater running so Cara's legs don't freeze. The radio is humming in the background, tuned to a local station that's currently playing a set of cheesy throwback love songs. Anticipation fills the rest of the cab, so much that I might have to crack a window if I don't get a sign about what's next here.

"Garrett?" Cara asks, her voice curious but faraway.

"Yeah?"

"Do you think Corey and Brooke are happy?"

Weird question, and not at all what I might have guessed would be a go-to topic right now. My face screws up. "I think so. Why?"

"I think so, too." She blows out a breath. "My parents aren't like that. I mean, they're happy or content, or whatever, but what Corey and Brooke have seems so much better. Like they're partners, so even if things get hard, they trust each other enough to shoulder it evenly. And they're in love."

I hold back a scoff. If only Cara knew that love isn't enough when you're talking about this way of life. I learned that from my mom, who once admitted she never stopped loving my dad. She just hated the life. Not only living with dirt in the house that never goes away and the dicey finances of running a farm, but the loneliness. All those long days, waiting up for a *husband*, only to have a *farmer* finally shuffle through the door, one who couldn't—or wouldn't—shut off that part of his brain for her, even for a few hours.

"It isn't about loving each other." My voice comes out harder than I intended, but I want her to hear the difference. "They both love the life. Falling for someone who gets that is what makes it work."

Cara twists on the bench seat to face me. "You love the life, don't you?"

"Yup. Probably have silt mixed in with my blood."

"Then why aren't you farming or ranching? Why are you working at the co-op? Everyone you've introduced me to thinks you're amazing. A few have mentioned that you're not doing what you should be—"

I flip on the dome light and the glare floods the cab. I catch a glimpse of her legs tucked up under her on the seat, causing her dress to ride up her thighs, but even that can't distract me from what she's trying to do.

Cara blinks a few times. "Ugh. Why'd you do that?"

"I wanted to see if you have your notebook out. Or your glasses on. Because it sure sounds like you're trying to interview me."

She shakes her head a little, her eyes ticking up toward the headliner.

"Or maybe I'm just trying to get to know you better. Through the fine art of conversation."

"Then ask me what my favorite movie is, or what kind of music I like. Hell, ask what I want for my last meal." I flick off the light. "Chicken-fried steak, by the way. Brown gravy, not white. Mashed potatoes with more brown gravy. Peach pie for dessert, made with Hotchkiss peaches."

Cara sputters out a little huff. "Let me get this straight. You'll drive me around to meet every other farmer in the county, let them all know I'm a decent person they should talk to, but if I ask *you* any questions, it's a hard no?"

Is she nuts? Of course it's a hard no. Giving Cara the lowdown on losing everything? Talking about how I never quite mustered the motivation to return to school but I can't name why? How I have a nightmare sometimes that I'm going to die at the co-op?

Hard. No.

At the very least, I'm interested in the opportunity to move the rest of this night inside the house, and I don't care how much women claim they want men to be vulnerable and shit, revealing all your failures and fuckups isn't a turn-on to anyone. If I answer her honestly, I'll get pity in return. And *fuck that*.

I take a deep breath. "Look, I like hanging out with you, and tonight's been great. Let's not screw it up. Besides, my story isn't the one you want, City."

Cara flips the light on as I did before. Her gaze is pinned to mine, not angry but determined, and I want to yank her across the bench seat and onto my lap because of it. She purses her glossy lips.

"How about this—you stop calling me City, and I'll give up asking you about anything of significance. Deal?"

I rear my head back. "The City thing bugs you? I didn't mean anything by it. I mean, I call Whitney 'Johnny Appleseed.' I call Braden, 'asshole.' And I don't even mean *that* as a bad thing. You should have said something earlier. I wasn't trying to be shitty."

"Well, all I hear is you pointing out the obvious: that I'm a rich girl from the city who couldn't find her way out of a tractor seat. I already know that. I have the mud-stained jeans to prove it. But if you're unwilling to have an actual conversation with me, then you don't get to give me one of your little nicknames."

My jaw drops open, slack because I don't know what to say. A few dying fish–like noises come out, but that's it. Cara turns her head and stares out the windshield. Great. I'm so not getting that dress up where I'd like it tonight.

What's worse is that I might have hurt her. Every time I used the name, which I thought was cute, I cut her down a little. Unintentional or not, it doesn't matter. I did. If there was a way to go back to the first moment I said it and erase it all, I would.

We sit quietly, the silence making it worse, mocking until I can't stand it and end up asking the lamest question possible, hoping to make it stop.

"What are you thinking about?"

Cara blinks, doesn't turn her head, but continues staring ahead. "I'm making a pros-and-cons list in my head so I can decide something."

"Decide what?"

Her head swings my way. "Decide if my plan to seduce you is worth it. If I crawled across this seat and sat right next to you, like I planned, if that would lead to something. Like *sex*."

Only the wild hum of wanting her saves me from chuckling at the idea she was going to "seduce" me, or the way she sounded annoyed when blurting out the words "like sex."

But that's trumped, too, by the way she's inspired something else: the sudden realization that I'm tired of pretending I don't want more than I already have. Because right now I want *her*. And for so long I've avoided or skirted past anything that might be a risk, telling myself over and over that my job, my life, all of it, is good enough. I've played nice and easy and content for too long, and I want something more now.

And I'm fucking exhausted from trying to keep my hands to myself when it comes to the woman sitting only a few feet away, who just announced she had a plan for tonight that involved sex. I want that so damn much, I'm bound to say the wrong thing a hundred more times tonight. Blame all the days that led up to tonight, plus my inability to think straight when I'm too close to her Creamsicle-ness.

I give my head a shake. I want her, and I hope she still wants me, so it's time to fix this shit.

"If you sat right here?" I point to the space right next to me. She nods. "Probably nothing."

Her face falls. She starts to fumble around for the door handle, clearly ready to wrench open the truck door and bail. I catch her before she does, taking her one hand in mine. Cara freezes.

"But let's say you did something else." I trace the pad of my thumb across the inside of her wrist. "Like crawled over here, threw those pretty legs over mine, and set that cute ass right on my lap."

Her breath hitches and my heartbeat kicks up, from a heavy thump to a wild hammering I can feel *everywhere*.

"If you did that?" I pause for a few beats and wait for her look at me, finding her wide-eyed in the right way.

"Then I'd know we both want the same thing."

Cara holds fast for a moment, like she's finishing up whatever internal debate she needs to, then she's headed my way, pausing only long enough to assess the amount of space between my chest and the steering wheel—as if there were any possibility she wouldn't fit. She's up on her knees and taking too damn long for my now-threadbare patience to handle, so I set my hands on her waist and haul her where she belongs. The faint sound of Cara's nervous exhales and the sound of my blood rushing southward is all I can hear when she starts to lower her body slowly. I keep my grip loose at her waist, holding back the urge to yank her down.

When she settles herself, I shift to center her weight where I want it, even if it feels as torturous as it does good. Cara takes a deep breath, urging her hips forward, then back again. My dick responds, and when she repeats the same rotation again, I groan to bite back the words rolling around in my head. Awareness flares in her eyes.

Yes, I want to tell her, that is my half-hard cock pressed to the heat of your pussy. Go ahead and rub all you like. Work it however you need to. I'll be ready when you are.

But Cara drops her hips and keeps them still instead of continuing to work her body against mine. She lifts her hands and eases her index fingers over my brows. My eyes fall closed. Her fingers continue downward, tracing the edges of my cheekbones, then my jawline, coming to stop before allowing her thumbs to graze my lips.

"I know I said I'd drop it, but I have one more question, Garrett. Then we can get on with this."

I let out a grunt that I hope makes it clear how getting *on with this* is my top priority right now, enough that I'd probably answer any question she asks. Hell, if she wanted to, I know Cara Cavanaugh could crack me open like an overripe cantaloupe. One good whack and I'd spill everything.

"You said your story isn't the one I want, and I think you're right. For the article, anyway. But for my own curiosity? You're wrong." My eyes flip open to find Cara's half-hooded gaze fixed on the play between her thumbs and my lips. "You don't want to talk about it tonight? That's fine. But maybe another night?"

I blink once, calculating how I can answer in a way that means we don't stop what's happening, but also doesn't promise more than I'm willing to give. Her thumb tugs down my lower lip, slowly and softly.

"Maybe." I answer hoarsely.

Cara whispers a thank-you, her lips close enough to mine to mean we don't say anything after that. We start in, lips crashing together, tongues teasing between moans. Her hands find my chest, rubbing her way down over every inch, until she lands them over my jeans and I jut my hips up, half intentionally and half instinctually. I wrap my arms low around her waist to keep her close, but she pulls back. Her eyes lock on mine as she starts to untangle my arms from around her.

She widens the spread of her thighs, settling when she's comfortable. When her hands touch the hem of her dress, my breath starts to come in labored bursts, my nostrils flaring with each one. Cara slowly drags her dress higher, until the material is bunched up and I can see the smooth fair skin of her thighs, the tight draw of her flesh, where she looks soft despite all the muscle tone I know is there. Hands twitching, I try to determine if this is enough of an invitation. If she can tell exactly how badly I want this. She must know, because she takes my hands in hers and lays them to the bare skin of her thighs. I barely manage a grunt before tightening my grip.

"Tell me what you want," I bite out.

As an answer, Cara flexes her thighs and starts to grind her body in the tiniest, hottest cock-tease of a move I've ever experienced. She gives up a whimper and yanks up her dress again, balling up the fabric in her hands and holding the fisted-up material against her hips. She starts to rock harder, desperate sounds coming from her mouth while she does. I draw my hands up high enough that my thumbs meet the edge of her panties.

"Is this what you want? My fingers here, pressed to your pussy?"

Cara digs her teeth into her lower lip and nods.

I move one thumb inward, taking two passes over the slip of what feels like a tiny and expensive excuse for panties. Slipping under the edge, I let out a low groan at my discovery there.

Slick. Warm. Soft.

Did I mention slick? Worth saying it twice—shit, twelve times—given how wet Cara is already. I grit my teeth and order myself to just do this for now. Finger her until I'm positive she wants more, then a little longer to be sure. And to do whatever it takes to keep from ripping my jeans open and yanking her onto my cock.

But Cara doesn't seem to think much of my self-imposed slow build, because after a few circles of my thumb to her clit, she's moaning louder, like she can't wait it out much longer. And while I know I need to temper *me*, if she needs more I'm not going to deny her. I use my other hand to pull her panties over and replace my thumb with the flat of two fingers, her sweet heat coating them in an instant.

Screw it. From her every sound and movement, I know I'm jumping the trigger here, but at least not with my dick, so I go ahead and slip my middle finger inside. I curl and crook a bit, nothing but the tip gently working the spot I know will help her find the edge. The moan Cara lets out is low and long, and when I add another finger, she doesn't hold back. She starts to ride my hand, hot and deep so my fingers can provide what she needs, and I take a cue from how she's moving, start to thrust my fingers in short pulses to match the pitch of her body. When her head drops back, I give a little more. When her mouth falls open, I give even more. When her brow furrows up and it looks like she's holding her breath, I give her everything.

"Cara." Her name comes out so roughly, it sounds like a command, and even though I'd never *tell* her to come, because demanding that would probably have the exact opposite effect, that's what I'm thinking. That I want her to give it up to me. Right now. I say her name again, the same rough tone, the same demand buried behind it.

She goes off like nothing I've ever heard, or felt, or experienced. A hundred times hotter and tighter, and when the best of it starts to taper, she tips forward to rest against me. She releases the balled-up material of her dress and sets her now-free hands to the back of the seat on either side of my head. Having her this way, drained and still letting out satisfied soft moans, feels so natural and right, I slip my fingers out slowly from inside her, intent on wrapping her up tight in my arms.

But she starts to languidly move her body around, curving her back and hips in satisfied catlike motions. My cock's enjoying the show—a lot. Unfortunately, Cara's moves have a little too much gusto and, tiny build or not, the distance between her and my steering wheel is only so wide. And what's in the center of the steering wheel? The horn.

Cara yelps when her back end bumps and the horn sounds, her squeal loud enough to compete with the horn's decibels. I yank her forward and start in on a prayer while biting my tongue so hard it's painful.

Please, God, make it so I don't laugh. She's hot and amazing and I want to fuck her so bad my dick might break off if I can't get it out of my pants and inside her in the next three minutes. So please don't let me laugh.

Cara shudders and drops her head to my neck, where she's

quaking under what I'm hoping is a mortified laugh and not tears. She lets out a pouty-sounding huff and I lose it, because she's so fucking cute, I can't stand it. I give a nudge of my shoulder to encourage her face up, but she refuses to follow.

"Cara, sweetheart." I snort. "Come on, look at me."

She shakes her head. "No. It's not fair. Why can't I be sexy? Not always, but if I could get ten whole minutes I'd thank the universe for the privilege."

A sweep of sympathy rushes through me. She could bounce her ass to the horn in a rendition of a Justin Bieber song and I'd still think she's beyond sexy. I smooth my hands down her back.

"You *are* sexy," I whisper, then guide her hand to the place where the proof of that isn't going away any time soon, even with the laughing.

"Put your hands on me, right here. Feel that?" She answers with a little hum of acknowledgment. "That's for you. *Because* of you."

She doesn't move her head from the crook of my neck, but her curious fingers grip me through my jeans.

"Can we go inside? Probably safer that way; who knows what I could bump into next?" I let out a soft laugh, but it dies in my throat when she speaks again.

"And I want to see you. Touch. Taste."

Her fingers start to tick upward, teasing at my belt. Fuck yes. Here we go, finally headed where I've wanted us to be, all damn night.

"Inside means you'll have to crawl off." I swat her thigh. Cara presses her knees to my sides with a dissatisfied murmur. A grin hits me at the sweet need in that sound.

"Got it. I can make this work. Grab your bag; we'll need house keys unless you want this on the front porch."

Cara dives for her purse, slinging it over her shoulder. I yank my keys from the ignition and toss them on the dash, then give her body a boost to mine. When Cara wraps her arms around my neck, I shove the truck door open and manage to get us both out so smoothly it's like I've done this a hundred times with her in my arms. I give her another boost to cradle her properly.

"OK, now wrap those legs around me nice and tight."

She does as instructed, and I almost regret asking, because the way she does—eager and urgent—means I'm in for one hell of a ride.

Then she starts to kiss me and it's a good thing I still remember everything about this place, even in the dark. Where the walkway is, how there's a stone about halfway to the door that's been upturned by an overgrown tree root from the cottonwood in the yard. The motion-sensor porch light kicks on when we come close enough and I drop her down, Cara digging through her bag to gather the keys, but her hands are trembling, so I grab the keys from her. I'm so primed that if she drops them, or the door sticks and she falters, seconds' delay might make doing this on the front porch a reality.

The door swings open a touch harder than I planned, which means it bounces back after hitting the adjacent wall. But Cara scampers in, darting around me and dodging the swinging door. She stops just inside, and then turns on her heel to face me. And, holy hell, the look on her face is everything I could ever ask for. Her chin tipped down, eyes bright and sparked with excitement, lips parted a fraction and a hint of impatience in the way her chest rises and falls with each breath.

I clear the threshold, kicking the door shut behind me. Stalking forward, I pull my coat off and cast it to the floor, then reach for her. My hands find her hips and I start walking, Cara shuffling backward in time.

Jesus, she's so *pretty*. This delicate beauty that looks fragile one second and strong enough to take your breath away in the next.

Such softness about her, but her body is taut almost everywhere. Arms and legs, the flat of her belly, the slope of her back downward. I catch a glimpse of her Pilates contraption and silently offer my undying gratitude to whoever invented that thing.

Cara bumps into the wall with a quiet thump. I grab her wrists in my hands, working them behind her so I can take both in one of mine, using the other to sweep a few stray pieces of her hair off her forehead. She wets her lips and I drive my hips forward with a shove, my cock settling against her core. Then I do it again.

"Fuck. Tell me you feel that, too."

Cara lets out a gusting exhale. "You'll need to be more specific." A little soft laugh. "I'm feeling a lot of things at the moment."

For demonstration's purposes, I offer another round. Also, my dick likes it.

"The way we fit together. Lined up in all the right places. It'll be so easy—this, *us*. My cock comes out, I pull one of your legs up and across my arm, and I'll be deep before you say 'please.'"

Cara drops her head back to the wall and it thuds. Hard enough that I scan the features of her face for any sign it hurt, trying to determine if I need to rub the back of her head and soothe away the sting. Nothing. Instead, she pushes her hips forward and straight into mine.

"Do that. What you just said." Her leg comes up, foot curling around my calf. "Plea—"

I'm nothing if not a man of my word. I cut her words off with a hard kiss, working my belt open at the same time. The button on my jeans slips free, and I all but tear down the zipper, using one hand to shove down my boxers. Freeing myself is a relief. Another kiss, more fumbling until I'm able to extract my wallet from a back pocket.

When I lean back to focus on ripping open the condom

wrapper, I catch Cara's gaze cutting downward, where my dick is up for whatever inspection she wants to perform—visual, oral, or tactile. Her eyes flare and she tries to fight back a little grin, but fails. Then her hands find me, both of them, those manicured fingers working in a near-perfect rhythm. My eyes fall shut and I freeze in place, my jaw dropping open on the loudest, most obscene groan that's ever left my lungs. She strokes and tugs almost too gently for what I usually like, but for now that's probably safer. Too much would make this condom beside the point.

"Garrett." My name on her lips is a reminder of what's happening here. I grab her hands and watch as they slip off my aching cock. A quick glance at her face, where I find her full-on smiling.

I grin back, then bait the hook. Because, lame or not, I'm just a guy who's about to go on a vain cock-motivated fishing expedition for a compliment. "What are you smiling about?"

She sets her upper teeth to one edge of her bottom lip, with a little disbelieving shake of her head.

"I'm trying to figure out if you have any weaknesses, a defect of some sort. You're funny and helpful, hot and smart. And when you bottle-feed a calf, I get jealous of the attention you're giving her. Now *this*." She darts her eyes to my cock, the one all but throwing its own ticker-tape parade to get her attention. "Is there anywhere you come up short? Anything you suck at?"

I roll the condom on and give myself a long stroke while I think.

"Bowling. I'm totally shitty at bowling."

Cara laughs and everything about me swells, inside and out. I lean forward. "Ready?"

She nods and I yank up her leg, set her knee into the crook of my arm, and step forward. Her bent leg is pressed between her chest and mine, showing off exactly how flexible she is. Another thank-you to the Pilates gods, whoever they are.

Everything I thought about how we would fit is true. Cara tugs her panties over and I take a slow push forward, the head of my dick slipping in, and just that snaps my sanity. When Cara lets out a soft wailing sound, I'm there, all the way and so deep I can't think straight enough to move. Then Cara's hands reach around and skate down under my boxers, her nails digging in to prompt me.

After that, it's just the two of us using each other in all the right ways. The greedy parts of her taking the demanding parts of me while our other limbs fight for purchase against each other. I move closer—because closer is better—and the angle changes. I'm driving deeper and harder, making sure to hit her sweet spot with every thrust. The lights go out in my brain when she tightens and pulses around me, over and over until her entire body starts to tremble and it feels safe to take mine. Pounding deep means the pressure barreling up from my spine when I come is so intense I have to flatten one hand to the wall for some stability. Cara's mumbling obscenities and prayers—and I'm doing the same thing, but louder.

After a few moments the world starts to align itself again. My eyes dart around the room.

Holy shit. I just had sex in the house I grew up in. For the first time. While there was plenty of me and my right hand going on in my bedroom during my teenage years, this never happened. First time for everything, I guess, no matter how bizarre the circumstances.

Cara seems to read my mind. Either that or she sees how my gaze has gone twitchy about our surroundings. She sets one hand on my chest, nestled between our bodies, and I skirt my eyes back to hers.

"Is this weird for you? You look like you just saw a ghost or something."

I give a jerky nod. "A little."

Cara's hand drops from my chest and I feel her trying to move away, so I let her leg down slowly. Her dress falls into place, exactly where I don't think it belongs. She looks to the floor.

"I get it. You don't have to stay." Then she's tipping her head down and tucking her hair behind her ears. I start to protest, but she waves it away. "It's fine. Really."

And just like that—with my goddam dick still half inside her—I'm dismissed.

14

(Cara)

I, Cara Cavanaugh, was not meant for amazing sex.

That's the only plausible conclusion to be drawn from the last thirty-six hours, in which I've done nearly nothing but dwell on and daydream about what happened two nights ago. I'm better suited for the perfectly adequate, just-fine sex I've always known. The sort that happens in a bed, missionary position, and sometimes results in an orgasm. *That* is the sex life I was intended for. Because this other thing? It's too much. No matter how hard I try, the dazed pleasure centers in my brain return to a darkened truck cab, a darkened house, and Garrett.

I've tried everything, including meditation. Sitting quietly in half lotus atop a couch cushion thrown on the floor, going all Zen when my mind goes off track.

Recognize the errant thought. Don't judge. Return to the breath.

Works for about three breaths. Then it's nothing but a lewd recall of Garrett, all of him. My body's reaction to his hand between my legs, fingers deep and full. His reaction to my hands on him, stroking as he fumbled with the condom. My leg held tight to his body as he slipped inside, then . . .

So much for meditation.

Then I decided to try my old standby: a pros-and-cons list, this one designed to determine if I could handle more Garrett in my life. If I could, what would that look like? If I couldn't, how was I going to avoid him in a town the size of Hotchkiss?

PRO: More Garrett means more of the Best Sex Ever.

CON: More Best Sex Ever will ruin me for other men of reasonable prowess and average endowment, who don't smell like clean-scented dirt and lust and sex. They wouldn't stand a chance. I'll die a lonely spinster because of it.

PRO: More Garrett would mean the chance to see him naked. I saw nearly nothing this go-round, and the idea I could leave without knowing what a naked Garrett looks like? Boo.

PRO: More Garrett would be fun, pure and simple. I *like* him.

PRO: More Garrett would mean I might get him to tell me his story. How he ended up letting go of his dreams and why someone like him, with so much potential, gave up on having more.

CON: If I get all of that? More of the Best Sex Ever, a naked Garrett, fun, and a glimpse into the real man beneath the easygoing grins? There is a strong chance I'll end up falling for him.

And that one con is enough. Because aside from my apparent inability to deal with the effects of amazing sex, I've also deduced that I'm not meant for casual sex, which is exactly what Garrett and I would be—the only thing we can be. Off-the-cuff and temporary, fun while it lasts, and entirely without the strings that come with considering more. And maybe if I didn't *like* him the way I do, or spend far too much time thinking about what makes him tick, then casual might be a possibility.

But, given the way my mind and my heart work, I'm not up for that sort of fun. Just one night with Garrett and I feel oddly like I have a hangover, a side effect I'm convinced has something to do with trying to play it cool when he went distant for a flickering moment just after he came, then trying to play it *super* cool when I assured him it was fine for him to go. And when I plastered the fakest all-good-here smile on my face after he kissed me then shuffled his way out the door, he looked confused and I felt wrecked. Add in the fact that I didn't come here to find a guy, but rather a story, and my decision is easy.

Find Garrett, tell him thank you for the Best Sex Ever, but let him know there won't be any more to come.

Time for a trip into town.

~ ~

The Hotchkiss Co-op is housed in a building that was once a depot station, now a nondescript storefront with aged wood siding and uninspired signage. The parking lot nearly outsizes the actual building, so I easily find a spot out front, a few spaces over from a lone Dodge truck. Garrett's truck is parked out back, and when I spy it on my way up to the front door, my body reacts, skin prickling in awareness and recollection.

Hell. That's going to be a problem. A heap of metal—just sitting there innocently—should not have this sort of power over me.

When I step inside, the space is well organized and far less messy than I expected for a co-op. The shelves and displays are neatly arranged, quite obviously kept after, and I can suddenly see that Garrett's hand is everywhere. Things might look humble at first, but if you look closely enough, there's care and attention paid to everything.

"You sure coddling moths are the problem? Bunch of guys are having trouble with mites this season. If it's mites, you'll need to spray. Organic, of course, but we have some new formulations in this year."

Garrett's voice emerges from a back room just before he steps out and drops a pile of small boxes on the front counter. He looks up to see me, his expression surprised at first, then pleased—and everything inside me ignites.

Stupid body. It doesn't understand our objective here. Abstain from the Best Sex Ever.

A customer ducks out from behind a set of shelves at the far end of the store, tossing a pair of work gloves on the counter next to the boxes.

"Whitney says this is what she wants. I mentioned the mites, but she claims I'm still an *apprentice*. And I decided to not push my luck by speaking again, because I love her, but pregnancy hormones—Christ. It's like trying to navigate a minefield on a high wire, and I'm not as nimble as I once was. If this is what her being twelve weeks along is like, I might have to start training again just to keep up."

When he turns to grab a gallon bottle of something off an endcap display, I get a good look at him and notice he happens to look a lot like former pro wide receiver Cooper Lowry. Almost his freaking doppelgänger. Same build, same shaggy blond hair, same hopelessly pretty face that made watching football games with my dad and the Cahill boys mildly more entertaining.

While their true fanaticisms are for college ball—*roll tide, y'all*—pro football is popular enough with our circle that I have more than a passing knowledge of the game. One too many of my Sundays have been spent watching the Bears in our families' shared executive suite at Soldier Field, or in the Cahills' lavish basement media room, surrounded by too much hollering and not enough commercials. But all those hours of my life lost means I know a fake Cooper Lowry when I see one.

"Good luck." Garrett chuckles. "Girl might be a little hippie sweetheart, but I'm sure she's a handful when she puts her mind to it."

Fake Cooper lets out a grunt as an answer, handing Garrett his credit card at the same time. Garrett runs the card and tears off the slip, taking the opportunity to look my way when Fake Cooper signs it. A lopsided smile, all for me, then he says my name by way of a greeting.

"Cara."

Dammit. The quiet familiarity in his saying my name that way—a low rumble laced with satisfaction—is not helping. I manage a blundering, awkward wave that probably looks more like a tic I can't control and pair it with a croaking hello. Fake Cooper hands back the receipt while squinting in my direction. Back to Garrett, then to me again. All while Garrett and I essentially strip each other's clothes off with our eyes.

Fake Cooper's phone buzzes, cutting the invisible tie between Garrett and me, both of us watching as he scans his phone face. A chuckle and a shake of his head, then his mouth breaks into a grin.

"OK. I'm out of here. The gorgeous, stubborn woman who's carrying my kid—but still refuses to marry me—wants barbeque. Right *now*, it seems."

When the store door jingles shut behind Fake Cooper, Garrett slips out from behind the counter to head my way. His approach, slow but casual, is still like a predatory prowl and I latch one hand on to an adjacent shelf to keep from launching forward to meet him halfway.

"Has anybody ever told that guy he looks exactly like Cooper Lowry, who used to play for Denver?" I muse.

Garrett closes the distance between us and puts one hand to my hip. "Doubt it."

"Really? Because it's uncanny."

His other hand finds my other hip, lowering both so he can tuck the tips of his fingers into the back pockets on my jeans.

"If they did say that, they'd probably feel pretty stupid."

"Why?"

Garrett leans close and kisses me. "Because that *is* Cooper Lowry."

My brow furrows up even as my eyes are still closed from the kiss. I work through the details of the last few minutes and flick my eyelids open.

"Wait a second. Is the Cooper of the Whitney and Cooper you know, actually Cooper Lowry? And did he say that this Whitney woman refuses to marry him? And she's having his baby?"

Garrett's face brightens in amusement and he gives me a nod.

"Is she in possession of all her mental faculties? Because Cooper Lowry looked like he thought it was the cutest thing ever that she was demanding barbeque. Pretty good sign that he's pussy-whipped. She has to be nuts to not marry him."

Garrett lets out a sharp laugh. "I can't believe the phrase 'pussy-whipped' just came out of your mouth." His hands slip fully into my back pockets. "But, yes, to everything you just rattled off. He is Cooper Lowry, Whitney does refuse to marry him, she's knocked up, and her brain is in working order. She's just not much for convention, claims marriage is a pointless institution."

"But he's *Cooper Lowry*."

Another kiss, harder this time, far less sweet than the first one. My hands land on his chest, intent on giving him a gentle push away. But when the heat of his skin beneath the worn T-shirt warms my palms, my fingers curl into the feel and all my other plans evaporate.

Finally, he pulls back with a muttered curse. Garrett casts his voice back over one shoulder.

"Bart! I'll be back in ten, OK?"

Behind him, a portly man lumbers out from a back office, his body taking up the entire doorway and then some. He brushes a wave in our direction without looking up from the clipboard he's scribbling on. "Take lunch if you want."

Mischief lights Garrett's face. "You hungry?"

He draws a lock of my hair to tuck behind my ear, just as I would have done on my own if my hands weren't still magnetized to his chest. I don't have an opportunity to answer before my hand is in his and we're headed out the door, quickstepping around the side of the building and over to his truck. Garrett yanks open the truck door.

"Crawl in, but don't go too far. I want you where you were two nights ago. Those pretty legs spread wide over mine."

I haul myself into the truck in a rush, somehow justifying the decision to do so by thinking that we'll be able to talk in here. In private. Alone. With my legs spread over his. As one does when they need to have a serious no-more-sex conversation with someone.

Garrett slamming the truck door shocks my senses. Big hands circle my waist and then I'm on his lap. A slow inspection of my body leads to his hands atop my thighs, tightening when he moves high enough to land where my legs meet my hips, his gaze lingering there.

"I haven't been able to stop thinking about you, Cara." He chuckles, almost darkly, raises his eyes to mine. "The whole night is on a damn loop in my brain. Do you know how inconvenient a hard-on is when you're trying to work?"

Yes, I do. Well, not a hard-on exactly—but I do know how inconvenient a loop of lewd thoughts can be when you need to work. That's why I'm here, I remind myself.

But Garrett doesn't wait for an answer, just presses his mouth to mine. We're alone and together, which means we're wild after one taste, my tongue teasing his and Garrett groaning to encourage me. But when his hands start to move up to niggle the buttons on my shirt, slipping one, then two, open, I know I have to stop this. If I don't, my shirt will be off before I know it—in broad daylight—and then doing what I came here to do will be impossible. I latch my hands to his wrists and Garrett goes stiff.

"Sorry," Garrett whispers, leaning back but allowing his hands to linger on the open placket of my shirt. He uses the tip of one index finger to skim there, then eases the material back until the lace edge of my black bra comes into view. I watch the bob of his Adam's apple as he works over a labored swallow.

"I barely had the chance to touch you here. I didn't get to see you, not all of you. I've been thinking about that . . . how we cheated each other out of the full show." His eyes come to meet mine. "We should fix that."

"Garrett, I can't . . ."

He rebuttons my top. "I could come over tonight. Or, you can come to my place, if you want. Fair warning, it's a straight-up redneck bachelor pad. But I'll change my sheets and light one of those candles that's supposed to smell like a waterfall or something, to air out the scent of my manliness. I can grill something for dinner and we'll hang out."

A pause as he sets his hands to the back of my neck, rubbing gently with his fingers, and I allow myself the indulgence of enjoying it.

"We can't do this."

Garrett's fingers stop moving. "Huh?"

Reaching up, I remove his hands and set them to rest on the seat. "We can't do this. Date. Kiss. Have sex."

His eyes narrow and he takes inventory of my expression, obviously confused. "Why?"

"What?"

He repeats the word, slower this time, with an edge to it. "Why? Did I do something? Not do something?"

I start to shake my head, then jerk my hands up to cover my

face so I can think, which is easier if I'm not looking at him. Garrett pulls my hands away, using one of his to trace a thumb over my lower lip.

"Unless I'm crazy, I thought it was good for you. I *felt* you, Cara. Around my fingers, against my palm, tight to my cock. And I loved every fucking second of it. So I can't think of a single reason why we'd stop. You'll have to explain to me why you think we should give this up."

I kiss the tip of his thumb, almost without thinking. "That's the problem. It *was* good for me. Too good."

Garrett's shoulders visibly relax and a smirk starts to tease across his mouth.

"But . . ." I tilt my head and wait a beat, ensuring I have his focus. "I'm not here for that. I'm here to work. This freelance thing is new for me, and I can't get derailed. Tell me you can understand that, how sometimes you have to give up the good stuff because there are more important things you need to do. That you have bigger things to accomplish."

His smirk fades almost immediately, replaced by his mouth leveling into a harsh, very un-Garrett-like line, shuttering his features into something empty but guarded.

"Important things. Bigger things." He blinks, lets his voice go flat. "I wouldn't want to get in the way of that."

"Garrett—"

He cuts me off. "Scoot off so I can grab my phone. I'll give you Whitney's number and you can set something up with her. She'll love your little hybrid car. You don't need me."

I awkwardly move off of his lap and watch as he scrolls through his contacts. When he finds what he's looking for, he doesn't turn my way.

"OK, City. Hand over your phone and I'll add this for you."

City. My jaw clamps tight. Guess we're back to that, then.

Meeting Whitney Reed in person only makes the whole Cooper Lowry thing even more confounding. Not that she isn't lovely and beautiful—she is. She's also a crunchy tree hugger with a nose ring who is dressed in a pair of worn-out leggings, a heavy zip-up hoodie, a trapper hat, and muck boots when I arrive at the orchard she and Cooper own—a look that I don't think it's too judgmental of me to say is not what one might imagine when typecasting a former NFL star's girlfriend.

Whitney ditches the coat, hat, and boots after we finish a tour of the orchard and head inside the decrepit farmhouse she and Cooper live in, tossing it all in a pile near the front door. She notes it when my gaze inadvertently lingers on her already hard-to-miss baby bump, giving an eye roll.

"Twins. Boys, I'm sure. And I'm working with Lowry genetics here, so stubborn and strapping are a given."

"Don't forget surly. And superior." Another eye roll from Whitney at Cooper's interjection from the kitchen, where he's perched at the stove, carefully extracting glass pint jars from a large stainless steel pot of hot water.

Whitney clears the small living room and sidles up next to Cooper, inspecting his work as he uses a dish towel to blot water off the top of each jar. He gives her a gently chiding side glance then kisses her forehead before craning over one shoulder my way.

"How'd it go out there? You get what you need, Cara?"

I take his question as an invitation to make my way into the kitchen, taking a seat at the vintage Formica table where Whitney has flopped wearily into a chair and gestured for me to do the same.

"Absolutely. Whitney's a great tour guide."

Cooper's eyes light and he cuts what I'm positive is a private, secret look at Whitney. "I'm aware."

He grabs four pint jars from the far side of the countertop, amidst what currently looks like the end of a production line in a small-scale canning factory. "Here, these are new recipes for an artisanal line of preserved goods I want to develop. This isn't our fruit; we're just playing around with recipes for now. There's a peach jam with lemon verbena and a quince ginger chutney."

Well, *obviously*. Because creating lemon verbena and quince concoctions are what record-crushing wide receivers are known for. These two must make sport out of defying conventions.

Cooper continues as he pushes the jars my way. "Make sure Garrett gives them a try. He's my best guinea pig; the kid will eat anything."

I'd already started to reach forward to draw Cooper's creations closer, but my hand freezes in midair at the mention of Garrett. Just like the thirty-six hours after we had sex, the thirty-six hours after I told him we couldn't be together have been no less challenging. Except this time it's regret that sends my mind wandering, which is far less pleasant of a distraction than daydreaming and replaying the naughty particulars of the Best Sex Ever. And when I wasn't dwelling on the regret that comes with hating the way Garrett wouldn't look at me in the truck, I was plotting ways to fix what I'd done—scheming a hundred different ways to earn a do-over with him and rationalizing away all the reasons I'd used to decide we should part ways in the first place.

Cooper and Whitney both fix on the way my slightly trembling hand hovers above the jars. I yank my hand back.

"I'm not sure when I'll see him. Garrett. We don't have plans, so . . ."

They exchange a glance, curiosity and concern, then Cooper gives a wave of his hand in the air. "No worries. I'll see him at some point."

He makes a move to gather up two of the jars, and suddenly

I see them as pint-sized opportunities. I may not be desperate enough just yet to use them, but if it comes to that, I will. If at some point I give in and decide that more Garrett is worth all that might come with, I can use these innocent jars of jam as an excuse to invite him over.

My hand shoots forward to block Cooper's. I clear my throat to be sure I don't sound as crazy out loud as I do in my head.

"I'll take them," I blurt out.

Cooper's eyebrows rise up warily. My not-crazy voice must still need some work. I try again, leveling my voice another notch. "I'll take them. Small town and he's the local golden boy. I'm bound to see him, right?"

15

(Garrett)

The first time I shot a compound bow was on my thirteenth birthday. It was a present from my dad that I'd worn him down about for months before that. In the ten-plus years since then, I've been through five different bows, learned how to fletch my own arrows, and worked hard to become a consistent shot at seventy yards. I've put in some time. Long gone should be the days when I was plagued by beginner's mistakes.

Mistakes like gripping the bow too tightly when I draw back, which means the bow will tip when the arrow flies and send it off course. Or punching the release instead of squeezing it, and rushing the entire shot. And forget follow-through. Because today, I've lifted my head too many times to count.

Chuck Adams, I'm not. Cameron Hanes? Nope. And Donnie Vincent's rep is safe from the likes of me. For those who don't know or care who those guys are . . . Katniss Everdeen could outshoot me right now with a blindfold on and President Snow breathing down her neck.

My latest arrow flings forward, headed toward the foam block target set up behind Braden's garage. It wobbles its way there and sinks into the upper right-hand corner, a good ten inches from the bull's-eye.

"Jesus fucking Christ." I let my arm drop heavily, my bow swinging loosely along the way.

Except for the jangle of Charley's dog collar, it's quiet from behind me. Even Braden gave up on the insults and commentaries about half an hour ago, which says a lot.

I could blame this pathetic display on a few different things. The low light of approaching dusk, my bow, or a bout of bad luck. Maybe my bum shoulder is the culprit, tweaked out of place yesterday after loading a pallet full of mineral bags into Kenny Euland's truck.

But let's be honest. The problem is me. A guy who's been in a bad mood since a certain city girl booted his ass to the curb.

"Just put the bow down; you're depressing me." Braden shuffles toward the house. "I'll meet you out front with beer. Pet the dog. She's good for this sort of thing."

When I hear the back door slam shut behind him, I whistle for Charley to follow me around the side of the house and onto the front porch, where a pair of log-hewn Adirondack chairs are set up. Braden lives outside of town near one of the area's mesas, in a cabin on a decent-sized plot of land covered in rocky outcroppings and scrub brush. The place suits him: a little rough and unwelcoming, but when you're here it's still a nice place to be. The late-afternoon sky is darkening, a swath of gold slowly disappearing into the far horizon.

Almost immediately after I flop into a chair, Charley finds a spot next to me and starts to nudge my hand with her muzzle. I give her a neck scratch and do the same to my own, a prickle of unease itching the hairline where my ball cap meets my skull. A six-pack of Coors Light, short by one, lands on the tree-stump side table between the Adirondack chairs, followed by a big bowl of the homemade snack mix that Braden makes to keep us from ingesting too many of the cancer-causing additives he's always soap-boxing about. He drops onto the other chair and kicks his legs out, tugging his wool knit cap down lower on his head before taking a long pull of his beer. I snag my own and crack it open, stare at the foam that seeps up.

"Let's just do this. I'll ask you once what's wrong and you can either share your feelings or tell me to drop it and we can talk about something else." I lean my head against the back of the chair and wait. "Cara?" he asks.

"Yup."

"You guys hooked up?"

"Yup."

He takes another drink and sticks his hand into the bowl, scooping up a handful of the mix.

"Seems you should be a hell of a lot less pissed off, then. A good lay is usually a salve for the mood. Instead, it's like you're doing an impression of . . . well, fuck . . . *me*."

I try to tamp down the fit of emotions that rise up, breathing deep before I answer.

"First off, she isn't a *good lay*. Don't talk about her like that. Second, my mood was fine—goddam great—between the time we got together and the time she ended it four days ago. Third, that's all I want to say about it. Thank you for your interest, Dr. Phil, but I'm done sharing now."

To Braden's credit, and true to his general personality, he drops it as promised. Charley nudges my hand again, setting her head on my thigh. At least there's *one* female who wants my attention. She gives up a little purring dog grunt when I rub behind her ears, and a little drool falls from her jaw onto my pant leg. Apparently, I'm a dog whisperer. If only I could manage something similar with Cara.

And the Cara situation was about more than the sex. I hated losing that, for sure—my dick was especially down in the mouth about that part. But even worse, I was losing out on more time with her. To top it all off, I was losing both things—the sex, and the time—because she had better, bigger things to do. She was working toward something more in her life, big dreams and real change. I was just the country fuck in a tiny town who had nothing going on. Today is the same as yesterday, the same as it will be when Cara leaves, and the same again ten years from now. Until she arrived in town and reminded me how good it was to have something to look forward to, I was fine with that. Now I was gnashing my teeth on envy and disappointment—at her and myself. A fucking terrible combination.

Braden drains his beer and gives the can a single crush, then launches it off the porch and straight into the bed of my pickup. Dick move, *and* he sinks it.

He grabs another. "Allow me to distract you with my own tale of shit, then." The tab cracks and hisses. "Amber Regan's producer called me earlier this week, wanted to talk *strategy* with me. And let me tell you, I should get a medal of compassion or something, because I did not once hang up on her. Even when she spent ten minutes using words like 'recapitulate' and 'brand identity.'"

I laugh—only a short chuckle, but it's nice to laugh about something for the first time in days. Braden presses on.

"Then she's like, 'Do you want me to send you a reel?' And I'm thinking she's talking about a fishing reel. Like some promo freebie they probably have boxes of, from being in bed with whatever company. So, I tell her, 'Sure, send it over.' I figure we can use it in the kids' fishing derby or some shit."

I finish my own beer and attempt the same toss as he did earlier. I overshoot it, consistent with today's track record, but the upside is that it hits the bedside of Braden's truck. Braden doesn't comment, only continues with his story.

"Yesterday, this package shows up and it's not a fishing reel. It's a *highlight* reel. Two hours of Amber Regan grand-slamming her way through multiple continents. Two. Fucking. Hours." His jaw is tight, flexing under what seems to be a tremendous amount of pressure, even for him.

"And? What did you think?"

Braden lets out a resigned sigh, shakes his head but doesn't look at me.

"Unless she's a damn good actress or they employ an award-winning editing staff, she seems to know what she's doing. Definitely not what I figured she'd be. I mean, as dick sexist as it sounds, I figured you can't look like that and be able to hold your own in the field. Didn't seem possible."

The way his face looks right now, I wouldn't be surprised if he's thinking something *sexist* about Amber Regan right this second. Sexist and wrong, in a hundred different ways. I consider rattling his cage about it, but before I can, my phone buzzes with a text. I slip one hand to the inside pocket of my coat and fish it out.

Cara's name lights up the screen, and inside my chest, things go tight as I swipe over the face to open it.

> Sorry to bug you. Power is out again. I tried the breaker, but it didn't work. Any other tips you could give me? If not, it's fine, I'll call an electrician in the morning.

The tightness in my chest ratchets up again because there are too many things wrong with this text.

a) She isn't *bugging* me. She never could, no matter what.

b) I have more than a tip for her.

c) I do not think it's *fine* for her to be over there without power.

d) She's not calling an electrician in the morning. I'm going over there tonight.

When I look up from the phone face, I don't even have to make my own excuse to bail. Braden raises a brow.

"That her?"

I nod. Braden looks at me solemnly and waves toward my truck, giving me his blessing. "Go. Turkey season starts in three weeks. You need to be able to hit something by then."

~~~

Well, that's interesting.

When I come to a stop in front of the farmhouse, the porch light is on. Same goes for the living room, where the lights are shining bright through the opened curtains. As I pulled up, I saw that the lone kitchen window visible from the side of the house was lit up, too.

Living room, kitchen, and front porch—all currently honoring Thomas Edison with their electrical functionality. I shut off the truck and peer toward the house again, doing my best to fight the anticipation I know I shouldn't let take hold. The fact the lights are on does not necessarily mean that Cara realized ending this was a bad idea. Maybe the breaker came through right after she sent that text. Maybe someone else came over to help in the meantime.

The cornucopia of light currently shining throughout the house definitely does not mean I should assume that Cara brought me here on a ruse because she misses me. Or wants me.

Because if I did entertain that idea, then I might also indulge the fantasy that she'll be waiting for me dressed in nothing but the little plaid shirt of hers that I'm a big fan of. Completely unbuttoned, with only a few inches of skin between her breasts exposed at first, showing off the flat of her belly and the trimmed strip below. She'll slip off the shirt and let it drop to the floor so I'm finally able to see her completely bare. Then she'll apologize for putting us both through the last few days away from each other, but I'll tell her she doesn't need to apologize—that being with her again is enough. Since this a fantasy, what happens next should be obvious. A blow job. Sloppy and enthusiastic, with the perfect play between her hands and her mouth.

But this is reality. I'm sure there's a much less interesting reason for what's going on here, so it's best to kill my growing erection now, instead of getting everyone's hopes up.

I knock on the door and only have to wait a few seconds before the door creaks open slowly. Cara peers out from the small space she's allowed the door to open, looking uncomfortable. I raise my brows and lift one arm up, raising my forearm to rest against the doorjamb. Cara sighs and opens the door the rest of the way.

And that fantasy I concocted? We're halfway there, with a few extras thrown in. Plaid shirt, the first few buttons undone, enough to remind me what her black lace bra looked like underneath it a few days ago. Her gorgeous legs are clad only in a pair of those tiny workout shorts, nearly covered by the shirt, so it almost looks as if she's not wearing anything. Better yet, she's wearing her glasses and her hair is a tumbled mess of slightly damp waves, smelling sweet and clean.

As expected, this means I want to dirty her up. Dirty her up so much that she won't be able wash all my dirty off of her for days. Unfortunately, her expression does not say she wants to be dirtied up.

I tilt my head and look over her shoulder, straight into the house. In the background, I can hear the echo of that opera music she likes.

"Things look plenty bright around here. I know you claim

you're good with words and any texts you'd send me would be clear as a bell, but maybe I'm a moron. Did I misunderstand what you meant by 'the power is out'?"

Cara flops her face into her hands. "No," she groans. "The power was out. But I didn't hear back from you, so I went out there and tried again. After a couple more tries, it worked."

"You know, you could have just called me and let me know you changed your mind. No need for all this."

Cara crosses her arms over her chest. "That's not what's happening here. I would have texted you again to say not to bother, but you never replied to the first one. I figured you were mad and ignoring my text was your way of telling me to back off."

Shit. I was too busy trying decipher why she was reaching out and crafting my own personal porn starring Cara to remember to text back, and the drive from Braden's isn't exactly five minutes away, even with how I was driving. I drop my forearm from the doorjamb and shove my hands in my pockets.

"Sorry. I was at Braden's, and the drive takes a while. When I got your text, I just bailed, completely spaced on letting you know I was headed over. My bad."

"Oh." Her features start to soften and she lowers her arms from crossing her chest. "I'm sorry for screwing up your night with Braden."

I let out a snort. "My night with Braden? You make it sound like we were halfway through our favorite chick flick and sharing a pint of Chunky Monkey." Cara's lips twitch. "How about I double-check the breaker box? Make sure everything looks good."

Cara steps back for me to come inside, peering down at her bare feet, and my gaze follows hers. Her toenails are painted neon pink—the last color I would have guessed. The surprise shot of color there is like another taste of who she is, and with each one

I want more. So many things I could discover about this woman
if I had the time, or her permission. Already I know that she's
a million different bits of fascinating—and I'd give anything to
know all of them.

We walk through the entryway and dining room, passing by
the spot where I had her pressed against the wall and sank inside
her only a few days ago, even though it feels like a lifetime. In the
kitchen there's a box of microwave popcorn sitting on the counter
next to a tub of butter and a small shaker jar of spice mix. An
unopened bottle of wine sits behind them.

Cara waits inside while I head out to check the breaker box. A
quick inspection reveals nothing out of the ordinary, like a half-
melted paddle or scorched metal. I slam the cover shut and walk
back inside, where Cara's waiting next to the microwave, her index finger poised to press the start button.

"Can I use this now?"

"Go for it. Everything looks fine out there." I point toward the
countertop. "Popcorn and wine for dinner? Your night looks only
a touch classier than what Braden was serving: Coors Light and
his special Chex Mix."

She turns on her heel and leans back against the countertop
edge, setting one foot on top of the other.

"Oh, yes. I had a very classy night planned. Binge-watching
Real Housewives, while eating popcorn and drinking red wine.
Now that I have power, the popcorn and TV are a go, but the
wine is still a problem. I didn't think to bring a corkscrew with
me, and there isn't one stashed in any of these drawers."

I grab the bottle and inspect the top. Setting it aside, I dig
out my multitool from my pocket, cut the foil with the small
penknife, then flip out the tiny corkscrew attachment. Cara gasps
and I cut a glance her direction to find her entire face lit up. A few
turns and a pull, and the cork pops free. Cara claps like I just did

something way more dramatic than opening her wine. I extend the bottle her way.

"A change of clothes in your truck and a magical corkscrew in your pocket. Is there any situation you aren't prepared for?"

I leave the magical corkscrew comment alone.

"Redneck shenanigans, I told you. We're like Boy Scouts with beer and camo. Geared up for anything."

She grabs a drinking glass out of the cupboard, then cuts a look my way from over her shoulder. "Do you want some?"

Maybe it's the light in here or my mind is simply playing tricks on me, but I'm convinced there's a flare of anticipation in her eyes. But as much as my dick likes the idea that there might be an opening for more here, the rest of me isn't quite on board. It's only been a few days since she made it clear that she has bigger, more important things to do with her time other than me, so I'd be an idiot if I stayed without bothering to figure out *why* she's asking.

Cara pauses before reaching for another glass, turning awkwardly to face me with her back pressed to the countertop edge. Wrong as it might be, watching her squirm a little under the weight of my steady gaze and silence isn't all bad from my viewpoint.

"Depends." I give her a slow once-over, just to draw out the moment. "Are you offering just to be polite? If that's what this is, don't bother."

Cara lets out a jaded snort and looks away for a split second before setting her glass down, then puts her hands to either side of the counter edge, taking a stance that somehow looks both casual and confrontational.

"I think we're well past *polite*, don't you think?" She returns the once-over I just gave her. "I asked because I thought it would be nice if you didn't take off right away. I asked because I've really missed seeing you—a lot—enough that the power going out gave me a legitimate excuse to text you, one that didn't involve chutney or jam. I asked because as much as I know it might not be the best idea, I want you to stay. So no, this isn't about my good manners. But that means you don't have to stay just to be polite, either."

Even though I have no clue what chutney or jam has to do with anything, my heart starts to bump around in my chest, an unsteady hammering beat to match the way I want to stalk over there and give us both what we want, while reminding myself to stay clear of exactly that. What tonight is, I'm not sure yet. But I'm damn sure that I'd like to stay and find out.

"Good. Then I also don't have to pretend that I like wine." I sling my ball cap and coat off, tossing them on the counter. We lock eyes, both of us giving in to relaxed grins. "I have some beer in the truck."

She gives up a soft laugh. "You have beer in the truck? Just randomly?"

"Not random. I keep a few stowed in my truck bed toolbox. Were you not listening earlier? Boy Scouts. With beer." I point to my coat. "And camo."

The microwave dings as I head toward the front door, hoping to hell she doesn't decide to lock the door behind me.

16

(Garrett)

Welcome to my very own wretched hell.

Cara's hand falls to my knee, using the position to urge herself up from where she's been curled against me for the last few hours, her head resting on my aching shoulder while she works over a red wine buzz and occasionally writhes around when she needs to stretch.

Unfortunately, because this is Cara, I'm willing to subject myself to the torture just to be near her. Torture that also includes *Real Housewives*. All of whom are fucking terrible. How a woman as smart as Cara finds this bullshit entertaining, I cannot understand. We're two hours in and I'm about one more Vanderpump away from losing my goddam mind.

As for my shoulder, it's killing me. Thanks to three dislocations from my high school wrestling days, my right shoulder is already junk. And after humping all those bags of mineral salt into Kenny's truck yesterday then shooting my bow today, the damn thing feels like it's about to go out again.

Cara leans up to take a sip from her wineglass, and I seize the opportunity to let out a quiet hiss of discomfort. I close my eyes and slowly adjust the position of my shoulder while twisting my neck to the left, praying that will dampen the worst of the pain before Cara takes up her spot again.

Just as I start to stretch, a heady waft of the Creamsicle scent I associate with Cara hits me.

Jesus. Now what? If I open my eyes, will she be sitting there sucking on a Popsicle?

Slowly, I lift one eyelid and take a cautious look her way. No seductive Popsicle licking, thankfully. Instead, she's sitting cross-legged on the couch, a small glass bottle in one hand, dribbling some sort of oil into her other palm. After setting the bottle on the coffee table, she rubs the oil between her hands and then extends one leg out, slowly drawing her palms over the smooth, toned skin on her thighs.

Slowly. Like, erotically, painfully, *slowly*.

Another pour of the oil into her hand. A new episode of those idiot *Housewives* is playing, and all her attention is on the screen, her eyes wide and her jaw tipsily slack as her hands follow the same slicked-up path, but on her other leg. I roll my shoulder again and consider that it might be better if it did go out. Then I'd be too distracted by the pain to think about the growing ache behind my fly.

Cara turns just as I grit my teeth and one side of my face crinkles up into a grimace.

"What's wrong?"

"Nothing."

"Well, that's a load of bull. Your face is all squished up. Are you sick?"

I shake my head but decide to grab my forearm with the opposite hand and outstretch it across my chest, pressing tentatively to see what happens. What happens is that it hurts even more.

Cara listens to me cuss under my breath, then scoots closer and draws her fingertip over my shoulder. "Here?"

"It's an old wrestling thing. I've dislocated it too many times, and when I was helping Kenny load some bags up the other day, I must have tweaked it or something. Not a big deal; eventually, it'll calm down." I release my arms and let them rest on my knees, leaning forward with my head dropped down.

"Take your shirt off."

My head lifts a little. "Excuse me?"

She grabs the bottle off the table and holds it up, giving it a loose shake in my direction.

"Take your shirt off and I'll rub your shoulder with this. It's scented argan oil." She thrusts the bottle under my nose. "Do you mind the smell?"

Do I mind the smell? No. Does she mind that I'm currently picturing her naked and drenched in this stuff?

I shake my head, answering in a rasp. "I like it."

"Scoot forward, then. It'll be easier if I sit behind you."

Cara wedges herself in behind me and starts to work my T-shirt up, the tips of her nails grazing across the skin on my back, and I try to figure out if what's happening is Cara's idea or the wine's idea. But her eyes aren't bloodshot, and she isn't slurring her words or fumbling with the hem of my shirt. She might be riding a decent buzz, but nothing says she's out of her mind drunk. And what she offered is a shoulder rub, nothing more.

I take over pulling off my shirt and lay it over the arm of the couch. When I turn back to make sure I'm not about to squish her, Cara is chewing on a thumbnail and sneaking a look at my chest. Her eyes tick upward and meet mine, a coy smile curving at her mouth. Shoulder rub, I remind myself, that's all she's proposed. But for a woman who a few days ago claimed we couldn't be together, she's certainly not shying away with her eyes at the moment.

"Make sure you tell me what you need. Harder or softer, OK? I want it to feel good."

I stifle a groan at all the ways I could interpret what she just said, none of which have anything to do with my stupid shoulder. She settles in and stretches her legs out so they're positioned to either side of mine. The sound of her dribbling oil into her hands, then rubbing them together is enough to make my cock thicken. And when she places an open hand to each of my shoulders, I have to hold my breath for a second, simply because her slippery, warm palms feel too good.

She starts in with long strokes, using her thumbs when she meets my neck. The scent of the oil wafts up with every pass. My shoulder starts to ease and release under her touch, along with every other inch of my skin she touches. She adds more oil and massages the length of my back, kneading down until her hands are easing under the waist of my jeans a little. I curve forward to encourage her and end up nearly slumped over from the relief. I'm a few minutes away from either moaning loudly or falling asleep, not sure which.

"Sit back," she whispers. I don't move. Her arms slither around my waist. "Lean back so I can get the front. I can't reach with you sitting like that."

My heartbeat starts to thump wildly because her hands are already exploring my chest and abs, her palms flat and her fingers spread wide. She gives a little tug to encourage me.

Finally, I lean back, trying to figure out how I can relax and still keep from putting all my weight on her. I reach for the edge of the couch cushions, grip my hands there, and let my arms do the work of holding my upper body off of hers.

"Come on, I can take it. Just relax."

Easy for her to say. She's not the one who's trying to forget hearing her say the words "I can take it" *and* keep his demanding cock in check.

And when her hands start to glide over my pecs, lingering the tips of her fingers over my nipples, I lose the fight with my sanity. When she does it again, but harder, my newfound appreciation for nipple play goes straight to my dick, where we're both a little surprised at the effect of her deliberate touch there.

She treks downward, over my abs and lower still, until my jeans become a barrier to going any farther. Another pass, abs to chest, chest to abs. This time, her fingers decide that, jeans or not, she's dipping lower. Her nails tickle the skin when she does. On her third round, she tucks her fingers deep enough that she's under the waist of my boxers.

My breath slows as my heartbeat continues to hammer. My head is a mess, battling between what I want and what she said couldn't happen between us again. My hard cock doesn't care, though, because Cara's hands are exploring and her body is pulsating with each unsteady breath.

But this was supposed to be a shoulder rub. That was OK. This, whatever the hell it's turning into, may not be. Not if she gives herself a chance to think beyond the wine.

I grab her hands. "Cara. What are you doing?" She lets out a needy-sounding whimper and does her best to free her hands from my grip. I loosen my hold but don't let go. "You said we can't do this."

Her mouth lands on my shoulder and she kisses a spot there. "What if I changed my mind?" she practically purrs. "What if I've second-guessed what I said the other day since the second I said it?"

She tugs free of my grip and puts her hands on my jeans, pressed boldly over my obvious hard-on. My own hands are frozen in midair.

"Are you drunk?" I choke out.

She chuckles softly. "No."

When she starts to make short work of the button and zipper on my pants, the rest of what I'm worried about comes out in a rush.

"Are you going to regret this? Show up at my work again and say we shouldn't have? Because I'm not going to be good with that. I'd rather just stop now."

Her hand slides into my boxers, still a little slippery from the oil. When she grips me and starts to move, I suck in a harsh breath as precum leaks from the tip on the very first stroke.

"Do you want me to stop? Because I don't. I want this."

I grit my teeth to keep from thrusting into her hold. "No, I sure as hell don't want you to stop. I just don't—"

"Hush, then." Cara lands her mouth on my earlobe, then kisses down my neck. "Lift up a little."

First the nipple play, now the neck kissing. All things I think of as more female pleasures, but right now they're doing it for me in a big way.

I give in. She isn't drunk, and we both want this. A lift of my hips and she pushes my jeans and boxers down until my cock springs out, bobbing there impatiently. The bottle of oil appears, and as her palm fills, I consider the possibility I might come from sheer anticipation. And when her hands take me, circling the head and slipping one over the other, I remember thinking of this the first day I met her. The totally inappropriate image of her done-up nails and a slow, slippery hand job. If anyone told me then that it was going to be a reality, I'd have said they needed to have their fucking head examined.

"I love your cock. The way you get *so* hard. How this part"—Cara traces two fingers gently to the underside of the head—"is *so* smooth."

Is she trying for a record? The world's shortest hand job? Because those words coming out of her mouth are a surefire way to earn a medal.

Cara tightens her grasp, and my lungs cease to function for a moment. She's just discovered my favorite grip, something shy of painful but so good for me. Most women don't know how hard they can work your cock and they'd never guess the abuse a guy sometimes inflicts on his dick when he's jacking off. But Cara found what I need without anything but her instincts.

Only one thing could make this better.

I'm so close that if I want to put a big cherry on top of this hand job, I need to take it now. Another minute or so, and this will be over.

Fuck it. I put my hands to hers and widen the spread between my legs. I draw one of her hands down. She cups my balls and holds there.

"How should I . . ." Her words trail off.

I take a labored breath in. "Tug or squeeze, anything you're comfortable with. Don't be shy, though. I need to feel it."

She starts with a squeeze. It's good, but not near what I need. A roll, then a little tug. My chest starts to heave. *"Harder."*

Cara moans, then grabs on and goes for it. Those mind-blowing instincts of hers do the rest. I groan long and loud—because I want to be sure she knows how perfect this is. Before I know it, she's doing everything all at once, jacking my cock and tugging on my balls in a perfect rhythm. I cast one look at her hands, knowing that's all it's going to take. Seeing the glisten of oil is enough and I spill into her hands with a near shout. She doesn't stop, only slows her strokes until I can't take it anymore. With a grunt, I grab for her hands with my own trembling pair, forcing her to stop before she kills me.

Cara tucks her head into the crook of my neck and lets out a murmuring exhale. Her teeth nip a tiny spot on my neck and my skin erupts under another wave of satisfaction. "Jesus. That was so hot."

If I ever figure out how to speak again, I'll tell her exactly how much I'm with her on that. For now, I'm going to stay here and try not to pass out.

After a few minutes, Cara's arms start to tremble a little, from where they're still around my waist. Our bodies are slightly damp against each other from exertion and my low back is cradled to her pussy, but *my* instincts tell me that the heat there isn't just because we're nested together. I sort out our limbs from each other and start to tug up my boxers and jeans a bit.

"Now you," I say, sliding off the couch and onto the floor on my knees.

Cara has her hands up in front of her, looking confused when I turn around and grab her legs so I can pull her toward me. "What?"

"Now. You."

Cara lets out a squeak when I make for her shirt, growling as I yank on the buttons with stupidly unsmooth fingers. When the last button comes free, I pull her shirt back and groan.

No bra. Just Cara and her small, firm tits on display, tipped with rosy, rock-hard nipples. I go straight for her, taking one between my lips and using my fingers to roll the other. Cara arches her back and I switch my hold, tweaking the first one, now slippery from my mouth, until she gives up a moan.

She's slumped down into the couch cushions so my abs are pressed between her legs, and when she tilts her ass up, she hits the wall of my body and grinds herself there with a few twists of her hips. Even if I'd like a little more time with her tits, we can come back to that later. The urgent press of her pussy against me is too much to ignore. Pulling her shirt off her shoulders, I toss it to the far side of the couch and start to work on getting these shorts off of her, curling my fingers at the waist and tugging them down over her hips. Cara's eyes flip open and we lock gazes. For a moment, everything feels weighted in that look, the two of us trying to decide if this—the chemistry, the heat, the way we can't stay away—is more than what it seems.

A few seconds pass, my hands still gripping the material of her shorts and hoping she'll lift her hips so I can finish this task. Instead, she locks her strong quads in place and tries to snap her knees together, but my body is in the way. Still, the message is clear. We are a no-go here.

My hands freeze. "What's wrong?"

Cara starts to mumble under her breath, then slaps her hands over her face and goes entirely still, quiet except for the sound of her shuddering breath.

Does she not want me to go down on her? Is that the problem? Some women aren't comfortable—I get that—especially not at first. So no pussy eating tonight? Fine. I can deal with that, even if I'm thinking I could spend a few hours down there and still not get enough.

"I am so sorry." Cara draws her hands down and peeks my way from over the tips of her fingers. "I don't know what I was thinking."

I catch up quickly. Fast enough that I feel my entire face go slack.

Holy. Fuck. Not this again.

Cara starts to rattle on about me being shirtless, how that caused a case of brain freeze, how much she wishes this were different. All I hear is an enormous load of bullshit.

"Stop." I grit my teeth together. "Just . . . don't. Please."

I remove my hands from her body and set back on my heels,

taking a good long look at her lying there, nearly naked and throwing a regretful gaze my way that does nothing but piss me off more.

I just let her stroke me off and came in her hands while she had ahold of my balls—in more ways than one. I came harder than I have in years, soaking up the entire experience, so weak and vulnerable that she got the best of me. Because this girl thinks I'm her dumb-ass redneck plaything. Some guy she can tow around by the dick and act like he's not worthy of licking her pussy. And I *let* her do it.

Grabbing my shirt off the couch arm, I yank it over my head and zip up my jeans. Cara dives for her own shirt and fumbles it on.

Fool me once, shame on you. Fool me twice—well, fuck that.

"Garrett, I'm so sorry. Please don't be mad. Please, just—"

I stand and put both my hands up in front of me until she shuts up. She's using one hand to keep her unbuttoned shirt closed with her feet tucked up under her. She looks tiny sitting there with me looming over her, which is what I need at the moment. If she stood up and our perfectly matched bodies came closer, it would be impossible for me to believe I have some power here.

"The first time you pulled this stunt, I took it. I didn't understand it, I didn't like it—but I took it." My jaw flexes tightly as I choose my next words carefully, knowing I'm about to draw a line between us. "Not this time. You might think I'm some stupid country boy you can fuck with, but I'm not. We're done here."

I don't wait for her to respond or question me, or hear her out when she starts in on a new round of apologies. I'm out the door and climbing in my truck before she can do or say anything else. My hands shake as I jam the key in the ignition and cold air rushes out of the vents when the engine turns over, sending it coasting over my bare arms.

Great. I forgot my coat in there. And my ball cap. Also—and this seems like the biggest problem of all—I left three beers in the fridge. Beers I could use right now.

Fuck it. I'll buy another coat, another hat. And a whole new case of beer, too.

A rough shove puts the truck in gear, but before my foot makes it from the brake to the gas pedal, the front door to the house swings open. Cara steps out onto the porch with my jacket, clutching it close to her chest. She halts there, barefoot and wearing tiny shorts, with her shirt now buttoned—but barely.

In the dark. In February. In Colorado.

And as much as I wish I didn't give a damn that she has to be freezing her ass off—I do.

I should drive away. Drive away at a clip that sets gravel spinning, leaving Cara on her own to figure out how stupid it is to stand out there in the middle of winter. That's what I should do.

But I can't. I can't because I'm a moron. Because I hate the sight of her looking lost. Because I hate feeling this way—pissed off and out of control—but when it comes at the cost of something, *anything*, with Cara, it's worse.

I throw a closed fist into the door trim panel and let the pain seep up before cutting the engine and returning to the porch. Stepping onto the second porch riser, I extend my arm, palm open, to retrieve my jacket. "Thank you. Go back inside."

Cara clutches the coat tighter to her chest and shakes her head. I flick my hand, silently demanding that she hand over my damn coat.

"I don't want you to go."

"Too bad. I told you, we're done here. I'd like my coat, but I'm happy to leave without it."

"Garrett . . ." Her head tilts to one side, with a plea in her eyes that sets me off.

"Fucking hell. What do you want from me? I let you jerk me off on the couch, then send me packing, just like you did last time. It's just my dick was in your hands, instead of inside you. Is that not enough humiliation for you?"

Cara's entire body seems to deflate. She shakes her head.

"I never wanted to humiliate you, Garrett. Never. But I didn't plan on this—meeting you and feeling all . . . like *this*. It's confusing. And I know that this doesn't have to be a big deal, but I suck at casual. I keep telling myself to let you do your thing and I'll do mine, but it's not working."

She drops her chin with a slow exhale, and almost looks near tears for a moment.

God. Why is this so complicated? Why are we fighting about this shit? What does she think is going to happen if she stops putting up roadblocks between us? She'll fall in love with me? That I'm such a primo catch she'll cast off her writing, her career, and her dreams? Come the fuck *on*. I'm not a primo catch, and she's not the type to give up on her dreams. Take it from someone who knows how it's done. There's a way to do it right, and you eventually learn to take today as it comes, forget tomorrow or next week or next year, because you're not counting on anything anyway. I've known Cara for two weeks, and I already know that way of life isn't for her.

So, honestly, she has nothing to lose. I'm not going to try to keep her, because she doesn't belong in a place like this, living a life like mine. I'm far more likely to end up gutted over losing a girl like her, not the other way around. She won't lose her mind over me, because her mind is too great a thing—it will remind her, always, of a greater goal.

I take a second to be sure I've evaluated this situation correctly, that it isn't my always-interested-in-Cara dick that's doing the thinking here. Cara's gaze has dipped to the ground, and her mouth is turned down at the corners. When I step up one riser, her eyes drift upward slowly and meet mine. I cross my arms over my chest.

"I'm not going to pull any punches here, because we're past that at this point. You're only here for a few more weeks. After that you go back to your life in Chicago." I tip my chin to be sure we're as eye to eye as possible. "And us fucking each other until you do won't change any of that. I think half of what you're worried about is because you're fighting this. But we both know you have things you came here to do and you're bound to end up back where you belong. Am I right?"

Cara shrugs. I run a hand through my hair with a huff.

"That isn't an answer. You doing *this*"—I repeat what she just did—"isn't an answer. Come on, be honest. Tell me where you live. Where you get your mail, the address you write down when someone asks. Where. Do. You. Live?"

She straightens up a bit. "Chicago."

"Yes. Now tell me what you're here to do."

"Write."

"Exactly." I lean in toward her. "And I won't get in the way of that, Cara. I promise. You keep saying you want this, so stop getting in the way of what's going on between us and trust that in the end, you'll still have your story. Stop overthinking this and just let it happen; then you don't have to worry about wanting it, because you have it."

Cara's eyebrows rise up. "But how would that work? Letting this *happen*?"

"It means we're together while you're here. We hang out, we go to dinner. We stay in and watch your shitty reality shows. We have sex. But you don't push this fuck-and-run thing on me afterward;

I stay the night. You suck at casual? Fine. While you're here we won't be casual; it'll be you and me, together, every day."

Her head rears back a few inches. "Every day? *All day?* But I have work to do. I can't just laze around all day and have sex with you. That's what I'm struggling with. Getting caught up in this."

A tired laugh escapes me. I take the final step toward her, clasping my hands to her face.

"Relax. I work fifty hours a week at the co-op, which means I can't stay here and be your personal sex toy, either. This is simple. I work, you work. After work, we do other stuff. Like, I don't know, make dinner. Go for a drive. Fuck like rabbits."

"Oh." Cara's gaze falls so that she's staring at my shirt collar and worrying her bottom lip, clearly mulling over my proposal in her brilliantly overactive mind. I could kiss her or keep talking, but neither of those seems like the right thing to do. It's better to give her some breathing room and let her debate the details for a minute.

So I wait.

One minute turns to two.

Another minute and my arms start to get tired from clasping her face. I start to wonder if she's reciting multiplication tables in her head. Silently singing her own opera renditions. Rehashing the latest *Housewives* episode or wondering how many different ways those women can find to waste good money.

Beautiful mind or not, if Cara doesn't speak soon, I'm going to kiss her. Maybe that'll remind her what's at stake here.

17

(Cara)

"This is simple. I work, you work. After work, we do other stuff. Like, I don't know, make dinner. Go for a drive. Fuck like rabbits."

PRO: This *does* sound simple. Deceptively so.

PRO: I like the idea of making dinner—with Garrett.

PRO: I like the idea of going for drives—with Garrett.

PRO: I like the idea of fucking like rabbits—with Garrett.

There's a small tear in the collar of Garrett's T-shirt, near the place where his left collarbone meets the fabric. I've stared at it for so long that I'd be surprised if he doesn't jostle me back to reality soon. Instead, his hands remain pressed gently to my face, thumbs drifting over my cheekbones. He isn't pushing, or pressing me for an answer. And if he's still as angry as he was before, he's damn good at hiding it. Or smothering it, burying it, and forgetting it. Or, as he just pointed out, I'm prone to overthinking things and he expertly *isn't*.

I blink twice, then tilt my face to see his.

"Yes. OK."

His face brightens in a flash, but he tamps it down just as quickly.

"I'm going to ask you one more time, to be safe. After that, we pretend like what happened earlier, didn't. We move on." He forces a neutral expression. "Are you sure?"

I give a jerky nod. Garrett replies by kissing me. Slow and teasing, proof of exactly how good he is at pretending and moving on. Because there's nothing furtive or bitter or hesitant in the teasing play of our lips together, even when what happened ten minutes ago should have inspired all that and more. His hands slip from my face to around my waist when he breaks the kiss and steps back. I remember that I'm still clutching his coat. I press it toward his chest and he tucks me into the crook of his arm.

"What now?" I ask quietly, knowing that no matter the plan we agreed to—the dinner-making, drive-taking, and rabbit-like behaviors—I can't manage a one-eighty without getting a little dizzy. I need his help to show me how it's done.

Garrett cuts his eyes skyward with a thoughtful pucker of his lips.

"Well, neither of us is currently at work. We ate popcorn for dinner. And it's a little late for a drive." His gaze comes to mine. "That only leaves one thing on the list."

Fuck like rabbits.

I try to keep everything in check. My erratic heartbeat, the tumble in my belly, the rate at which my lungs want to suck up all the oxygen in the county. We've already had sex. That ship has sailed, but even so, this is different. Intentional. Less like falling victim to a weakness for him and more like I've been handed a dirty Choose Your Own Adventure book.

If you think more sex with Garrett is the best idea ever, turn to page thirty-nine. If you prefer torturing yourself by staying away from him and watching Real Housewives *at night for the next six weeks and never finding out what he was going to do if he'd gotten all of your clothes off, then turn to the last page. The end.*

"You aren't still hungry? We only had popcorn."

Garrett does what I would have, eventually. He tucks my hair behind my ears.

"I'm not hungry. So, unless *you're* hungry, I just want to go inside and be with you." He pauses, searching my eyes. "Unless you're not ready. Maybe you need a night to yourself?"

A night to myself? After all the angsty drama of tonight? After I've finally come to the conclusion that a not-casual-but-temporary Garrett is better than no Garrett at all? No way. I'm turning to page thirty-nine—and he's coming with me.

I take his hand and drag him through the front door, which Garrett kicks shut behind us. The house is nearly dark except for the glow of the television lighting the entryway and the stairs leading up to the second floor. My bare feet are silent on the stair treads, but his weight and his boots mean there's a creak and shuffle behind me as he follows. At the end of the hallway is the bedroom I've been sleeping in, the one with big windows that face east and let in the glow of a Hotchkiss sunrise every morning.

Tonight, the only glow is from a yellow-cast light fixture in the center of the ceiling. Garrett scrubs a hand down his face and tosses his coat on the floor next to the bed. His eyes track across the room and he shakes his head languidly. I draw a hand up to faintly touch my lips.

"No. Way."

He chuckles. "Yes way."

"This was your room?"

Garrett nods and his eyes tick up to the ceiling with a laugh. "Just for eighteen years or so. Give or take." He steps close enough that he can slip a hand to my hip, fingers tucking under the hem of my shirt to meet the bare skin above the waist of my shorts. "Why'd you pick it?"

"The windows."

He tilts his head. "The sunrises?"

I nod and slip my fingers in the soft curls of hair above his ears, and his eyes drift shut. These unruly locks are the ones that always sneak out from around the edges of his ball cap. Most times, when he takes it off, there's an inevitable bit of hat-head going on, but it never stays that way for long, eventually settling into a pile of messy softness.

"Is this still too weird for you? Do you want to go to your place? The place you live now?"

Garrett shakes his head and his eyes draw open. "I'm fine. I spent a lot of time thinking about getting laid in this room, anyway. Full circle or some shit."

"But this place—"

"Stop." Garrett digs his fingers into the bare skin on my hip, hard enough to interrupt my words. "I don't want to be anywhere but right here, right now. We don't have to worry about anything else. Just *now*."

I find my eyes tracking away from his, guarding the parts of me that will always look to a plan, for answers to my questions, for more. "I'm not so good at that. The *now* thing. My brain likes jumping ahead."

Garrett kisses my forehead. "I know. I already figured that out. We'll practice, OK?" His hands come to toy with the buttons on my shirt. "Tell me exactly what you're thinking—don't debate it, just say whatever pops into your head."

The words are out before I can mull them over into nothing.

"I want my clothes off. But I want you to do it."

Garrett doesn't hesitate, undoes the two lone buttons I managed before chasing after him earlier. My shirt hits the floor and he takes my hand, leading us over to the bed. He sits down on the end of it, leaving me to stand in the space between his legs. The bed creaks loudly under his weight and he casts a wary look at the mattress, and then bounces a little to re-create it.

"I'm not sure this bed can withstand what I had in mind; I may have to hold back a little. I thought the guy that bought this place was loaded. Did he end up that way because he's cheap?"

Another test bounce on the bed and it sounds like a spring somewhere underneath has sprung for the last time.

"He's not cheap, he just has a wife who's in charge of all things decorating. But they have seven houses and one of them is always under renovation, so she's *very* busy. I'm sure if she knew that Davis paid that real estate agent to cobble together a few things for my stay—and none of it was bespoke or Italian or eighteenth-century something—she'd have a heart attack."

I start to shimmy my shorts off, because talking about Davis or my life back home isn't what I want right now. Garrett's hands latch on to mine, gently shoving them away.

"You said you wanted me to do it."

"Well, you were too busy bouncing around on the bed. I'm tired of waiting."

Garrett hooks his fingers to the waistband on my shorts and starts to pull them down. My breath lurches when he has them halfway down, then leans in to blow a soft breath to the space between my legs.

"I've wanted to slip these shorts—your jeans, anything—down your legs since the second I met you."

The shorts hit the floor and I manage to kick them out of the way, even as his hands have started a reverse course. Fingers trailing up the back of my calves, behind my knees, my thighs. He stops where my legs meet my backside and tightens his grip.

"Now what?" Garrett asks. I try to think, but it's hard. He makes a little scolding sound. "No thinking. Just say it."

His lips press to my low belly, followed by his tongue tracing a hip bone as his hands continue to curl at the backs of my thighs. Garrett's hands are big enough that with a turn to move a bit deeper, his fingers nudge against my core, my legs going a little wobbly when he does. That becomes more than enough to declare what I want next.

"I'm naked. I'm wet. Do you need more direction than that?"

Garrett groans. My weak legs and impatience send me toppling into him, until he hits the bed with a thump. I crawl over him and my mouth finds his. We start to fumble, hands trying to cover too much all at once. Garrett suddenly sits up, taking me with him and tossing me to one side, then covers my body with his and shoves one leg between mine so his thigh is pulled up to meet my core. When the denim on his jeans rasps there and the cotton of his T-shirt rubs across my nipples, I drag my mouth away on a gasp. He starts to kiss his way down my neckline, but I push on his chest to stop him. Garrett startles back, and then stiffens. I trace my fingers to the knot of bone tensing under his clenched jaw.

"Your clothes are in my way. I want them off."

I give him a shove and Garrett all but leaps off the bed, yanking the back of his collar to strip his shirt off, attempts to toe off his boots at the same time, growling when he realizes it won't work. I drop a hand between my legs to keep myself occupied. A moan comes out when I do and my eyes drift closed.

"Oh, Jesus Christ. Don't do that." Garrett's boots thump when he tosses them across the room somewhere.

I hear the jangle of his belt coming undone, a zipper lowering, and the tear of a condom wrapper. The sounds only heighten everything I'm feeling: the anticipation, knowing I don't need to back off or hold back, the way my body is more than ready for this. My fingers start to work in tight circles, with a light touch that's what I need but not quite what I truly want.

"Fucking *wait*. Wait for me, Cara. That's my job now; getting you wet and primed is what I do while we're together. I'll do it, just give me ten seconds to get my damn jeans off."

I sigh softly and still my motion, but keep my hand exactly where I want it.

Garrett nearly launches onto the bed once his jeans find the bedroom floor, immediately dragging my hand away, but not replacing it with his own. Instead, it's a slip of latex, his cock head working circles where my fingers just were. My back arches and my legs drop open, hoping for more as quickly as possible. He takes himself in hand and thumps himself to my clit, his own personal reflex test on my body, because my knees shoot up and a lurid groan leaves my throat. Garrett chuckles, dark and wicked, him asking, *Did you like that?*—without saying a word.

When his body comes to lie on mine, I realize I was too busy touching myself to see him naked. And that's not OK. I've thought about him stripped down far too many times to miss the show tonight. I give a shove to his abs and he lets out an *oof*.

"What? Condom's on. We're fine."

"Stand up."

He freezes in confusion, then drops his head to my collarbone and rocks it there.

"No. Why? Christ, you're killing me, Cara."

"I didn't get to see you naked."

"Look later. I'll strut a catwalk for you, if you want. After."

"Now."

A growl—half annoyed, half crazed. He puts a hand on either side of my head and pushes up, his overachieving biceps flexing. I stop myself from demanding he complete twenty push-ups over me first. Or plank himself there until I say stop. That might be a bit more than he can take.

Garrett stands at the foot of the bed, puts his hands to his hips, and cocks one knee out. I lift up enough that I can rest back on my forearms.

Hello, Garrett. This was worth testing his patience. In fact, the frustration on his face merely adds to the view. He's hard every-where. Abs and arms, pecs and legs. And his cock. His cock is *very* hard. As in, angry and annoyed, hard.

He throws his arms wide. "I'm a hell of a specimen, yeah? This work for you?"

I grin, lips pursed shut.

"So we're good?" A jerky nod from me and Garrett exhales. "Thank Christ. Then spread your legs, please."

My legs are wide in an instant. Garrett seats the head of his cock and pushes inside. And maybe it's because he's on top of me, his body and weight adding to the experience, but it feels like more. More to handle—or simply more of *him.*

"Fuck. Wrap your legs around me." Garrett thrusts deep when I do, just once. "Tighter. I know those pretty legs are stronger than that."

I put my arms around his neck for leverage, giving everything I can—and he takes it. The bed is creaking loudly and squeaking like something important could come loose at any second. And if this is Garrett holding back to save the furniture . . . then, *ohmyGod.*

When his voice falters into him groaning in my ear, I focus on the sound of Garrett working hard, taking everything, and giving more than I knew was possible. His pace starts to turn jerky, but his sounds and every thrust are enough. When he hears me come, his body presses harder to mine, taking two more pun-ishing thrusts before going still. A low curse rumbles into my ear.

After that it's quiet. Nothing said until he comes back from the bathroom after taking care of the condom and slips under the covers with me. I move over to give him room.

"Don't even think about it." A big arm circles my waist, yanks me closer, drawing my back to his front. "I sleep naked. Hope that's OK."

With the length of his body to mine, still half-hard and nestled between my legs, I decide it's more than OK. Pretty sure this arrangement of ours is going to work out *just fine*.

18

(Garrett)

As a guy with a mom who can't get enough of cheesy romantic movies, I spent more than my fair share of time as a kid suffering through her film choices, which means that I'm familiar with the tried-and-true formula for those flicks. About halfway through most of them, there comes the part where it's a bunch of clips strung together of the guy and girl doing cute stuff together, like having a snowball fight. Maybe hitting a baseball game, where they share a hot dog and she wipes mustard off his nose, right before she catches a fly ball. All the while a catchy but sappy song plays in the background.

My life.

There haven't been any snowball fights or baseball games in the last two weeks with Cara, but there has been a Hotchkiss High basketball game, an unintended water fight in completely inappropriate weather, and an afternoon shooting sporting clays at a local course. She's from Chicago, where some of our nation's strictest gun laws were born, so I'm not sure if it's irony or straight-up poetic justice that she's a natural with a shotgun in her hands.

Today, I head straight back to the farm right after work, without even bothering to hit my place first. A stash of my clothes are already piled up on the floor on my side of the bed, so I have everything I need. When I step through the front door, a flood of the feral cat opera music I'm starting to appreciate is blasting through the house from a small portable speaker Cara has sitting on the coffee table. She's curled up on the couch with her laptop open, her glasses on, typing away at the keyboard confidently like she's all but kicking ass on her word count for the day. Her daily word count goal is five hundred, by the way, which I thought sounded easy—and made the critical mistake of saying so out loud. I was wrong.

The words have to be *quality* words, I was told. Right after she threw a glare my way and yanked her glasses off, tossing them aside so she could explain—in detail—why I was so, so wrong.

Which is why I don't speak when I enter the house tonight, because I've learned it's best to leave the genius to her work. I skirt straight through the foyer and the dining room, put away the groceries I brought with me in the kitchen, planning to then make my way upstairs for a shower. When I round the corner to head up the stairs, Cara is standing there, her face almost expressionless.

"Can we go for a drive? I packed up a picnic-style dinner. Sandwiches, chips, and I made some lemon bars."

I take an inventory of her face again. Usually Cara's face gives up everything. Happy? Her dark brown eyes do this glittery thing that makes her whole face look like it's reflecting sunlight.

Pissed off? A tiny nostril flare, followed by her scrunching up her nose.

Horny? Twofold. First, her lips part and she traces the back of her teeth with her tongue. Then she picks a body part—my chest, my hands, once it was even my bare feet—and fixes her gaze there until I can't take it anymore and give her a good reason to switch her focus.

But tonight she's a blank sheet. Not sure I like it.

I try and choose my words carefully, never having met this version of Cara before and not quite sure what she's looking for.

"Are we going for a drive because the words are going well? Or because they're not?"

"Neither." She strides off toward the kitchen. "We should go soon."

So much for a shower. She stood next to me, though, so if she had an issue with my eau de co-op she could have sent me upstairs. Cara peeks her head back out and looks my way, brows raised. Guess I need my coat. Like, now.

Cara reappears, a small cooler clasped in her hands, dressed for what is bound to be a chilly picnic in a pink hoodie with a puffy vest layered over the top, black leggings, and a pair of knee-high muck boots. And the same disturbingly vacant look on her face.

I don't know what Cara weighs, but I'd venture a guess that I've got a good eighty pounds on her. Still, I'm shaking in my boots.

<hr />

Our drive takes us to a state park about fifteen miles outside town, where there's a small pond surrounded by waist-high scrub oak and not much else. The pond is well-known by locals, less so by tourists, and this time of year it's typically deserted in the evening. I ease down an access road on the west side, then back my truck down to the pond's edge.

The sun is starting to set, so we'll only have about an hour to enjoy the view. It's definitely not what most would think of as picnic weather, but we're both layered up enough to stave off the nip in the air, and the sunset will be worth it. We both hop up on the dropped tailgate and I set the cooler between us. Cara pulls out the sandwiches and small baggies of chips, hands one of each of my way. Cara pulls back the butcher paper on her sandwich.

"I've never been fishing."

"Seriously? Not even as a little kid?"

She takes a bite and shakes her head, staring straight ahead and lazily kicking her legs back and forth beneath the tailgate. I take a quick look back toward the cab of my truck, where a fishing pole sits in my gun rack. A small tackle box is in the truck with a few salmon eggs and a couple of spare lures. More than enough stuff to keep her occupied until the sun sets, even if she snags the line on every cast.

"If you want to wet a line, we can."

Cara cocks one eyebrow, high enough to clear the top of her glasses. "Is that a euphemism? For oral sex?"

One side of my mouth tips up. "No, dirty girl. I meant that I have gear in the truck and a pond lies five feet away. You probably won't catch anything, but that doesn't mean you can't call it fishing."

"Gee, thank you for your tremendous confidence in me."

"Not a comment on *you*, a comment based on the conditions. They haven't run water in here or stocked it, plus it's too cold out. Just don't want you getting your hopes up about catching anything."

Cara takes another bite of her sandwich then wraps the remainder back up in the butcher paper, puts it aside, and shimmies around like she's already preparing herself to cast.

"I don't care. Show me anyway."

I set my sandwich down and take a look at the sky. Better work quick.

Grabbing the rod, I hand it to her and start to rummage through my tackle box for the jar of salmon eggs. Cara starts whipping the rod through the air so forcefully it makes a sharp slicing sound with each of her pretend casts. I bite down on my tongue and let her go for it—that way I can see what her natural instincts are—until one particularly overzealous "cast" means I'm nearly beaned on the head. Even though the hook is safely clipped to the keeper, I might lose an eye if I don't reel *her* in a little.

"Yo, dial it down there, Bill Dance. Keep that thing under control or you're going to be calling me Popeye."

Cara stops the rod in midair and looks over her shoulder. "Sorry. I like the way it makes that zingy, whisking noise. Who's Bill Dance?"

That zingy-whisking noise. Fucking adorable. Every time she says things like that, I have to remind myself how soon this will be over by counting the weeks we have left until she leaves, because if I don't, then doing whatever it takes to keep her forever sounds like a good plan. I find the salmon egg jar and unscrew the lid to poke two fingers in.

"Pro bass fisherman."

"People fish *professionally*?"

Sidling up next to her, I take the rod from her. Releasing the hook from the keeper, I slip on a few salmon eggs, and Cara's attention is on my hands, except for the occasional dart of her eyes to watch my face. I can feel her gaze like always, and if I could bottle the way my body hums under that sweet inspection, I would.

"Yes, people fish professionally. Now come stand over here."

Cara slips under my arm to stand in front of me, where we hold the rod together so I can guide her through the basics. After only a few instructions, it seems like she has the feel down, so I step aside and let her loose. And, because this is Cara—because I think she was quite possibly born in the wrong place on earth—she proceeds to drop a long-arced, beautiful cast that lands with a gentle splash into the water.

I leave her standing in the soft sand near the water's edge and grab our two foldable camp chairs from inside the bed-mounted toolbox, along with a small bottle of whiskey that's stowed deep underneath the rear seats. Usually I only pull it out when it's time to celebrate punching an elk tag, but tonight seems like it's worthy of an exception.

Cara lets out a snort when she sees what I've gathered.

"Honestly, someday, I swear you're going to drag a movie projector and concession stand out of the back of that thing. Or maybe a bistro table and a string quartet."

"Come summer, maybe I will."

Not that Cara will be here to see it if I do. I shake off that thought and work on setting up the chairs at the water's edge instead. I take a seat to watch her and swallow a small sip of the whiskey, then hand it her way. Cara takes a drink and returns it. We're quiet for a bit, nothing but the hum of nature around us.

"I'm wearing my glasses tonight."

I grin, more to myself than anything. "I'm aware."

"Do you know why?"

"Because you know I think it's hot? You enjoy watching me watching you, when you wear them?"

Cara laughs but shakes her head at the same time. "It's because I'm feeling inquisitive. Do you know what about?"

The whiskey bottle is pressed to my bottom lip and there's a sting there from the liquor, but it's no match for the sting in my gut when I note the determination in Cara's voice. Now her weird blank-faced act from earlier makes sense—the woman was giving me her poker face, all so she could get me out here for a goddam interview or something. I take another drink. Bigger this time.

"You," she says, confirming everything I just figured out.

It takes a second for the burn of that shot of whiskey to clear. When it does, I lower my voice. "Don't, Cara."

She brushes off my warning and reels in, then casts again.

"I had planned on doing this at some point after we had sex one time. When you're naked and drowsy, all doped up on the aftereffects of our fantastic sexual compatibility. Then I decided that seemed a little praying mantis of me."

My head drops back to meet the unforgiving metal edge of the camp chair, and I study the sky above me where it's now dark enough to make this conversation feel menacing. Also, *annoying*.

"Here's what I know. Garrett Strickland, twenty-five, Hotchkiss native. Local golden boy with academic *and* athletic scholarships, who was supposed to do big things. Then his dad dies. He comes home and things go to shit. He has to sell the family farm, and even when he could have gone back to school, he doesn't. Instead, he stays put and gets a job. A job that shortchanges everything he's capable of and tanks everything he planned on."

Jesus Christ. I don't know whether to congratulate her on managing to sum up my entire life in a paragraph, or tell her to fuck off. I settle on sarcasm.

"Crack reporting there, Cronkite."

"Not really. All that crap is obvious. What isn't so clear is *why*."

Without even posing a direct question, Cara manages to cut to the heart of what she wants to know. Why did I give up? Was I lazy? Was I carrying around some sort of hidden pain I needed to dig up and deal with?

Or was it something that the writer in her would find way less interesting? Like that I'm not the kind of guy who needs much beyond what I have?

Except maybe a YETI cooler. I'd like one of those.

I let out a long exhale. "I know you want a big, revealing answer, here, Cara, but the truth is that I'm a simple guy. You might think my life is tragic and pathetic or something—but I don't. No big mystery, no deep, dark emotional turmoil. What you see is what you get, that's all."

Cara reels in and sets the rod on the ground next to her chair, then walks over to stand in front of mine. She points toward my chair.

"Is this thing strong enough to hold both of us?"

I set the whiskey to the side and open my arms, thinking this might the best route to redirecting the conversation. "I have no idea. But my ass will hit the ground first if it isn't."

She crawls into my lap, straddling me so we're face-to-face. The chair stays put and doesn't collapse to the ground. And like always, her moving around in my lap means that my cock starts to get interested in what's happening—even when my brain and my gut instincts say that we shouldn't give her anything but a cold shoulder, otherwise she'll keep pushing.

Cara drapes her arms around my shoulders and uses the tips of her fingers to tease the hair on my neck. My shoulders immediately relax under her touch—so much for that cold-shoulder plan.

"I don't think your life is tragic or pathetic, Garrett. And I love the what-you-see-is-what-you-get quality of who you are. I'm just curious if you ever think about doing anything else. I mean, why don't you buy a farm?"

A bitter laugh comes out. "Why don't I buy a farm? Are you serious?"

"Yes." Cara's face is entirely earnest. Christ, she *is* serious. No matter how much time and effort she's put into learning about folks around here, there's still a lot she doesn't understand.

I sigh. "Because I can't. It's impossible, financially. Dirt isn't cheap. The money I have would make for a laughable down payment, and banks aren't exactly standing in line to write paper on that kind of risk. Guys like me are priced out of owning farmland these days."

The place between her eyebrows creases together. "How did Corey and Brooke do it? They're young and they own their own farm. And what about Whitney?"

I put my index finger to the creases and gently rub to smooth them, then run my finger down the ridge of her nose.

"Corey and Brooke have Brooke's dad. He's an established farmer with equity and a credit history. He was able to back them so they could buy their place. Even with that, they're still not pulling in enough income to farm exclusively, so Brooke works part-time at the bank and Corey teaches a few engineering classes at the community college in Delta. And Whitney's a whole other story. She bought her place on her own, but that's only because it was an abandoned hellhole, so she got it as a total steal. Then she almost lost it to foreclosure because she had one bad season. Cooper saved her place."

"Oh."

Disappointment colors that one word. As if she believed a swift kick in the ass is all it would take to get me going on a bigger path—and she wanted to be the one to give it to me. After that, I'd step right up to buy three sections of irrigated land, with water shares and mineral rights.

Her hands come to my chest, settling a little too close to my heart for where this conversation is headed. I fight the urge to grab the whiskey bottle and take another slug. She waits a few more seconds, then plants a soft kiss on me—a kiss that all logic shouts I should run from, as fast as I can, because like that poker face of hers, it's a trick. A trick I'm determined *not* to fall for.

"Play a game with me."

"No thanks." I grunt.

"Come on." Her fingers start to walk up my chest, across my

shoulders, and up to my cheeks. She pauses at the hollows below my eyes, stroking there gently until my lids droop closed.

"Just a little game. Nothing scary."

I open my eyes and give her a halfhearted glare. "You are aware that I can't say no to you, right? It's kind of shitty how you're using that to your advantage right now. You're a goddam snake charmer or something."

Cara drops her hands from my face, presses her palms together in a prayer, then zigzags them through the air playfully, all while waggling her brows like a goofball. I roll my eyes. She returns her hands to me, this time threading her fingers through my hair.

"Close your eyes," the snake charmer whispers. When I do, she starts in again, voice still lowered. "Relax. Picture your life a year from now. You can have whatever you want. You can be anyplace, do anything."

My body starts to hum anxiously, and every inch of my skin wants to shake off whatever this feeling is. Cara leans forward and kisses me, so softly it seems like a dream. Her hands are in my hair, her mouth on mine, and her tits are pressed to my chest. She keeps talking, a kiss between each question, never pausing long enough for me to answer.

"Where are you?"

"Are you alone?"

"Who's with you?"

"Are you happy?"

Finally, she leans back a fraction. "Tell me, Garrett. What did you see?"

The whiskey, Cara's gentle questions, her kissing me, and I don't know which it is, but I'm too raw to fight the vision that hits me.

And that vision is green. Soft green. A wheat field in late spring—and it's going to be a good year. A white house set back off a dirt driveway, humble and rough, small enough that it doesn't ask much of the guy who lives there.

That's what I see. Cara repeats her question. I swallow thickly. "I don't know."

"Garrett, don't do th—"

I cut her off. "No. I can *see* it, I just don't know where it is." I feel her pleased gaze through my closed eyes. "It's green. Rolling hills. A wheat field."

She doesn't push after that, but I find myself waiting for her to ask the other questions again. If she did, I might tell her the truth.

"Are you alone?" No.

"Who's with you?" You.

"Are you happy?" Yes.

When she doesn't, I shove my hands into her hair, pull her close, and kiss her. And it's like I'm telling her everything when I do.

Cara pulls back from the kiss, but stays close enough that the curve of her mouth is against mine. "Let's go home. I feel like showing my gratitude."

"Is this my reward for sharing?"

"Something like that. But what I have in mind isn't suited to this locale. My knees will get dirty."

My cock goes thick in an instant. I try to shift so she doesn't feel it all at once—can't have her thinking that tonight's emotional mining expedition and this hard-on are in any way connected. The next thing you know, she'll have me journaling my feelings and researching tantric sex—and talking it all to death while I do.

I give her a grin. "Had I known that was the reward, I'd have opened up earlier. In fact, I have other secrets, if you want to keep digging."

Cara laughs. "I'm sure you do."

I yank her closer, set my lips to the shell of her ear. "When

I was eight, I stole a dirt bike magazine from a gas station in Grand Junction. When I was thirteen, I borrowed my mom's station wagon in the middle of the night and ran over one of our neighbor's mailboxes. Junior year of high school, I trespassed in two farmers' fields because this girl who was here for the summer said she wanted to have sex in the back of a truck and . . ."

19

(Cara)

My phone chimes with an email as I head down the driveway to Garrett's place—the modular, not trailer, as I first called it. In my defense, how was I supposed to know that his place sits on a *foundation* and that makes all the difference? Not exactly knowledge I've ever required before now.

After slowing to a stop in front of the rickety porch that extends from the front door of the modular, I glance toward the cup holder where my phone sits. My mother. Subject line: *Aspen - Little Nell / Apogée.*

I don't even have to open it to know the details. My parents are coming to Aspen, I'd guess. While there, they'll be staying at their favorite boutique luxury hotel and dining at their favorite French restaurant. All likely under the guise of my upcoming birthday on the thirteenth, but more likely because my mother wants to shop and my father wants to wear jeans with a sport coat and drink until he doesn't care about anything.

Instead of clicking on the mail icon and confirming how right I am, I'm distracted when a booming laugh from across the way catches my attention. Parked over near a shed, Garrett, Braden, and Cooper are gathered around Garrett's truck, tailgate down with Garrett perched on it and the other two each leaning on a bedside. All three are dressed in hunting gear—brush pants with lace-up boots, and base layer shirts under camo coats. Dead things—turkeys, I'm assuming—line the truck bed behind Garrett. An opened cooler rests on the end of the tailgate, the likely source for the beers they're drinking. I check the clock on my dash. Not quite lunch, and nowhere near what my parents would consider an appropriate cocktail hour. Apparently, hunting means it's five thirty somewhere.

Camo, dead things, and beer swigging at eleven a.m.—on a Sunday. And contrary to everything that defined my life before coming to Hotchkiss, I'm surprisingly charmed by the whole display.

Sundays have become a date day of sorts for Garrett and me, given that it's one of his days off, and I quickly discovered that for most rural farming or ranching folks, it's also the day that church and family take priority. Cell phones are turned off and only those tasks that can't be ignored are dealt with, and if a writer like me tried to move in on that time, it would be the fast track to a freeze-out. So I spend my mornings doing a long reformer workout and catching up on emails, maybe a little drafting if I'm behind on my word count. Garrett usually hunts or shoots his bow, then we meet up midday.

Another raucous laugh from the redneck congregation that I shouldn't find attractive, but do. It's a big ol' mess of cliché masculinity over there, and all my primal lady urges respond. So evolution must be to blame when I ignore my phone, step out of the car, and sex-sleepwalk my way over there. Garrett's eyes are on me the entire time, with a grin that fades into something more promising with each step I take.

Cooper and Braden are making an attempt at idle chitchat,

but from the bit I'm able to comprehend—beyond the buzz in-spired by Garrett's prowling gaze—their conversation isn't exactly lively. Mostly it's a volley of one-word comments and grunts.

Garrett sets his beer aside, widens the spread of his thighs in invitation. "Hi."

The urge to crawl into his lap and draw my legs astride him—because I know what comes with the spread of his legs like that—is immediate and wild. A needy pulse that reminds me what it's like when he drives up into me, the way it can wipe out sound judgment and all reason on the first jerk of his hips.

"Hi," I manage.

"I have something for you."

I bet you do.

My eyes widen, skirt to Cooper and Braden, who are both staring into their beer bottles. Garrett gives up an almost impos-sible-to-hear snort, and then clears his throat.

"It's in the house. On the counter. For tonight."

I consider what it could be. Nothing but lewd images come to mind. I give Garrett another look, adding a twitch of brows to ei-ther side as a reminder that we have an audience. He does nothing but press his lips together and fight the urge to laugh.

A beer bottle hits the truck bed, courtesy of Braden, where it clangs loudly. He reaches for the dead turkey that's closest to him and grabs it by the foot, above a rather menacing-looking spur. Cooper does the same with the bird closest to him. He adjusts his ball cap and reaches for his coat where it's draped over the truck bed next to him.

"Looks like it's time for Braden and me to be somewhere other than here."

Garrett grins, all for me, and doesn't respond to Cooper's ob-vious suggestion that the two of us are throwing off such ridic-ulous sex vibes that we would clear out a church service. Braden tips his chin my way and slaps Garrett's shoulder hard enough to throw him a bit. And then they both simply walk off. Men. If women part ways like that, then you can be sure someone is mad at someone.

Two trucks start and then it's just the two of us. I groan. "You can't look at me like that when there are other people around."

"Like what? Like I want them to leave so I can take you in the house for a nice, long round?"

"Yes. Like that."

"Why? I got what I wanted; they left. Now we can go in the house and you can tell me what you were thinking when you walked over here—that way I know exactly how to give it to you. Everybody wins. Explain to me what the problem is here, why I can't look at you like that."

My head drops into my palms. "Because . . ."

I try to think of a good reason. Nothing happens. Probably because Garrett's arms have wound around and slid down to my backside.

"I don't know. Just *because*."

Garrett stands and our bodies meet, he rocks his hips to mine. "Well, OK, then. Just *because*. Got it."

An hour later, Garrett tugs on his jeans but leaves them unbuttoned, a detail I'm able to note even from where I'm sprawled out naked on his bed—and a touch dizzy, despite being entirely prone.

"You stay there and rest. Take a nap. I've got to clean my bird and then I'm going to start prepping for the dinner I'm going to make you. Need to run into town and hit the grocery store. You want anything?"

I flop my head about on his pillow because words are too much work. The bed dips under the weight of him and one of his hands slips up the inside of one of my calves, then traces slowly upward, between my legs and over my belly, a quick stop at my breasts, before cupping the back of my neck.

"Did you see your stuff on the kitchen counter?"

My eyes fall closed. "No. My eyeballs were on your butt when we came into the house. That's what happens when a redneck throws you over his shoulder."

Garrett chuckles, his face pressed in my hair so when he does, his breath tickles my scalp.

"Ah, yes. I forgot." A kiss to my forehead. "Take a look while I'm skinning my bird. If it isn't what you want, I can get other stuff while I'm out."

Another kiss and he's gone. I urge myself out of bed with a huff, slipping on my shirt and grabbing my phone off the floor. My mom's email lights up the lock screen again, and I figure I can't put it off any longer. Two clicks and it opens.

Cara,

I hope this email finds you well and accomplishing what you had hoped. After speaking with Amie, we've decided to come to Aspen for your birthday. We have three suites at The Little Nell, plus reservations at Apogée for dinner on the 12th. I assume you can drive from Davis's? If not, please advise and we'll arrange for the charter to bring you in.

Mom

Ah, classic Nan Cavanaugh. No surprises here, nothing particularly motherly or enthusiastic—what she's sent me is essentially a jazzed-up itinerary. And, as usual, it feels like I'm about as crucial as the hotel concierge to her plans. Perhaps I've been in Hotchkiss long enough for it to have rewired some fundamental part of my makeup, because driving over to Aspen sounds about as fun as a root canal. The one upside I can think of is a few hours with Amie at our favorite spa there, where the facials include caviar and the hot rock massages use stones imported from Norway—it's as decadent as it sounds and Hotchkiss hasn't changed me so much that I'd turn my back on *that*.

After pecking out a short reply to my mother that matches hers in the emotional detachment department (*Sounds lovely. The drive is easily manageable. I'll arrive on the eleventh. Cara*), I drop the phone to the bed and pad out to the kitchen.

While Garrett's place is definitely rough around the edges, it's also clean and comfortable. The furniture is spare but no more so than what I've already grown used to at the farmhouse. A couch and coffee table sit in front of the requisite large-screen television, and the only other furniture in the living room is a rack of dumbbells and a weight bench in the corner. On mornings when he hasn't left early to help the Eulands or go turkey hunting, Garrett grunts his way through an hour of lifting. Sometimes, I watch. Sometimes, I lie in bed and listen.

On the kitchen counter, I find what he's been so determined about making sure I inspect.

Three boxes of microwave popcorn. One plain, one movie-theater butter, and one kettle corn. Three bottles of red wine. A cab, a merlot, and a pinot noir. And a sticky note with a heart on it, stuck to the top box of popcorn. It's the simplest of offerings, but entirely perfect. I trace the heart with one fingertip as my own flutters away.

The front door kicks open and Garrett strides in holding two near-failing paper plates full of raw, slightly bloodied, meat.

So much for all my feel good heart fluttering and manly appreciation, because this hunting thing just got real—and it's gross.

Garrett sets the plates near the sink and starts to rinse off the meat. "Did I get it right?"

With a smile, I stare down at the sweet little gift set he's curated for me. "It's perfect."

"I'm glad." A returning smile is in his voice. He continues cleaning the meat, dropping each piece into a large metal bowl, where I can smell a heap of garlic and herbs. "I had no clue on the wine, but this is Colorado wine country, so it wasn't hard to find a vino geek at the liquor store in Paonia to guide me."

I let my finger trace the heart again. "Now if you only had *Real Housewives*. Then this night would be complete."

Garrett sets the bowl in the fridge and moves to wash his hands. He tears off a paper towel, wipes his hands dry, tosses it in the trash, and leans back on the counter. "On the DVR. Should be the last three episodes you haven't seen."

My finger freezes in place over the heart. I cut my eyes his way to see if he's joking. He's not. Because he's giving me his soft eyes, the ones that emerge when he's either postorgasmic or sleepy. He's giving me *Real Housewives*, wine, popcorn, and soft eyes. Everything inside me goes all . . . *verklempt*.

My face shows it, too. And Garrett doesn't know what to make of it, because he shoves his hands in his pockets and looks down at the linoleum floor.

"Unless you watched some episodes while I wasn't there, you should be on the one where they go to Dubai. Looks like, *as fucking usual*, the two Lisas are about to go at it and Kyle's pretending she wants to stay out of it. And Erika's taking those gay dudes along."

Oh God. He's trying to sound put out by the whole thing, but his attention to the details—the Lisas, Kyle, Erika's glam squad—

betrays whatever sardonic take he was trying for. This day just keeps getting *better and better*.

I give my head a slow shake. "Could you take your shirt off when you say that?"

Garrett's eyes shoot up to meet mine. "Take my shirt off?"

Drawing a hand up to my forehead and pretend to dab away some very feminine perspiration—the glistening kind that would accompany a woman being simply *overcome*.

"Yes. Because the only thing that could make this better is if you were shirtless while you provide this detailed synopsis of my next *Real Housewives* episode."

He offers an eye roll but a grin is tugging at his mouth. I pad my way over to him and press my hands to his chest.

"Are you sure this is all about me? Or are you harboring a secret love for *Real Housewives* and this is a way to cover it up? Am I your reality-show-obsessed beard?"

Garrett cocks a brow. "No. I do not love them. I think they're all terrible. But *you* love this shit and I love—"

His jaw snaps shut. Panic flickers in his eyes as my heart starts to beat overtime, my mind tracing an imaginary heart with our names etched inside.

Carefully, he starts in again. "I love making you happy. Even if it pains my eyeballs and tortures my hearing to watch those women do what they do."

"Sure," I crow, my tone a little too jovial to cover up what I think just almost happened, and the potential implications of it. But I decide to let it go—for now. "Keep telling yourself that."

❧

Garrett doesn't have a dining table—no surprise there. This means our Sunday dinner is served in the living room, with us on the floor around the coffee table. I take a seat atop a couch cushion because it adds a Moroccan flair to what might otherwise feel college-dorm-like. Garrett tries it but claims he feels like a toddler in a wobbly booster seat and tosses it aside.

Tonight, unlike the other nights we've eaten dinner together here, there are candles on the coffee table and Garrett's done all the cooking. Normally, it's a joint effort—he does the grilled cheese while I heat the soup, he scrambles the eggs while I manage the toast and coffee. But given that the menu centerpiece is wild turkey, I didn't know how to help with anything beyond opening the wine. Other than that, I stayed out of his way by drafting a few pages based on my visit yesterday with a local vineyard owner and sending out three email proposals to small magazines to hopefully line up my next freelance assignment.

Garrett sets a square plastic platter in the middle of the coffee table, piled high with skewers of herb-marinated turkey breast cutlets, each one wrapped around an asparagus spear and then covered with a bacon slice. A bowl of roasted potatoes sits next to a plate of those refrigerated croissant rolls, and two small dishes of some sort of sauce. Not only does everything look good, the smell of applewood smoking chips filling the air for an hour as he worked outside at the grill had already piqued my taste buds' interest. Although it hasn't overridden my hesitation about eating something I saw with its feathers on just a few hours ago.

"You ready for this?"

I take a deep breath. "I think so."

Garrett starts to dish everything out for me, setting a skewer, a spoonful of potatoes, and one roll on my plate before handing it my way, spying my apprehensive expression when he does.

"Come on. You probably pay twenty bucks a pound for meat at Whole Foods that isn't as free-range, fresh, and organic as this stuff."

He plates for himself, then raises his glass of beer to me, and I grab my wine.

"To Cara Cavanaugh. For coming to Hotchkiss, meeting a guy like me, and getting a taste of this life."

Our glasses clink. We each take a sip and I push my gaze to the plate in front of me, hesitating. After a deep breath, I take up my fork and start simple, with a potato wedge. Garrett slices into his turkey, stabs a forkful, and dips it in the sauce. A good-sounding grunt leaves his mouth.

Now or never, I guess.

I start with a small bite, ensuring there's plenty of bacon covering the sliver of turkey. I dunk it in the sauce and stare at the fork for a moment, then close my eyes and eat up.

I wait for the inevitable *gamey* flavor people always talk about to hit my tongue, but it doesn't. In fact, it's good. Maybe better than good. The meat is more flavorful than any Thanksgiving turkey or turkey burger I've eaten—not quite as tender, but not tough, either. My eyes flip open and I give my fork a surprised look.

"You look shocked." Garrett's voice sounds both pleased and mock-insulted.

I take another bite, bigger this time, and chew slowly, ensuring I truly taste it. Another bite, more sauce.

"I am. I figured it would be, I don't know, gamey or something? People are always saying that. I don't even know what it means exactly, but it doesn't sound complimentary. But this is so good. It tastes . . . *clean*."

"That's because it is. No antibiotics, no growth hormones. Plus, I think shooting them with a bow helps, too. And what you do after is important, cleaning and getting the meat cooled down quickly. I don't kill anything unless I'm going to eat it, so I don't screw around with that part."

I point at the dishes between us, take my latest bite and dip it. "And this sauce is amazing. What's in it?"

Garrett slows his chewing and swallows. He finishes and points his fork toward the bowl.

"That?"

"Yes, the sauce. What is it?"

He smirks. "*That* is something very special. Something I only serve my finest guests." He gives a tilt of his head. I widen my eyes to prompt him.

"Ranch dressing."

My face falls. "Ranch *salad* dressing?"

He lets out a huge laugh. "Yes. Ranch salad dressing. The kind from a *valley* that's apparently *hidden*. But not from a bottle. Not anything so ordinary for you, Cara. This is the stuff from a packet. I mean, I put some effort into this. I had to add the milk and the mayonnaise, then mix it all up, and let it sit in the fridge for an hour."

I slap him in the chest with the back of my hand and he snorts. Garrett continues to chuckle between bites, then sets his fork down and kisses my temple. Given that I just did my out-of-touch-rich-girl thing, it seems like the perfect time to mention my trip to Aspen.

"So . . ."

Garrett parrots back, "So . . ."

"I wanted to let you know that I'm leaving on Friday."

Garrett freezes, his glass poised under his bottom lip. Our eyes lock and his mouth parts a little. His arm drops, stops short of the table, then he sets his glass down deliberately and his eyes drop to his lap.

"I thought you were staying until the end of the month. Until April."

My face crinkles up. Oh, hell. I set that up wrong.

"Jeez. No, not *leaving*, leaving. I mean, just for a few days. My family is coming to Aspen for a long weekend, so I'm going to meet up with them. I'll leave Friday and be back on Wednesday."

Garrett releases a gusting breath. I do the same. We look at each other, relieved, then wary—because we see exactly how relieved we both are.

And that's not good. Because if leaving each other for good unnerves us both, then we're in trouble.

20

(Cara)

There aren't many things I've longed for since leaving Chicago for Hotchkiss. Not my king bed or the Japanese soaker tub in my master bathroom. Not the Pilates studio down the street from my condo or my favorite brunch place, where they serve salted caramel brioche French toast and sriracha-infused Bloody Marys.

But *this*, I missed. Somehow—I'm sure Garrett bears some responsibility here—I'd forgotten its powers. The way it can right your bad day or soothe your frazzled nerves.

The mani-pedi.

I bite back a moan when the spa technician's hands make their way up from my heel, pause to knead the oddly tense back of my ankle, then move up along my calf muscles. I've already luxuriated my way through a ninety-minute aromatherapy massage and hydrating herbal wrap, and a Colorado arid climate reparative facial, and had all the parts of me that required it waxed smooth. Now this. My eyes fall closed, relishing in the wafting scent of lavender essential oils from the foot bath.

"OK, Cara Jane." Amie plops, somehow elegantly, into the treatment chair next to mine. "During my massage, I was thinking."

"You're not supposed to think during a massage. It's against the rules," I say, voice monotone.

"Rules, schmules. But first, pick one for me, please."

The click of nail polish bottles draws my eyes open. Amie has two bottles clasped in each hand. In her right, two shades of pink, nearly identical, save for the hint of pearl in one. In her left, a bottle of midnight blue and one of cherry red. We both know pink is her usual choice, but I note how her left hand seems extended a bit farther.

"The blue one. It's edgy without looking like you might have a Joy Division tattoo somewhere on your body. Mom will hate it."

Amie snorts and passes the bottle to her technician with a thank-you. She adjusts herself into the spa chair, wiggles her shoulders around and then re-knots the sash on her fluffy robe with a rather rough yank. Just like she always does.

I would know. At home we have a standing twice-a-month date at our favorite spa. Where we indulge in our love of mani-pedis, get our eyebrows threaded, and sometimes enjoy the occasional massage. So on top of the indulgence and pampering, I miss this, too. A few hours with my sister, who knows what I look like when I ugly cry, laugh until I cry, and cry without shedding a tear. Because sometimes it's more than enough to feel *known* by another person, in ways you could never explain.

Amie completes her nesting ritual and takes a sip of the champagne from the glass sitting next to her. "Anyways. I was thinking that you should invite Garrett to dinner tomorrow night."

My gaze kicks up to the ceiling. *"What?"*

"You should invite Garrett to dinner."

I tip my head her way, expecting to see some evidence she's joking. She isn't.

"Are you serious? Invite Garrett. To Apogée. With our mother." After saying it out loud, I try to picture it. I do, and it's only a snapshot, but that's enough. It's *bad*.

Amie's voice holds none of the alarm mine did. "Of course. Don't you miss him? Wouldn't it be fun to spend your birthday eve night with him? In your suite?"

My body answers before I can. Mostly by way of weird, breathy, half-obscene sounds that emerge when I think about Garrett spending the night in my hotel suite. The two of us in the big bed with the soft sheets. The two of us in the big bathtub with the wood-burning fireplace in front of it. Oh God. I bet Garrett can build the best fire. He probably doesn't even need matches.

Despite liking that picture way too much, I still know it's a bad idea. I try and think of a sound, specific reason that will smother out my hormones enough to abandon this ill-advised scheme.

Suddenly, a singular, unmistakably cultured voice cuts through all the clamoring in my mind.

"Cara, I bought you a dress at Burberry while I was out. They're tailoring it to bring in the bustline so it won't look deflated on you. I'll have the concierge pick it up in the morning and send it up to your room after they do. It will be just right for dinner tomorrow night."

And there's my reason. My mother. Standing there in full make-up, every curl of hair still in place despite having just emerged from her own deep-tissue massage. Even in a spa robe, her trademark poise remains unmussed.

I avoid an adolescent sigh by focusing on my toes, where a coat of bright violet nail polish is being applied, muttering an obligatory thank-you.

"Cara's inviting one of her Hotchkiss friends to dinner tomorrow night, Mom," my traitorous sister chirps. "We need to let the restaurant know we're six instead of five now."

My head jerks up and I hiss in her direction. "Amie!"

Mom runs her hands over the front of her robe, smoothing away nonexistent wrinkles. "Of course. Does she have any dietary restrictions? I'd planned on the chef's tasting menu for all of us."

"*He*," Amy offers.

My mother's hands freeze. Her eyes rise up and meet mine. "He?"

I take a labored swallow, reminding myself that this is my twenty-eighth birthday. I'm certainly old enough now to invite a man to dinner if I feel like it, without offering an explanation. Even to my mother.

What's done is done, then. Might as well go with it.

"Garrett. And no restrictions that I know of. He eats just about anything."

Her eyes narrow at the familiarity implied by my last sentence. She cinches the sash on her robe tighter around her waist and replies flatly, "He eats just about anything. How lovely."

When she turns on a heel and clears the room en route to her facial, I pick up a particularly fat issue of *Architectural Digest* magazine off the side table between us and whack Amie's arm with it. She doesn't even flinch, merely giggles and tugs on her diamond-stud-wearing earlobes.

I let the magazine hit the table with a flat thud, then down what remains in the champagne flute sitting next to me before emptying hers, too—hoping it comes off as dramatic as it was intended. Another laugh from Amie.

Only one thing to do now. I grab my phone and fire off a text.

Feel like taking a drive to Aspen?

21

(Garrett)

I'm not sure if it's this restaurant or my shirt that's making my skin itch, but something sure as shit is.

The shirt is a light blue Ariat button-down that was a Christmas present from my mom two years ago, gone unworn until now, because I never had a reason to wear it. But dinner with Cara Cavanaugh's family at a place like this? Time to dig out the shirt. And wear it tucked in. This is Colorado, so jeans are acceptable anywhere, although I made sure to wear my least-trashed pair, along with boots that do not have dried mud in every stitch.

As for the restaurant, Apogée is uppity and French, housed in a renovated Victorian-era house at the end of a block in downtown Aspen, the kind of place where dinner will take three hours and you'll pay through the nose for the privilege of every minute. And when you leave? Still hungry.

I left myself time to spare for the drive from Hotchkiss to Aspen and arrived almost a half hour early, then sat in my truck for a while before finally coming inside the restaurant, still wondering why I said yes to this dinner in the first place.

The short answer is *Cara*. The Cara who made my day when I saw her text come through, right up until I read it and realized what I was in for if I said yes. But she's the same Cara I missed seeing for the last few days and the same Cara I can't say no to—even if that means I end up perched on an antique bench in the lobby of a pretentious restaurant like this one.

The bench is rickety as all hell, and the unfriendly woman greeting guests shoots a death glare my way every time I move and it creaks. Her black hair is pulled back in a painful-looking knot at her neck, and she's dressed in a bloodred dress with knee-high black boots. She's coldly beautiful, and I find her *terrifying*. I've been holding my breath and sitting like there's a bomb under the bench ever since she instructed me to sit here while I wait, hoping to keep the glares to a minimum.

I check my phone again, scratching my neck as I do, cursing the stiff shirt collar and my rumbling, empty stomach. Who sits down for a dinner like this at eight o'clock at night? People who don't have to get up at five a.m. to help Kenny Euland tag calves, that's who. Still, here I am—with my neck starting to chafe and my stomach demanding a cheeseburger in the next five minutes or it's going to start growling loud enough to be heard back in the kitchen.

A vision of that burger fills my mind as the front door swings open and a gust of cold night air rushes in. A tall man with a full head of dark but salt-flecked hair steps inside, holding the door as a petite blonde wearing a knee-length black coat with a fur-lined collar brushes past him. She stops two feet away but doesn't seem to notice my existence, tugging off her leather gloves and tucking them into a black purse she has clasped in the crook of one arm.

Another blonde follows—basically a younger model of the first, her blonde hair pulled back like the hostess, but on this woman it comes off as elegant instead of severe. Flanking her is a guy who looks like he's one vote away from his first Senate term, with dark hair and a nice suit, pressing his hand to her lower back as he stares quizzically back at the doorway.

"Where did she go?"

The older blonde sighs and shakes her head, lips pursed and her jaw drawn tight enough that I can see her delicate jawbone flex.

"How did we lose her between the car and . . ." The younger blonde's words trail off when she swings her gaze across the room, smiling when her eyes land on me. And when she does, the set of her mouth and the way her entire face turns bright in a way I'm familiar with—I know exactly who I'm looking at.

Cara's younger sister.

Cara's claimed more than once that she and her sister Amie look nothing alike—but she's wrong. Sure, the hair color, eye color, and heights are different, but that's too obvious. Underneath that, in the way they move and say everything with their expressions, they're practically twins.

Amie's mouth starts to form what looks like a greeting for me, but she's cut off by the future senator. "Here she is."

My eyes sweep to the doorway and Cara's there, still half turned toward the outside, like she's looking for me. Her father gently pats her shoulder. When she turns, she sees me immediately.

And maybe it's the hunger pangs doing the talking here, but I want to clear the distance between us and kiss her without a bit of warning. Without worrying about her family or the terrifying hostess, or anything else. All this and we've only been apart three days. Three days and I'm already out of my mind thinking about my hands up in her hair, doing a little damage to her pin-straight look tonight, so different from the just-out-of-bed look I like and know best.

She's wearing a dress that might require a little damage, too. Fitted, borderline tight, it hits just below her knees. It's black and white, with a weird-looking flowery pattern on it that reminds me of a bad tablecloth. And while I'd never say so, I don't think it's my favorite look on her—not that she doesn't look gorgeous, she does. She just doesn't look like *her*. This dress is too Stepford Wife, too worthy of a strand of pearls and the right amount of judgment to match. She also looks like she can't move, let alone breathe. She looks stuck—trapped inside a dress that's wearing her, instead of the other way around.

Now, her shoes . . . those are a different story.

Cara's long legs look even longer when she's sporting a pair of black heels that are high enough to seem treacherous, but look damn hot. The strappy things that crisscross her feet and wrap around her ankles only ratchet up the hotness.

When I stand, the antique bench creaks in relief. Cara lets her eyes eat up my frame and each of my senses soaks up the experience: the sight of her, the orange Creamsicle scent of her, the way I want a taste. I go straight to her side, hoping her family will understand, and when my hand finds hers, it's just the two of us. For a moment we're in a little bubble, alone, neither of us wearing clothes that obviously make us want to scratch our skin off.

"Cara." Her mother's voice bursts the bubble. "Introductions, please."

Cara and I both straighten. She sighs while keeping her eyes on mine and I give her hand a squeeze. A *let's do this look* passes between us.

"Sorry. I'd like you all to meet Garrett Strickland." Cara starts to tick off each member of the party and I get something different from each. A curt nod from her mother, a firm handshake from her father, and a goofy smile from Amie.

But the future senator says almost everything I need to know with a handshake and a grin—one that says *don't fuck with her* and *welcome to the jungle*, all at the same time.

⁓

Amuse-bouche, my ass. My mouth *does not* find this bacon-wrapped roasted banana bite at all amusing. When the team of waiters set these tiny pewter plates in front of us, I almost laughed at the pretentious bullshit that came with presenting what looked like someone's first-day kitchen fuckup. Then the head waiter stepped back and announced: "An amuse-bouche." His eyes locked on mine. "To entertain the mouth." After that, he said something else in French but didn't bother to translate.

I labor through chewing the mushy banana in my mouth and search the table for something that might help clear away the taste once I finish. But there's not even a bread basket on the table. All that's in front of me is my water glass and a little teakwood bowl filled with pink-colored salt nuggets. I begged off ordering a beer—despite Cara's mom asking twice already if I was sure I didn't want one—because I have a long drive home coming later. But that was before this not-mouth-entertaining banana thing.

Cara's hand finds my thigh under the table and gives a squeeze above my knee. Using her other hand, she moves her wineglass a few inches over in my direction. I grab the glass and take a gulp, swishing it around in my mouth as subtly as possible.

"Garrett, are you positive you don't want a beer? I'm sure they have something . . . *domestic*."

Cara fingers grips my knee and her nails dig in. "Mom, please stop asking him if he wants a beer. He's a grown man. If he wants a beer, he will order one."

A split-second glaring match ensues, ending only when a flicker of confusion and disappointment lights in Mrs. Cavanaugh's eyes and she looks away. I draw Cara's still-claw-gripped hand in mine and skate my thumb over the back until I feel her relax.

"I'm fine, Mrs. Cavanaugh. But thank you for asking. Again." She nods and the neutral eye contact I get feels like a victory, a bonus over what I've gotten up to this point.

Another sweep of my thumb to Cara's hand and I glance her way, waiting for her to see me. When she does, there are little furrows across her forehead and her mouth is turned down at the corners. I don't think I've seen her this way before—even when she's writing and the words aren't going well. And all the techniques I employ on those nights to distract her, I can't use here. I can't kiss her neck or rub her shoulders, can't tickle her until she's out of breath from squirming. I definitely can't make her squirm in other ways.

Amie interjects before I do something stupid like haul Cara into my lap, kiss her, and wrap my arms around her until her head is tucked to my neck.

"So, tell us more about Hotchkiss, Cara. How is your work coming along?"

The legion of servers have cleared the amuse-bouche plates and are now placing slightly bigger plates in front of us. In the center is a cracker the size of a poker chip, topped with salmon roe and a dollop of something foamy. I groan silently.

Fucking bait on a Ritz cracker.

Cara waits until the server sets her plate down, her brow loosening when she answers. "Well, my working draft is coming along and I've interviewed quite a few people already, but I still have more lined up. And I think I'm finally starting to fit in a little, which makes talking to people easier."

I finish chewing my Ritz bite and grab a sip of water. "You're totally fitting in. I mean, Kenny calls you 'darlin'.'"

She snorts. "Kenny calls everyone 'darlin'.' That's not exactly a sign of my seamless integration into the community."

"But he means it with you. I've known him since I was five, but I see him these days and it's all 'Cara, Cara, Cara.'"

"Jealous?"

"Yes."

"Good."

"Damn near as jealous as I was when that heifer got fresh with you."

Our protective bubble sweeps over us again. Cara smiles and I lean in an inch or so, making her all mine for the moment.

"A heifer? As in a *cow*?" Cara's dad has been nearly silent since we sat down, but when his too-loud question pokes a hole in our bubble, I look up, steal a look at his empty scotch glass, and understand why. He's teetering on the edge of drunk, that's why.

"Our Cara, the girl who was kicked out of Campfire Girls in the first week because she refused to put her book down and leave the tent? She experienced some sort of cow interlude? I want to hear this story. Do tell."

Cara groans. "Let's not."

"Come on, City." I stretch an arm out and drape it over the back of her chair, setting my hand to her shoulder. Cara gives me a wry but playful look. I turn my attention back to the table.

"Her first time out with me we went to a cattle rancher's place. Kenny Euland's. The same guy who cares only about Cara now, despite having known me since I was cruising around on a Big Wheel." I lift an eyebrow in her direction. She jumps in.

"It's calving season right now, so these guys are super busy. We're talking twenty-four-seven. Garrett helps out when he can; they need as many hands as they can get."

One look and she hands it back to me. "Anyway, we're out

checking pastures, looking for any problems, checking on the gals to see if any of them are close or look like they're going to have trouble delivering."

Cara grabs a quick sip of her wine. "Garrett parks the truck and starts tossing out these feed pellets. These things are like catnip to cows, so suddenly we're surrounded. But I was holding my own."

"*Until . . .*" I add.

Amie's eyes dart between Cara and me. Same goes for the fiancé, both of them grinning. Cara drops her head and uses her napkin to cover her face, speaking through the cloth.

"Until . . ."

Ice rattles in her father's scotch glass and a server materializes out of nowhere to replace it with a fresh one. A ruddy blush is across his features now, but he's still with us. Her mom? I'm not sure. The lemon-faced but vacant-eyed look she's sporting makes it hard to know if she's totally checked out or entirely tuned in.

Cara drops the napkin back to her lap, giving up a dramatic sigh. I move my hand to the back of her neck, letting my thumb rub tiny circles near the slope of her collarbone.

"Until a randy heifer came up behind me and started poking me. The cow was right . . ." Cara opens her arms wide then uses one hand to wave at the space where her fine ass is. "Right *there*. I didn't know what to do. I thought it was Garrett at first."

I sputter a little. "You did? Seriously?"

She gives up a jerky nod and a booming laugh escapes me. Amie slaps her hand over her mouth to keep from howling, but her fiancé joins right in with me.

"I did." Cara's eyes light up when I give a sly grin that admits the idea of me groping her ass that day wasn't *too* far-fetched. "But the wet snorting sound was my first clue that it wasn't Garrett. I screamed, took off, then tripped and face-planted into a puddle of mud and cow pies. I was covered in it."

Amie gives in and laughs, loudly and unreservedly, followed by Dad adding in a scotch-soaked chuckle of his own. And when Cara tips her head my way, her temple resting on my upper arm, it's like we've done this all before, a million times over. Sat at a table and told a story together, with the sort of timing that would earn us envious looks from couples who can't do the same.

But I know it's just that. A feeling. Something more than what it is. An anecdote between two people who don't have anything but a few more weeks together.

After what feels like nine hundred one-bite platefuls of weirdness, the server declares that our dessert soufflés will arrive shortly—an announcement which everyone but me makes excited noises about. I thought the thimbleful of berry sorbet we just ate *was* dessert.

Can't blame a guy, really. Not after a salad course that looked like someone tossed a handful of weeds on a plate then sprinkled some beer nuts on top to garnish it, followed by a sliver of smoked trout with pickled-something on it that tasted mostly like vinegar, and then a glob of duck-flavored mousse smeared on a piece of melba toast. And the pasta course, which was one—*one*—ravioli on a plate, stuffed with something orange and mushy, drizzled with olive oil and a single shaving of Parmesan cheese. The entrée was enormous by comparison. A supposed elk tenderloin that tasted a lot like bison to me, surrounded by three baby red potatoes and the same number of roasted carrots.

Still, everyone else at the table has leaned back in their chairs to stretch in what I think is the rich-people version of a food coma.

Cara downs the last of her wine and turns my way, letting the other conversations carry on without us.

"Hi," she whispers.

My mouth hitches up on one side into an easy grin. I lean forward a few inches. "Hi."

"Are you miserable?"

"No. I'm not miserable." I kick one eyebrow up. "I am starving, though."

Cara stifles what I know would be a real laugh if we were alone. I tuck my hand into hers under the tablecloth, setting our intertwined hands high on my thigh.

"Before I forget, Brooke called me looking for you. She wants to give you some info on a guy with a farm in Kansas she thinks you should meet. Her dad's second cousin by marriage or some crap like that. Make sure you call her when you get home."

Home. That word nudged its way in there without my permission, and I'm not sure if backpedaling will make it worse, so I leave it alone, thankful that it's nothing compared to my near-slipup a few nights ago. Although I'm sticking with the story that the *Real Housewives* are to blame for the *I love you* that almost came out of my mouth—the show is fucking ridiculous, so talking about it must have a similar effect on my common sense. And falling in love with a woman who doesn't live here and is leaving sooner rather than later would be beyond stupid.

Cara moves our hands deeper into the space between my legs, and I realize that if she noticed how I said "home," she doesn't care. Plus, her hand is closer to my dick now, so thinking about much else is impossible.

"Kansas? What part, did she say? Close enough for us to day-trip when you have time off?"

"I didn't ask. But Kansas is a haul, so—"

"What in God's name could be in Kansas? Other than corn-fields or . . . whatever it is they grow there."

So much for thinking there were other conversations going on around us and we might become invisible to everyone but each other for a minute. Apparently, Cara's mom's radar was still tuned in. Not sure how moms do that, but they do.

Cara's entire body turns taut, like she's looking for an escape route. She pulls her hand from mine, sets it on her lap to fidget with her napkin. "A possible lead for another interview from a friend of mine in Hotchkiss. She mentioned it to Garrett."

"*Another* friend in Hotchkiss? Have you been hired by the Chamber of Commerce yet?" Mrs. Cavanaugh mutters before leveling me with a look that makes it clear she doesn't like the roots Cara's dug in Hotchkiss.

I'm enemy number one for the moment, the guy who's helped her daughter settle into a town that's too far away from where she wants her and doing things she apparently doesn't want her daughter wasting time doing. "Perhaps that will be a good stop on your drive *home*. After all, before you know it, it's time for you to head back for Amie's wedding."

"I know," Cara manages. Too quietly, too meekly.

Mr. Cavanaugh's glass—his fifth, but who's counting—hits the tabletop with an uneven landing he rights before the ice cubes topple out. "Speaking of you coming home, Cara Jane—"

Ah. My chest starts to swell and a smile hits my lips. Cara's middle name is *Jane*. I love that. It sounds all musical and pretty.

"—you need to set up your quarterly appointment with Ron Dunlap. Meeting with your investment advisor is part of the agreement Granny Jane and I had when she established the trusts for you and Amie. As trustee, it's my job to make sure you don't neglect these things."

"Dad. Not now, please." Cara rolls her eyes, her tone strained.

But Dad's officially too blitzed to notice. He's talking way too loud, and now his eyes are watery. Being shit-faced means he doesn't hear the plea in his daughter's voice or see the cringing blush on her cheeks, any of the clues that might keep him from continuing to talk about what is apparently Cara's big fat bank account.

"In a few short years, you'll gain access to your entire trust, Cara. You need to be prepared. Money doesn't manage itself; you have to—"

Cara lurches up from her chair, nearly knocking it backward until I shoot my arm out to keep it upright. "Excuse me for a moment."

Cara skirts between our chairs and clears the room. Amie watches her bolting exit, then looks my way with a silent question: *Are you going or am I?*

I'm on my feet in a split second. "Be right back."

I scan the entryway for Cara but don't see her. A staircase leads up to a second floor, and I pause there, capturing the hateful hostess's attention. Suddenly, I want to do anything I can to wipe that smug, pinched smirk off this woman's face.

"Hey. Is the john up there?"

Her face goes slack and she looks a little confused *and* totally horrified. For a moment it looks like she's about to skewer me with a rant, but then she seems to decide I'm not worth the effort. She gives a limp flick of one hand toward the stairs.

I take the stairs two at a time, and they creak loudly, which I hope irritates the hostess even more. Ducking down the hallway, I come to a stop outside the ladies' room door and wait for the sound of water rushing in a sink to stop. The door creaks open and Cara checks her reflection in the mirror before stepping out, coming to a sharp halt when she sees me. Her eyes are tired and a touch red, but thankfully nothing indicates she's been full-on crying in there.

"You OK?"

She lifts one shoulder and looks right through me. I try again.

"Is it the soufflés? They do seem to be taking a long-ass time. Rest assured, I'm sure when they finally come out, they'll be the best three teeny-tiny bites of chocolate you've ever tasted. They'll probably garnish them with the world's smallest raspberry and a microscopic sprig of mint. Maybe a dollop of whipped cream the size of a miniature donkey's teardrop. Fair warning, when I scarf all that down, you're going to have to roll me out of here."

Cara laughs, takes two steps forward and crashes into me, wrapping her arms tight around my waist. My hands come around her, one sweeping down over her hair, which is as silky as it looks, so I do it again. Her dress feels nice, too. The kind that means I want to know how easily it would rip open if we were alone.

A shaky exhale leaves her. I set my hands to her hips, grounding her with a firm grip. "Why are you freaking out right now?"

She exhales loudly, tips her head down to tuck herself closer to me.

"I'm sorry about all of this. Dragging you up here to endure my family and French food on little plates while my mother foists beer on you and my dad discusses our finances like everyone in the world has a trust advisor. I should have known better. But Amie wanted to meet you, and I missed you, so I convinced myself it wouldn't be that terrible. I was wrong. It's *so* terrible."

I let out a quiet snort, pull her closer so I can kiss her cheek, then urge her back enough that we can see each other.

"Cara, sweetheart, I knew what I was getting into by driving over here. Did you honestly think I didn't know I was going to stick out like a sore-thumb redneck tonight? Come on, you know me a little better than that." I bump her chin gently with my thumb. "I know who I am. I know where I fit and where I don't, so you don't have to worry about me—I can handle myself. But I wanted to see *you*, so here I am."

"But my mom with the *beers*. Like you're incapable of enjoying wine or scotch or simply some water. And my dad. Jesus, he—"

"Your dad's half in the bag. Not the first or last time I've spent the evening with a guy who's shit-faced. And I think your mom's just trying to figure us out. She's not sure whether she needs to erect a steel fence between our chairs or figure out how to hustle you home to Chicago on a red-eye tonight. She's feeling possessive, that's all."

A scoff from Cara. "My mother has never been possessive of me. Amie? Maybe. But not me."

Tucking a stray lock of her hair behind her ear, I tilt my head and study Cara's face to see if she believes what she just said. When her eyes suddenly won't meet mine, I realize she does.

"You're way off base there. She might not understand you, but she loves you. Loves you hard enough that she's getting a little mama grizzly on us tonight. I can't blame her—it's impossible to know you and not want to sink your hooks in, make sure you don't get away."

Cara's eyes rise to mine again, all the spark and light I like to see there shining through. Her hands slip up and over my chest, then tick down the center, stopping to toy with the top button on my shirt before pressing her body to mine. I remind my dick that we're in the hallway of a fancy restaurant, but he doesn't seem to hear me. Given that my cock is deaf and I think Horny Cara might be plotting her arrival on the scene, we probably need to get out of this hallway as quickly as possible.

"Better now? Are you ready to go back down there?"

She shakes her head slowly, undoes a button on my shirt, and tucks her fingertip under the stiff material. Heat radiates from that spot so intensely I can feel it in my toes.

"Tell me what you need, then." Cara gives a jerky nod toward the entrance of the restaurant. I swallow hard. "Yeah? You sure?"

She teases the center of her upper lip with the tip of her tongue, whispers that she's *so sure*. I follow up with a question that makes it clear I need to get out of this restaurant as soon as possible, because the fact that I even consider it means this place is getting to my brain.

"What about the soufflés?"

Cara undoes another button. "They take *forever*, trust me. No one will even notice. Where's your truck?"

"Out back. In the lot where I'm pretty sure the kitchen staff parks. It looked like it belonged there more than it did out front between a Tesla and a Range Rover."

"Tell me you parked in a dark corner of the lot."

I grin at her. "The darkest."

22

(Garrett)

Stupid fucking dress.

It might show off the beautiful lines of Cara's body, and the fabric might feel good under my hands as I trace her form, but it's also a terrible design if you want a quick fuck in your truck before the soufflés make it to the table.

Cara makes a grunting noise that might not sound hot if it weren't because she was trying to, yet again, hike up her dress far enough to straddle my lap. She's up on her knees, the top of her head brushing the headliner, perched on the bench seat next to me, where I'm struggling to keep from latching my hands on to the bottom of her dress and splitting a seam open to fix the problem at hand. I can imagine the sound of the fabric tearing and my dick hardens even more when I do.

This was so much easier the night we ate barbeque and she was wearing her shirt-looking dress thingy. If she had that dress on right now, we'd both be coming down off the high of an orgasm already.

"I *hate* this dress." Another tug, combined with a shimmy of her hips, attempting to work the fabric up from where it's stuck a few too many inches down from where we both want it.

I try not to laugh but can't stop when she thrusts her hands into little fists and then basically pratfalls backward to the bench seat. Thankfully, she lands on a down coat tossed there, which protects her head from whacking the door trim panel. She gives a frustrated wiggle to stretch her legs out on top of mine.

"Is it rude to say I agree with you?" I place one hand to the inside of her legs and say a silent goodbye to any hope for more here. "Because I hate the dress, too. I'd like to rip it into a hundred little scraps of expensive fabric. Then it would just be you in whatever you have on underneath. And the shoes. I'd like you to keep the shoes on."

She groans. "*Not* helping. In retaliation, I feel compelled to tell you I'm not wearing anything underneath."

I choke out my own groan. "Stop. I'm begging you."

Cara lets out a devious but teasing hum. "It was a practical decision. This dress is so tight that even my slinkiest things were showing. Although I did debate putting on a bra for a bit. Mostly because I was worried about seeing you and my rowdy nipples saying, *Hi, Garrett, we missed you, please touch us*, the second you entered the room."

With a smile into the darkness, I drop my head to meet the seat back. The cab is barely illuminated by a stream of light off a tall lamppost in the far corner of the lot where my truck is parked. From here the rear entrance to the restaurant is visible, a few of the kitchen staff milling around out back for a smoke break. The lot is full of trucks like mine and cheap beater cars, the opposite of everything Cara and I just escaped inside the restaurant. Here in my truck, we're just us. The *us* that exists already, even after so few weeks knowing each other. The *us* that understands how we don't make sense, but somehow we also do.

My hand slips higher, tracing the skin of her inner thigh until my wrist hits the bottom edge of her skirt. Cara murmurs something sweet but impatient, and with the heat of her near my fingers, I know exactly what she needs to turn that sound into sweet satisfaction. She needs a release, a few minutes where she's less in her head and more in her body, when she doesn't have to think or worry she's anything less than perfect.

I know if we stumble out of this truck to go back inside and her mom says something cutting again or her dad's lips are loosened even more by another scotch, shit's going to get stupid in there. Cara will end up screaming or crying—or both. I sure as hell don't want that.

I decide to reassess our situation here. While her skirt might not make it up to her waist so that she can straddle me, I think there's enough room to give her what she needs with my hands. A little creativity and I might even be able to get my face down there. I slip my hand straight forward until the tip of my middle finger grazes the place where all her heat is centered. Cara makes a whimpering noise, then slaps one of her hands over my mine.

"Garrett, please. I'll die if you start something we can't finish."

"Who says I'm not planning to finish?" Another tease, this time higher. "Pull your dress up as far it'll go. I can make this work."

Cara doesn't protest or pause, just uses both hands to do what she can. We only gain an inch or so, but anything feels like a victory. I adjust so that I'm half leaning, my weight on one forearm so that my other is free to reach for her. Cara drops her legs open a bit more, and I slide my hand forward.

And at first I'm too focused on positioning myself to notice anything else, but when I ease my hand up, I realize something's different. She's smooth, but even more so than what I've come to expect.

"Christ, you feel different. Did you . . . You're so smooth. It's like fucking silk down here."

I emphasize my point by running my fingertips over her mound, then down both sides, and then use my full hand, fingers spread wide, to cup her pussy with my hand. Cara twists her hips, letting out an appreciative sound.

"I got waxed yesterday. Brazilian. I didn't know if you like this sort of thing; maybe it's too porn star for your taste."

I slip my hand out, pressing my fingers to her lips to quiet her from speaking such nonsense, and she sucks on the tips. My dick rears up when she tongues the flats of my fingers in the same way she does when she's doing other porn-star-type things.

"Do *you* like it? 'Cause you didn't need to do it for me. I appreciate your pussy no matter how it's landscaped. Trimmed, edged, bonsai, whatever."

A soft laugh from her. "Thank you, that's good to know. But yes, I do like it. This is my usual look, actually."

"Yeah? You haven't . . . I mean, I haven't seen you this way since you've been here. Again, not complaining—observation only. A complimentary, grateful, worshipping observation."

"Tell me if I've missed it, but I haven't seen a waxing studio in Hotchkiss. Is it near the co-op?"

I slip two fingers inside her just as she finishes her smart-ass comment and the last few syllables break down into a long groan. That's what I like to hear. My thumb comes to her clit, gentle to start, slow strokes and circles.

"Well, I'm a fan of this look, so you know. And if you let me turn on the cab light, I'll let you watch me prove it."

She grabs a fistful of my hair. "Don't you *dare* turn that light on." Her hips shove up an inch or two, chasing the feel of my fingers inside her. "Because as much as I'd love to watch you prove it, I will kill you if you do."

I move around to slide back and do my best to lie close to her, and then adjust her legs to accommodate the new position.

Keeping my face up, I press my chin and mouth below the edge of her skirt. The hem is digging into my nose, but I don't care. My tongue finds her, circling twice before centering all my attentions where Cara needs it most—and when I do, she lets out a wild moan.

Bingo.

I continue with my fingers, shorter strokes now, a pulsing rhythm I know she likes, then use my tongue to lick and suck as best I can. Cara starts to pant, her hips shoving toward my mouth when I suck her clit tight. Her taste covers my tongue, my chin, and her thighs are bracketing my head, keeping me where she wants. I turn every move deeper, faster, and more until she gives up a gasp that wants to be a scream but can't be, not here. I soak up the feel of her, the way she's letting go, even if it's only for a moment, because I'm the one who gave her what she needs. And I love knowing that I did.

I kiss her there once more, until she's completely spent and entirely limp, telling me thank you, and mumbling that she's ready for her soufflé now.

23

(Cara)

Had I known that an orgasm between the entrée and dessert is what it takes to make dinner with my family more palatable, I would have employed this strategy years ago.

Garrett and I slip back into our seats just as the soufflés arrive. My dad has entered into the mute, pensive phase of his drunkenness, and my mom is too preoccupied with glaring at Garrett to direct any other comments my way. I'm too dazed to notice much beyond my spoon digging into this creamy chocolate concoction. Garrett might think this place is a joke, but his dish is already empty and now he's eyeing mine—so there's no denying that Apogée's soufflé game is strong.

Despite my daze, Amie's Cheshire cat grin and the way she keeps nudging her index finger toward the crown of her head, is a little hard to ignore. I narrow my eyes and try to decipher the cryptic gesture. Is she making a halo with her finger? Is she claiming she's an angel? That I am? When the last forkful of my dessert hits my mouth, I set the fork down and hiss in her direction.

"What?"

"Your hair," she whispers. "There's something in it. It looks like *feathers*."

My hands fly to my hair, extracting a few downy white feathers. Garrett tries to hide his snort by pretending to napkin off his mouth, then reaches for the offending fluff to examine it.

"Goose feather," he stage-whispers. "Must have been sticking to my coat. Sorry."

He isn't sorry.

Neither am I.

I'm also not sorry about begging off after-dinner drinks at the Caribou Club with my family. Not when the alternative is Garrett in my hotel suite, building me a fire and getting this obnoxious dress off. We make our goodbyes, all of them going exactly as I expect: Amie and Tayer are lovely to both of us, Dad only gives a drunken wave in our general direction, and Mom ignores Garrett while pointedly reminding me of our appointment at an atelier tomorrow afternoon, where I'll do my best to play the part of a quiet dress-up doll while she picks out a wedding rehearsal dinner outfit for me.

Garrett eases his truck out of the restaurant parking lot onto the main drag in Aspen, headed toward the opposite side of town where my hotel is. Frankly, he's driving a little too slow for my taste, but I busy myself by concocting a pros-and-cons list in my head. Sex before or after he builds me a fire? Sex before, during, or after the bathtub soaking? Before I know it, Garrett is slowing at the driveway entrance to the hotel. He squints out the windshield.

"Where do I go now?"

I gesture toward a large red awning at the front entrance. "Pull right up to the front. The bellman will call the valet."

Garrett notes the wacky grin on my face and looks confused. He pulls in and two bellmen quickstep over to the truck, faltering long enough that it's obvious they're trying to decide if we're lost.

Only when one of them recognizes me do they snap into action and my door is opened in a flash. I hop out before the bellman can offer his hand and land gracefully on the asphalt, turning back to find Garrett looking even more puzzled.

"No kiss? You're just going to leap out? I'd drag you back in here and fix that, but this guy standing next to my truck door and staring is throwing me off my game." His eyes dart toward the bellman, who looks like he's already unsure about what to do with Garrett's truck once he has the keys. "Guess he likes to watch."

"He's waiting for you to get out and give him your keys. Please tell me you aren't thinking he can't be trusted with your truck. Come on, hurry it up, my suite awaits. I'm in room ten *sixty-nine*, which I'm convinced is a promising forecast of some sort." I toss him a goofy wink to match the wacky grin.

Garrett's face falls. "Oh, shit." He reaches his arm out toward me, only to let his hand drop to the bench seat. "I can't stay. I told Kenny I'd be at his place at five to help him tag calves."

"What?" My face falls, mirroring his expression. My body does the same, hips slumping into the edge of the seat.

"You said *dinner*. I didn't know you wanted me to stay overnight. I can't just . . ."

His words fade quietly off and I realize that he's right. Our text exchange did not include me mentioning anything about the very involved plan I had for *after* dinner. All I did was ask if he felt like driving to Aspen, to which he asked if I was joking, to which I replied that I was hoping he would come to dinner. After that it was date, time, and location.

Garrett begins to apologize again, but I cut him off with a shake of my head.

"You're right. I never even mentioned this, I just assumed. When Amie orchestrated this scheme she was talking about you and me in my suite and then I was picturing you building me a fire, without matches somehow, and there's this big tub in the room that both of us could fit in, and then I thought about breakfast in bed for my birthday with—"

"Wait." Garrett holds a hand up and draws his eyes closed. "It's your *birthday*?"

"Well, technically, it's not my birthday for another hour or so." He mutters a curse as his eyes open, one hand coming to the back of his neck and working over the tension that must have taken up residence there. "But it's fine, Garrett. You aren't a mind reader; I should have been clearer."

"But—"

"It's *fine*. Just come over here and kiss me. Then get going. You need to get home."

He shoves the truck into park and scoots across the bench to kiss me, looking pained when he does. I give him my best *I'm fine* smile the entire time, even as he drives away.

Once I'm in my room, it's time to choose. To pout or not to pout.

PRO: Pouting would be justified, I think. As would wallowing, stomping my foot, whacking a pillow, and ordering a smorgasbord of poor food choices from room service.

CON: Pouting won't fix anything. I won't feel better, I'll feel worse.

CON: Pouting is for toddlers. In less than an hour, I'll be twenty-eight.

Decision made. There will be no pouting. I will act my age by building my own fire, drawing my own bath, and perhaps giving myself another orgasm.

In the master bath, I saunter over to the wood-burning fireplace and prop my hands on my hips to evaluate what I'm dealing with. A black stand holds fireplace tongs and a poker, both in nearly new condition. A copper bin on the floor is filled with wood, from twigs to quarter-split logs, along with a sheaf of newspaper and long-reach matches tucked in one side. Attached to the bin is a placard.

Need assistance?
Butler service is available by dialing #200.

Pssh. Assistance? I don't need assistance. I may have used said butler service before, but not tonight. Tonight, I'm doing this on my own. I have my wits and my determination, and that's enough.

And I have Google. Just in case.

Without stripping off my dress—although I might seriously consider using it as kindling—I kneel down on the cool tile floor and unlatch the fireplace's glass door, then consider how to go about things. Probably should have paid a bit more attention when I did solicit a butler to do this.

I grab a few twigs and toss them in there, followed by a log. I toss on three more, because if one is good, four must be better. After that, I proceed to fill up all the remaining space left with balled-up newspaper. I lean back to admire my work. Looks good to me. Time for the matches.

Extracting a long-handled match, I strike the tip against the rough side of a slate tile on the fireplace and watch it light to life. I choose a spot to set the flame, then lean forward to set this thing ablaze, right as a series of thumps sound at my suite door. I pause but don't hear it again. It didn't sound entirely like a knock, perhaps I was hearing things. Back to work, then. Another lit match in hand and—dammit.

The sound comes again. Louder this time. Maybe it's Amie.

One quick puff and I extinguish my match, skip to the door, and yank it open.

Not Amie.

Garrett.

Garrett with his hands full, holding a six-pack of beer in one hand and two small logs in the other, his foot outstretched and ready to thump the door with the toe of his boot.

"I called Kenny. Said I couldn't get there until noon tomorrow because it's your birthday. He said to tell you happy birthday . . . *darlin'*."

A grin creeps across my face. "I love Kenny."

"Kenny? That's who's getting the love right now? I managed to source beer and what's required for a fire from the crap stashed in the back of my truck, and I get nothing?"

"Oh, you're getting something. Don't worry about that."

"Like getting that dress off before the door shuts behind us?"

I give the door a shove to open it wider and Garrett nearly leaps inside. By the time the door slams closed, I'm already walking away, wrangling the zipper on my dress as I do.

~⁓~

"But let's say there were no matches. Not here, not in your truck. Could you?"

"Inside? At night? No."

I make a disappointed sound and stick my bottom lip out. One of Garrett's hands emerges from under the water, along with a handful of bubbles, which he bops me on the nose with. I'm between his outstretched legs in the oversized tub, my back resting against his chest, covered in bubbles up to my neck.

"Christ. I admit that I can't start a fire without matches under these extremely shitty conditions you've laid out, and you sound like I just told you there's no Santa Claus. Cutting me off at the balls here, Cara. I didn't realize you were so tough to please."

I blow the bubbles away by pushing out an exhale. "*Au contraire.* I'm very easy to please. I couldn't ask for anything more right now."

Garrett laughs, low and relaxed, his hands returning under the water to cup my breasts. "I'm sure this crazy-fancy hotel room has something to do with it."

I pause and scan the room, knowing that this place has nothing to do with why I'm happy. My happiness is about something else tonight. It's bigger and better than thousand-thread-count bed linens or butler service.

"I think it has more to do with *you*. I think if we were in the tub at the farmhouse, I'd be just as happy. Maybe more."

Garrett's palms come to cover my nipples, but he doesn't do anything more. No rolling them or pinching, nothing but him touching me intimately, feeling me up because we both like it.

A kiss lands on my temple as Garrett draws one hand away and reaches for his beer, the cold bottle covered in condensation. The fact that he's drinking cheap beer in a fancy hotel-room bathtub, totally at ease with who he is, is a big part of what I've fallen for when it comes to him. He is who he is, no excuses or apologies. And I'm learning from his example, figuring out how to be me in the same way.

Which, I suddenly get, is why dinner tonight was so painful. I've spent my whole life worrying about how I've never felt quite at home in the world I come from—but for the first time I've gotten a taste of what life might be like if I wasn't struggling to make it work. In Hotchkiss, there is an ease in the way of life, a slower pace that isn't about laziness, but simplicity. And for all the ways I was known to everyone I'd met there as the city girl, no one had yet to act as if I needed to be someone different. There—and with Garrett—I'm able to just be me. All of me. The rich girl, the writer, the klutz, the babbler, the woman. Tonight, I was back to struggling with how to fit in, wanting my parents to somehow be different, and wishing it all weren't so hard to manage.

"I think I know why I freaked out at dinner. The real reason," I say slowly.

Garrett hands the beer around to me. "Yeah?"

Taking the beer, I hold it in my hand and stare at the condensation around the neck.

"When we were upstairs in the hallway, you said that you know who you are. Where you fit and where you don't."

A hum from Garrett and I scoot farther into the water, nestling myself deeper into him.

"I thought it was about you, the way my family was treating you. But the truth is, it was about me. *I* didn't fit. I like who I am in Hotchkiss, the way I don't feel like I have to try so hard. Doing this freelance thing, going my own way—it's changed my perspective on everything. Even how I am with my own family."

Garrett reaches up to sweep some curled tendrils of damp hair back from my cheekbone.

"OK, so you figured that out tonight. Maybe I'm missing something, but what's the problem here? Does any of that change your life?"

I scan the ceiling and think. "I love my family. I might hate nearly everything my mom says, or how tone-deaf my dad is about the rest of the world, but I love them. And Amie's my rock."

"OK . . . and?" Garrett draws the word out, asking for more.

"What if going my own way takes me too far away from that world, too far away from them? What if I can't have both?"

Garrett's lips press to the crown of my head, and his arms wrap tight to my body. He waits until I relax into his hold, letting go of the tension that comes with admitting what I just did: that I might want a different life, one that is so unlike what I've known it might mean giving up something else.

"In a million years, I can't imagine your family letting go of you, Cara. They're smart people, and they love you, end of story. They'll want to know you, no matter what."

His mouth comes to the shell of my ear, that nearness reassuring me as much as his words do.

"You *can* have both. You can have everything you want. So be you—whatever that means, wherever that takes you."

In the morning, I'm awake before the alarm, tucked into Garrett's side, where he's sprawled out and breathing deeply. The room is warm, sunlight streaming in through the windows that face the bed. Garrett shoved off some of the bedcovers in the night so his naked body is exposed down to his hips, the ridges of his chest and abs on display. A faint trail of light brown hair starts under his navel and extends down, disappearing under the sheet.

I set my hand to his chest and press it over his heart. A slow and steady thump, so like the way I think of him. Reliable and steady, easy and honest. I lift my palm and let my fingers trace circles there, passing over his nipple a few times.

A sleepy grunt from Garrett puts me on pause. He moves around in a manly wiggle, spreads his legs wider, then shoves the covers down enough to expose the first few inches of his half-hard cock. His hand slips down to rest at the juncture of his thigh and pelvis, thumb razing the side of his length. He stills. I put my fingertips to his nipple again, curious if what's happening here has anything to do with my touch.

Another grunt. Another man wiggle. Only this time, his hand blindly takes up residence around his cock, drawing down and up. Then his hand flops away, leaving this now very awake part of him to bob there unattended. And I'm sure it's my very awake hormones doing the thinking here, but it looks so *lonely*. Like it needs company. Company that I and my mouth are suddenly quite interested in providing.

It's possible his cock can hear my dirty thoughts, because a drop of precum beads the tip as, I swear, he hardens and lengthens more. All without his touch or mine.

Jesus, the male anatomy—it's *fascinating*. Not that the female anatomy is any less of a wild wonderland; it is. My body's current state is proof enough of that. It wants company.

I tap Garrett's shoulder gently but get no reaction. I try again, poking my index finger a touch harder and adding in a little jostle for effect. Still nothing.

"Garrett," I whisper. Another jostle. *"Garrett."*

Finally, he mumbles something, so I kiss his chest and trace my fingers like I did before. His hand goes to his cock again, grasping the base like it's part of a subconscious morning check-list, ensuring it's still there and in working order. He gives himself a slow stroke, then turns his eyes my way, barely opened a sliver.

"You OK?"

"I want you." I kiss his nipple and his hand moves up slowly until the head is in his grip. "I need you."

He licks his lips. "OK."

That was easy. *OK.* No pause, no follow-up questions. No checking to see if I'm sleeptalking. Just *OK.*

He reaches my way, half grabbing and half patting to encourage me over to him. Thanks to my newfound appreciation for sleeping naked, no time's wasted for me to strip, and I can move straight to kneel between his outspread thighs, kissing my way down his chest. Then his cock is against my lips and the scent of him, musky and salty, makes teasing him seem unproductive, so

I lay my tongue flat to the bottom of his cock, take one pass up, and suck him deep. Garrett's hands immediately knot into my hair, tightening fistfuls of it in his grip. My mouth waters enough to turn every new pass slick and sloppy. Garrett groans and lifts his hips to help me along.

"Jesus *Christ*. I love the way you suck my dick, Cara. You work it so good. The best fucking head *ever*."

Despite the accolades, after another few strokes he gently pulls my head back. Reluctantly, I give him up from my mouth, using my hand to draw down his shaft to cup him lower, firmly and with a tug, just the way he likes. Garrett's eyes roll back in his head on another groan. I loosen my grip, waiting until his eyes meet mine. His hands come to stroke leisurely—tip to base and back, with a twist of his wrist to circle over the head each time—as mine drop away.

"You're wet, huh?" I nod jerkily. I am. I *really, really* am. I don't even need an exploratory touch to confirm, I can already feel the slippery glide of my smooth skin there. Garrett's eyes darken.

"Then bring that pussy up here and come get what you woke me up for."

After snatching a condom off the bed side table and rolling it on him, I'm there. Riding him until he pulls me forward, our chests pressed to each other, and he takes over.

I sink into the feeling of being taken while still sitting atop him, Garrett's breath against my ear, slow and steady with every easy thrust he offers. My heart pressed so near to his that I can't help my next thought.

I want to keep him.

I want to keep Garrett Strickland. Not merely for a few more weeks, not only until I leave. I want to *keep* him.

Forever.

24

(Cara)

While it might only take a few hours to drive from Aspen to Hotchkiss, it truly is like going from one world to another. Downtown Hotchkiss is absent of any tiny boutiques, so instead of Loro Piana and Moncler, you'll find the big spenders around here at the farm supply store.

And forget grocery stores full of gleaming produce, well-curated cheese displays, and shelves lined with imported condiments bearing labels written in foreign languages. This grocery store has seven aisles, sallow lighting, and worn industrial carpet on the floors. But like so many other things about this community, there is something freeing about its simplicity, the way it makes a store with twenty-five different kinds of mustard seem not only wasteful, but ridiculous.

I arrived in town from Aspen a few hours ago, unloaded my bags at the farmhouse, and set off for the grocery store to stock up on some essentials. Aisle five happens to be where the oh-so-essential condoms are. The same place I'm currently struggling to do the math on how many boxes we'll need to finish out my remaining time here.

Sixteen days . . . multiplied by Garrett's amazing recovery rate . . . carry the three for my discovery that multiple orgasms is a thing . . . divided by the number of hours he works at the co-op, and . . . no wonder I was a liberal arts major, because math is *hard*.

I toss an extra box in my cart—better safe than sorry. A quick scan to determine if I have everything I came for. Yes, but things are also looking a little processed. The closest thing to a vegetable in here is a box of sun-dried-tomato-flavored crackers.

I hustle my way back toward the produce section to grab a few apples, rounding the corner too quickly and nearly crashing my cart into the backside of Braden, who is scowling at an overripe avocado and squeezing it gently in one of his big hands. To avoid hitting him in the butt with my cart, I end up crashing into a display stand where the other sad avocados are piled up.

Braden slowly turns to look over one shoulder and raises a brow.

"Sorry. I was trying to avoid hitting your . . ."

I twitch a hand toward his behind. Braden follows the gesture with his eyes, still gently fondling the avocado, and my face starts to heat. Braden's brooding hotness and his particularly intense brand of scrutiny could make even the strongest-willed woman a little wobbly. While his hotness doesn't do anything for me, the scrutiny has an especially unnerving effect.

So I do what I always do when I'm unnerved. I babble. A lot.

"I wanted to get some apples because my cart was looking a little packaged and processed. I figured I could jet back over here and load up on things without an expiration date printed on them. I think I'll skip those avocados; they look like about a week past guacamole and about two hours away from drawing fruit flies. Garrett's not particular, but even he might balk if I tried to serve up something using those things. I mean, he might actually say no. And Garrett doesn't say no to anything, at least he never has to me, except when I'm prying and—"

"You talk a lot. Garrett never mentioned that." Braden's eyes flick downward and scan my cart, where three boxes of condoms sit like obscene cherries on a sundae. "But he's a redneck chatterbox himself. The fact he can't talk much has been a nice break from his usual flapping."

"What? Why can't he talk?"

Braden sets the avocado back on the display, picks up another. "He's sick."

"Sick?" The word comes out squeaky and panicked, but Braden doesn't notice; he simply continues to squeeze his way through the avocado display. Garrett and I have been incommunicado in the three days since he left my hotel suite on Monday. I knew he was working, and he knew I was trying to get in some quality sister time with Amie, so we've each been doing our thing. Apparently, part of his thing has involved getting sick.

"What's wrong with him? Is he OK? Does he need anything?"

Finally, Braden gives his attention to me instead of the guacamole starters.

"Those are rhetorical questions, right? Because I'm the guy friend, so this isn't my department. *You* are the girlfriend. All I know is he's complaining like a big-ass crybaby."

Girlfriend. I heard the rest, but my brain keeps rewinding to that word. Garrett's bestie just referred to me as his girlfriend, and I want to quiz him on why. Did Garrett call me that? Does Braden think that? Does he see what we don't? Underneath his gruff, prickly exterior is he an all-knowing seer of the human heart?

I'll study on that later. All I need to know right now is what Garrett's mango lassi Popsicle is. The comfort food he needs when he's sick. Everyone has something their mom served up on a TV tray while they convalesced wearing footie pajamas and watching cartoons. Even *I* have a thing. Granted, the special mango lassi Popsicles were made by our housekeeper and presented on a silver tray with crystal handles. But my mom *told* her to make them, which was her way of showing concern. So what is Garrett's mango lassi Popsicle?

"His what?"

I shake my head, wishing I hadn't accidentally said that out loud given my audience.

"I'm trying to figure out what his mom would make him. Everybody has the thing their mom made them when they were sick, right?"

Braden rolls his eyes, starts to respond. Before he does, his eyes track over my shoulder and his entire face hardens as a string of muttered curse words leave his mouth. Slowly, I peer over my shoulder to see what could possibly make Braden crankier than usual.

And I'm not a guy or anything, but on the receiving end of his stare is a woman who most men would *not* scowl at.

Drool over? Stumble toward in a daze? Drop onto one knee and propose to? Those things, yes. These would be the reactions of normal men to the blonde across the store.

Her hair is a tumble of beach-blonde waves pulled up into a messy bun, showing off a set of bright blue eyes, big dark eyelashes, and a peaches-and-cream complexion. She's clad in a pair of black leggings with a camo coat on but unzipped where the top she's wearing underneath shows off her seriously plentiful breasts. She's laughing at something the dark-haired and heavily tattooed woman next to her just said, and I can't decide if I'm more jealous of her cup size or how shiny her hair is. Total toss-up. She's like a beauty queen wrapped in cool, outdoorsy packaging—and factoring in Braden's reaction, I quickly figure out who she is.

This must be the TV huntress girl, the thorn in Braden's already thorny side. Amber something. When she glances our way, her smile broadens and she gives a little wave in our direction. Braden grunts and turns my way.

"As I said before, this is girlfriend department shit. But if you really want to know what wee Garrett's mom would make him, you could just call her. She works for the city over in Grand Junction, in the payroll department. Ask for Paula Strickland—she never went back to her maiden name."

He shoots a dejected look at the empty basket he's been clutching and another at the sad avocados. "But I have to get out of here before I do something that will land my ass in jail or on the unemployment line."

He awkwardly jangles the basket, looking for a place to dump it. When he doesn't find anything, I extend my hand. "Give it here. I'll put it back."

"You're a fucking saint, Cara. You are so out of Strickland's league it isn't even funny. You know that right?"

I yank the basket away. "You're kind of a jerk. You know that, right?"

"I absolutely do."

His long legs make short work of the store and he's gone. Good grief, he's wound tighter than an eight-day clock. Amber Regan and her smiles and her big *personality* would probably be good for him.

I set his basket in my cart and fish out my phone. Back to the matter at hand: getting an answer to what Garrett's mango lassi Popsicle is. My reporter instincts kick in, and after a quick search, I find the city of Grand Junction website, scroll through their departments and track down the HR department phone number, dial, and ask for Paula Strickland. Then I'm on hold, and while I wait, I realize what a stupid idea this.

I'm not a reporter right now; I'm just a pushy-slash-presumptuous girl randomly calling the mom of the guy she's sleeping with. Whom I've never met. At her place of employment. To ask about comfort food. I don't even know how to open the conversation. Ms. Strickland? Paula? And after that, how do I introduce myself? As Garrett's girlfriend? As the woman with three boxes of condoms in her shopping cart, all purchased with her son in mind? Or as a woman who is leaving in a few weeks but is starting to worry that she's not going to be able to give him up?

Jesus. What was I thinking? The on-hold music—an elevator version of "My Heart Will Go On"—continues to play in my ear and I'm a split second away from hanging up.

"Hello, this is Paula."

Dammit. I suck in a sharp but quiet inhale and blurt out an entirely fact-based greeting, hoping that might make me feel a little less like someone whose internal compass for what's socially appropriate is currently off-kilter.

"Hello, Paula. My name is Cara Cavanaugh. I'm a friend of Garrett's."

There. That was just right. All the facts and nothing that alludes to how well I know her son. Well enough that I've endeavored to make a detailed inspection of every freckle on his pretty body, especially the cluster that resides low on his right hip bone and resembles the Little Dipper constellation. Those freckles and I have gotten close. Biblically close.

"Cara Cavanaugh? I'm sorry, sweetheart, but have we met? If so, I'm embarrassed to say I don't remember. Although Peanut hasn't brought a girl over to meet me in years. I think I would remember."

Wild delight creeps through my chest and flushes over my face in an instant. For two reasons. One—be still, my ever-swoony heart—his mom calls him *Peanut*. I can't decide if this is something I should tell him I know, or something I should keep tucked away in the happy parts of my brain, along with an image of a boyhood Garrett, all gap-toothed smiles and floppy hair and impossibly grubby clothes.

Secondly, I'm apparently not just the latest in a string of girls seduced by Garrett's easy way and honest heart. Even if I haven't met his mom, neither has anyone else. Suddenly, it feels like I'm a very special snowflake.

"No, no. We haven't met. I've only just met Garrett when I relocated to Hotchkiss for a bit while I'm working. We've only known each other a month or so."

"Oh!" Paula lets out a strange peep. Like a baby chick but more excited. "You're the girl from Chicago. You went out to Kenny's with him. You're *tall*."

That earlier delight turns to triumph. He told his mom about me. I *am* a very special snowflake. The most extraordinary, remarkable, haute couture snowflake to ever land on Garrett's tongue.

No. No thinking about his tongue. Not now.

"That's me. I was calling because he's sick and I was curious if there was anything I could make for him. You know, a comfort food. He has a cold or something, although I just got back into town and I'm going entirely off Braden's assessment of the situation, which was—"

Paula interjects flatly. "Full of compassion and curse words, I'm sure." She laughs quietly. "But the answer to your question is lemon chicken orzo soup. Peanut calls it the *magic soup*."

Let the heart melting being. *Peanut* and his *magic soup*. Thank God for this shopping cart because my knees are about to give out from the schmaltz of swoon going on in my chest. Paula rattles off the ingredients and a few basic instructions. Sounds like I'm dealing with a pretty basic chicken soup, but orzo takes the place of egg noodles, dill replaces parsley, and a hit of lemon juice rounds it out. I thank her and promise to provide an update once I've seen her Peanut with my own eyes.

"And Cara?"

"Yes?"

She lets out a chuckle. "Good luck."

"I'm sure it will be fine. I've made regular chicken soup before, so this shouldn't be too much of a stretch."

She sighs. "No. I meant good luck with Peanut. He's a pill when he's sick. If there was a contest for crankiest sick person ever? He'd wear the sash and earn the crown."

~

She wasn't kidding. Not even a little bit.

Garrett Strickland is an obstinate, grumpy, crabby sick person. He's a teething baby wrapped in the body of a grown man, waffling between whiny and cantankerous so quickly my head is starting to hurt.

I was greeted with this: "FYI, never sneak into a redneck's house, City. This isn't Chicago, and our approach to home security does not involve ADT. More like CZ. Or S&W."

For the record, I did not sneak. I knocked. Twice. Then I let myself in through the always-unlocked door. Then I bumbled around in the kitchen for ten minutes or so before he crept out from his bedroom wearing just his boxers and a T-shirt with his hair a mess and holding a .45 in his hand. It was pointed downward, but still. I was able to put to use the knowledge I'd gained from a few days spent at the local outdoor shooting range with Garrett in order to note that the safety was on—and the fact that I now know how to distinguish a specific handgun from others and be able to visually identify that the safety is on shows exactly how much my life has changed in the last few weeks.

He shuffled back into his room, and I stood there a little dumbfounded while I listened to the sound of his nightstand drawer opening and him returning the piece to where it normally resides.

Back out he came. "Do you hear that? Why are those birds chirping? It's the middle of the day, for fuck's sake."

Followed by, "Feel my forehead. Please. Cara, baby, I think I'm dying."

After he flipped the channels on the television for approximately two minutes, he tossed the remote onto the coffee table with a growl. Then he whined for a blanket. Then he declared he was dying. Again. I sent him back to bed.

That was two blissfully quiet hours ago. I was able to finish up the soup prep, then settle into my place on the couch and fire up my laptop to organize some notes and do some research on reclamation work at abandoned mining sites for a spec piece I've been noodling on, inspired by the controversies brewing down around Durango. I lost a few days of work time while I was in Aspen, but I'm still on track overall, and the editor at *Purpose & Provisions* is happy with the pages I submitted with my last progress report.

As it turns out, Garrett and I together became a good thing for my work; aside from his help with interviews and understanding this world, he did more. He pushed me when I needed it, pulled me along when I got stuck, and let me off the hook when it was for the best. He's become a solid beta reader, too—I've finally gotten him to tell me when he thinks something I've written isn't quite right, instead of blanketing his opinions with some version of *you're the writer, not me.*

Garrett shuffles out of the bedroom, not looking much like

the solid guy I just described. He's dressed in a pair of loose sweat-pants and a fresh T-shirt, his hair wet from a shower. He pushes his bottom lip out in a pout when I pat the couch cushion next to me, setting my laptop on the coffee table. Garrett drops heavily onto the cushion and tips his head to rest on my shoulder.

"Feel a little better?"

He grunts. "Like one percent better. Maybe two."

I kiss his forehead then push some still-damp locks of his hair over to one side. "I made you some soup. How about we eat some and finish watching *Red Dawn*?"

"What kind of soup?"

"Lemon chicken orzo."

His head cranes my way, hazel eyes brightening a bit. "You made the magic soup?"

Cranky or not, the sweet hit of adoration there means I want to keep him more than ever. Even more than I did when we were in bed three days ago, as much as I probably will days from now when I realize he's given me his cold germs. I kiss his forehead again.

"That I did."

"How did you know?"

"Well, *Peanut*, a little bird told me."

Garrett groans. Then he nestles down onto my lap, gives me a tired smile and a murmured thank-you.

That's when I understand what a spectacular mess I've created for myself, because this—leaving him and going home—is going to hurt. Badly.

25

(Garrett)

"**Y**ou *like* her."

Here we go. I probably should have followed Cooper and Cara out into the orchard rows. But my favorite apple farmer is fighting a bout of morning sickness that's got her looking peaked and keeps her from trekking about too much, so I decided to stay back at the house with Whitney while Cooper shows Cara the new wind machines.

Cooper's investment in the enormous portable fan contraptions couldn't have been more timely. A cold front rolled through a few nights ago, and this time of year their apple and pear trees' tender buds are beginning to bloom, so any dip below freezing means they could lose yield for the year. Cooper's been up every two hours for the past week, checking the temperature and turning on the fans when needed. By mixing the cold air with the warm air that rises naturally off the trees and ground, the fans can help retain a few of those critical degrees.

But seems I'm about to find myself at the mercy of a woman who's at least a foot shorter than me, sports a nose ring, and just spent the last ten minutes looking like she might faint or puke—

and while she shouldn't be a formidable opponent, I'm considering bolting off the porch step to avoid this conversation.

Whitney made some herbal tea that smells like mushrooms and pinecones, but thankfully tastes like almost nothing. I accepted because she offered, while knowing I hate tea. So the fact that it tastes like water is a good thing.

"Look, Johnny Appleseed. I know I'm sitting here holding this mug of herbal tea and we just talked about getting your first ultrasound and whether or not you can find organic prenatal vitamins, but make no mistake, if you follow that statement up with anything that includes the words *like-like*, I'm leaving. I have to keep my man dignity intact, no matter the cost."

Whitney laughs, bumps her elbow into mine. "Don't fret. I wouldn't dream of doing anything that might put your masculinity in jeopardy. I'm just saying, *you like her*. Not a commentary, not even a question. A statement of the obvious."

Inside, I admit to the truth. I like Cara. A lot. I like her *too* much. A hell of a lot more than I expected to when we started out and way more than I should since she's leaving in less than two weeks. In fact, if I did let the herbal tea and all the new-baby banter take hold, the idea that I'm well past *like* and nearer to something way more fucking complicated, isn't a stretch.

I decide to take the easy way out. "It's kind of impossible not to. She's very likable."

Whitney takes a sip of her tea. "Well, I think it's great. I was worried you might end up on one of those farmer dating sites at some point. Not that there's anything particularly wrong with that, I just prefer it if my love stories don't involve selfie profile pictures and computer algorithms."

I set my mug off to the side, then scratch the back of my neck and fidget with the bill of my ball cap.

"You can drop it with the love-story stuff, Johnny, because

there's still a damn good possibility of my ending up with a pro-file on FarmersOnly.com at some point. Assuming that I hit the lottery and somehow end up farming again. But either way, Cara will be back home. In Chicago."

Whitney protests quietly, but I cut her off before she can say more. Because if I let her push forward with that thread, she might somehow convince me there's hope for more with Cara, and I know better. I keep my sights set on the trees that fan out in front of Whitney's house, enjoying the view and forcing down the ache in my chest. Cooper and Cara emerge from one of the far rows in the distance, ambling slowly back in our direction but still well out of earshot.

"Garrett." My name comes out of Whitney's mouth like she's harping *and* consoling me.

"Whitney." I parrot back her name in the same tone, then ex-hale sharply. "Look. I knew she was only here for eight weeks. Has it been great? Yes. Does it suck that she's leaving? Fuck yes. But that's the way it is. What am I going to do? Ask her if she wants to move into my modular with me? I don't even have a garage for her to park her fancy SUV in. You think if I promise to scrape the frost off the windshield for her in the winter, that would be enough for her? Because that's about fuck-all I have to offer."

By the time I'm done, I've raised my voice too much, reveal-ing how much it kills me that I have so little to give Cara. So far all I've provided is some directions, a few introductions, and orgasms.

And my cold. I did give her that. But even there, I came up short. She made me the magic soup, and when I asked her what she needed to feel better she croaked out something about mango Popsicles and footie pajamas. I ended up bringing home a box of shitty store-brand Popsicles in a variety pack because that's all I could find, tossing out all the ones that weren't orange and prayed mangoes tasted similar. As for footie pajamas, I lent her a pair of my sweatpants, then put a pair of my wool hunting socks on her feet and tugged them up over the sweatpants and proclaimed them to be redneck footie pj's. Next thing I know, she's teary-eyed and covering her face with a pillow. Talk about fucking up the simplest of things.

Out of the corner of my eye, I see that Whitney's mouth has dropped open a little. She draws it closed and skirts her gaze back toward Cooper and Cara, where they're inspecting a low branch on a pear tree.

"See that guy over there? The stubborn, grouchy, brawny, handsome one?" Whitney asks. I grunt like the asshole I've suddenly become.

"He happens to be *the* Cooper Lowry, former NFL player and all-around high achiever type. He has a plan for his *plans*. I, on the other hand, have on occasion slept in my vehicle because I was either too broke or feeling too flighty to do otherwise."

Whitney tilts her head to rest on my shoulder, her eyes still on Cooper.

"But when it comes to the two of us making a life together? Doesn't matter. Not one bit."

A few hours later, the four of us shuffle out of Whitney and Cooper's farmhouse, fat and drowsy from dinner. We stop in the driveway to say goodbye, Cara and Whitney doing the girl-hug thing while Cooper and I do the guy-handshake thing. Once the girls separate, Cooper steps in behind Whitney and puts his arms around her waist, hands to her belly, and the protectiveness in that gesture is hard to miss. They're starting a *family* together. Jesus. My head goes a little fuzzy at the thought of kids, the way they need you for everything and how not knowing if you're going to be able to give it to them must be scary as hell.

Cara spies my expression and flops her hand out. In addition to the fuzziness of considering the reality of kids, the craft beer shit Cooper likes packs a wallop, and I'm definitely feeling the two I drank with dinner. With Cara being a wine girl and Whitney not drinking, it's a good thing Cara became the de facto DD for the night.

"Keys, please."

I fish them out of my pocket and set them in her palm. Whitney's eyes go wide and she twitches a finger our direction, gesturing at the exchange.

"Oh my God. Is she driving your truck?"

I tilt my head back, trying to process Whitney's question and why she sounds so surprised. Then Cooper smirks and my buzzed brain puts it all together. And it's true, Cara is the first woman, ever, to drive my truck. Tonight isn't even the first time, either. The first time she ended up behind the wheel it was because I lost a bet.

She asked to drive my truck, sweetly, claiming it was on her Grand Valley to-do list, along with driving a tractor, which she managed to tick off her list with Brooke. I flinched but was smart enough not to launch into all the reasons I've never let a woman drive my truck. Cara would think they sounded sexist, and she'd be right, but she also isn't from a world where your truck matters.

Cara proposed a wager. She said I couldn't watch her do a thirty-minute Pilates reformer workout without eventually dragging her off the contraption and putting her through another type of workout. I accepted, knowing my truck was at stake.

I lost. Ten minutes in and I couldn't stand another second of Cara in those tiny shorts, her ass in the air, her mile-long legs outstretched. She claimed her prize. And she looked damn good sitting behind the wheel of my truck, enough that I snapped a picture of her with my phone as she drove, because not only was it cute and sexy—it was like she belonged there.

Tonight, though, Cara at the wheel is a purely practical decision. "I'm a little buzzed. Better to play it safe."

"But she's driving your truck. And *you* are going to ride shotgun while she does it. Screw our *like-like* discussion. I've never been granted the pleasure of driving Cooper's truck. Never. I'm currently spawning his offspring, which he's fine with, but driving his stupid beast of a truck? *That* I can't be trusted with."

I give up a long groan and Cooper snorts, wraps his arms tighter to Whitney.

"Babe. Let it go."

"But maybe she doesn't understand the significance here." Whitney gestures toward Cara. "I mean, I didn't know the whole guy-and-his-truck-shall-never-be-parted thing before I met you. Cara should know what this *meammdfph*—"

Cara starts to twirl my key ring around her index finger, a smugly amused smile on her face because without even spelling out the details, she knows the score here: Garrett, zero. Cara, truck keys. And my balls.

One of Cooper's big hands gently slides over Whitney's mouth. "Babe, you're killing him here. Seriously."

He kisses the top of her head, pretends to growl angrily when Whitney nips his hand with her teeth, before turning his attention back to us.

"We're glad you guys stayed for dinner. Now I'm going to take my girl in the house and try to convince her for the one thousandth time to marry me. And after this whole truck-driving conversation, I think she's *totally* going to be up for it this time. Things could get crazy. And loud. You two should bail while you can."

Cooper starts to walk a playfully squirming Whitney back toward the house while I open the driver's door for Cara so she can crawl in. Once I'm loaded in on the passenger side, Cara pauses before putting the keys in the ignition, distracted by Cooper hauling a loudly giggling Whitney up into his arms.

Cara lets out a quiet laugh. "On a scale of one to ten, those two make *zero* sense."

"Pretty much."

Cara's hand drops to her thigh, keys still clutched in her fingers. "I bet this place is gorgeous come fall."

"It is. Late summer and all the way through to Thanksgiving. Too bad you won't be around to see it. But Cooper's been ramping up their social media stuff, I'm sure he'll post pictures come harvest time."

Cara doesn't respond, doesn't move, only stares straight ahead, gaze settled on nothing in particular. Just Cara staring blankly.

"I could come back."

The words are almost monotone, nearly emotionless. But underneath, I know that's not the case, something else is happening here.

She's baiting me.

Cara's waiting for me to say something dramatic, tell her how much I want her to come back. Or, better yet, tell her not to go in the first place. Drag her onto my lap and confess exactly how much these weeks have meant to me, the way they've cracked open parts of myself I've kept locked tight for years. The parts of me that want more than what's good enough. The part that still wants some land to make my own, a first planting and a first harvest—and someone exactly like her to share all those moments with. She wants me to admit that I'm falling in love with her.

And the fact that I am doesn't count for shit. Because loving her won't change the truth of our situation. A country guy and a city girl who live in very different worlds.

We still have time to unravel this thing. Enough days and nights to cut ties and do what's best for both of us. And if I do it right, then someday Cara will just be the woman in the expensive SUV on the side of a county road—a beautiful stranger and nothing more.

I'll start tonight, using the greatest emotional war tactic known to man: almighty silence.

After a few moments of weighted quiet, Cara seems to take the hint. Her face falls and the sight of that alone is almost enough to make me break, let everything that's in my heart spill out onto the floor of this truck. Almost.

Cara sets the keys into the ignition and mumbles under her breath. "Or not."

26

(Garrett)

As it turns out, figuring out how to free yourself from someone else's heart sucks. There's no way to detach and disconnect without acting like a jerk most of the time, and if you're still having sex with that person, it's a hundred times worse.

But it's working. So well that by today, the day before Cara is set to leave, I manage to leave the house for work without the two of us saying anything more than "good morning" to each other. My plan to cut ties is a complete victory. Which should be a good thing, right? But instead, it feels like I'm an evil genius who's hell-bent on triumph and getting exactly what he wants, but can't quite deal with how all his success feels so fucking shitty.

Cara's spent most of the day packing up boxes and loading them into the storage pod that's sitting outside the farmhouse, ready for them to pick up and transport back to Chicago tomorrow morning. When I pull down the driveway after work, the door on the storage pod is up and the front door to the house is wide open. Cara emerges carrying a large box, peering around it to make sure she doesn't trip down the porch steps. The storage pod is nearly full with her belongings, including her reformer.

She slows to glance my way but doesn't stop, stepping into the metal crate and setting the box down in an open corner. I make my way over to her as she's headed back into the house for another load.

"How in the hell did you get your reformer out here? Did you dismantle it?"

Cara skirts past me and clears the porch risers with one long jump. "No, Brooke and Corey stopped by earlier to say goodbye. I conned Corey into helping me wrangle it in there."

"Oh." She sidles past, carrying another box, and doesn't even look at me. "That's good. Probably helped you get a head start on loading the rest of this stuff."

All I get is an offhanded mumbling as she rearranges a few plastic bins to make room in a corner. She steps back and surveys the pod, then it's back into the house. Not a second wasted to stop and look me in the eye, or do anything other than act like I'm in the way of what she's trying to do.

When she saunters back out, I step into her path and reach for the box.

"Here, I'll take this one. How many are left? If we get this knocked out quick, I'll go get us some barbeque and we can watch *Real Housewives* while we eat. I can get you wine, too, if you need some."

I set my hands to the sides of the box and make to take it from her, but her grip tightens and she takes a half step backward.

Cara's eyes shut tightly. "I've got it."

"I know you've got it; I can see you holding it. But I can help. Just hand it over and the two of us can tag-team the rest. It'll go quicker if we do this together."

"No." Her eyes flip open. "No tag-teaming, no doing this together, no you helping me. I need to do this myself. Without you."

My hands fall away helplessly. "What? Why can't I help you load these boxes?"

"Because . . ." Cara takes a long inhale, holds it, finishing her thought on an exhale. "Because after tomorrow, I won't have you around anymore. No more Garrett to help me find my way or fix my electrical problems or talk me down off a ledge when the words aren't coming or buy tropical Popsicles for me when I'm sick. Tomorrow I'll be Garrett-less. And I'm feeling a little screwed up over how much that's going to suck."

She long-steps to the side, ensuring she can move around me. I hear the box drop to the floor with a thud, and then she's stomping toward the front door again. She stops at the threshold, keeping her back to me.

"Go shoot your bow or something. Do whatever it is you did before I showed up in town. Because if you think I didn't notice what you've been doing, you're an idiot. You have to get used to being without me, too—and you picked a shitty way to go about figuring out how to deal with that."

The front door slams shut behind her.

My work is done here. Things have unraveled; the ties are cut. And it's a total clusterfuck.

⌒〜⌒

I don't go shoot my bow. I do, however, lie on my couch in the dark and stare at the ceiling like a weirdo, bogged down by the idea that Cara is leaving, right at a time when she doesn't seem to like me much. The shitty reality of losing her had been hovering under the surface for weeks, and I'd wasted our last days together, thinking if I held her at arm's length, that would make it easier. Instead, things were harder than they ever needed to be, and it's all my fault.

At midnight I try to force myself off the couch and into my bed. But I can't, because in my bed, Cara's scent will be there, along with every memory of us together in my sheets. By one a.m., I've completed a depressing jerk-off session inspired by one of those memories, a particularly long and filthy night that included Cara using my headboard to balance herself as she rocked her pussy against my face. She came so loudly I thought she was about to stroke out.

By three a.m., I'm in my truck and on my way back to Cara. I kill the headlights when I pull down the driveway, slowing to keep the motor from roaring. I find the front door unlocked, a sign that either Cara was waiting for me, knowing I'd come to my senses—or that she's truly one of us now, distanced enough from her old life to feel safe keeping her doors unlocked. Both theories help me from feeling like a creeper when I slip inside the house, drop my coat and toe off my boots at the bottom of the staircase, and make my way up to the bedroom.

When I step into the bedroom, though, I'm not sure what to do. Is it OK to crawl in bed with her? Naked, like I normally would? Probably not, given that when I last saw her, she was pissed at me and I deserved every bit of it.

I should wake her up first. But how? Should I sit on the bed and wait until she opens her eyes? Maybe not. That seems a little sparkly-vampire-stalker-ish.

"Cara." I whisper loudly, hoping it's enough to wake her. She doesn't move. I lean forward. *"Cara."*

I notice how the bedcovers are rumpled and one of her feet is peeking out from an upturned edge. This I can work with, because my sweet Cara is *crazy* ticklish.

A few featherlight traces across the sole of her foot inspire a twitch. I try again. "Ca-ra."

Suddenly, she startles, half shooting up from the bed and

throwing one hand over her chest. She adjusts her eyes to the darkness, leaning forward to focus on me.

"Garrett, what are you *doing*?"

"Trying to wake you up."

"Why?"

"Because I want to get in bed with you, but I didn't want it to be creepy."

She flops back to the bed with a huff. "Why would it be creepy? We've slept together nearly every night for the last eight weeks."

"Because I screwed up and you're mad at me. Because you told me to leave earlier."

Cara flips the bedcovers back. "Just get in here."

"Can I be naked?"

"Well, seeing as I'm currently naked because I was waiting for you to come back, I think it's fine if you are, too. Ideal, really."

My clothes are off in a flash, unzipping and tugging until everything is in a pile on my side of the bed.

Before I slip in, my eyes linger on Cara's naked body, exposed where the covers are pulled back and highlighted by the slivers of moonlight peeking through the window shades. She's lying on her side with her back to me, and like always, she's so beautiful it turns my breath harsh and desperate. I calm the urge to grab her roughly and hold her tight until I've smothered away all the distance I forced between us over the last few days.

Her fair skin combined with the moonlight means she almost looks like she's glowing, all the way from the taper of her slim calf, up and over her taut thighs and the dip of her waist and up to her shoulders, broken up only by her dark hair against the white pillow. The length of her bare back is both pretty and sexy, and knowing the softness of her skin there so well, means I immediately want to rub the head of my dick across the entire span of her lower back and tease the crease of her ass.

Cara turns in the sheets, tips her head back to look my way. "What are you waiting for?"

My hands ball into fists at my sides. "I'm looking at you."

"Will you be done soon?" she whispers. "Because I've been waiting for hours."

I give in and release my balled-up hands, put one knee to the mattress, and slide in to lie down on my side, my chest to her back, one hand sliding over her hip. I dip my hand low on her belly, then spread my fingers wide so my hand covers the entire space from hip to hip. I kiss her cheek, then pause, breathing deep to pace myself. We've done this so many times before, so many different ways. We've fucked hard, fucked slow, banged dirty and rough, and been so gentle with each other that it doesn't feel anything like fucking.

But no one of those ways will be enough tonight. I want all of it at the same time. A rough fuck that's as slow as it is dirty, as heated as it is wild. I want to get so deep she thinks she feels my cock in her throat, then pull back to give her just the head, my thumb over her clit when I do. I want her to feel all the things I'm feeling. The heat, the disappointment, the ache, the hunger, and the regret.

Above the rest, I want her to feel one thing.

Me. Taking her, loving her, and asking her to forgive the way I've ruined these last few days by trying to forget how it feels to know her.

Cara starts to move restlessly, her ass nudging back toward me. I meet the press and rub my dick across her soft skin, letting my hand slip lower still, leaving her belly and teasing between her legs. She moans and tilts her hips back again.

"Are you still mad at me?"

She exhales heavily. "I wasn't really mad at you to begin with. I'm sad."

I bury my face in her neck and drop a soft kiss under her earlobe, taking in the sweet Creamsicle scent of her hair and skin. "I screwed up. I'm sorry."

"I know," she whispers.

Cara puts one of her hands over mine, urging them lower. I slip my middle finger to the space where I'm used to finding evidence of how good I'm making her feel, but tonight she's nowhere near ready. All her sadness, the hurt I caused, is showing up here. Another wash of regret settles in my chest. I swallow hard and let the feeling sit there.

"Cara." My voice cracks because I'm pleading with her, just by saying her name. Asking for forgiveness.

She lets out a slow breath and sinks her body closer to mine, like she's turning everything over to me. I draw my hand out from between her legs and wet my fingers in my mouth, keeping my touch slow when I slip them back in place, shifting my other arm around her so I can cup one of her tits. My palm meets her nipple and finding it pointed and hard is a relief. Rolling her tight bud between my fingers helps, a slickness building between her legs. I wet my fingers again. A few more well-paced teases and she's there. A fucked-up sense of accomplishment rages through me—because I fixed this, gave her what she needs instead of taking it away.

I start to extract my hand and her entire body stiffens. Her hand latches on to my wrist. I drop a kiss to her hair.

"It's OK, I'm not going anywhere. Just need to get wrapped up."

"You don't have to," she whispers, her hand still holding mine.

My entire body freezes in place. She can't be saying what I think she is.

Tonight? This is when she decides to toss out the option of letting me have her that way? Bare and deep? Tonight?

My mind starts to battle with my dick and my heart, all at odds with each other. My dick is all but screaming his agreement.

My brain says that we haven't talked about this and now, with my dick leaking precum against her soft skin, is not the time to try and make a sound decision on the topic.

But most of all, my heart has one thing to say. Fuck *no*.

We cannot go without this time. Not when this is it for us. Going bare inside her would be for the moment we decide this *isn't* the last time—when we know there will be so many more times, we'd go broke from buying condoms. Feeling Cara that way, while knowing it's a one-time pleasure? That would gut me.

I shake my head almost imperceptibly, not even sure she can see my response in the semidarkness, and reach over to the nightstand, groping blindly until my hand finds the box we put there. Cara's hand is on my dick, stroking slow and tight as I fish around, finally grabbing the box and shaking it so a foil wrapper lands on my chest. Gently, I remove her hand and slip the condom on.

Cara starts to twist my way, but I stop her. Missionary might seem like the right way to say goodbye, her underneath me, our chests close while I drive deep and hard. But just like the idea of having her bare, it's too much.

I use my weight to put us back where we were. My chest to her back, one arm tucked under to reach her breast, the other over her waist. I grab her thigh just above the knee, pulling her leg back so she can hook her ankle behind my leg, opening her to where my demanding cock has already settled, the head slipping across her palm when she tries to guide me inside, but I put my hand to hers. She moans as I try to keep from doing this all wrong, too hard or too fast for what tonight is about. Finally, I let go and push inside.

One stroke and everything snaps apart. She's pushing and urging herself back to me, I'm shoving and driving forward, both of us breathing hard. She says my name, begging for more. When I give it to her, my hand leaves her breast, moving up to find more leverage. My hand lands between her neck and shoulder. I set it there as loose as I can, but pounding into her drives my grip higher. To her throat, where I falter. The wild impulse to hold on to her there, hard and tight, surges up, and I try to push it away, slowing the pace of my thrusts and stroking my thumb across her neck, still fighting the craving to claim her and hold on for as long as I can.

And when Cara arches her body, moving her hips back to take my dick deeper and pushing her throat into my palm, I know she feels what I do. No fear or panic. No demands or control. Just the give-and-take of two people who aren't sure how they're going to go on without each other.

My pace kicks up and Cara starts to make the sound she does when she's close. Her sounds, her pussy clenching tight around me, the rush of heat that comes when she's there . . . all of it sends us both over the edge, both of us loud and wild, alive and savoring.

My hand remains high on her throat, nearly cupping her chin. And when I come back to myself—the daylight me—I try to pull away as quickly as I can, without scaring Cara more than I probably already have.

But she puts her hand over mine, keeps us there for a moment, then urges our intertwined hands up to her mouth. A kiss to my palm follows.

And my fucking heart cracks open.

⁓

An hour later, we're both still awake, knowing sleep will mean we're losing precious minutes and hours together.

Cara has moved onto her belly, her arms up and resting around her head on the pillow, the bedsheets pushed down to her waist.

I'm on my side, my hands tracing her skin. I draw the sheets down all the way, leaving her naked down to her ankles, and start to take inventory with all of my senses. Starting at her right hand, I trace the back of her hand with my fingers. Then her wrist, her elbow, her upper arm. I kiss across her shoulders and her back, soaking up the feel, the sight, the smell of every inch of her skin.

She twists her head a bit to see me better. "What are you doing?"

I slide my hand over the curve of her waist and the sweet roundness of her ass, then start down the backs of her thighs, making sure I take my time with her legs.

"Memorizing you. So I don't forget a thing."

27

(Cara)

Full sunrise arrives far earlier than I want it to. Garrett leaves for work after promising he'll be back to say a real goodbye on his lunch hour, and after he's gone I try to sleep again, but can't. Finally, I drag myself out of bed and grab my phone, checking emails and sending a text to Amie to let her know my plans for heading out.

When I click the phone to sleep, the lock screen shows today's date. April first.

Fitting, since I'm still waiting for the April Fool's Day joke I want to kick in. Garrett showing up later, pretending we're about to say goodbye, then laughing and looking at me like he doesn't understand how I could fall for the whole thing, because he wouldn't dream of letting me go.

But he hasn't even kept the door open to more between us. No hints or comments, no invitation to visit, no vague remark about my always having a place to stay if I'm in town. Instead, he spent our last moments before sleep last night tracing my entire body with his fingertips and his lips—all because he said he wanted to memorize me. Remember me.

And all I could think about was the one thing that too often goes hand in hand with remembering.

Forgetting.

~

After loading up a few remaining things into my car, I stop in the kitchen and fill up my water bottle, then take a glance around the room, which is empty of my belongings now. I walk through to the living and dining rooms and take the same inventory. All are empty of any sign I was here—exactly the way I found them.

I allow myself one last look at the place that became my home while I was here. Then I step outside, toss my water bottle in the car, and head back to take a seat on the porch. The trees that surround the house are starting to bloom—tiny green buds on the oaks and small pink blooms on the apple trees. The rumble of a truck I know so well sounds in the distance. I close my eyes as it grows louder and louder, finally opening them when it goes quiet.

Garrett steps out from the truck in his rural uniform: a red T-shirt that shows off the contours of his chest, a pair of dusty jeans, and scuffed boots. A sweat-stained ball cap on over his light brown hair, a few hunks of slightly curly hair escaping from around the brim. No coat, because Colorado has decided it's spring. Sunny and warm, a cloudless sky above.

"Hey." Garrett pauses on the flagstone walkway, halfway to me.

"Hi." Standing up, I wipe my palms on my jeans and close the distance between us.

Then we're eye to eye, and the memory of the first night we were together comes back in a rush.

"Tell me you feel that, too."

"The way we fit together."

"Are you all set? Everything loaded up?" I nod, watching the way his lips move when he talks. "Nothing left in the house that I need to carry out here for you? Did you remember your maps? You'll need them if you're going to Kansas from here; the GPS in your car might not show the area this guy is in. And what about your bag—"

"Don't." I drop my head. "Don't talk about stupid stuff right now. I don't want to skip over this part."

"What part?" Garrett's voice becomes so muted the words are almost hard to hear.

I look up to find his eyes, wait a beat to be sure he's paying attention.

"The part where we say goodbye and it hurts. Hurts so much I can't breathe. The part where you let me see that you feel it, too."

Garrett's jaw ticks tight. Then he gives in, drops the mask of being a guy's guy, and shows me, with only a slump of his shoulders, what I asked to see. My eyes start to sting and his face falls.

"Come on, City, don't cry. Please. It tears me up to see you cry."

Immediately, my hands reach up to gather fistfuls of his shirt. I ball the material tight in my hands and give a yank, knowing my voice is harsh, and knowing I want him to hear it.

"Don't you *dare* call me City. Not right now. Don't say goodbye to the girl who showed up here two months ago. Say goodbye to *Cara*."

Garrett's arms gather me up, then his mouth is on mine and we're kissing. Kissing in a way that makes my heart beat too fast and my skin feel as if it's both burning and freezing. He pulls back but keeps our foreheads pressed together, using his fingers to tuck my hair behind my ears.

"I need to say something, Cara."

A rush of expectation tears through me. Maybe this is it. The moment, the declaration I've been waiting for.

He leans back, drawing his hands to the base of my neck, and his eyes flicker to where his thumbs have settled near my throat, his hold so close to where it was last night. Garrett lingers there, stroking his thumbs slowly, eventually resting them against my clavicle.

"I don't quite know where to start." My eyes rise to his, but I stay quiet. He has the words, I know he does, he just has to find them.

"You showing up here was the best thing that's happened to me in years." Garrett shakes his head slowly, like he's still trying to reconcile it all for himself. "You reminded me what wanting more feels like. The way it scares you and gets your blood pumping in a way nothing else can. And I needed that more than I realized."

Another swell of hope, with less uncertainty now. He *gets* it. He *feels* it.

"So even though I know you don't belong with me, that you belong to another life in another place . . . thank you. Thank you for coming here and being with me. No matter how short it was."

I wait for him to say more—the part where he asks me stay—but nothing happens. He doesn't ask me to love him, he doesn't say that he needs me. He doesn't say anything else at all.

Garrett is letting me go.

⁓

A day later, I'm in another state. And whoever coined the term "fly-over state"—and all the derision that goes along with it—was a moron. They've likely never been to northwestern Kansas, either. Because if they had, they would be hard-pressed to find what I'm currently staring at anything but gorgeous.

I'd always pictured Kansas as hopelessly flat and dusty, but instead there are miles of rolling hills. The fields are planted, and here in one of Gerald Ramsey's wheat fields, the stalks stand about a foot tall, rich green in color and thick like a lush carpet. A spring rainstorm is brewing in the distance, and Gerald claims they need this rain. He just hopes it's the right kind of rain. Gentle and steady, for long enough but not too long. And no hailstorms or tornados, thank you very much.

Gerald is part of Brooke's extended family—and while she had only met him a few times, she claimed he was the sort of rural-life character whose plain-spoken ways would be worth my time, and even if it couldn't be a part of my Grand Valley story, I'd at least be able to see what the fields of Kansas look like this time of year. When I pulled up to Gerald's house, I found a white-haired man who stood at least two heads shorter than me, but managed to grip my hand with his knotted, arthritic one so hard my fingers ached. Then he looked me over and asked in the bluntest way possible *what the hell a woman like you is so interested in farming for*.

And I needed that sort of bluntness in the wake of leaving Hotchkiss, otherwise I would fall apart. The drive from Hotchkiss to Denver was a blur. I stayed the night in a clean but basic motel room, enjoyed a stale donut and weak coffee from the breakfast buffet, and was in the car again by six a.m., cruising down I-70 in traffic until things turned sparse at the state line. I made my way north to Kansas Highway 36, and after that the radio picked up nothing but country music, church services, and conservative talk shows. I went with the country stations, but realized quickly what a mistake that was. Country songs about love and guys who don't ask for much? *Not* what this girl needed to hear for three hours straight while driving through places so rurally beautiful it made her chest ache.

Gerald's truck growls up from behind me and I turn to find him cruising down the two-track, slowing to a stop next to me. "You all set there, Miss Cara?"

Gerald had left me to take a few photos and scribble some notes while he took a quick drive over to his machine shop, with plans that we would head back to his house after that and sit down to talk for a bit. Tucking my camera into my backpack, I sling it over one shoulder and climb in the passenger seat of his beat up Chevy flatbed, then drop my bag to the floorboard and roll down the window on my side.

The air is humid and thick. It smells like heat and mist and silt, the dark clouds in the sky turning darker with each passing minute. In the distance I can hear what I now know—thanks to Garrett—is the hum of industrial fans at the local grain elevators.

Gerald pops a cough drop in his mouth from the bag he has sitting on his dashboard, amongst a clutter of papers, a wrench, a red shop rag, and other assorted pieces of his life. Tucked into the edge of the rearview mirror is a photo of a couple in black and white. A Saint Isidore pendant hangs below from a leather cord, bouncing each time we hit a low spot in the road, sometimes hitting the windshield with a flat thwack.

"I think you brought the rain with you, Miss Cara. We like folks who bring the rain."

I laugh and run a hand through my hair, tucking a few strands behind my ears. "Glad I could be of use."

We roll to a stop in front of a large two-story farmhouse, disproportionately longer than it is wide, stretching narrow toward a cornfield behind it. A smaller house sits across the way, on the other side of the driveway, a square one-story showing its age with rough paint and an even rougher roof.

"This house is what we always call the big house. Over there is our little house. I grew up in this one, but when I came back from Korea, my wife and I moved into the little house. Stayed there until my parents passed."

Gerald opens the front door and I follow him in. "That's how it's been done around here for a hundred years. Kids get married and stay in the little house, then move in here when it's time."

"Does anyone live there now? Your kids?"

He stops to set his coat on a hook inside the doorway. "Our Bobby didn't make it home from Vietnam. He was our only one, so it's been empty for years. Had a part-timer a while back who lived there for a bit, but he didn't work out."

We pass through a dark living room, the windows still covered in heavy draperies I suspect Gerald's wife hung in that room a few decades ago. In his kitchen, a small table is as covered in stuff as his dashboard was, and the countertops are the same—Crock-Pots and toasters, coffee makers and a stack of phone books, plates and bowls, empty mason jars lined up in neat rows.

Gerald clears a stack of magazines off a kitchen chair and rear-ranges a few things on the tabletop, and then pulls the chair out for me.

"You drink coffee? There's a pot here, plus some of those cookies there." He points toward a blue metal tin sitting opened on the table.

Garrett's caution about always taking what's offered rings in my head, even when the cookies look like they haven't seen a lid in months and the coffeepot shows a dark, suspect ring of tarnish lurking at the top of the glass carafe.

"I'd love some coffee, thank you. Would you mind if I record our conversation?"

He tells me to do what I need to do, then pours two cups of coffee and sets them on the tabletop, pushing the tin of cookies my way with one of the bulbous and knotted knuckles on his painful-looking hands.

"My Sarah loved these. Takes me a while to get through a tin on my own, but I can't help myself from buying them when I'm in Colby, over at the Walmart."

I take a cookie and dip it in the coffee, eat it in two bites. Gerald tries to fit a finger through the mug handle but can't manage it, wrapping it up in both hands instead and bringing the mug, slightly trembling, slowly to his lips.

I set my notebook out but drop my pen to the page and leave it there, lean back in my chair and cast a glance out the window above the sink where raindrops are on the glass.

"There you go. My rain has kicked in."

Gerald nods. "Needs to keep on for a bit."

The room is quiet, not even the tick of a wall clock. He pops another cough drop, this one extracted from the chest pocket on his button-down denim shirt. "You ever been to Kansas, Miss Cara? Brooke said you weren't a farm girl."

"This is my first time here. And I have to tell you, it's nothing like what I expected. It's so hilly and green, so beautiful."

"I'll say thank you, even if I don't have a thing to do with it."

I tilt my head. "Oh, I don't know about that. All that green out there is because of you. If it weren't for you, it might be a sub-division or an oil field."

Gerald's face turns hard. "I'll be damned if that happens. I'd say over my dead body, but I'm going to make sure they can't do it even after I'm worm food."

When his eyes light, I know that whatever he's about to say is why I'm here. I grab another cookie and set it on my notepad, taking a sip of coffee.

"See these hands?" he asks, holding up his gnarled fingers. "Can't do a damn thing with them. Fixing fence or running a tractor, these claws of mine won't cooperate."

"Is it painful?"

"Course it is." A bleak chuckle. "Anyway, Doc Hart in town told me I got to start thinking about what's next. I told him a plot next to my Sarah was *what's next*. Doc didn't think that was much to laugh at. Said I had to think about what to do with this place."

I slide my cookie off the notepad and notice a dark spot of oil soaking through the paper.

"Did you come up with anything? A plan?"

Gerald is quiet as he attempts to stretch his fingers out of their hook-like positions. "I won't sell. Not to one of these big guys, at least. I don't give a good goddam if this land goes dry and I have to will it to the county as a damn preserve, I won't hand over more land to guys in suits and ties who will tear down this house and work this land like it's a two-bit whore." His eyes come to mine. "Sorry, miss."

I wave him off. "Don't be. So if you don't want a corporate farm here, who do you want? Another local farmer?"

He shakes his head. "Most of these local guys are one step away from the big boys. I sell to them, a few years from now and they sell out. Same damn result. What I want seems like it should be simple, but I've yet to find it."

I raise my brows, pick up my pen.

"A young man who wants this life so damn much he thinks there's clay under his nails even when there isn't. And not some kid from the city who thinks farming sounds like a neat idea. They wouldn't last a day out here. I want someone who knows this life, all the shit that comes with it, but wants it anyway."

My body starts to sink into the chair, a clear picture of just that guy coming to mind and weighting me in place. Gerald scratches the back of his neck, and that familiar gesture—Garrett's absent-minded go-to when he's thinking on something—gives more reason for my body to sink even lower.

"Someone who would let me live out my days in this house and sometimes indulge an old man's stories, let him believe he might have a lesson to pass on. A kid that might let me putz around in the machine shop on my good days, check in to make sure I'm not dead on my bad days. I find that kid? He can have this place for a song. Just so long as I know he wants to make this his own. For as long as his damn hands will let him."

In a flash I can see it all: Garrett, right here, amidst the green and the hills. Gerald still here, every day until he's gone.

Two guys. One farm. A million reasons why it could save them both.

28

(Garrett)

Thwack.

Christ.

I drop my arm, bow swinging loosely in my right hand, and take a good look at my arrow downrange. Currently sticking into the wooden post *behind* the 3-D elk target that's just thirty yards away.

I missed the whole target. The whole elk target. A big animal— and this target is sized to match.

The peanut gallery behind me is unnervingly quiet. Cooper and Braden say nothing, which is worse than having them toss insults my way. I turn and open my arms wide in a silent gesture for them to let me have it. Braden waves me away.

"Move." He steps up, draws back, and anchors. Holds steady and squeezes the release. All looks good. Except for when he jerks his head up at the last second.

Swoosh.

Braden's arrow misses the target, swishes through the tall grass to the right, and disappears. Not sure which is worse: my arrow stuck in a wooden post or Braden's in the grass. We may have to file a missing persons report on his, because it could be anywhere in that field—and almost impossible to spot when the shaft is camo-patterned and the vanes are brown.

Cooper steps forward, shoots a look downrange, and shakes his head.

"Jesus Christ. I thought you two were going to help me get *better* with my bow. Are you showing me what *not* to do?"

Braden and I just stand there silently. Cooper is a newbie to archery hunting, and while he filled his turkey tag and killed a nice bird this season, Cooper Lowry doesn't do anything halfway. He quizzed us for hours before settling on which bow to purchase, then did the same with the quiver, the arrows, the release, and the sight. Since then he's invested in enough targets and bales to open his own archery range if he wanted to. We're standing in an empty field across from his and Whitney's house, on the land he purchased for them to build a new house on and eventually expand the orchard. For now it's empty and all ours to demonstrate our apparently worthless archery skills.

I shuffle forward and commence to pulling my arrow from the wood post. A good yank sets it free and I inspect the field tip, twisting to tighten it down. Braden stalks past, eyes glued to the ground, grumbling as he looks around for his arrow.

Cooper sidles up next to me, adjusting the hay bale behind the target. He looks Braden's way, sets his arm atop the foam elk's back, and leans on it.

"I know what your problem is, but Braden's a mystery. Guy's usually steady as a rock out here."

To be fair, *everyone* knows what my problem is. You can't escape the prying ways of a small town, especially when a certain long-legged woman is suddenly conspicuously absent and my mood is coincidently sour enough to curdle a gallon of milk. Long gone is the guy who was content with everything—his life, his world, his complete lack of a future, or anything new and interesting.

And, trust me, I've tried to find that guy and forget Cara in all the usual ways. I tried drinking her away for a few days, right after she left. I tried busying her away by working on my truck, shooting my bow, and helping Brooke and Corey and Kenny and Whitney—anybody who would take my help—so that I was busy twenty hours a day and exhausted when I got home. I even tried dragging Braden to the Mesa County Fair on rodeo night, thinking a few pairs of painted-on and blinged-out jeans might help. I came home sick to my stomach and missing Cara more than ever.

I cast a thumb in Braden's direction.

"Braden is still trying to recover from the whirlwind phenomenon that is Amber Regan. I think he thought that she would come out here and scout, go home, and he wouldn't have to deal with anything until they came back out to shoot the show. But TV production shit apparently doesn't work that way. He says it's like having a hot neighbor who talks too much and keeps knocking on your door in the middle of the night."

On cue, Braden rises up from the hunched-over position he was in and lets out a sharp shout, then starts to walk around in the field again.

"And you? How are *you* doing?"

I send a dry look Cooper's way. He rolls his eyes. "Whitney told me to ask. She says you're not being *forthcoming* with her. She's worried about you."

"I'm fine."

"Fine," he echoes flatly.

"Yup. Fine."

Braden starts to kick at the ground aimlessly, dirt flying up with every frustrated swing. "Fucking guy needs to get laid in the worst way," Cooper mumbles, tipping his ball cap up and running a hand through his hair before setting the hat back in place. "As for you, we both know what you need."

I lift a brow and wait. Cooper's expression is matter-of-fact.

"You need a treasure map to your balls. I suspect they're in Chicago, but that's just a guess." He glances across the field, over to the house, where Whitney is waiting for him—and always will be.

"Don't wait too long to go looking for them. She might forget who they belong to."

Braden never found his arrow.

He kicked the ground a few more times, cursed again, then stomped back over and announced he was going home. I stood around like an idiot, hoping someone might give me a project to do so I wouldn't have to go home yet, until Whitney stepped out onto the porch with a gleam in her eye that was directed just at Cooper, and I wasn't blind to what it meant. It seemed that her perpetual morning sickness had pretty much passed and she suddenly wanted to make up for lost time.

Normally, I would have made myself scarce, but then I started thinking about Horny Cara and the only-for-me looks I used to get from her and ended up zoning out at the memory, hanging around the field until Cooper eventually told me to scram.

At home, I check the mailbox before going inside to . . . I don't know what. Stare at the wall? Listen to feral cat opera? Watch *Real Housewives*? Fuck it. Maybe I'll just drink.

The mailbox flops open, a bunch of junk mail and catalogs, most of which are for other people who used to live here. The only things that are mine are a cell phone bill, a Cabela's catalog, and a large envelope addressed in casual but precise handwriting I recognize immediately. Whether it was from seeing her legal pad scribbling or the sticky notes she used to leave around the house for me, I know it as well as my own. One of those notes is still tacked to my refrigerator, where I avoid looking at it but can't bring myself to throw it away, either.

> *Beer in the fridge. Be back by five. A drive later?*
>
> *xo, CC*

Breathing deep keeps me from dropping the rest of the junk mail on the ground and leaving it there. I make it inside, clear a spot on the countertop, and toss the rest of the mail to the side, placing the envelope down in its own special spot, where I can stare at it.

What the hell is she sending me? By *snail mail*? I slide a finger under the flap and try to open it neatly, thinking if I don't that would only be more proof of how wrong we are for each other. That Cara deserves a man worthy of her, a guy who doesn't open his mail like an ape. A man who does it carefully and thoughtfully, in a straight line. Jesus, who the fuck am I kidding? That guy would have a letter opener—a pearl-handled one—and I just have my stupid bear-paw hands.

After sufficiently fucking up the envelope, I pull out the

contents and find a very impressive magazine, larger and thicker than most, printed on heavy paper with a matte finish. On the cover in the bottom right corner, I spot why she sent me this.

Last Generation Profile: A Kansas Farmer Looking for Answers
By Cara Cavanaugh

She did it.

Not that I doubted she would—but *she did it*. A note is tucked inside the front page of the magazine, written on fancy-looking personalized stationery.

Garrett,

So, here it is . . . my first published article as a freelance writer. Now, don't panic, I didn't abandon my Grand Valley write-up—that one is much longer, so it's still in edits and is set to run in the next issue. But my trip to Kansas yielded this piece, and while it's only two pages, I'm pleased with how it turned out.

I've also enclosed a copy of my full interview with Gerald Ramsey, the farmer that I profiled here. Gerald is "good people," as you would say. Honest and modest, he says what he means and means what he says. You two would get along like there's no tomorrow.

Take a listen . . . I think you'll hear what I did.

And when you do, you'll know exactly who Gerald is looking for.

Spoiler alert: it's you.

Love, Cara

29

(Cara)

"So, with all our best wishes for an amazing forever . . . to Amie and Tayer."

The room erupts in a low, dignified rumble. Clinking glasses, muted voices, the sound of a few guests laughing a little too loudly and a little too early in the evening for a society wedding in downtown Chicago at the opulent Palmer House. I'm sure my mother's already managed to identify the offending parties and has set her sights on them with a laser-beam glare, ensuring they don't ruin *her* perfect wedding.

Will gives the crowd a nod, then sets his glass down before taking his seat, shooting a quick look my way from over the heads of Amie and Tayer, his brows raised in what seems to be a question. I smile back, offering a low-key thumbs-up to reassure him that his best-man speech was perfect. He wipes mock sweat from his brow and grins.

When the orchestra starts in again, Amie and Tayer are off, doing what's expected of them tonight. Smile and kiss, greet and circulate, dance, and kiss some more. Amie gives my shoulder a squeeze as she steps away.

"Promise me you'll dance at least once tonight, Cara Jane."

Despite all the hectic demands that came in the final weeks before the wedding, and our well-behaved but still whirlwind bachelorette glamping trip, my sister looks exactly as I knew she would today: beyond gorgeous and elegant, entirely poised while still enjoying this day for all that it should be. And she's definitely doing justice to her custom Carolina Herrera lace trumpet gown, its delicate re-embroidered lace contrasting with the flutter of tiny organza feathers that cover the skirt, and the glimmer of rose-gold embellishments throughout. Even my Carolina dress is a dream, silk and tulle in the softest shade of blush, in a similar silhouette to Amie's but without all the adornments that only belong on a bride.

I tip my head back to see her, cock a brow. "Can I choose the song? Because I've been listening to a lot of country music. And, let me tell you, that Luke Bryan knows how to pen a gem. I'm thinking the one where's he's asking that country girl to *shake it* for him would be a hit with this crowd."

"Please do. Just so long as I know you're having a little fun." A tilt of her head and a smile, full of nothing but love.

"I'm sure more cake will bring a smile to my face. Go on now. Take your new husband and go be beautiful and dazzling."

Amie mocks a curtsy for my benefit and sweeps off with Tayer at her side. I scan the room and try to determine if there's anything I should be doing right now—some maid of honor task I'm neglecting. But we're nearing the point in the evening when the stodgiest guests will start to check their watches and plan an escape, while the less-genteel folks will start figuring out how best to cajole someone up to their hotel room. I simply have to decide if I'm going to drink and wallow away my evening here, or go home and do so in the privacy of my condo.

PRO: Drinking alone in a hotel room sounds like a crack way

to end the night. Celebratory. Going home and drinking alone sounds depressing.

CON: Hotel suites make me think of Garrett. Garrett thoughts are off-limits.

PRO: Immersion therapy is an actual thing. The opposite of avoiding would be spending the night in a hotel suite, alone, to help you forget.

CON: Heartbreak is also a thing. An actual, living, breathing, heartbreaking thing.

"You're doing that thing, Cara." Will plops himself in the chair next to me, abandoned when Amie left to be dazzling.

"What thing?"

"Where your lips get all twisty and pursed. The thing that means you're pro-coning something in your head."

A little groan escapes me, one that tapers into a snort. "I'm debating drinking. Not whether I should drink or not. Just the location of said drinking."

"Do you need a pen? You could scratch it out on the back of this menu card." Will casts a small piece of card stock to the table-top in front of me, makes as if he's patting his tuxedo for a writing utensil. I flick the card away with a laugh. Will looks across the room and clears his throat.

"I read your article."

My body perks. One happy distraction—other than Amie's nuptials—I've had from Garrett thoughts these past weeks has been the excitement of seeing my Gerald Ramsey piece in print.

"You did?"

I try to keep the anticipation out of my voice. The needy, *please tell me it was good, but only if you truly mean it* tone that always comes out sounding squeaky.

Will nods, then smirks. "Don't make that face. It was really good, Cara. You know it was." I shrug, but a stupid grin follows.

"It was different from your stuff at the newspaper. I don't know exactly how to explain it, but it was like it was more *you*."

My hand drops to his forearm when I tell him thank you, the touch feeling so normal and so equally odd at the same time. Will looks up and catches the eye of a dark-haired woman sitting at a nearby table. She's porcelain doll tiny, with high cheekbones and a sprinkle of freckles across her nose.

And she's his date.

Vivienne. The sister of a lawyer at his firm, she's confident and smart, only drinks chardonnay, and is short enough that even in four-inch heels, she barely meets his shoulder. She's perfect for him—and I couldn't care less. Observing them together, even kissing a few times during the rehearsal dinner, sent nothing into my heart or my gut. Mostly, I watched them like I would a documentary, waiting to see if I would feel something. I didn't.

"So where is he?" Will leans back in his chair, scans the crowd.

"Who?"

He waves toward the room and my eyes follow the gesture.

"The guy. Your Colorado boy. *Garrett*." I crook a questioning brow his way. Will cracks another smile. "Seriously? You think Amie and Tayer haven't given me a full report? Come on, I know everything, Cara Jane. And it sounds like he handled Nan like a champ at dinner in Aspen, so I'm intrigued. Point him out."

I drop my eyes and start to fidget with the bracelet on my arm, straightening it on my wrist. "He's not here."

"Really?" he asks, genuine surprise in his tone.

"Really."

Will narrows his eyes my way. "Did you break up?"

I vaguely want to flop forward and face-plant into what's left of the salted butterscotch *pot de crème* I snagged off the dessert table. "No. Not *break up*. I mean"—I sigh—"I live here. He lives there."

"And?"

"And, what I just said. Here, there."

"And that's why you're not together? The here, there thing?"

I could try to explain there's more to it, but I don't know if that's true or not. And even if it is, sitting with my ex at my sister's wedding is not the place to figure that out.

"Yes. That's why we're not together."

Will furrows up his brow, assesses me, and then thrums his fingers casually on the table. And after so many years of knowing him and his black-and-white, legal-eagle mind, I know he's about to say something pointed.

"Well, that's a dumb-ass reason if I've ever heard one."

And there it is.

⌒〜〜

After seeing Amie off amidst a shower of rice grains and good wishes, I decide that another minute in that hotel is the last thing I want. An hour later, I'm home with my pretty dress sitting in a pile on the floor next to my even prettier shoes, my hair still styled in today's updo and a full face of photo-ready makeup, all while wearing a T-shirt I stole from Garrett's—one I'm sure he'll never notice is missing since the man has nothing *but* T-shirts. With the TV on as background noise, I set about painting my toenails a bright shade of happy yellow for no reason other than just *because*. Because it's been a long day, because my beautiful baby sister got married, because I miss Garrett and I'm currently not bothering to pretend like I don't. I feel like missing him tonight—just because.

A half-empty glass of wine is on the bedside table along with my phone and a bowl of popcorn. I swipe a final coat on my big toe and take a peek up at the TV, where a group of dating show cast-offs are trapped in "paradise" together and someone—not of the female persuasion—just started to drunk cry. Recapping the bottle of polish, I set it on the nightstand and stretch my legs out, then take a gulp of my wine. As I set the glass down and make for my popcorn, my phone rings. My eyes zero in on the display.

I look at my wineglass to make sure it isn't empty. If it were, that might explain why I'm seeing things. Because if I'm not, then that means Garrett is calling. Before I have time to process anything fully, I realize the damn thing is about to go to voice-mail. My hands latch on to the phone, poking and sliding to be sure that doesn't happen.

"Hi." I answer, heart beating too fast and my voice a little breathless.

"Hey. It's Garrett."

"I know."

He chuckles and my skin erupts in a tickle. I'd almost forgotten how much I love that sound.

"I got your letter. And the magazine." He clears his throat. "It's amazing, Cara. I'm so proud of you. You made it happen."

Quite a few people—Will tonight, others before—have said the same thing. Congratulated and encouraged me, told me they were proud and impressed, but from Garrett, the compliments are weightier. Whether it's because he was my guide through so much of this or how much Garrett's opinion on nearly anything matters to me, I don't know—but his praise means everything.

"Thank you." My mind jumps to the article, then jumps again. "Did you listen to the interview recording?"

"Yeah. You were right, Gerald sounds like good people. Reminds me a little of my dad."

He drops it there. Doesn't tell me if he heard what I did or if he could see himself as the kid Gerald described as clearly as I could. All the ways that I've always wanted to know Garrett better—

convince him to tell me more—rise up like usual. And if I were still in Hotchkiss, I might push those thoughts away and resist the urge to ask for more.

But I'm not. I'm here, back where he thinks I belong, all because he let me go. So screw holding back. I don't have anything to lose by asking—not anymore.

"And? What about the rest? The guy he's looking for to take over his land. The guy that sounds exactly like you. Did you hear that? And if you say no, I'll know you're lying."

Garrett's side of the line goes quiet, all except the faint sound of him breathing.

"God," he eventually sighs. "I fucking miss you, Cara. So much. I miss you and I'm in love with you, and I can't shoot an arrow straight or stop feeling miserable—because you're gone and it's killing me that I lost you."

His attempt to change the subject works. It works rather well, because my heart stops for a few beats, then restarts with a thump that feels like it might rupture a few of my ribs.

"You didn't lose me, you let me go," I finally clarify.

"Fuck, I *never* let you go, Cara. Not where it counts."

I try to stay calm, having wanted to hear all of this so badly it's made getting out of bed a chore some days. And I still want those words . . . I just really wanted to hear them *two months* ago.

"You're not the only one who's been miserable, Garrett. I've been hurting, too. Since the day I left."

"I'm sorry. I never wanted that—for you to hurt. Ever." He pauses to let out a heavy exhale. "I don't have anything to offer you. Nothing. Had I asked you to stay, I would have been asking you to settle. And I'd have woken up every damn day wondering if this was the day you'd figure out how much you gave up to be with me, for us to be together. Do you get that? Why I couldn't ask you to stay? Stay for *what*?"

The pieces of Garrett I'd been trying to understand since I'd met him—what made him give up so much and accept so little—all fall into place. It was simple, really.

Fear.

Garrett Strickland was running scared. He had lost too much all at once—his father, his farm, his future—so he went home to where it was safe, where life was predictable and people knew him as the easygoing guy who never wanted for more than he had, so that was all he had to be.

Figuring that out means I could answer what he just said in a few different ways. I could soothe him, say something that doesn't take him to task for more or demand that he refuse to back down from his own goddam life. But that's not what he needs.

"For *you*, Garrett. That's what I would have stayed for. For you. For us."

"What *us*?" He counters cynically. "The *us* where you're living in my shitty modular, waiting for me to get home from my dead end nine-to-five at the co-op? Or the real bullshit fantasy where I'm farming and you're trying to play farm gal but hating it? Which *us* is it you would have stayed for?"

I bite my tongue for the seconds it takes to keep my temper. Stubborn, shortsighted, presumptuous *man*. If I didn't love him as intensely as I do, if I didn't believe that he loved me the same way, I'd tell him to have a nice life and hang up this phone. But I believe that he's more than this moment, when he's underestimated what he deserves and what I'm capable of, when I still believe that we're meant to share a life together.

A slow exhale means I'm ready, steady enough to say what I need to.

"You're a pain in the ass, you know that? If you remember correctly, I spent a lot of time, by *choice*, at your shitty modular. The only problem I have with your job at the co-op is that I think you stay there *because* it's a dead end. And you know I don't want to play farm gal. I just want you to be you, and me to be me. The two of us supporting each other, living out our dreams—together."

He starts to cut in, but I stop him. "That night in Aspen, you told me I could have everything I wanted. You can, too. And I know you're enough for me, right now, no exceptions. But if you don't, we won't stand a chance. So if you think you need to be more, go figure out how to do that."

We both take deep breaths when I pause, the sound echoing across the line and the miles between us. But I'm determined to have the last word, knowing that's what we both need in this moment.

"And if I were you, Garrett? I'd start by taking a trip to Kansas."

30

(Garrett)

My hand is shaking.

Shaking so much I can't do anything but focus on trying to make it stop. Because the last thing I want to do is ink this twenty-year land contract with a shaking hand, and have my first signature as a land owner look like I was scared to death—even if I am.

"Hell, son. Take a deep breath. Can't have your signature ending up looking like mine. I've got an excuse: I'm a thousand years old and my damn hands are worthless. You can't claim either."

I drop my head and chuckle. Across from me, Gerald Ramsey reaches for the candy dish in the center of the table, flicks through it, and selects one with a wrapper that looks like a cartoon strawberry. His gnarled fingers work to unwrap it enough to toss the candy in his mouth.

The closing officer at the head of the table lets out a little giggle and leans back in her chair, but doesn't rush me. I take a hard look at the paper, take that deep breath Gerald instructed, regrip the pen in my hand, and set my eyes to the blank line. A grunt sounds from the corner of the room.

"Jesus Christ, Strickland. I'm hungry and you promised celebratory beer. Move this shit along."

Braden is slouched in a chair with his legs stretched out and crossed at the ankles in front of him, his head tipped back and his ball cap set over his face like he's catching a nap. He's here because he's Braden—a good guy with a truck, one he'll put to use if you need some help moving your shit from Colorado to Kansas. He'll load up your crappy couch and sagging mattress into the truck bed, make sure everything is tied down securely, then fill up the cab with your shotguns and reloading supplies, and make the nine-hour drive with you to your new place. And he'll even keep his complaining to a minimum—that is, until you're in a small-town title office and he's hungry and you promised him beer once the closing was finished. Then he's nothing but grumbling and grouchy.

"I *was* ready. Then you started bitching. Now I have to start my calming exercises all over again. Have a piece of candy and shut your trap."

Another giggle from the closing officer. Even if this is rural America, might be safe to say she's never had a group like ours at the table. A few too many curse words for polite company, dirty jeans and dirtier boots, three guys without a lick of sense or swifts enough to do anything but be who they are.

I put the pen to the paper on the line where it says I'm buying one section of Kansas farmland, a 1977 Farmall tractor, a combine with corn header, plus two UTVs that have seen better days but remain serviceable. And two houses—the big one where Gerald will stay, and a modest place across the way where I'll live. All of that for a price that seemed too good to be true with a down payment most sellers would laugh at.

But Gerald didn't. He looked me in the eye and told me what we were doing was about more than money. So I tapped most of what was in the savings account I had from settling up my dad's estate to use as a down payment, knowing this opportunity was worth every dime and that my dad would have thought the same. The land contract means Gerald will owner-carry the rest of the price over the next twenty years, taking monthly payments at a more than reasonable interest rate.

Everything feels right suddenly—meant to be—so much that when the ink hits the page, my signature looks fine. No shaking scrawl or jittery evidence of how unlikely this all seemed only a few months ago, just my name in a strong hand that shows I'm ready for this.

Finally.

⁓

I slam the tailgate shut on Braden's truck and step around the bed, where he's tossing his duffel bag onto the backseat. My truck is parked nearby, so I open the toolbox and extract two beers from the cooler in there. Braden shuts his door and I hand a beer his way.

"One for the road."

He cracks the tab and foam seeps over his fingers. He switches hands, shakes off the suds with a flick, scanning my new place as he does.

"You'll need a roof before winter."

I nod, my mouth twisting into a frown. So it begins, the never-ending list of things a farmer has to deal with. Fixing what breaks when he has to, putting what he can on the back burner, figuring out a way to pay for all of it. A fact my mom reminded me of when I told her about Gerald and his farm, and the opportunity for me to buy it. I could hear the caution in her voice—but she could hear the excitement in mine. And even if she thinks Kansas is too far away for her taste, she knew what having my own land would mean to me, so she helped me pack up my place . . . and bawled like a baby (or a good mom) when Braden and I headed out.

I look up at the roof, spying a few spots where shingles are missing. Still, the roof will have to wait until next year. Hopefully a little patchwork before winter will get me through.

"I need a lot of things. Might need to wait for spring to have a roofing party."

"Turkey season?"

I shrug, raise one brow to him. "I don't know. Would a Kansas bird tag be enough to drag your ass back out here to stay for a weekend? And help me replace my roof while you're here?" I sweep my hand out toward the wheat field in front of us. "I'll let you hunt on my place."

My place. My land. It's crazy how things can change so much, so quickly.

"I'm not paying a trespass fee," Braden grumbles.

"Wouldn't dream of asking."

He throttles the last of his beer, tosses the can in the bed of my truck. "It's settled, then. I'll be back in the spring." Braden climbs into his truck, shuts the door, and starts the motor. He drops an arm to the top of the steering wheel and looks my way. "Congratulations, Strickland."

I toss my empty into his truck bed, then cross my arms over my chest. "That almost sounded sincere. Now get the fuck out so we can hug."

Instead, Braden drapes his arm out the window and reaches forward a handshake.

"You sure you'll have room for me in the spring? Or will this place be full of throw pillows and decorative candles?"

I drop his grip and shake my head. "Who knows? I'd let her stuff the place full of throw pillows if that's what she wants. But it took a while for me to get here, so I can't blame her if she's moved on. All I can do is tell her the door's open, you know?"

Braden nods. "I'm putting the truck in gear now. Then I'm going to take my foot off the brake and coast away, just in case you try to hug me when I say this." The truck creaks as he slips his foot from the brake. "She belongs with *you*. You belong with *her*. You signed your life away today, Garrett. Now make sure you have one to come home to."

The truck rolls away for a few feet more, then Braden finds the gas pedal and a cloud of gravel dust billows behind him as he drives away. I turn around and put my hands in my pockets, taking a deep breath as I survey my new existence.

The late-afternoon sun is a rich orange color, setting slowly off to the west. My truck is covered in Kansas dirt and parked in front of my new house, that sunset glow framing both.

The night Cara and I went fishing, she wanted to know what I saw when I closed my eyes and pictured a future of my design— what it looked like, where it was, who I was with, and if I was happy. And I could see it that night, clearly, but I didn't know where it was or how to get there.

That place was here. When she asked me to imagine what my heart wanted, this was it.

There's just one thing missing.

Taking a few steps back, I pull my phone out and snap a picture, then start to type out a text to go with it.

My truck, the house, the sunset—everything's there in that picture, everything she needs to see to know I'm where I belong, all thanks to her.

Calling this place home now. Thank you. If you feel like taking a drive, the door's unlocked.

31

(Cara)

My phone buzzes as the nail tech finishes applying my top coat, and I groan. This will inevitably be when one of the two magazine editors I'm freelancing for will have decided to send over revisions on the articles I've submitted, I'm sure of it. Both of them, coincidentally, have impeccable timing and short fuses. And I currently cannot reach into my spa robe to extract my phone without screwing up my nails.

They'll have to wait. It's Sunday afternoon, after all—the day of special spa time.

Still, when the reminder sounds two minutes later, I nearly give in. Amie strides into the room at that moment, with a serene post-massage look on her face.

"Amie Jane, please grab my phone for me. It's buzzing and making me feel guilty."

She puts her hands to her hips. "No *working*. It's our day. With my honeymoon and you all nose-to-the-grindstone, we've barely seen each other."

I tip my head and paste on a pleading expression, knowing she's right, because even with those two freelance writing assign-

ments submitted and awaiting approval, I've also contracted with
three online journals to write monthly features and book reviews,
upping my workload substantially—but also satisfyingly.

"I'll make you a deal. If it's work-related, I give you full permission to send a reply that politely advises I'm unavailable until
tomorrow. I just don't want it to look like I'm ignoring them." I
lift one arm up and scoot my hip her direction so she can reach
the pocket.

"Promise?" I nod. Amie slips the phone out, unlocks the face,
and scans it with narrowed eyes. She peers closer. Then her jaw
drops open.

"What?" Amie makes an odd gurgling sound, like she's trying
to say something but doesn't quite know what. "Is it bad? Why are
you making that face? Tell me!"

She thrusts the phone face my way.

A picture of Garrett's truck, parked in front of Gerald Ramsey's
little house, with a Kansas sunset glowing softly in the background.

I read the text—the invitation in it—and my heart is there
before my breath can catch up.

He did it.

Amie lets a grin spread over her face, and when my widened
eyes meet hers, she's already yanking on the sleeve of my robe to
encourage me from the chair. Before I know it, I'm in the spa
locker room, using my now shaking hands and screwed-up nails
to yank on my jeans, tug on my tank top, and grab the rest of my
things from the walnut-wood locker.

"Cara."

I groan inwardly. My mother, inconveniently along for today's
Sunday spa day, a ritual normally reserved for Amie and me alone,
but hijacked by Mom under the guise of wanting to discuss with
us the fete she's putting together for Dad's upcoming birthday.
Today of all spa days, when everything in my world has turned on

a dime and I'm now hell-bent on nothing but getting to Kansas so I can have all of what I've been hoping for.

I toss my bag on the floor and set about pulling on my sandals, casting another glance at the gouged and marred polish on my nails. "Mom, I have to go. I'll call you next week about Dad's party, but right now I—"

"Cara. Jane. Cavanaugh."

Uh-oh. She's taken on her chiding voice. The one that plagued my adolescence and is best dealt with by giving in. My shoulders sag and I turn her way, expecting to see the expression that usually accompanies that tone—exasperation mixed with disappointment.

But instead, my mother is standing there looking entirely unlike her normally composed self, her posture slack and her gaze almost distressed. Her eyes dart to my nails.

"Your nails are a disaster. Come here, let me fix them."

She waves a hand toward the long countertop decked out with complimentary spa products and tools, sets about plucking out a cotton ball from a huge apothecary jar and searching for the polish remover. Because God forbid we risk my leaving here looking anything less than perfect. I follow her hesitantly, determined to find a way to clear out of here as quickly as possible. Stepping in behind her, I see her reflection in the large mirror above the countertop, her brow furrowed until she finds the bottle she's looking for.

"It's fine, Mom. Please, I really need to go. Garrett just texted me and—"

"Please, Cara," she implores. Her eyes raise and our gazes meet in the mirror. "He gets to have you forever. Let me have this moment before that happens. I just want to fix your nails before you go. Please."

Her eyes are watery and weary, and for the first time I see in my mother's face what I was convinced for so many years wasn't particularly present for me.

Love. Fondness. *Feeling.*

My eyes start to sting. Because the sight is so unexpected, because this moment is a reckoning of all those years we spent at odds. Because I know that, in a strange way, she's offering her approval—to the life I want to live and the man I want to live it with. I thrust my hands out, offering them up to her, entirely grateful for what she's trying to say—in the only way she knows how.

"I'd like that."

Maybe this was a mistake.

Maybe bolting out of the spa doors, driving home in a rush, and taking just enough time to shove a few mismatched things in a bag and take off on an eastbound interstate . . . was a mistake.

Surely showing up on Garrett's doorstep a mere fourteen hours after he sent his text would look a little crazy. I flip down my visor to assess my hair (a rat's nest) and my face (even worse), and then flip it shut and peer at my bare nails with a resigned sigh. I'm a mess. Five months apart and I show up looking like this.

I scan the area—noting that his truck is nowhere to be found—and contemplate my next move, drumming my nails on the steering wheel, exhausted and jittery all at the same time. He *did* say the door would be unlocked. I could, technically, scoot in the house and do some damage control, then set myself on his doorstep and wait. Except his caution about sneaking into a redneck's house seems relevant here, given that I'm showing up unannounced.

Decisions, decisions.

PRO: A bathroom sink, a splash of cold water, and a hairbrush would do wonders at the moment. All three are sure to be behind that front door.

CON: Garrett could show up while I'm in there—looking like a vain, beauty-conscious home invader.

PRO: The ability to see Garrett for the first time in five months without looking like a sea hag.

PRO: Bathroom sink, cold water, hairbrush.

Done. I throw the car door open and step out, peek around to be certain Garrett's truck isn't parked somewhere I haven't noticed. Then I scoot up to the front door and give the handle a wiggle. Unlocked, just like he said.

I give the handle a twist and start to open the door, slowly. Exactly like a home invader.

"Haven't I told you about the dangers of sneaking into a redneck's house, City?"

Shit.

I turn slowly. And there's Garrett—just like I left him. T-shirt and jeans, ball cap and boots. Standing there with a pair of work gloves in his hands and a huge grin on his face.

"I'm sorry. I wanted to brush my hair, and I didn't see your truck, so—"

"You came," Garrett interjects. "And fast. Like, really fast."

The double entendre in what he just said—unintended, I think—means my already frazzled mind conjures up a hundred different puns in response, but I decide to save them for later.

"I drove straight through." I thrust my hands out and proceed to jabber on with information I'm sure he couldn't care less about. "I was at the spa but messed up my nails trying to get dressed. I had to take the polish off."

Garrett looks quizzically at my nails, then takes in the rest of me, scanning my length, and I can't tell what he's thinking when he does. "But you're here."

I drop my hands. "Of course I'm here. Why wouldn't I be?"

"I don't know. Maybe you'd moved on."

"I didn't."

We both go quiet. Garrett lets his gaze fall to the ground as if he's regrouping, then straightens his posture and looks right at me. "I'm just going to put this all out there, right now. No small talk or beating around the bush. So you know where I stand and what I want. OK?"

And like the day we said goodbye, my heart starts to rush full of hope. I try not to let it, but it happens without my permission. I give Garrett a nod and do my best to stand entirely still, without locking my knees, in case they decide to give out.

"I'm so in love with you, Cara. You made me want more, then created this amazing opportunity for me to have everything I ever wanted and gave me a swift kick in the ass when I needed it. You told me to do this for me and for us. I did. The only thing that's missing now is you."

He pauses long enough for me to think it's my turn, the moment when I toss myself off the stoop and into his arms and Pavarotti shows up side stage to send us off into the sunset with the proper libretto accompaniment.

"But . . ."

My plan to toss myself his way starts to fizzle. What? No "buts." Is he crazy? You can't declare yourself like that and then get a bunch of "buts" up in there.

"But I want you to *want* to be here. For yourself. I don't want you to give up anything to be with me. I want you to be you, and me to be me . . . just like you said. This won't be easy, this life. I need you to promise me you'll think about that and whatever you decide, you'll do it knowing you've been honest with yourself."

Garrett's shoulders release on a long exhale. Speech over, I think. I cock my head and level him with my best straight face. I'm guessing grinning like a goofball will negate what I'm about to say and he'll think I'm being impulsive, which I'm not. All of what he's worried about—the work, the choices, the truth—I've already thought through all of it. For months I've imagined the best- and worst-case scenarios of a life with Garrett, and in the end, there was no question in my mind. I know that all our worst days together will always outweigh any of my best days without him.

"OK."

His brow furrows up. "OK?"

"Yes. OK. I didn't bring my stuff with me, obviously, so I'll need to head back to deal with those things, arrange to have my things shipped out, decide what to do with my condo, but . . . OK."

"But you didn't think about it," he sputters. "I know you, Cara. You have to work this over in that beautiful mind of yours. Pro and con the shit out of it. You haven't done that."

I make my way down the stoop, head slowly in his direction. He looks nervous.

"You're wrong. I've had five *months* to think about it. I have an entire spreadsheet of pros and cons on this topic. The pros win. I've just been waiting on you."

Everything about him—his body, his expression, the grin that's quirking on his lips—returns me to the day when we met on the side of that county road in Hotchkiss. When he thought I was just a lost rich girl from the city and I thought he was just a guy with washboard abs, bedroom eyes, and directions.

When I reach him, my hands slip to his chest, pressed to his shirt, which is covered in dust, and I love the smell of him, the way he feels, the *realness* of him—just like this. Garrett as he's always been, the Garrett he'll always be.

And when his arms wrap around my waist, I know he sees me, just the same. Cara, as he's come to know me, as he's always loved me.

Garrett tips his chin down, sets his eyes on mine.

"I hope you're ready for this, City."

Am I ready?

Hell yes.

Loved *Second Chance Season*? Turn the page for a sneak peek at
the third book in the Grand Valley series,

Ready for Wild

Available October 2017 from Pocket Books

1

(Braden Montgomery)

"*Forget it. Luck is with me today, I can feel it.*"

"*Luck? Take a look at this face. It was meant for television.*"

"*Age before beauty, you two. And pass the doughnuts.*"

The partially closed doorway to our conference room muffles the voices inside, yet I'm able to overhear just enough of my co-workers' conversation that I stop short outside the door. Luck? Television? Age before beauty? The doughnut talk, though, *is* familiar.

When I open the door and step inside, nothing in particular looks different. The small, stuffy room is windowless and always reeks of burnt coffee and something sickeningly sweet. Today's culprit is an open Dunkin' Donuts box in the middle of the conference table where my three game-warden colleagues—Julia, Drew, and Egan—have settled in, each wearing khaki button-down uniform shirts embroidered with the Colorado Parks and Wildlife logo. Since the Dunkin' box is already half-empty, it's likely that everyone at the table is already working on their second artery-clogging snack of the morning, washing it down with their third cup of bad coffee.

All of this is what I expect to find in this room when I make the drive from my base in Hotchkiss to the main office in Grand Junction for staff meetings with our boss. And yet . . . something isn't right.

Today, the mood in the room is different. Instead of mumbled conversations and not-quite-awake expressions, everyone's energy is off—as in, wild-eyed and eager, *off*—and it's making me twitchy.

I don't fucking like it.

Julia looks my way with a doughnut in her hand. A few flecks of granulated sugar fall from her chin when she pins me with a grin that's way too animated, even for her, plumping her always flushed cherub-cheeks even more. With her short auburn hair in rumpled curls, a soft build, and the out-of-style eyeglasses she keeps on a chain around her neck, Julia always brings to mind my elementary school librarian—a woman I couldn't help but love with all of my little kid heart because she was the keeper of the books. As a result, I find it nearly impossible to frown on anything about Julia, even when that grin makes me nervous.

"Morning, Braden!" Julia calls out.

"Morning," I answer flatly, warily taking in the equally jolly expression on Drew's face.

Drew is fresh out of college and probably too good-looking for his own sense. He typically pairs his uniform shirt with dark denim jeans he cuffs at the bottom, and his boots always look brand new, not a speck of dirt on them no matter the weather. And this might be the seventy-five-year-old cantankerous asshole who lives inside my thirty-two-year-old body talking, but with his precisely trimmed beard and his square-framed glasses, he looks like every cliché hipster you meet in a craft brewery taproom. The kind of guy that *makes* things in their spare time—like reclaimed barn wood cornhole boards or bottle openers fashioned out of recycled mountain bike chains, junk that only sounds ingenious to other bearded-guys of his kind. I still haven't figured out how Drew ended up working as a game warden instead of doing something with, I don't know, websites. Or *apps*.

Even Egan, the seasoned veteran of our group, looks like he's merely counting the days until retirement—literally—by using the calendar he has in his office for exactly that. The first thing he does each day is draw a big red X through the date on the calendar, knocking one more day off from the two years remaining until he's eligible for full pension benefits. Today though, he's smoothing the front of his shirt and sitting up straight in his chair, opening up a spiral notebook on the table as if he's planning to take notes.

Again, I don't fucking like it.

I keep my eyes shifted their way as I walk toward the coffee brewer, waiting to see if one of them is about to jump onto to the tabletop and break out into song or anything else just as bizarre.

When I step up to shove my travel mug under the pour spout, I nearly knock over a huge color photo that's been set up on an easel just off to one side. The photo wobbles and I reach out quickly to keep it from falling to the ground. Once it's steady, I train my focus on figuring out what the hell it is and why it's here—in the goddam way.

I step back and scan the photo. A woman with a big smile, big curls of blonde hair, and bright blue eyes stares back at me. She's dressed in a hot-pink camo-patterned tank top and a pair of impossibly short white denim cut-offs, while holding a compound bow in one hand. She's also wearing some sort of high-heeled sandal-looking things, posing with one hip cocked out in a way I think must be an uncomfortable position to stand in for longer than ten seconds. All of this, while standing in the middle of a sagebrush-covered field, a ridgeline of snow-capped mountains in the background. Along with what I think are photoshopped whitetail deer and some mountain squirrels lingering about behind her at sunrise, of course, like she's some half-dressed, witless Disney princess.

But who cares, because an outfit like *that* obviously makes sense if you're headed out to do some shooting on what looks like a cold morning. Forget jeans, a sweatshirt, a ball cap, and some decent boots—just throw on as little clothing as possible and bumble out there in some heels. I'm sure the wildlife won't notice when you fall down every other step and make enough noise to send them into the next county.

Ugly text is splashed across the top of the photo in varying shades of hot pink and carbon gray, in a garish, almost unreadable script font.

Watch RECORD RACKS every Sunday
Exclusively on the AFIELD CHANNEL

My nose wrinkles and my lip curls. I point my index finger accusingly at the photo, my gaze now frozen on certain areas of the blonde's tank top I feel a little pervy staring at but can't quite bring myself to look away from.

"What. Is. This." I growl.

Behind me, Julia claps her hands together like a seal cub and makes a strange chirping sound. "You don't know? That's Amber Regan, she has a hunting show on the Afield Channel. Isn't she gorgeous?"

I grunt by way of answering the obvious. Even dressed like a ridiculous, sexed-up advertising cliché of a sports*woman*, I can't deny that something about the image hits me hard, and in ways I haven't felt in a long time. So much that if I hadn't decided a few years ago that my Chesapeake Bay Retriever dog Charley is the only female I'm interested in sharing my bed with, I'd consider making some room for Amber Regan.

Unfortunately, she also has a hunting show. As if the killing of an animal should be both exploited and glossed-over, edited until it looks like responsible hunting is something that happens in twenty-two minutes and includes obnoxious whispered voice-overs. And I don't say that because I'm anti-hunting—it's the opposite. It's because I *am* a hunter.

But I hate hunting shows, the way they make all of us look like blood-thirsty morons hell bent on nothing but a new mount for the living room wall. Those shows are just one of the many reasons I don't have cable, only rarely sitting my ass in front of my crappy television to watch the one channel I pick up with an antenna. Even reading hunting magazines is sometimes more than I can stand, simply because they spend too much time writing about success and too little time on the reality of what happens in the field.

In reality, sometimes you don't get a shot, never see hide nor hair of what you're looking for. Sometimes you take a shot and you miss. Even when it all goes as it should—good shot, clean kill—you still have to walk up to a dead animal, stand over its now limp body and own what you've done. *That* is the truth of hunting. And if you don't feel that responsibility so intensely your heart hurts and your eyes water, then you shouldn't be a hunter. Just keep your hands clean and buy a steak at the grocery store if you're unwilling or unable to feel anything about the meat on your plate.

I peer at the photo and decide Amber does look vaguely familiar. Her bow is the same brand I shoot, so I must have come across her image before in a magazine ad. None of this however, explains why she's on display here—in all of her poster-sized, sleek, high-res glory.

"Her being gorgeous and prancing around TV doesn't explain . . ." I swipe my hand through the air in front of the picture. "Whatever this is. Or why it's here. Blocking the coffee."

"Everybody here?" Our boss Tobias strides into the room before anyone can reply to my rant, taking a quick inventory of the room and answering his question for himself.

Tobias drops a stack of folders on the table and drags out a chair, watching as I make my way over and drop into a seat across from him. He shoves up the reading glasses perched on his nose to sit atop his head, smoothing down his bushy Magnum P.I. moustache with one hand.

"Let's get the obvious out of the way. I figure if we don't, none of you will pay attention to anything else I have to say."

His hand slips to the breast pocket on his uniform shirt, removing four skinny plastic straws that have been cut in varying lengths and taps them on top of the file folders.

"As I think most of you already know, I received a call last week from the Denver office. Amber Regan, star of the show *Record Racks* on the Afield Channel, is interested in featuring an archery elk hunt in Colorado this season. She and her team will be out next month to scout locations and they've asked that CPW provide some guidance on the area. I need *one* of you to spend the day with them, show off public lands in your units, and offer insights on herd population." He holds up the plastic segments. "Hence, the straws. It's the fairest way I could think of. Short straw wins."

Julia seal-claps again and leans forward, her hand already outstretched and reaching toward the straws. Drew and Egan follow her lead. I stay rooted in place, something near rage rising in my lungs, filling them so much I can't take a full breath. You have *got* to be shitting me. Amber Regan. Here. Bringing all of her bullshit to town and managing to somehow drag this State into the mix.

Tobias works the straws so that the tops are in a straight line, obscuring the bottoms from view. "OK, everybody in. Draw your straw and—"

"Wait," I bark.

All eyes cut my way and Tobias lets out a tortured sigh. My feelings about this sort of thing are nothing new to him, but the look on his face says he was secretly hoping I would play along this time. Not so much.

"Why do we have to play dog-and-pony show with her? And why is she even looking at units around here? Send her up north so they can show off the trophy bulls in unit 201. Better yet, let whatever high-dollar outfitter she's in bed with do this for her. All she's supposed to do is show up and shoot anyway. That's how this crap works."

Tobias pinches the bridge of his nose with his free hand, draws in a calming breath.

"She's supposedly taking a new tack this year. Going on DIY hunts that aren't a sure thing, getting her hands dirty, and doing the work herself. But this comes from the top, so we don't have a choice either way. She's hitting up four areas in the state, including 201. It's only February, so she has some time to think over where she'll end up for her hunt come this fall."

"But—"

Tobias cuts in. "No more discussion. Just draw. We have other things to cover today and I'd like to get through it all sometime this century."

My chest clenches tight as if someone's attempting to wrestle my heart out of my rib cage. This—the way I can't gather enough breath to keep from feeling a little dizzy—must be the sensation that comes with selling your soul.

Not that anyone else seems to care. They've already each snagged up a straw and started comparing lengths. Egan's face falls when he sees he's out of the running and all that bright-eyed light from five minutes ago goes dim with a harrumph. Julia thrusts a fist up victoriously when she beats out Drew, leaving him scowling at his straw while she proclaims that she knew it would turn out in her favor.

"Not so fast." Tobias turns to me, the last straw still in his cupped hand. He jiggles it my way. I shake my head.

"No."

"*Braden.*"

"No. Consider me a conscientious objector to this whole thing. I don't want anything to do with it."

"Just take the damn straw, Montgomery. This needs to be fair and square, I don't want you coming back later whining that you didn't get to play."

With a scoff, I narrow my eyes. "No chance of that. Trust me."

"Braden, come on. Don't worry about it, I'm destined to win. Luck is on my side," Julia crows.

Luck. Like that matters one bit. I don't believe in luck or fate or divine *anything*. Luck is for suckers and romantics, dreamers and believers.

I do believe in draw odds, however—the statistical factors that drive so much of my job. Only so many hunters who apply for certain tags to hunt are granted one, all based on how the population of whatever species they're after is thriving and what best serves long term conservation. Part of my job as a game warden is to keep an eye on those hunters that do have a tag and make sure they're playing by the rules.

As for my odds right now? Those aren't in my favor. Four people in the game, two of them already out. I'm at fifty-fifty. It's simple math. But Tobias is clearly running out of patience and I like my job, so I'd prefer to keep it.

With a grunt, I snag the last straw from Tobias's hand and hold it up.

All measly two-inches of it.

My jaw drops and Julia's does the same, all while Tobias tries to rein in the shit-eating smirk on his face. Fucker. Boss or not, that's what he is in this moment. Because he knew *exactly* what he was holding.

"Congratulations," Tobias deadpans, and a chorus of groans from the rest of the room follows.

I might believe that luck is for suckers, but right now, one thing is for sure—today, *I'm* the sucker.

Acknowledgments

As always, thank you to Victoria Cappello and Elana Cohen, who each continue to provide expert guidance and support. And thank you to everyone on the Pocket Books team, who all do so much to ensure these books are the best they can be. An extra special thank you to Janet Robbins Rosenberg for sharp, comprehensive, and thoughtful copyedits. Thank you also to Lori M. for beta reading *Second Chance Season;* your notes were spot-on and key to strengthening these characters.

To every reader, reviewer, and blogger out there: *thank you.* I hope you know how amazing you are. Thank you for reading, thank you for reviewing—and most of all, thank you for chatting with others about the books that you love.

To Warren . . . thank you for being the Garrett to my Cara. If it weren't for you, I'd *still* be wondering how those ducks got down there.